SHE WAS AS STRONG AND ADVENTUROUS AS ANY MAN

Valentina. She was fresh from a convent, but she sure didn't act like it.

Not in the front lines of battle, where she handled a gun as good as any man.

And not in the arms of Ben Wilkerson, where she was as much a woman as a woman could be.

But loving her made trouble for Ben. Before she came into his life, Ben had only himself to worry about in the vast conflict that swept Mexico. Now, with this fearless girl on his hands, his task was doubled and his chances of surviving this bloody carnage were cut in two. . . .

BLOOD
AND
DUST

⓪ SIGNET BOOKS (0451)

SAGAS OF COURAGE AND PASSION

- ☐ **BLOOD AND DUST by Robert Steelman.** A young man of incredible heroism caught in a savage war—an epic adventure in the tradition of Louis Lamour. Out of the action and excitement of the past and the timeless passions of the human heart come a rousing adventure and the story of a young man growing to manhood as a nation reshapes its destiny. (400520—$3.95)

- ☐ **BRANNOCKS #2: WINDWARD WEST by Matt Braun.** Three brothers and their women ... going their own ways ... until their paths crossed and their conflicts exploded. This is their saga as they followed their dreams through the American frontier where only the strongest survived. "Takes characters out of the old west and gives them flesh and blood immediacy—Dee Brown, Author of *Bury My Heart at Wounded Knee*. (147014—$3.50)

- ☐ **TOBACCO ROAD by Erskine Caldwell.** This is the saga of Jeeter Lester, his shiftless family, and their ribald adventures with the other earthy men and women of Tobacco Road. "A master illusionist ... an impression of absolute reality ..."—*Time* (152581—$3.50)

- ☐ **DIRT RICH by Clark Howard.** A sweeping Texas saga—gushing with money and sex, violence and revenge. The Sheridians. They had nothing, wanted everything, and got even more than they lusted for. A man of courage and a woman of passion who never gave up on their dreams in a big, glowing saga bursting with all the stuff of life ... "A winner! A must read!"—*Houston Chronicle* (148010—$4.50)

Prices slightly higher in Canada

Buy them at your local bookstore or use this convenient coupon for ordering.

NEW AMERICAN LIBRARY,
P.O. Box 999, Bergenfield, New Jersey 07621

Please send me the books I have checked above. I am enclosing $_____
(please add $1.00 to this order to cover postage and handling). Send check or money order—no cash or C.O.D.'s. Prices and numbers subject to change without notice.

Name _____

Address _____

City_____ State_____ Zip Code_____
Allow 4-6 weeks for delivery.
This offer is subject to withdrawal without notice.

BLOOD AND DUST

Robert Steelman

AN ONYX BOOK

NEW AMERICAN LIBRARY

PUBLISHER'S NOTE

This book is a work of fiction. Names, characters, places, and incidents either are the product of the author's imagination or, if real, are used fictitiously.

NAL BOOKS ARE AVAILABLE AT QUANTITY DISCOUNTS WHEN USED TO PROMOTE PRODUCTS OR SERVICES. FOR INFORMATION PLEASE WRITE TO PREMIUM MARKETING DIVISION, NEW AMERICAN LIBRARY, 1633 BROADWAY, NEW YORK, NEW YORK 10019.

Copyright © 1987 by Robert J. Steelman

All rights reserved

 Onyx is a trademark of New American Library

SIGNET, SIGNET CLASSIC, MENTOR, ONYX, PLUME, MERIDIAN and NAL BOOKS are published by NAL PENGUIN INC., 1633 Broadway, New York, New York 10019

First Onyx Printing, October, 1987

1 **2** 3 4 5 6 7 8 9

PRINTED IN THE UNITED STATES OF AMERICA

To the wholly fictional

BENJAMIN THOMAS WILKERSON

whose tombstone in Chihuahua might very well read: "Born in Texas—but his heart now lies here with his old friends"

Author's Note

Blood and Dust is a novel and does not pretend to be history. While I have tried to make it as factual as possible, history does not often accommodate the novelist. Consequently, for story purposes I found it necessary to change the order of events, telescope time, synthesize characters to the extent of rolling two or three into one, and invent a hypothesis concerning the presence of U.S. troops in Mexico in 1916. So while this book is not completely factual, I believe it is true. Truth is sometimes more informative and more compelling than fact.

I am here obliged to mention the rich source material of John Reed's fascinating firsthand accounts in his book *Insurgent Mexico,* William Weber Johnson's monumental *Heroic Mexico,* and other references that are listed in the Bibliography.

ROBERT J. STEELMAN

San Diego, California
April 17, 1985

— 1 —

It is September now, and the summer rains have ended in my Mexico. The air has been washed clean and clear, and smells like good wine. Our two great volcanoes, Popocatépetl and Iztaccihuatl, lie sleeping—a sleeping maiden, the one; the other the warrior who guards her. The two float in space, their snow-frosted peaks like sails on the ocean, seen from far away. Soon, in October, regular as clockwork, the rivers in Durango will fill with snow water from the Sierra del Gamón and the Sierra de la Silla, that high country where Pancho Villa's División del Norte used to hide from the Federales when things went against us.

The floods of cold milky water irrigate the valleys but wash out painfully constructed roads the farmers need to bring their produce to market. In Mexico, every boon has a disaster to go with it. But the farmers, *la gente*, whom General Villa fought for, plod cheerfully on in the face of disaster. *"Mala suerte!"* they say with a wry grin. *Bad luck*! Then, stoic and enduring as always, they go back to work.

They are fine people. I have lived out my years among them, and do not miss McNary, Texas, in Hudspeth County, where I was born and spent the first thirteen years of my life. I don't even care that in the EEUU they have just elected President a man named Nixon—Richard Nixon, I think. That all seems very far away.

The sierra is pockmarked with caves. A man can ride up any *barranca* and find a perfectly livable cave. That is where we hid in those old days when the Carranza troops were looking for us. I sit in my chair, blanket over my knees, staring at the blue horizon and remembering. Legs spread wide, the general was pissing against a sandbank alongside the railroad tracks to Ciudad Juárez. The stream roiled in golden foam. A nearby bandit jumped away in alarm, swearing, while Villa laughed, that high-pitched sound that was almost a giggle. The big Jalisco sombrero was tilted far back on his kinky reddish hair as he swaggered around with that funny pigeon-toed gait. The general was heavy and awkward on the ground, but riding Siete Leguas, his favorite mare, he became transformed into grace and lightness.

"*Señor?*"

It is Magdalena, the housekeeper, coming out of the house with rolls and chocolate for my breakfast.

"Chocolate!" I grumble.

"*Sí, señor*. Have you taken your medicine this morning?"

Still remembering, I say, "He used to poke fun at Carranza because Carranza drank chocolate. 'Coffee,' he said, 'is a man's proper drink.' He called Carranza and the fancy men around him '*chocolateros*.' "

"The medicine, Señor Wilkerson! Dr. Velásquez says—"

"Ah, *hijuela chingada*!" I grin as Magdalena scuttles away, shocked at my language. *Chingar* is really not so bad; Mexican men use it as we would use "pshaw" in English. It is a common word, and refers to what a man does to a woman in bed. We used to use it whenever anything went wrong. "*Ay, chingado!*" Fucked again! Anyway, that is what always happens to the good people of Mexico. *Fucked again*! Now that I am old and sick, I am reduced to using obscenities to shock poor old Magdalena. But I have seen better days, killed men, rode hard with the general all over Mexico, known great battles— and defeats, too. Now things are quiet, too quiet. The cats sleep in the patio, the town of Parral dozes in the siesta. I also doze.

After a while, I sip the chocolate and think of George McFall, dead at Torreón, playing his fiddle—a hero. Back then he sat on the creek bank playing Scottish tunes while I sweated in the Chihuahua sun of late summer, washing river gravel with water from the creek. I was fourteen years old, almost fifteen, and a runaway from Grandpa Johnson's little farm in Hudspeth County, Texas. Old for my age because of all that happened to me, I had thrown in with Mr. McFall in El Paso. Mr. McFall told me the rivers in Mexico were full of gold, but so far we hadn't found any. That is, *I* hadn't found any, because all Mr. McFall did was set on the bank and play "Annie Laurie" and "The Piper's Lament."

Not only was there no gold, but we had run out of the cheese and sardines and crackers we bought with the last of our money when we came across the border at El Paso.

"I'm starved!" I complained. "And tired! I ain't going to do any more work while you—"

"There is no such word as 'ain't,' laddie. Listen, have you ever heard 'The Warrior Boy'?"

I blew out a long breath and sat down. "I ain't worried about my English." Sweat dripped from my nose and every bone in my body ached. "You promised to teach me some more Spanish!"

"You've got to learn English first, laddie. Sometimes I despair of you." He stopped sawing on the fiddle, held up a bony finger. "Hist!"

I histed.

"That's the coal train from Ciudad Juárez. It's whistling for that little telegraph station down below."

"That's the foolishest thing I ever heard of," I said, wiping my face with a shirttail. "As hot as it is in Mexico, why ever would they need coal?"

"You can rest a little if you want, Ben," he conceded.

That was all right with me because I was already resting.

Laying down the battered old violin, Mr. McFall sprawled on the bank, hands clasped behind his head, looking at me through his cracked spectacles. "You know, Ben, you are really a beautiful child!"

"I ain't—I'm not a child! I'm going on fourteen!"

Mr. McFall was bony. Everything about him was bone and gristle—face, hands, big feet. He had the bushiest white eyebrows I ever saw, and white-tufted ears that made him look like an owl. He could give an owl cards and spades, too, on the wisdom bit. He was smart, and educated. He knew all about the stars and Italian operas and a certain knife you use when you're eating fish.

"A little old for a cherub," he went on, "but with that long blond hair and blue eyes, Botticelli would have used you for a model, except for that dirty shirt and worn-out jeans."

"Bottle who?"

"Botticelli painted angels that looked like you, Ben. Curly blond hair like silk . . . eyes so blue the sky would envy . . . perfection in face and body—"

"Stop it!" I said. "Dammit, I—" My eyes started to mist; they stung. Angel? I was tainted with crime, like a bad piece of meat—and the stink of it would stay with me forever. I hadn't told Mr. McFall about it, of course. It was my own private grief, and I wouldn't tell anyone. Embarrassed, wiping my eyes with the shirttail, I stuffed it back in my jeans.

"Ben," Mr. McFall said, "if I've offended you, I didn't mean to." He pulled at his woolly eyebrows, a way he had of doing when he was puzzled. "It's just that an old man like me appreciates young beauty! Nothing carnal, you understand—it's only a matter of aesthetics."

I didn't answer, just picked up the iron pan and went to swirling water and gravel around again. Mr. McFall took up his violin.

"Any color yet?"

I shook my head.

"Well, keep at it, Ben. You know my fingers have got the arthritis or I'd help. The cold water chills them."

Arthritis don't bother his violin-playing, I thought. Then I stiffened, sniffing the breeze. "Do you smell what I smell?" I asked.

He tried the air himself. "When you get to be my age your smeller doesn't work so good. What do you smell, laddie?"

"Meat! Meat roasting! I smell meat, Mr. McFall!"

He tried again, shook his head.

"It's coming from down below, down the valley!" I was excited. My mouth watered.

"I declare!" Mr. McFall said. "I think I smell it too! Oh, how delicious!"

I dropped the iron pan. "I think I'll sashay down there and see what's going on."

"No, Ben! Who knows—they might be *bandidos*!"

"I'm nimble," I said, "and starved into the bargain. You wait here while I go down and take a look. It's probably only a party of woodcutters, and they might be willing to share."

It was foolish, of course, and I lived to regret it. Or did I? Certainly that fool decision changed my life, and who's to say if it was for better or worse? Anyway, that smell! It was fat and rich and juicy and I was starving, or thought I was, which to a young boy is just as bad. At that age you feel things ten times as keen as grown folks do; everything is magnified.

As it dropped down, the burbling creek was lined with willows. I skulked on bare feet from cover to cover, following that meaty smell. Licking my lips, I thought I could even taste it. As I crept closer I could see through the willow fronds jigsaw pieces of activity—men moving about, horses, the orange wink of a cooking fire. Someone laughed, a man cursed, horses stamped and neighed.

Bandidos? Maybe. With the crazy political system in Mexico there were a lot of bandits—both good and bad. Mr. McFall said President Huerta was a bandit, though I didn't know about that. Parting the bushes carefully, I peered through the rank-smelling willows. Oh, that delicious smell . . .

When a big hand clamped down on my neck I squealed like a pig. I was slight of build for my age and this big brown-faced man picked me up by the neck like a chicken and stared at me.

"*Qué haces, chamaco?*"

I understood that much Spanish. *What are you doing, boy?* I tried to explain, but he had such a grip on my neck that all I could do was gurgle and turn blue in the face. Finally he let me go, and waved a machete that looked seven feet long.

"*Pues, qué haces?*" he demanded.

"I . . . I . . ."

Impatient, he struck me across the face with a leathery hand. He had a glass eye, and it went one way while the other looked straight at me. Dammit all—I started to cry, but bit my lip and gave him back stare for stare.

"I'm a United States citizen and you better not do that anymore!"

"United States?" He spat. "*Al diablo con* United States!" Collaring me, he dragged me through the willows, across the creek, and threw me down in the circle of squatting men. I rolled into the fire where they were roasting meat on sticks. They laughed when I scrambled to my feet, beating out sparks in my ragged jeans.

"*Qué tienes, Juanita?*" a man asked, chewing on a meat-laden bone. Another grinned, wiping a greasy mouth, and said, "*Un pajarito muy extraño, no?*"

To them I guess I *was* a strange little bird. I wished I had that little bird's wings, to fly away. I was scared, and felt like I was going to wet my jeans. My captor, Glass Eye, put the blade of his machete against my throat and sawed a bit.

"*Diga, chamaco!*"

They didn't speak any English, and with that bad eye of his I wasn't sure if my captor would misjudge where his machete blade was. My teeth chattered.

"Don't! Please! *Por favor*! I'll go away! I didn't mean any harm—I was hungry, that's all!"

Backing away from the terrible blade, I stumbled and knocked a stick loaded with meat into the ashes. Angry, its owner jumped to his bare feet and rushed at me, swinging a rifle butt like a club. He reared back, poising himself for a downswipe that would spatter my brains all over Chihuahua, when a shot sounded. My executioner's gaze wavered. He squinted thoughtfully upward at a hole in the brim of his straw hat.

"*Basta!*" the newcomer said, sliding the pistol back into a handsomely worked holster. He turned to me. "American?"

"*Sí!*" I babbled. "I mean, yes! I'm from Hudspeth County in Texas, and never meant harm! I was hungry, and I told Mr. McFall I'd just come down here and visit these folks that was cooking meat—"

"Hungry, eh?" The man was slim and dark, small-boned, but wiry. He was neat in khaki riding breeches and a silk shirt open at the neck. Taking a chunk of meat away from a sullen *bandido*, he handed it to me. "What's your name, kid?"

I tore into that meat like a cur dog. Between mouthfuls I said, "Ben, sir. Benjamin D'Artagnan Wilkerson."

"D'Artagnan?" He smiled, showing a line of white teeth neat as his clothes. "You'll make yourself sick, Ben, if you don't stop bolting down that goat meat!"

I looked at what was left on the stick. "*Goat* meat?" Goats were smelly and dirty.

"*Cabrito*. Young goat!"

I figured I had enough goat meat for the moment. Still and all, maybe they'd let me take some back to Mr. McFall. He said he had eaten things in Paris like snails and frogs. Surely he wouldn't mind a rasher of goat meat.

Good Lord! Mr. McFall! He was still up the creek, I remembered, waiting for me to come back! What should I do? I didn't want to give away his whereabouts, now that I myself had been captured. How was I going to warn him?

It turned out to be no problem. Mr. McFall, clearing his throat, stepped out of the willows and waded across the creek, holding his old violin like a club.

"I heard a shot. If any of you gentlemen has harmed this child, I'll—" He drew back a little when Glass Eye stuck a pistol in his face. "Watch that piece, sir! It could be dangerous!"

He was a cool one, all right. The slim man frowned at him and asked, "Who the hell are you?"

"George McFall, sir, this young man's mentor and adviser. I am late of Memphis, Tennessee, where I conducted classes for young ladies in music, deportment, and various cultural subjects. And whom have I the pleasure of addressing?"

The slim man twisted up a cigarette from Bull Durham and lit it with the swipe of a match on the seat of his breeches.

"Name's Mix. Tom Mix."

"Glad to meet you, Mr. Mix."

"Maybe *you* can tell me what you and the boy are doing in these whereabouts!"

Mr. McFall waved an airy hand. "Just looking for gold, sir, in the creekbed up yonder." He pointed with the violin bow. "We haven't found any yet. The boy is lazy, as boys will be, you know. But we have hopes, and—"

"For all I know, you both might be Huerta spies!"

"Oh, no, sir!" Mr. McFall turned to me. "We're not spies, are we, Ben?" He had picked up a bone and was worrying meat off it.

"No, we ain't, Mr. Mix. Just American citizens kind of prospecting, although why they call it prospecting I don't know, because there ain't—isn't—aren't anyone with as little prospects as us!"

"Well, we'll see. The general will want to take a look at you." Mr. Mix gave an order. The brown-faced men, in ragged straw hats and dirty white jackets crisscrossed by bandoliers, mounted up.

"You two will have to go shank's mare," Mr. Mix said. He swung a booted leg over a wide-nostriled black mare that looked like an Arab—as fine a horse as is in the picture book. Some of the bandits rode ahead, laughing and joking. When Mr. Mix pointed down the valley toward the distant railroad tracks, Mr. McFall and I stumbled along the rocky trail, Glass Eye keeping his good eye peeled on us.

"I don't like this at all, Ben," Mr. McFall whispered. When he stumbled over a rocky ledge, I helped him up. "Mexico is a land of passion and violence! We're apt to get a dose of lead poisoning for our pains." He began to wheeze with the effort. "At least, laddie, you'll leave this world with a full stomach! I only got a smidgen of that meat."

"Goat meat," I said.

He looked at me. "Goat meat? Well, it does have a certain bouquet."

The patrol led us down the canyon through thickets of catclaw. It was hot; the heat bounced back and forth from the steep walls of the canyon. Somewhere the cool little creek disappeared underground. A big crow followed us down the canyon, cawing like a rasp biting into metal. I knew that was bad luck. My thing shriveled up into my belly, and when I spoke, my voice seemed to squeak and shrivel too.

"I'm sorry to have got you into this, Mr. McFall. I was a fool!"

Trudging beside me, he patted my shoulder. "Well, it's a new experience anyway, Ben. I may write a book."

Write a book? He would have to send the manuscript to the publisher with postage from the heavenly gates, and if I ever got to read it it would be in a rest period from stoking the fires of hell.

Finally we came out of the canyon and onto the flat plain where the Central Railroad of Mexico ran. The coal train from Ciudad Juárez sat on the siding, surrounded by more bandits. Waves of heat floated off the black iron of the boiler, making everything look wiggly. A shabby wooden shack baked in the sun with wires leading down to it; the telegraph station. In front of the shack a group of anxious men surrounded a runty bearded *bandido* who had a broken telegraph sounder in his lap and was reeling off magnet wire trying to repair it. In the doorway of the shack lay a flat crumpled body in a pool of blood. Eyes that didn't see stared at the sun through cracked spectacles. Flies were buzzing around the corpse. I swallowed hard. I have since seen a lot of death. Blood and death and crumpled bodies are part of the scenery in Mexico, but the only blood that moves me now is my own; I am very edgy about my own. But then I was fourteen going on fifteen, and had never seen a dead man.

Glass Eye gave me a shove toward the dusty Dodge auto alongside the tracks, where a group of men were talking. Beside the Dodge car a big man in a wide sombrero was pissing on the sand. The stream would have done credit to a horse. Mr. Mix spoke to the big man very respectfully while he pissed, calling him "Hene*ral*." That was how the Mexicans pronounced "General." Beside me Mr. McFall muttered, "That's him!"

"Who?" I whispered back, trembling. My own thing had gone so far up into my bowels that I'd probably never see it again.

"Villa! Pancho Villa! Born Doroteo Arango in Durango. The revolutionary that's fighting President Huerta!" Seeing me so scared, Mr. McFall tried a little joke, but it fell flat. "Arango from Durango, one might say, speaking poetically."

Besides Mr. Mix and the general, a third man joined in the discussion. I knew who he was without anyone telling me; El Carnicero, the one they called "Pancho Villa's Butcher." Mr. McFall had an old copy of *Excelsior*, the Mexico City daily, with a picture of him—a man named Rodolfo Fierro. The Butcher had a cruel set to his mouth, piercing dark eyes, and a blond forelock that kept falling over his eyes. He appeared quite a dandy, with little bells on his spurs and a carnation in his lapel. I knew about carnations; Grandma Johnson used to raise them before she lost her mind. Fierro had a lot of butcher's equipment on him. A heavy pistol was on each hip, a rifle in one hand, and about a ton of bandoliers across his chest—so many they looked like they would sink him right into the sand.

Mr. Mix seemed to be arguing our case with the general and Fierro, but you could tell he was losing out. *"No, mi general!"* But Fierro joined in, eager for blood, I guess, and finally Mr. Mix just shrugged and gave up.

"What are they talking about?" I whispered.

Mr. McFall sucked in his breath. The Adam's apple dodged up and down in his throat. "They . . . they have determined to kill us, Ben."

"Kill us?" My voice squeaked up and then down.

"They think we are spies for President Huerta, who is now in power in Mexico City."

Benjamin D'Artagnan Wilkerson, I thought, you are going to die today in the sun-drenched Chihuahua desert! It's obvious your crimes have caught up with you. Maybe I didn't deserve to die because I was a Huertista spy; I wasn't. But I had plenty of other crimes against me, and they had found me out. "The wages of sin is death,"

Grandpa Johnson said. I'd drawn my last paycheck, then. I didn't tremble anymore; I was paralyzed, staring glassy-eyed at the scene, the last earthly scene I'd ever see. There was the hot steamy engine, the string of cars loaded with coal, the dead telegrapher, the lounging Villistas eating tortillas with Campbell's pork and beans spread on them, the man trying to fix the telegraph sounder. One group had a deck of cards and was gambling for cigarettes on a blanket. No one cared that a young boy, almost fifteen, and a nice old man were going to be snuffed out. Mr. McFall put a hand on my shoulder.

"Stiff upper lip, Ben!" His voice sounded odd and strained. "We've all got to go sometime. It's not too important whether it's now or then." He held the old violin to his chest. "I want them to kill it too, so it dies with me."

Mr. Mix came over to us. "I'm sorry," he explained. "There's nothing more I can do. The general is planning an attack on Ciudad Juárez, and he figures you're spies that might give away his plans."

I think I started to blubber, but choked it off because Mr. McFall sounded so calm, like he was discussing the price of eggs.

"We are not spies," he explained, "and I told you that! I would suggest to General Villa that there can be severe international repercussions if American citizens are murdered in Chihuahua."

Mr. Mix shrugged. "Does anyone know you two are down here? Or does anyone care?"

Mr. McFall tugged at his eyebrow. "You have us there, sir!"

Fierro the Butcher sauntered over and shoved us toward a clump of straggly bushes. *"Adelante!"*

Mr. Mix gave a last handshake to us. "I'm sorry as hell, but you shouldn't have come into Chihuahua when the revolution is going on! The best I can do is report to the United States consul in El Paso when I get back across the border. Give me your names."

"George Henry McFall. Born Leith, Scotland, 1857."

I started to speak, then changed my mind. Finally I

said, "It don't make any difference anyway." No one would miss me, at least not in Hudspeth County, Texas.

Shaking his head, Mr. Mix walked away, spurs jingling; to me it sounded more like tolling. General Villa was examining maps spread out on a table. Fierro growled at Mr. McFall and told him to stand in front of a mesquite. Mr. McFall stood there, tall and pale and bony, holding the violin in front of him like a shield.

"Not in the face, please, *por favor*. The chest, sir. *El pecho*, if you please!"

I couldn't stand it. If I had to die too, we might as well die together. I ran to Mr. McFall and stood beside him, holding his hand. Fierro dragged me aside with an oath. *"Vete!"* he snarled, sighting in on Mr. McFall.

I resisted. "Goddammit, I've got some rights around here!"

He smashed me across the face with the butt of the revolver and I dropped like a sash weight. Nose bleeding, I struggled to my knees. The whole world was spinning round; the coal train soared overhead and everything was upside down.

"No you," Fierro said in English. "No you, nice boy!"

Half-blinded, blood dribbling into my eyes, I wobbled to my feet and tried to reach Mr. McFall. But I was giddy, and fell down again.

"No!" Mr. McFall called. "Stay away, Ben!"

Something stirred in my battered mind. I remembered that bearded *bandido* trying to fix the telegraph sounder. And Mr. Mix had said, "The general is planning an attack on Ciudad Juárez." Why would they be marking time in the desert unless the telegraph station was part of the plan? They probably needed that sounder to send an important message or something. And the telegrapher was dead!

"Wait a minute!" I yelped. Staggering up again, I seized Fierro's arm just as he fired at Mr. McFall. The shot went wild, hitting a rock and whickering off into the desert. Fierro cursed and swung at me again with the butt of the gun, but I was staggering, so he missed me this time.

"Don't interfere, Ben!" Mr. McFall cried. "Let him get it over with, for God's sake! I don't care anymore!"

Unsteady, I grabbed Fierro and almost brought him down with me. "I can fix it!"

"*Qué?*"

Because I had hold of his gun arm, he couldn't do anything.

"I can fix it! That sounder!" I squalled.

He didn't understand me. I twisted away, running drunkenly toward the telegraph station.

"*Alto!*" Fierro shouted. Shooting, he pursued me. I was dizzy and confused, running in all directions at once, but the spurts of dust at my heels gave them wings. I crashed into the old Dodge automobile and fell at General Villa's feet.

"I can fix it!" I howled. "Let me fix it!"

Mr. Mix was sitting on a pile of ties, smoking. The general looked at me, puzzled, and then at Mr. Mix.

"Fix what?" Mr. Mix asked.

I pointed. "That—that sounder! I can fix it! You need it, I know. And if you don't stop that idiot that's took it all apart, he'll ruin it so it can't ever be fixed!"

Fierro grabbed me by the collar but the general pushed him aside while Mr. Mix and the general jabbered in Spanish. Saved for the moment, at least, Mr. McFall emerged from the bushes, pulling at his eyebrows and carrying the precious violin. Fierro glowered at me like a cat cheated of a plateful of mice.

"What do you know about the telegraph, kid?" Mr. Mix asked.

I guess I babbled. "There was this . . . Mr. Ballew . . . worked for the railroad in Hudspeth County. He only had one leg. He taught me how to send the Morse code they use on the Texas and Western Railroad and I made my own sounder out of tin cans and some wire he gave me and I used to go down to the telegraph station on the siding where he worked and—"

"Whoa!" Mr. Mix said. "Slow down, kid. Let's get this straight. You can fix that thing—that sounder?"

"Yes, sir. I can." After all, I had once built a sounder, hadn't I?

He talked to the general. General Villa looked at me with greenish eyes under his heavy brows. *"Es verdad, chico?"*

"It is exactly *verdad*," I said. "I am an *experto* telegrapher." I thought that was the way to say it in Mexican.

"If you're pulling someone's leg," Mr. Mix warned, "you'll be sliced up into little pieces with a machete and fed to the lizards. But if you're on the level, get over there fast and fix that damned thing—quick!"

I ran to the shack as if the devil was after me, wiping blood from my eyes with a sleeve. The Villistas moved aside and the man with the sounder handed it over with a sigh of relief.

Thank you, Mr. Ballew, thank you for teaching me about the telegraph and how sounders are made and for the Morse code which I got to send and read about as good as you did. And thank you, Mr. Dinwiddie, my schoolteacher in McNary, for bringing me old copies of Electric World *that told me how to make my own telegraph station.*

While they gathered around to watch, I sat down, legs crossed and the sun frying me. The sounder was nearly ruined; it looked like someone had stomped it flat. Maybe the dead telegrapher had tried to destroy it when he saw the Villistas coming. Brushing away the splintered remains of the sound box, I saw what was left and swallowed hard. Fine wire everywhere, in tangled skeins; the coil was half-unwound. That idiot! Still, the brass yoke and fittings were sound. It's pretty hard to do anything to good sound brass, even with a boot heel. The man with the glass eye squatted beside me. When he saw what I was doing with the wire he held out his hands obligingly, the way I used to do with Grandma's yarn when she was knitting.

"Bueno," I said. *"Garcías."*

He grinned, and the glass eye spun awry in the socket. *"Gracias,"* he corrected. *"Gracias, joven."*

I stole a glance at the general and Mr. Tom Mix, trying to avoid seeing the telegrapher's corpse. Mr. Mix kept shaking his head while the general waved his hands and seemed to be pressing an argument. Mr. McFall stood to one side, patient as an old dog, holding the violin to his breast and plucking his eyebrows. Fierro the Butcher lolled in the scanty shade of a giant saguaro, spinning the cylinder of his revolver and humming to himself. The tongue darted out of his mouth every once in a while like the forked tongue of a Hudspeth County rattler, which are the meanest rattlers in Texas and probably elsewhere, although I hadn't been much elsewhere.

"*Bueno*," I said again. That was a handy word. "Good."

A tall, thin officer with a beaked nose walked over. "The general getting impatient," he said in English. "Train must be in Ciudad Juárez before come night."

I had the coil almost finished. Some of the wire had broken and I skinned the ends with my barlow knife and spliced them real neat. Finally I slipped the repaired coil back on the iron core and connected the coil ends to the brass binding posts on the wooden base.

"Finished, *chamaco*?"

"Yes, sir. Now I'll take it in the shack and connect it to the line."

I stepped gingerly over the dead body, which looked to me like it was starting to swell in the hot sun. The telegrapher might as well have been an old boot, for all any of these ruffians cared. I would have prayed for the man except I knew from what had befallen me back in Hudspeth County that I was outside the pale, as they say. I had murdered a human being, and that was against the Ten Commandments as well as Hudspeth County law.

In the dusty telegrapher's shack there was a tin plate of beans on the table and a half-bottle of beer. The sun shining through the dirty windows made golden patterns on the walls where it went through the bottle. The peeling boards were pasted full of old newspaper clippings and pictures, and there was a goldy-looking frame on the table with a woman and two small children in it.

"*Apúrate!*" the long-nosed man urged. "Hurry up, *chamaco!*" Time goes quick! The sun almost behind the sierra!"

I smelled the familiar sharp odor of acid batteries. Luckily the brass sending key was all right, and the relay. When I tied the final wire into the sounder and closed the key, the sounder began to clack like mad. I took a deep breath.

"It works!"

Long Nose clapped me on the back. *"Bravo, chamaco!* What they say in Ciudad Juárez, eh?"

Taking a pencil and a sheet of paper from the desk, I began to write. I didn't understand it, of course; it was all in Spanish, except for the few telegraphers' symbols that are standard anywhere. But I wrote it all down and handed it to Long Nose. He hurried off to show the general while I listened again to the clatter. *Donde* something . . . *el tren*, that must be "the train" . . . *carbón*, that was probably "coal."

The general himself came to the shack, bulking big in the tiny place. Long Nose, whom I found later was Colonel Luis Aguirre Benavides, the general's private secretary, wrote in a notebook while the general dictated. Colonel Aguirre Benavides (that's something funny—in Mexico the father's name comes first, then the mother's) tore off the sheet, written in a very fine hand, and said, "Send that, *por favor, joven.*"

It was encouraging of Colonel Aguirre to say "please." I had a growing hope that maybe I had become important to the Villistas, and was too useful to kill. Opening the key, I sent the message. The sounder started its clicking again. I wrote it down and handed it to Colonel Aguirre, who read it to the general. I began to suspect that General Villa couldn't read or write.

The general nodded, stroking his mustache and looking at me with his slightly bulging eyes. *"Ah, qué bueno!"* he cried. With Colonel Aguirre following he shambled heavily out of the shack, scattering the brown faces which had been peering in.

Activity boiled. The locomotive started to steam. Two desperadoes in the cab held pistols to the head of the engineer and fireman, who was throwing coal into the firebox as if the devil was after him for letting the flames of hell go slack. Villa's men drove the dusty Dodge auto up a makeshift ramp onto a flatcar, doing the same with the horses, which they led into boxcars. Then the whole ragtag gang piled on top of the boxcars, singing and firing guns into the air. One man dragged a sheet of rusty tin to the top of the boxcar and they started a fire on it to cook beans and heat tortillas.

"By Harry, you've done it, Ben!" Mr. McFall cried, seizing my hand and dancing a hornpipe. "You've saved our bacon!"

I looked around for that bastard Fierro but he was busy helping with the horses. "For now, anyway," I admitted.

I approached Colonel Aguirre, who was making a desperate effort to call the roll. No one paid much attention to him.

"Sir?"

He didn't look at me, just went on mumbling, checking off names.

"Is that all? If so, then my partner and I will be going."

He waved me away. *"Muy ocupado, muy ocupado!"*

"Well, then," I said, "we'll just light out. We were glad to make your acquaintance."

But Mr. Tom Mix took my arm, motioned to Mr. McFall to follow, and led us protesting into the single passenger car. It was full of frightened citizens huddled in one end. The general and his staff had taken over the dusty plush seats and were reading maps again.

"We've got a gold operation back there on the creek. All our traps are back there—the tent and pots and pans and a hatchet and my good copper-toe boots and—"

"Shut up," Mr. Mix said, "and listen, both of you!" He pushed us into seats as the car jerked forward. As the train speeded up, the last thing I saw was the telegrapher's body cooking in the sun and a coyote dodging around the shack, creeping toward the body and sniffing. Mr. Mix took out his sack of Bull Durham and rolled another cigarette.

"Don't be foolish, you two! You got out of that kettle of fish very nice, kid, and saved your father's hide. The general likes you. Colonel Aguirre says he's thinking of making you the general's telegrapher."

"Mr. McFall's not my father!"

"No," Mr. McFall said, "though I'd be proud to be." He took out a dirty handkerchief and wiped blood from my forehead. "By the way, what is that song the men are singing?"

Mr. Mix blew a cloud of smoke. " 'Adelita.' Kind of a love song." He turned to me. "You were looking for gold, eh? Well, the general has got bags of it in the baggage car. And the general is mighty generous to people he likes. He's a great man, Villa, and you can get more gold that way than grubbing in a fucking creek!"

"But I don't understand what's going on! If I'm to be his private telegrapher, shouldn't someone tell me what's happening?"

Mr. Mix drew deep on the cigarette and tossed it out the window. Playing very softly, Mr. McFall tried to finger out "Adelita" on the violin.

"All right. Guess it won't do any harm now. You see, the train was on its way from Ciudad Juárez to Chihuahua City. The general seized the train and figured to send a message to Ciudad Juárez that the train was being fired on by rebels and would have to come back. Then he'd load up the train with his soldiers and when they rolled into the station at Ciudad Juárez they could take the city by surprise."

"Very ingenious," Mr. McFall murmured, tightening a string on his violin.

"Only the damned telegrapher tried to be a hero and got shot for his pains, except first he kicked the hell out of the sounder and put it on the blink. We were stuck here till you fixed the sounder and sent the message to General Orozco—and he said: Okay, train, come on back. *Sabes*, kid?"

"I *sabes*—sure."

"They needed you, kid. That's why you're a sort of second-grade hero and have got a chance to make something out of yourself if you keep your nose clean."

I understood. That is, I understood until the train stopped

to take on water and Mr. Mix rose. "Got to leave you folks now."

"Where are you going?" Mr. Mix appeared to be our only real friend.

"Get my horse out of the boxcar and make tracks." He took out a comb and ran it through sleek black hair.

"Tracks? To where?"

"The good old USA! Didn't you ever see me in the moving pictures?"

Moving pictures? I remembered about moving pictures. A man in McNary rented a storeroom once and hung up a sheet and charged a nickel to see something about a train robbery.

"Are you really in the moving pictures?"

He nodded. "Worked for the moving pictures on some orange groves out near Los Angeles, a place called Hollywood. Paid me a hundred dollars a week, too, to wrangle horses and look pretty!"

"Why did you leave?" Mr. McFall asked, hitting a clinker on his fiddle.

"Got tired of the fucking orange trees, came to Mexico with some other cowhands on a dare! But I'm low on funds now, and those fur-and-garment Jews want me back."

"Aren't you coming with us, then?"

"Christ, no! The general's been trying to persuade me to stay. But do you think I want to get my ass shot off when I'm on my way to be famous again, and with more money too? Those moving-picture Jews finally came around." He grinned, showing a lot of white teeth, and gave me a friendly shove. "Remember what I told you, kid. Stick with Villa!" Running a finger through his black hair and shaking himself all over like a feisty dog raring for a fight, he swung down the iron steps, smooth and easy, like a good rider getting off a horse. For a moment he paused under our window.

"Stay clear of Fierro, kid! He's a bastard, and likes pretty boys like you!" Then he was gone, looking for his horse. As the train lurched ahead, we saw him galloping across the parched desert toward the border.

"Well!" Mr. McFall said. "I'm sorry he's gone. Mr.

Mix saved your life and you saved my life, laddie, and it kind of seemed that I ought to have saved Mr. Mix's life somehow to complete the circle."

Stay clear of Fierro, kid! He likes pretty boys like you! It seemed I was out of the frying pan into the fire. My stomach kind of rose up and then fell again, sickeningly. I did not want to be General Villa's personal telegrapher. I did not want to go to a battle in Ciudad Juárez. All I wanted was to go home to Hudspeth County and be with Ma and Grandpa, though the old man would probably whip my ass good with his razor strop and then turn me over to the sheriff to be hanged. But the coal train had begun to pick up speed and the passing landscape was only a blur. I wished I could pray, but no God worthy of his salt would ever listen to a wretch like me.

— 2 —

If you think the lurid past I spoke of was juvenile exaggeration, let me tell you about Ben Wilkerson. I was born in 1899, and named Benjamin Thomas Wilkerson. Grandma Johnson used to call me "Ben Tommy"—can you imagine that? It was even worse than "Benjy." Anyway, at an early age I decided that anybody with a plain-Jane name like Benjamin Thomas Wilkerson would never amount to anything. I tried a lot of other names with more juice to them, and while I was reading *The Three Musketeers* I decided on "D'Artagnan" for a middle name. I kept the "Benjamin" and the "Wilkerson," of course; "D'Artagnan" was just for me to know and dream about.

I did a lot of dreaming, and it made Grandpa Johnson mad. He used to whip me fairly often. My pa died in an accident at the big sulfur mine just west of the little farm where Grandpa raised pigs and goats and wheat and corn. Grandma Johnson, Ma's mother, sat in a rocker all day and stared at the wall. She'd had some kind of brain fever since the year the crick flooded us out and Mom had to take care of the old lady like a baby—feed her and change her and everything. Cleary was my big brother, and Cleary said Grandma's brains had turned to cornmeal mush. Anyway, she was a nice old lady before her brains softened. I figured Grandma must know everything on the newspapers pasted on the wall to keep out drafts, but with mush brains I guess she couldn't make much sense out of headlines like PANAMA CANAL STRIP ACQUIRED or JAPANESE IMMIGRATION SUSPENDED.

Cleary didn't appear to like me much, either, but I think

that was because he was drunk most of the time. He made corn liquor and had about a dozen mason jars full of it under his bed. He sold some of it and made a little money that way, but most he drank. Then he'd get kind of crazy and take down his shotgun and load it and swear he was going to look for McCrackens. The McCrackens had land next to us, and Cleary claimed they set their fence on our property. When Cleary got like that he wouldn't listen to anybody. Ma and I would go out in the barn and wait for him to cool down. Usually, though, Grandpa would hear him ranting and come in from feeding the pigs and take the shotgun away from him. Grandma never paid Cleary any mind; she just sat there staring at the wall.

Grandpa was a tall, skinny man with a fierce white mustache and eyes that were cold and hard and blue as marbles. He'd been a chaplain in the War Between the States. You didn't want to cross Grandpa; he wasn't scared of anybody or anything, because, he said, "When you've come in a wagon all the way down here from Tennessee and fit rattlers and high water and the hog cholera and Texas bullies with more guns than brains, there ain't much you're afraid of anymore!"

He and Cleary used to argue all the time about the house. Grandpa had built the house from oak he gathered from the mountains and sawed and fitted up long ago. He used to tell about how he mortised every joint so it could be fastened together with locustwood pegs. He built the barn, too, and the smokehouse and the corn crib. "There ain't a single solitary nail in any of my work!" he used to claim. "No iron to rust!"

Cleary would take another swig from his jar and jeer at Grandpa. "Them locust pins gonna dry out and the whole kit and caboodle'll fall down!"

Then Grandpa would say, "It ain't done for these twenty year, has it? Good for another ten, at least, and by that time me and the old lady'll be dead and gone and our immortal souls flew up to that Golden Kingdom in the sky!"

Cleary would rag him about the Golden Kingdom and Grandpa would get mad and take down the big Bible from the shelf and read Cleary where it said about the Golden Kingdom. That never settled anything.

Maybe Grandpa thought the house was good for another ten years but Ma had doubts whether she was. Before Pa died and we had to move in with Grandpa I remember her as real gentle and loving. Anymore, she complained all the time, and got thinner and thinner. There were grease spots on her dress and she took a lot of Dr. Miles's Nervina. "Well," she'd say, turning from the cookstove and wiping sweat with the hem of her apron, "this house may last another ten, but I doubt I will!" Lips set grim, she'd haul Grandma out of her chair and say, "Now, just look! You've messed yourself again already! I got to clean you all over!"

Seems like the only time Ma put on a clean dress was on church-day or when Mr. Dinwiddie came to visit. Mr. Dinwiddie was my teacher in the one-room McNary school. When Ma heard his mare she'd shuck off the old gingham dress and put on the flowered shift she wore to church on a Sunday, along with the good shoes wrapped in newspaper in the closet. By the time the teacher got on the porch, she'd be sitting in a rocker reading Grandpa's Bible.

"Well, good afternoon, Mr. Dinwiddie!"

Hair combed and face splashed with water, I'd linger close by, wriggling with delight. Mr. Dinwiddie was a young man—only nineteen or twenty or thereabouts. He was slender and dark with nearsighted blue eyes and steel-rimmed spectacles; stoop-shouldered, Ma said, from too much book learning. Ma said there were a lot of things in books that common folk like us didn't need to know. Mr. Dinwiddie was always putting things in the children's heads, a lot of folks grumbled, and the people of McNary hadn't made up their minds about him. Still, he came cheap—thirty dollars a month and room and board at the Ballards' place down the road. Mr. Ballard was superintendent at the sulfur mine.

"Good afternoon, ma'am. May I come in?"

I was breathless with anticipation, seeing books and magazines under his arm. Mr. Dinwiddie wanted me to read lots of books, and I did, but my favorite reading was the copies of *Electric World* he sometimes brought.

Ma would pick up a jug and take out the corncob. "Do you care for a cup of whiskey, Mr. Dinwiddie? That road out from town is awful hot and dusty."

"Ah . . . no, ma'am. Thank you kindly."

"Cleary's best! Good white corn and rye and heavy malt! He sprouts the malt hisself, and double-stills the liquor!"

"I just stopped by to see Benjamin, to bring him some books." Taking them, I bobbed my head in bashful gratitude. I idolized Mr. Dinwiddie and always tried to talk refined like him, though Cleary made fun of me when I used a big word. "And here's a recent copy of *Electric World*. I understand Ben has made himself a little telegraph set."

Ma bustled to the stove. "I'll just brew us up a little ginseng tea, then. Oh, that stuff the boy's got up in the loft? All them wires and things?"

"I suppose so, ma'am."

Pumping water into the cracked enamel pot, Ma shook her head. "I declare, Ben's got his cranium so full of learning I fear it'll overheat his head someday and give him an apoplexy!" She stirred yarbs into the pot. "He ain't never around no more when he's needed. He's up in that loft reading a book or down to the railroad pestering Mr. Ballew or—"

"The telegraph operator . . . yes. I understand Mr. Ballew gave him some wire and things. Well, Ben has an inquiring mind, ma'am."

"I'd a whole lot rather he'd inquire into some of the chores around here!" Ma handed Mr. Dinwiddie the best cup and they set together.

I guess it was true; I did a lot of reading and dreaming, though I think no more than any healthy boy with a bump of curiosity. When I was supposed to be chopping weeds or cutting wood for the cookstove I'd just as likely be stretched out on the corn-crib roof, my favorite spot, dreaming, reading, looking at the clouds. I would hear

Grandpa and Cleary in the garden patch, thinning out carrots or something.

"Now, where's that boy?" Grandpa would grumble, leaning on his hoe. "He's got a supply of disappearing pills, I think! Set him to a task and before you know it he's disappeared in thin air!" I'd make up my mind to come down in five minutes and go back to the chores, but I didn't have a watch and it was hard to tell when five minutes was up.

"You got to take him in hand again, Grandpa," Cleary would say, "soon's you find him!" Then he'd laugh.

"Ben ain't at all like Cleary," Ma went on. "Cleary's only nine years older but he's a worker—leastways when he's sober. Traps coons and bobcats and muskrats and gathers ginseng and trades for sugar and salt and tobacco and canned goods at Hawley's store, things we need around here."

Mr. Dinwidde finished his tea and stood up. "I'm afraid that's the last issue of *Electric World*, Ben. My subscription has run out. And there's other news, too. Ma'am, I won't be teaching the children anymore, this fall. I've only had a year of college, you know. Well, an uncle of mine died and left me a little money. In a few days I'm going back to college in Austin to get my degree."

For a minute I didn't understand. *Electric World* was such a wonderful magazine. It told about Mr. Marconi's wireless invention and how to make a telescope and had diagrams of electric motors and pictures of Mr. Edison's talking machines and such. It beat Grandpa's Bible and *Pilgrim's Progress* all hollow. I was leafing through it, excited, when what Mr. Dinwiddie said sank in. *No! Please don't go!* The world started to come apart on me. Teacher Dinwiddie had shown me a new world, a world of *The Three Musketeers* and *Roughing It* and poems by Mr. Henry Wadsworth Longfellow and tales about the Roman Empire.

"I guess they'll soon hire another teacher. There's still a month before the school term starts." Mr. Dinwiddie put a hand on my shoulder. "Maybe someday you can be a teacher yourself, Ben, and teach the McNary children!

33

You go back to school and study hard, now! Read all you can, find out all you can. I've got great hopes for you!"

I was disconsolate. Maybe Mr. Dinwiddie leaving was what started my downfall; I've often thought it was.

"Anyway," Mr. Dinwiddie went on, "I'll bet you'll enjoy going, seeing all your friends. Weren't you sweet on Prue Ballard, Ben?"

My face got red and I mumbled something stupid. Prue Ballard, the prettiest girl in the school, had long chestnut curls and a full sweet mouth and soft brown eyes. I'm not sure she even knew I existed. But I worshiped her from afar. By McNary standards the Ballards were rich. They had a house with wallpaper and it was said that in the parlor was a big glass dome on a stand with stuffed birds inside. Once, sitting behind Prue, I touched a curl that lay on my desk. The feel of it lingers still in my fingertips—soft, silken, thrilling. And the way she walked! I didn't know much about sex things, but her proud walk sent an electric thrill through me that was not described in *Electric World*. Once I dared to poke my foot forward under the desk and touch her high-laced black shoe. I shudder still at what happened.

Keep your dirty feet off me, Ben Wilkerson!

I hated her for that. Yet I could not help but remember the softness of the chestnut curl, the touch of my bare foot on her shoe—Prue Ballard's shoe.

That same exciting day Mr. Dinwiddie paused writing sums on the blackboard. "What's that? Prue Ballard, did you speak?"

"No, sir."

Mr. Dinwiddie went back to his sums on the blackboard while some of the kids giggled behind their hands.

"Now, you must always remember to carry, whenever the sum of the column is . . ."

Well, I knew all about sums and carrying and stuff like that already. Red-faced, I buried my nose in the arithmetic book. *I touched her, anyway!* And my feet weren't dirty, either, except for a little dust—road dust. Still, Prue Ballard had only become more distant, more unattainable, more goddesslike. I worshiped her. Sometimes my passion for her made me feel very queer in my groin. What was that feeling, anyway? Well, I had another arrow to my quiver. Old Mrs. Cady, the conjure-woman, had told me what to do.

"Now," Mr. Dinwiddie said, "I must be going."

"Stay for supper, teacher!" Ma urged. "We got sidemeat cooked with a mess of turnips, and a gooseberry tart in the pie-safe. Grandpa and Cleary will be in soon and we'll all sup together!"

Mr. Dinwiddie shook his head. "I'm sorry, ma'am. Thank you for the invitation, but Mrs. Ballard will be expecting me and I've promised to help Prue with her multiplication tables tonight."

Prue! Prue Ballard! The love-knife turned slow and sharp in the fresh wound. Maybe Prue herself would be sitting next to Mr. Dinwiddie at supper! And Mr. Dinwiddie himself once said he had his own girl in Austin. The unfairness of it!

Mr. Dinwiddie rose to leave. "Give my regards to Mr. Johnson and Cleary, ma'am." We followed him out into the dooryard. "And you, Ben . . ." Mr. Dinwiddie got on his white mare. "Make me proud of you someday!"

"Thank you for the books," I mumbled.

After he was gone, Ma said, "Whatever is the matter with you, boy? You act like a sick cow. Is it that Ballard girl again?"

"Maybe," I said, disconsolate.

"I don't want you fooling around with her, now! The Ballards is quality, and you ain't got no business with the Ballards! The Good Book says 'each to his own kind,' each to each. It says that real plain in the Bible, although I don't remember exactly where right now." She rapped me on top of the head with a knitting needle. "Remember, now!"

Fooling around? "I ain't . . . I didn't do anything!"

"See that you don't, then."

After supper I climbed the ladder to the loft, feeling sad. The future was black—Mr. Dinwiddie leaving, Prue Ballard humiliating me, the devil working his wicked ways inside me like Grandpa said. All that was left was my homemade telegraph set on the shelf beside my cornshuck mattress. I had sawed a piece from an old horseshoe, hammered it flat, and wound it with wire Mr. Ballew gave me to make the core. A piece of a broken spokeshave, hinged at one end and supported by a spring, tapped on the homemade coil when current from the battery Mr. Ballew also gave me was set free by the crude telegraph key. The key was my own design, fashioned from a strip of tin can mounted on a wooden block. This was station BW on my own Benjamin D'Artagnan Wilkerson South Texas and Chihuahua Railroad. Moodily I touched the key, hearing the reassuring click of the sounder. I wanted desperately to talk to someone—anyone. Bemused, in the darkness I worked the key in the Morse-code symbols old Mr. Ballew had taught me. At first, I didn't realize what I was tapping out. Then I knew. *I . . . love . . . you.*

Who did I love? I didn't know, exactly. Downstairs, Cleary was drunk again and arguing with Grandpa. When my brother Cleary was drunk, he could make fine music with the songbow he fashioned from a chinaberry branch. The limber bow was strung with a cord, and when Cleary held one end of the bow against his teeth like a Jew's harp he could make different notes by opening and closing his mouth. They always wanted Cleary at the play-parties.

> I wish I was an apple,
> A-hanging on a tree,
> And every time my sweet love passed
> She'd take a bite of me.

Cleary only played that song because Grandpa said it was sinful.

> She told me that she loved me
> And called me sugarplum.
> She throwed her arms about me
> And I thought my time had come!

There was lightning in the west. Some weather must be making up. From down below I heard Grandpa complain,

"My joints hurts like fire, they do!" Ma was washing dishes in the tin pan.

I . . . love . . . you. I sent that message over and over, like it was a magic spell or something, a message that might straighten out my love yearnings.

A fanciful thought struck me. I had some wire left over. Maybe I could run the wire through the trees down toward the railroad tracks. Maybe it would reach Mr. Ballew's shanty and then we could talk to each other when he wasn't busy with railroad traffic. Excited, I climbed out on the roof of the kitchen lean-to. It was near dark and the air was cool and fresh. Crickets chirped, an owl fluttered by, one of Cleary's coon dogs raised his head from between his paws and whimpered.

"Shut up!" I hissed. Old Posey stared at me for a minute, then went back to sleep. I tied one end of the reel of wire to the chimney and jumped down into the tall grass. Inside the house I could hear Cleary arguing with Grandpa.

"I know what's wrong with Ben. He's got girl thoughts, I bet! I remember when I was his age. Oh, my pecker'd get stiff as a ramrod when I—"

"Cleary Johnson, you shut your mouth!" Ma cried. "I declare, such talk in my house!"

My feet were cool in the dew-wet grass. I still remember that delicious swishing cool; maybe it's fixed in my mind because what I did that night led to such disaster. Unreeling the wire, I rounded the corn crib and shinnied up the big sycamore at the end of the cornfield. At the top I pulled on the wire and saw it come up taut, clearing the corn crib, shimmering in moonlight.

Of course, there wasn't enough wire to go all the way to the railroad; I guess I'd known there wasn't. But it was a start. Mr. Ballew would probably give me more wire if I asked him nice. Satisfied for now, I climbed back down with a feeling of a job well done and made my way over the kitchen lean-to to my bed. Cleary was drunk, it sounded like, and was singing. I guess Grandpa and Grandma and Ma had gone to bed. Through my open window came a cool breeze that smelled like rain, and there was distant lightning. I remember to count between the flash and the sound of thunder . . . *three, four, five, six, seven, eight*—boom! It wasn't far away, the rain.

Weary, I stretched out on the cornshuck mattress and played my mouth-harp very softly and finally dreamed the terrible dreams of youth.

Mr. Tom Ballew had lost his leg under the cars a long time ago. I paused outside the shanty, listening to the telegraph chattering inside. Morning sun silvered the rails; they came together in the distance like an arrow pointing west.

"I'm here," I said when the clatter of the sounder stopped and Mr. Ballew closed the key.

He was maybe fifty, a lonely and bitter old man. "No kin," he would say, sitting in the rickety chair outside and smoking his pipe. "No woman to fry my bacon and make coffee, no one to talk to—"

"You can talk to me," I always offered.

"What woman would want an old one-legged man anyway? Can't blame 'em!" Knocking out the dottle in his palm, he sighed. "What the hell you want, Ben?"

"I . . . I . . . just come by to visit." I would have to be careful and not come on him too quick about the needed wire. Sometimes when he was feeling real low he'd chase me out of the shanty with his crutch and cuss me. "Two legs, eh? Think you're smart! Git out of here!" But mostly we were friends.

Early-autumn sun was shining at the edge of a bank of dark clouds. There was a flash of lightning from cloud to cloud, and the sounder suddenly chattered. I waited a respectful time and then said, "They're calling you."

"No, they ain't."

"But—"

Mr. Ballew pointed with his pipe toward the distant clouds. The sun had been swallowed up, and lightning flashes laced the blackness. "Sometimes lightning gets into the telegraph wires and sends a lot of crazy stuff."

"Lightning does that?" I was fascinated, and had forgotten all about the wire.

"Sure does."

"But I heard an X and a C and something that sounded like Q—or maybe L!"

Joking, he said, "Chinese words, maybe! They got lightning in China too, I guess."

I picked at a wart on my finger. I probably got that wart from the dead frog in my matchbox. Mr. Ballew seemed so sad this morning that I wanted to share something with him. I took the matchbox out of my shirt pocket and opened it. Mr. Ballew sniffed the air, drew back.

"Jesus Christ, boy! You been sprayed by a polecat or something?"

I showed him the little frog. "It ain't . . . isn't quite ripe yet, but—"

"Good God! It's ripe enough for me!"

I tugged gently at the leg of the frog. "Mrs. Cady . . . you know, the one they say is a witch? She told me if I took a frog and let him rot good so he'd all fall apart, then you could put the bones in a little sack and fasten it to a girl's dress when she wasn't looking and then that girl would love you!"

I'd told it just as general information but Mr. Ballew knew better. "That Ballard girl, eh?"

"I guess." I couldn't meet his eye and my face got red. I'd only thought maybe he could use a frog to get him a woman.

"Witches! Dead frogs! Spells and conjures!" Mr. Ballew heaved himself out of his chair and stood on one leg like a crane. Waving his crutch, he said, "Get along home, boy, and don't bother me!" Hobbling back into the shanty, he mumbled as he went, "Ain't bad enough I got to sit here all day listenin' to a clacky telegraph sounder—I got to put up with silly talk about witches and conjures!"

I didn't get my wire.

We were getting ready for church on Sunday. Grandpa put on his old gray soldier coat with the brass buttons he was so proud of. He'd fought with Longstreet's corps at Gettysburg and Chickamauga and Petersburg. Cleary, in his underpants because it was sultry, sipped at his mason jar and picked at Grandpa.

"The niggers say, 'Don't study war no more,' Grandpa! How you come off going to church of a Sunday morning in that old soldier coat?"

"I don't allow you to provoke me," Grandpa said, buttoning the coat right up under his chin and picking up his good felt hat, fresh-brushed by Ma. "Keep an eye on Grandma, Cleary, whilst we're gone."

Cleary drained the jar. "Hell, she ain't goin' no place, is she?" He went into the bedroom to get another jar from under his bed.

Ma and I were ready, Ma in her flowery shift and a pink silk tucker, gray hair tucked under a straw hat with a red ribbon. I had on a white shirt and nearly new jeans and the precious copper-toed boots Cleary bought me one winter when the pelts he trapped were real thick and lush and brought a lot of money. Ma gave me a dime to put in the collection plate.

"You bring around the wagon, boy?" Grandpa asked me.

"Yes, sir, I did."

We got into the wagon behind the mule, Grandpa and Ma on the seat and me on a feedsack behind. I could hear the church bell in McNary. It's surprising how far you can hear a church bell on Sunday morning. As we wheeled out of the yard, Grandpa's hard blue eyes caught a glimpse of my shiny copper wire hanging up in the sky.

"What in the Lord's name is *that*?"

"Just some wire, Grandpa," I explained. "I hung it up there like a real telegraph wire."

He clucked to old Jupiter. "We come home, boy, you take that dinged thing down—you hear me? It's like kind of a graven idol, running up into the Lord's heaven like that. Anyway, it probably scares the chickens and the goats."

"Grandpa, it ain't—"

"Mind your grandpa!" Ma told me.

"Yes'm."

Reverend Caldwell's sermon was a real rouser, all about

40

hell and damnation. Thunder outside, and flashes of lightning through the church windows gave it a kind of heavenly confirmation. I like a real stem-winder like Reverend Caldwell—I always did. Life in West Texas wasn't very entertaining and I think that's why so many went to church.

Outside it was sprinkling a little. The wind rose, whipping Grandpa's gray coat around his knees. Ma held a hand to her hat as we hurried across the churchyard and there were sprinkles of cold rain. Grandpa didn't hardly wait to talk to the Teasdales, the Ellises, and the Rollinses, like he always did. Climbing up on the wagon in a hurry, he picked up the whip. "Come along, you two. Hurry! Looks like it's going to be a gully-washer!"

Old Jupiter was trotting as fast as he could and we were halfway home, just passing the McCracken place, when I saw smoke drifting up through the sycamore trees. "Something's burning, Grandpa," I said. "Look over yonder!" I could smell smoke and see a tongue of flame licking high into the trees.

Grandpa sawed old Jupiter to a stop, looked, sniffed the air. "Godamighty! It's our place!"

It *was* our place. Flames roared at the shingles Grandpa had hand-split long ago, and as we wheeled into the yard the loft—my loft, where I slept—fell in with a roar and a shower of sparks.

"Cleary!" Ma jumped down off the wagon, tearing her shift on a splinter. "Cleary's in there, and Grandma! Oh, my God!"

Grandpa ran up on the porch, calling, "Cleary! Where are you, Cleary? Oh, Lordy! What will we do?"

The parlor wasn't on fire—yet—but it was full of smoke. I followed Grandpa into the smoky blackness, hearing him cough and spit as he searched for Grandma and Cleary. Gasping for breath, I dropped to my knees, where the air was fresher. Ma's bottle of Dr. Miles's Nervina, sitting on the shelf, exploded and blew sticky stuff all over me. Below the blanket of smoke I could see Grandma still sitting in her rocker, staring at the wall.

"I found her!" I cried. "Grandpa, I found her!"

Grandpa was wandering through the kitchen. "Cleary, boy! Where are you? Oh, Lord . . . let me find Cleary!"

Grandma just sat in her chair. I tried to explain fire to her but she just kind of smiled and went on rocking. I had to fight to haul her out of the rocker that had been home to her. "Goddammit!" I yelled. "Come out of there, Grandma!"

She was heavy and kind of billowed around like a pudding. Finally I got hold of her leg. She fell almost on top of me but I dragged her out the door, her trying to hang on to an arm of the rocker and smiling, like she was real happy. I left her sprawled on the porch, dress hiked high around her fat thighs. Ma ran to her and pulled down Grandma's dress.

"Take her out in the yard!" I said, and ran back into the house, bumping into Grandpa, who was dragging Cleary by the straps of his overalls. Cleary looked awful. He was all red and peeling. Long strips of skin hung down from his face and arms, and his mouth sagged open. His overalls were on fire and when Grandpa dropped him in the yard I ran to the well and got a dipperful of water to throw on the smoldering overalls.

"He's dead," Grandpa cried. "Oh, Lord . . . the boy's dead!"

As if to confirm his words, a gush of flames exploded out of the house and I could smell corn liquor; Cleary's mason jars had blown up. My hands burned and I looked at them in a kind of daze. They were blistered. Big fat bubbles were beginning to rise on them, and Dr. Miles's Nervina was sticky all over my shirt.

"He's dead!" Grandpa yelled, and dropped to his knees, clasping his hands in prayer. His gray coat was singed and one side of his mustache had been toasted brown. A little rain started to fall and sooty black streaks ran down his cheeks. "Oh, Lord . . . receive Cleary Wilkerson who is dead this day of the devil's fire!"

Buggies and wagons began to roll into the yard. Mr. Claude Teasdale started a bucket brigade but it wasn't much use; the whole house was ablaze. Men ran back and forth to the well carrying buckets, tin cans, bottles—anything that would hold water. But it only turned to steam when they threw it through the door. Finally they gave up.

"Someone get Doc Birkett!" Mrs. Rayford Ellis suggested.

Luther Teasdale, who had been bending over Cleary, shook his head. " 'Twon't do no good. He's dead. Suffocated by the smoke, probably."

Some of the women were helping Ma with Grandma. She no longer had her rocking chair so they set her on the edge of the watering trough and she almost fell in. I saw a dull sheen in the dirt and picked it up. It was the end of my telegraph wire, melted so there was a shiny nub on the end.

They were still arguing over Cleary. Someone found a mirror and held it to Cleary's scorched lips. Cleary's coon dogs howled. Holding the wire in my burned hands, I tried not to look at Cleary but couldn't help it. His overalls and shirt were nearly burned away and the skin was blistered into curls like wood shavings. The drizzle turned into a downpour. As the drops fell on the smoldering timbers with their locustwood pins, Mrs. Mose Allison dropped to her knees in the wet grass.

"Lord, why? And it happened while we was in your house a-worshipin' you!"

"Ain't no fog on the mirror," Mr. Teasdale decided in a hushed voice. "The spirit has done left the body, that's a fact!"

"Maybe," someone suggested, "if we was to roll him over a barrel, like when the little Gumble child fell in Cinder Crick—"

"Didn't do no good then," Mr. Rayford Ellis, the blacksmith said. "Don't hardly see how it'll help now."

"I'll get a barrel out of the barn," I offered.

No one seemed to hear me but Grandpa. He was staring at me with those cold blue marble eyes.

Mr. Ellis took a pinch of sniff and stuffed it between his gum and lips. It was raining harder. The women carried Grandma, still smiling that foolish smile, up on the porch, about all that was left of the oak-and-locustwood house.

The men still hung around Cleary's body, trying to say things of comfort.

"Rain has drained all the lightning out of the clouds now," Mr. Ballard said. I hadn't seen him come. His buggy was in the yard, and Prue Ballard was sitting in it with an umbrella over her head. "One stroke hit the tin roof of the pulley-house at the mine, but the lightning rods drawed it off. Metal attracts lightning, that's a fact!"

I was still holding the melted end of that telegraph wire in my hands. Grandpa got up off his knees and pointed his finger at me.

"Beelzebub!"

They all stared. I could see, almost feel, Prue Ballard's soft eyes on me.

"Beelzebub!" Grandpa snarled. "This is a Beelzebub of a wicked, willful child! The devil worked through this child to destroy, to burn . . . to kill!"

"Ben?" Mr. Teasdale asked. Mr. Ellis spat and asked, "Whatever do you mean, Mr. Johnson?"

Grandpa snatched the end of the wire from my nerveless fingers and pulled hard. The other end was in the sycamore and it came loose and spun down in shiny coils. "This here wire drawed the lightning! I told the boy to take the unholy thing down, going up into God's Sunday air like it was, thumbing its nose at the Lord! This here wire was the devil's instrument, and this here child the agent of the devil!"

There was a general sucking-in of breaths. Drawing away from me, the people started to murmur among themselves.

"The devil has took possession of this child!" Grandpa yelled. "The devil has worked his will through this child to destroy, to burn . . . yes, to kill! Kill Cleary Wilkerson!"

"Now, wait a minute!" Mr. Rayford Ellis objected. "This here is silly, Mr. Johnson! It was just an accident, that's all!"

Mrs. Ellis joined in. She gave me cookies sometimes. "Now, don't blame it on the boy! My goodness!"

Grandpa wouldn't have it. Pointing his bony fingers at me, he started to chant in tongues, his voice breaking into a high pitch. "Beelzebub! Beelzebub!" There was a lot more funny words that tumbled all over each other as spittle flew from his mouth and wet his beard, only I could never reproduce them. "Beelzebub! Beelzebub!" That's all I can remember.

Heart pounding, scared to death, I ran. Stumbling, slipping in the rain-wet grass, I fell and picked myself up to run again. Sobbing, filled with panic and horror, I blundered through the stinking shoemake bushes across the road and lost myself in their green embrace. *Doom, doom, doom for all time, for Benjamin D'Artagnan Wilkerson, the Beelzebub, whoever or whatever Beelzebub was!* Hiding in the shoemakes, my heart trying to pound its way out of my shirt, I put my hands over my ears, still hearing that relentless chanting ever higher and higher. God help me! I thought. I've burned down Grandpa's house and murdered my brother Cleary Wilkerson!

— 3 —

There's a lot more, of course. In fact, when I wandered away from McNary I was so despondent that I tried to hang myself under a railroad bridge near El Paso, but the rope was old and rotten. All I got out of it was skinned knees and elbows from falling in the rocks.

Maybe it sounds comic now, but few can understand the depths of despond a fourteen-year-old boy can sink to. If there was any way to measure my gloom—for example, some kind of electrical despondency meter to put on me and measure my despair—I'd have driven the needle off-scale and probably blown up the meter in a puff of smoke. But right now I was on a Mexican railroad train headed for the Battle of Ciudad Juárez and it was the day before my fourteenth birthday.

You wouldn't have thought these people were going to a battle. They were all singing and cracking jokes and eating tortillas and drinking some beer they found in the telegraph station. The beer was warm and foamed all over everyone. No one cared except the scared passengers the general let off when we stopped once for water. The soldiers played dominoes and a game called *conquién* in the aisles—it looked like what we called cooncan. Quarrels broke out. From time to time guns went off and Mr. McFall and I cringed. But it was only the soldiers on the roof shooting jackrabbits.

Everyone was singing bawdy songs. With my scanty Spanish I picked out the words of one of them:

> There were three whores sitting in a *silla*,
> Saying to each other, "Viva Pancho Villa!"

A *silla* is a chair, you see, though why three ladies sitting in a chair is so funny I don't know, except that everybody roared with laughter.

There were a lot of women soldiers on the train. It seemed odd for women to go to war, but there they were, wearing gingham dresses, mostly, with big straw hats, but weighed down with cartridge belts and pistols just like the men. One of them—an old gray-haired woman with a big wart on her nose—took a shine to me. Her name was Victoria.

"Tienes hambre, niño?"

Well, I wasn't any *niño;* I was practically fourteen—but I was hungry. She went away and came back with beans and tortillas and a chunk of the sugar candy they call *piloncillo*. She didn't pay any attention to Mr. McFall; just squatted beside me and patted my knee while I ate.

"Guapo," she mumbled from time to time. *"Muy guapo."*

I didn't know what that meant. But Mr. McFall, watching me eat (I knew he was hungry too, and after Victoria left I gave him most of my beans), explained it meant, "Handsome—very handsome." Well, if she thought I was *guapo* it was all right with me, although I never thought of myself as particularly handsome.

As the train approached Ciudad Juárez I could see city smoke in the distance. The train stopped occasionally and everyone got out with crowbars and sledges and tore up the rails behind them. It was clear they didn't intend to come back that way.

Besides all the roughly dressed soldiers on the train there were other interesting people. One, I found later, was the grandson of a man called Garibaldi who Mr. McFall said liberated Italy. This young man was a commander of one of the Villa outfits, and he was a real dandy. He stuck out like a sore thumb because he wore a tan riding suit, kind of, and a green velour hat turned up on one side with a feather in it. Another was an American newspaper reporter, a Mr. Wickwire. He was from the El Paso *Morning Times* and was assigned to follow General Villa.

"I don't relish the idea of getting killed right across the river from my house," he said, mopping his brow with a handkerchief. "I've been shot at enough in the last month. When the shooting starts, you two come with me and we'll skip across the river out of harm's way." He was a funny little man, bald as an egg except for a gray fringe around his ears, with nearsighted eyes peering through iron-rimmed spectacles. I figured it would be just as good for him to go home to El Paso instead of staying for the battle, because I didn't think he could see very well anyhow. But that was my mistake; Henry Wickwire, in his dirty plaid shirt and leather puttees, turned out to be one of the best reporters around.

"We're very near the city," Mr. McFall said, eating the last tortilla. "I'm nervous, Ben. Are you? I've never been in a battle."

"Me neither," I said. My stomach felt queasy and I was considering whether to throw up the food old Victoria had given me.

"Let's keep an eye on Mr. Wickwire, shall we? Wherever he goes, we'll follow him."

"All right," I said.

It was almost dark. Someone lit the swinging oil lamps in the car. To steady my nerves I took out my mouth-organ and played a few chords, but my mouth was pretty dry. Ahead I could see dim lights—the lights of Ciudad Juárez. The man with the glass eye staggered along the aisle. He smelled sour with beer, and was punching cartridges into the magazine of his revolver. He grinned at me without the grace of teeth.

"*Hola, joven!*"

"*Hola, señor,*" I said back.

He had the funniest glass eye I'd ever seen. Old Mrs. Cady, the witch-woman, had a glass eye, but it stared straight ahead while her good one looked around. His good eye stared straight ahead, but the glass one swoggled around in every direction, like it was too loose, and not a good fit.

"*No pistolas?*"

"*No,*" I said, "*no pistolas.*"

"We're noncombatants," Mr. McFall explained. *"Nosotros no vamos pelearnos*. We're not going to fight."

Glass Eye looked incredulous. "No . . . fight?"

"No, sir," Mr. McFall said. "We're neutral, you see, as U.S. citizens."

"No fight?" Glass Eye demanded. He roared with laughter. Lurching back down the aisle, he returned in a few minutes and dumped two Colt revolvers and a pair of bandoliers full of bullets in our laps. "Everybody fight!" He slapped Mr. McFall on the back.

After he left, Mr. McFall looked with distaste at the weapons. "This is getting very sticky, Ben!"

With a boy's curiosity, I took a cartridge belt and slung it over my shoulder. Then I picked up a revolver; it was empty and I plucked cartridges from the bandolier and pushed them into the cylinder.

"I wish you wouldn't do that," Mr. McFall said. "It makes me nervous."

Now we were sliding past buildings in the outreaches of Ciudad Juárez. A moon was rising and in the faint glow a man came out of a signal tower and waved at the coal train as it passed. Then he turned suddenly and started to run back into the tower; I guess he had seen the cars were filled with Villista soldiers. If he had a telephone, and he probably did, there would be all hell waiting for us in the city! But a shot rang out from on top of our car and the man in the signal tower threw up his arms and fell over the railing. Maybe this looked like a ragtag army, but they sure knew their business.

"Take those damned things off!" Mr. McFall begged. "Somebody will mistake you for one of those Federales and shoot you!"

I kind of liked the way the heavy bandolier lay across my chest, and the sag of the *pistola* at my belt. I had a .22 rifle once that Cleary bought me when he was in a good mood, but that was a popgun—nothing like this.

"In a minute," I said. "Wait till we get a little closer."

Well, we got closer almost before I knew it. Brakes locked and screaming, the coal train slid along the platform. It was dusk and there were only a few dim electric lights in the station. Whooping and yelling, coal-dusty Villistas poured from the cars, firing so many shots in the air I figured they wouldn't have any left for the battle. In the dim light I saw Mr. Wickwire outside our window, beckoning. There wasn't time to disarm myself; Mr. McFall was on the floor behind me, breathing hard.

"Too late!" he gasped. "The way he was making a flat shirttail, Wickwire's halfway across the river by now!"

Orange spurts pierced the smoky gloom inside the station. The racket under the corrugated iron roof was deafening. Another shot broke one of the swinging oil lamps in the car and dribbled kerosene on me. Wiping the oily stuff from my face with a sleeve, I looked around. We were the only people in the old passenger car. The rear end, where General Villa and his staff had been, was burning.

"We got to get out of here," I decided. Putting a leg over the windowsill, I dropped to the cinders beside the track. Mr. McFall was slower, and I reached up a hand to help him. Just then a shadowy figure alongside the tracks lit something with a match. It flared long enough for me to see a uniformed Federal soldier heave something into the air. Spitting fire, it soared through a window and exploded inside the car. Mr. McFall disappeared in a gush of smoke and flame. Dynamite, that was what it was! Maybe they thought the general and his staff were inside.

Sick at my stomach, I grabbed the sill and hoisted myself up.

"Mr. McFall! Where are you?" I cried.

In the fire-lit smoke I couldn't see anything. My ears rang like church bells from the explosion. Dropping down on the cinders, I ran like a rabbit. The pistol and cartridge belt weighed me down but I set a pretty good record for a hundred yards, out through a door that hung on one hinge and directly into the belly of a fat Federal soldier crouched behind a pile of railroad ties.

He fell over backward, rifle going off into the air. I kept going at high speed, completely out of control. All I knew was that if I kept running I was still alive.

I didn't know where the Villistas were; there seemed to

be only Federales around, milling in the streets of Ciudad Juárez, looking confused. Compared to Villa's men, the Federales looked like real soldiers. They were kind of simple-looking country people, but they all had high soft-leather boots and tan jackets and big felt hats with some kind of insignia on them.

On a side street was a small public garden lit by tiny electric bulbs. I dodged in there and hid under a kind of kiosk I guess was for band concerts because there were cornets and trombones and a bass drum lying on the floor that must have been left when the shooting started. There were a lot of little refreshment stalls lit by petroleum wicks or colored-tissue-wrapped candles that flickered in the night wind, but no one to tend them. Away to the north, close to the river, a lot of shooting was going on. I had no intention of trying to cross the river to safety right then. I would just sit under the bandstand, stinking of kerosene, and think about poor Mr. McFall.

He never had a chance. That stick of dynamite must have blown him to kingdom come. My eyes started to mist up. Mr. McFall had been good to me and taught me a lot. He wasn't much on the business end of a shovel, saying it ruined his fingers for playing the violin. But he shared and shared alike with me when I was hungry and desperate in El Paso, and was almost like the father I lost when I was a baby. *Take those damned things off!* Those were his last words to me. Well, I would take off the damned gun! No use pretending I was a warrior; blood made me sick.

It started to rain, a light misty drizzle. The candles guttered out. Somebody must have put the central electric station out of business too, because the few electric lights glimmered off. I wormed my way out of the bandolier. That pistol was fascinating; big and oily and deadly. For the last time I picked it up and squinted along the barrel. That was when I heard a frightened squeak, like a mouse.

"Who's there?" I called, my heart beginning to race. People say something about a person's heart being in his mouth when in danger. Mine was in my chest where it belonged, only it was pounding so hard I thought it would bust out right through my stinking shirt.

"Who's there?" No answer. Well, it might have *been* a mouse! Mice could very well have a home under the bandstand and sneak out, after everyone had gone home, for crumbs and bits of food.

Still I heard a lot of rustling and scraping. If it was a mouse, it was a damned big one! Picking up the loaded revolver, I aimed it into the blackness under the bandstand. What did you say under these circumstances? If it was a person, "Hands up" wasn't practical; there wasn't enough room under there. "Surrender"? That sounded pretty theatrical. "You're under arrest"? I wasn't a policeman. Scared, and trying to think what to say, I accidentally pulled the trigger. The whole underside of the kiosk lit up; every sagging rotten board could be counted, and there was a jungle of spiderwebs.

"Me rindo!" a voice called.

Me rindo? Rendirse, to surrender.

"All right!" I said sternly. "Drop your gun or whatever you're dragging there and advance and be recognized!"

It was the dirtiest and most tearful small soldier I ever saw. She was one of Villa's women soldiers, and was scared to death. When a stray shot ripped through the underpinning of the bandstand, showering us with splinters, I don't know which one of us was more scared. Right then I wished I had a swig of Ma's Nervina tonic.

On hands and knees she scuttled toward me, dragging an old musket. I took it away from her and laid it down.

"Good Lord!" I said. "Lady or whatever, what are you doing under this bandstand?"

Of course, she could have asked me the same question. But all she did was snuggle up beside me like a scared pup and hide a tearstained face on my shirt. It was embarrassing.

"Tengo miedo, señor!" That meant she was scared.

I wasn't any *señor*; I was only thirteen years old, but that *"señor"* kind of pleased me.

"You're supposed to be out there fighting like the rest of the *soldaderas*!" I told her.

"Qué?" She turned un-Mexican blue eyes up to me, puzzled, and wiped her nose with the sleeve of a ragged shirt.

"Usted . . . ah . . . tu debes . . . uh . . . pelear. Fight! You're supposed to be out there shooting that gun at the Federals and not hiding under here! If that Fierro bastard finds you under here he'll shoot you—and probably me too, for harboring a fugitive or whatever it's called!"

She tried to get closer. *"Mande, señor?"* Her big straw hat scraped against one of the beams and it fell off. I never saw so much blue-black hair. In the dim light it fell down in waves, like I guess the ocean, though I'd never seen the ocean. It smelled . . . I don't know exactly how it smelled, but after all these years I remember it; dirty as she was, she smelled wonderful. To me that flowerlike scent means to this day Valentina, only then I didn't know her name. Black hair cascading down, and blue eyes—I'd never before seen a Mexican with that combination. It was pleasurable.

I stared for a minute, and then said, "We're in a fix, us two, and I don't know what to do, and I'm sure you don't either."

Somehow, with her clinging to me that way, I felt a responsibility. "Just a minute, *niña.*" Maybe she was a *niña*—a child—but she had that swelling around the chest like Prue Ballard. Though small, she might even be old as me. Crawling toward the edge of the kiosk, brushing cobwebs off my face, I looked around.

"Hey!" I said. "Look!"

She didn't want to come, but I grabbed her wrist and pulled her after me. *"Mira!"*

The Federales no longer milled around in the plaza. They were huddled in a tight circle, ringed by Villa's *soldados.* In all their finery they were being pushed and herded like sheep by the raggle-taggle Villistas. Foremost among the captors was wart-nosed Victoria, prodding sullen men twice her size with an old shotgun. Glass Eye was there too, keeping an eye on strays and uttering what sounded like terrible threats. The arms of the Federales lay in a tangled pile in the middle of the plaza; the autumn rain came down harder and harder, veiling everything in a kind of haze.

Dirty and cramped, the girl and I crawled out from under the bandstand, our dirt turning to mud. The lights in the plaza winked on again; someone must have restored them at the power station. The prisoners were rounded up and led away somewhere and the Villistas rejoiced in victory, throwing their arms around each other, dancing, singing to the music of a small band of musicians on the lately vacated bandstand. No one minded the rain. Ciudad Juárez was ours! Well, not ours; I hadn't had anything to do with it and I didn't know whether it was good or bad for Pancho Villa to take Ciudad Juárez. Still, I was caught up in the joy of the moment and ran about clapping people on the shoulder and being embraced in turn.

Suddenly I stopped, my mouth open. It couldn't be! Hardly believing my eyes, I stared at the bandstand. Mr. George McFall was standing before the *mariachis*, who were playing "Adelita," the favorite song of the Villistas. He was directing with an occasional flourish of his violin bow while scraping out something that didn't seem to agree with what the rest of the musicians were playing. Above the racket of cornets and guitars I think I recognized Mr. McFall's tune; it was "The Campbells Are Coming."

"Mr. McFall!" I screamed.

He stopped his scraping, peered about. "Ben! Ben Wilkerson! My boy!"

Hurrying down, throwing his arms around me, he tried to hold me and the violin and the bow all at the same time.

"Where have you been?"

"Where have *you* been?" I demanded. "That dynamite . . ."

Taking off his spectacles, he huffed on them, rubbing the glass with his sleeve. "Yes, the dynamite! That was an experience!" Come to think of it, he did look sort of battered. His face was sooty and some of his hair was burned off and there was a smoky smell to him. "Well, do you know what happened, Ben?" Still rubbing his glasses, he stared at the girl. I hadn't been aware she was still clinging to my arm. "That blast blew me right out the opposite window and into a clump of bushes! I was startled, as you might well understand, but mostly unhurt. I walked about looking for you, but with no success. Then these musical gentlemen came along, and I joined them." He hooked the spectacles over his ears and asked, "Who is this young lady?"

"Well, I don't know," I said. "She . . . she just somehow attached herself to me."

"Romance, eh, laddie?"

I was embarrassed, but was saved from further embarrassment when old Victoria, dropping her shotgun, hurried over to embrace the girl, both of them laughing and crying at the same time. I tried to follow the chatter but it was one too many for me.

"They appear to be friends," Mr. McFall explained. "The girl's name is Valentina something-or-other."

The Villistas were plundering the refreshment stands, helping themselves to roasted meats and pastries and colored sweet water from big glass jugs. *"Arriba!"* they were all shouting. *"Arriba* Pancho Villa!" Around the plaza Villa's men shot locks off shuttered shops, broke in, looted. Everyone took armfuls of stuff whether they needed it or not; it was all free. They dressed themselves in fine garments—short jackets with silver buttons, big Jalisco sombreros, fine leather boots to replace straw sandals. The *soldaderas* pranced about in fancy gowns trimmed with delicate lace, bare feet crammed into silk dance slippers. Old Glass Eye came up to me carrying, of all things , a typewriter! I don't know what he intended to do with it; I was sure he couldn't even read. But he wanted his share of whatever was available.

He tried to give the typewriter to me. *"Toma!"* he urged. "Take, *chamaco!* Take!"

I refused very politely. *"Muchas gracias,"* I said, but Mr. McFall whispered in my ear.

"Take it, Ben, for God's sake! These people can get angry very quickly! He would resent it if you refused his present. After all, isn't it your birthday? Your *cumpleaños*?"

By George, it was! It was after midnight, and today was my birthday. I took the typewriter—a good one, an Oliver— like Mr. Dinwiddie's back in McNary, Hudspeth County.

"Eh?" Glass Eye's fake orb spun like a top. "Eh? You say? *Cumpleaños? El joven?*" He pointed at me, and his face, wrinkled like a dried mud flat, broke out in a grin so wide I thought his face would fall off.

"*Cumpleaños! El joven!*" He shouted to Victoria. "*Cumpleaños!*"

The old lady had been dressing Valentina in a looted green gown with lots of lace. She came over, pulling Valentina after her, the girl still in dirty bare feet and wearing the tattered straw hat. Others followed, gathering about me. Glass Eye (I might as well give him the name everybody called him, Ojo Parado, which means "Fixed Eye," like it was fixed to look straight ahead all the time, only it didn't, and kept rolling around in the empty socket) —well, Ojo Parado kept yelling, "*Cumpleaños! Compleaños!*" and they hoisted me up on their shoulders and carried me around in the rain. I tried to get down but in the excitement of winning the battle they wouldn't let me. Someone had the bright idea of breaking into a bakery and they stood me on the floury baker's table while they rummaged through the glass cases and stuffed themselves on fancy cakes and sweet rolls and cream horns and cookies with icing on them.

They brought me a huge thing that must have been a wedding cake a rich man had ordered. It was three feet across, I think, decorated with swirls of red and pink and green and blue, and had a little bride and groom on top. Ojo Parado swept aside the little figures and dug out a chunk of cake, handing it to me. Someone ran to a nearby store and found red candles. Ojo Parado stuck them in what was left of the cake and lit them. "*Cumpleaños!*" everybody kept yelling. "*Arriba compleaños!*" Oh, it was crazy! Later I realized it was a kind of hysteria after the battle, but it was still crazy.

Mustache smeared with pink icing, Ojo Parado started singing, very softly, stroking my hair like I was a child. The others stopped their racket and their eating and gathered around. Some took off straw hats, others only stared at the burning candles.

I know now that what the old man was singing was "Las

Mañanitas," the lovely song that Mexican parents sing early in the morning on the birthdays of their children. At daybreak father and mother creep silently into the child's room and sing the song. In English it goes something like this:

> Awake, my love, awake!
> Look—the dawn is here.
> All the birds are singing
> And the moon will disappear.

It is a beautiful song. Years later I sang it to my own "grandchildren." There was silence in the room except for the old man's cracked voice, singing a song he probably remembered from his childhood. Those bloodthirsty Villistas stared at the candle flames and in the eyes of each I thought I could see something touching—remembrances of home and family, so far away, other happy birthdays and *fiestas*, love of children left behind while the parents fought for their freedom, even a wistful hope that there would someday be enough food and a little plot of their own land and education for their children. Maybe I overreached myself in the emotion of the moment, but I still think those things were there, in their eyes.

When the song was done they all pressed forward to shake my hand. Old Victoria held me close and put her wrinkled cheek against mine. Valentina just looked at me, then cast down her eyes and followed Victoria away. Silently, others filed out. In the distance I could still hear shooting. But in spite of that it seemed very quiet in the bakery, littered with the remains of the birthday feast.

"Happy birthday, Ben," Mr. McFall said, picking up his violin.

Lest you think the capture of Ciudad Juárez was all sweetness and light, I must tell you what the last spattering of gunfire meant. The Butcher, Rodolfo Fierro, had taken some fifty of the Federales into a walled enclosure and offered them their freedom if they could get over an adobe wall two meters high before he killed them. As they scrambled, he shot them all with his pistol, stopping only for a moment when he had a cramp in his finger. It was said that General Villa was very angry with him, but he needed Fierro too much to punish him. Rodolfo Fierro was necessary to the general, and both of them knew it.

We hardly realized it was near dawn. The rain had stopped but the air was heavy and moist. Filmy mist arose from the river. Across the Rio Grande the city of El Paso was beginning to wake. While most of the Villistas still slumbered we could hear the grinding of cart wheels, the toot of a locomotive from the El Paso railroad yards. Smoke rose from factory chimneys. In the east the sky was pale rose as the sun, still hidden, struggled upward. Mr. McFall and I sat on the edge of the deserted bandstand eating rolls spread with a bottle of raspberry jam I found in the plaza. I still had the Oliver typewriter.

"We had better get out of here," Mr. McFall remarked. "Our trip to Mexico has been interesting, and I don't regret it. Mexico is a land of great beauty—beautiful people and beautiful mountains and beautiful things of all kinds. Unfortunately, it is also a land of blood and violence. They are endemic to the land."

"What is 'endemic'?" I asked, eating the last of the roll and licking my fingers.

"We had better go," he said, picking up his violin. "I'll explain on the way to the river. And throw away that typewriter, please."

At the bridge we found the entrance guarded by Villa's men. "*No pasen!*" one warned, waving a fine sword that had probably belonged to an officer of the Federales.

"But we're American citizens!" Mr. McFall protested.

One of the guards raised a carbine and gestured menacingly. We retreated. "Well!" Mr. McFall said. "They obviously have no regard for international goodwill and understanding!"

While we loitered near the bridge, the dawn grew. It would be a fine crisp November day, dust and smoke washed from the air by the rains of the night before. It would be a better day if we could figure out how to get across the river. I wanted to go home; I had had enough of

Mexico. I was hungry, too—that roll hadn't been enough for my young stomach. I guess Mr. McFall was hungry also.

"Let us think of food, Ben," he said. "Sometimes that helps. What food do you fancy?"

"Chicken," I said mournfully.

"Fixed how?"

"Fried. Fried so it's crusty and brown and when you bite into the meat it kind of smokes!"

He considered that. "Well, I would like oatmeal."

"Oatmeal?" I was astonished.

"Yes, oatmeal. Fixed by my sainted mother in Leith, Scotland. Hot, with butter on it, and rich cream." He sighed, blew his nose. "And mother bustling about the kitchen in her apron, mixing up scones for the oven."

I had never heard of scones and was about to ask when there was a bustle at the Stanton Street bridge. A big touring car came across from the El Paso side, starred flags fluttering from the fenders. Sitting in it was a military man, very stiff and straight, collar buttoned up tight and a lot of colored ribbons and medals on his chest. Beside him was a little dried-up man wearing those pinch-something glasses that glinted in the sun that had by now cleared the eastern mountains; he wore a high silk hat. They were obviously important personages because the guards fell back and long-nosed Colonel Aguirre, the general's secretary, was there to welcome the visitors. The colonel got into the car too and they all drove away in a spatter of mud.

"Now, who could they be?" Mr. McFall wondered. "An American officer, very high-ranking, and someone that looks like a diplomat of a sort!"

I didn't know, and didn't care. "The river isn't very deep upstream," I pointed out, seeing reeds growing in it. "We could probably wade across."

Mr. McFall looked. "Yes, I think you're right. I don't swim, but if it isn't too deep I could probably make it. It's worth a try, anyway. I'm tired of Mexico too." Getting up, he put a hand on my shoulder. "I'm sorry there was no gold in Mexico, Ben—at least for us. But we *have* had a rich experience."

"I guess so," I agreed.

Casually we sauntered upstream, dodging behind the willows, where we couldn't be seen from the bridge. Someone was following us, I was sure, but I couldn't see them; I just had a feeling. "Someone's trailing us," I said.

"Oh?" Mr. McFall said, looking over his shoulder. "I don't see anyone. Who would care about us?"

Together we slid down a muddy bank, Mr. McFall holding his violin high. My bare feet sank into the ooze and a frog hopped away, croaking, which startled Mr. McFall so he nearly fell. I reached out to help but just then a shot was fired. It splashed in the river ahead of us, sending up a fan of spray.

"*Alto!*" a hoarse shout came.

We halted, standing still, not looking around.

"*Manos arriba!*"

We raised our hands, turned slowly. On the bank stood a skinny Villista corporal with a pockmarked face, along with two or three other soldiers in borrowed finery. The corporal jerked his head in command and we struggled up the muddy bank, which was hard with our hands over our heads. Being this close to the U.S. and safety, we didn't want to take any chances on getting shot.

They prodded us with their guns and led us back to the plaza. Behind the broken windows of the Corona Coffee Shop sat Rodolfo Fierro with a silver pot and a plate of pastries before him. He didn't even look at us, went on dipping his roll in the cup and sucking the coffee out. We stood there, us and the corporal and his guards, waiting. Outside, Villa's men were loading booty into wagons—paintings with gilt frames, bedsteads, musical instruments, sewing machines, shovels and hoes, bird cages, along with case after case of ammunition and piles of captured arms, including a small cannon.

Finally Fierro turned, dabbing at his beard with a napkin. "*Bien!*" he said, pressing his stomach to release a delicate belch. "You run away, eh? You two?"

"We didn't run away," Mr. McFall protested. "We are American citizens, and belong rightfully across the river!"

Fierro rose, smoothing his tailored uniform jacket with the brass buttons.

"Tais-toi!" he said to Mr. McFall in the French language that high-class Mexican people sometimes used to show they were refined. "I talk to *joven*!" Sauntering over to me, he put a manicured hand on my head. I shrank away, and Fierro grinned.

"You don't like me?"

I didn't, of course. If there was ever a man that exuded evil, it was Rodolfo Fierro. And why he was interested in me, I wasn't too sure yet; I mean, about details.

"You will like," he decided. Motioning to the guards, he said something brisk and commanding. Taking my arms, they bore me out the door. Mr. McFall followed, protesting, but one of the guards pushed him in the chest with the butt of his rifle and Mr. McFall fell down, wheezing.

"Where . . . where are you taking me?" I quavered. Was I going to be shot for good this time?

Whipping his boots with a leather crop, Fierro walked ahead and spoke to me over his shoulder. "You not run away, *joven*! Bad, very bad! You belong our División del Norte. You telegraph, you. The general want you to be telegraph, eh?" On the way out he paused at a wrecked flower stand and picked out a carnation for his buttonhole.

Finally he turned into a looted clothing store, the shattered window still bearing a paper sign in red letters: VENTA GIGANTE—big sale. The guards turned me loose and while Fierro searched among the jumbled piles of clothing, Mr. McFall passed outside the broken window quickly, like a ghost, then was gone again. Fierro finally located a man's tweed jacket and a pair of whipcord riding breeches, along with some high leather boots and a striped silk shirt.

"You put on, eh, *joven?* Need fine clothes, you. Important boy now. No bare feets or dirty shirt no more, eh?"

Scared, I looked around for a private place to put on the clothes. There was a curtained recess in the back of the store. Clothes over my arm, I headed for it but Fierro grabbed my arm. His lean face contorted in what might have been a smile, but his voice was low and hard and somehow excited.

"Here, you, *joven!* Now! Change here!"

I didn't want to undress in front of all those men. Quickly Mr. McFall passed the window again. Red-faced, humiliated and embarrassed, I shucked off my shirt and pants and stood bare in front of them. One of the guards laughed, but Fierro wasn't laughing.

"Bueno," he muttered.

I remembered what Mr. Tom Mix had told me when he left the coal train. *Stay clear of Fierro, kid! He's a bastard, and likes pretty boys like you.* Suddenly I knew what my fate was going to be. I threw down the clothes and tried to run but there was no place to go. The guards pinioned my arms while El Carnicero dressed me, me struggling all the while. My flesh crawled when I felt his hands on my skin. I started to scream but he cut me off, slapping my face with a hand smelling of cologne.

"Now," he said, "you go to bathhouse! Pretty boy . . . very nice . . . wash good! Look like general special telegrapher, eh? The general be pleased."

They let me go then, the skinny rat-faced corporal following me. In the plaza I turned around, looked back. The guard was still following me.

In my new clothes I dodged behind a deserted booth and into the bushes. Running around behind the shops, I came out in an alleyway and looked around the corner. Sitting on a broken chair, legs crossed, rifle across his lap, the pockmarked guard looked at me with amusement. When I moved slightly, he moved too, quick like a cat.

Mr. McFall hurried down the street, looking into smashed storefronts and poking into piles of rubbish. Seeing me in the alleyway, he came up, breathing a sigh of relief.

"There you are, Ben!" He mopped his brow. "I was afraid you—"

"Get across the river somehow," I said in a low voice. "Get across, quick! I'm in big trouble!"

He touched the expensive tweed jacket. "How fine you

look! The coat is a little large for you, but it's excellent material—wool from Scotland, I should say!"

"Never mind wool from Scotland! Get away before they do something to *you*!"

Violin tucked under his arm, he frowned. "Ben, what's wrong?"

"I . . . I can't get away myself." I nodded toward the guard. "I'm practically a prisoner. Fierro says I'm an important person now, General Villa's private telegrapher. So you get across the river somehow, before it's too late! Please!"

"An important person, Ben?"

"Yes," I said. I was important to Rodolfo Fierro, I knew with agonizing certainty. But I couldn't bring myself to explain to good, patient, kind Mr. McFall. He probably wouldn't have understood anyway; I doubt if they do things in Scotland like Fierro planned for me. People from Scotland, Grandpa Johnson once said, are very religious and hard-nosed about sex.

"But I can't leave you, laddie!" Mr. McFall protested. "I won't leave you! After all, I'm the one who talked you into coming down here to Mexico in a vain and foolhardy search for gold!" He shook his head. "I should have known better! Man's search for gold has always led him into trouble and tribulation. Well, anyway, I'll stick with you, Ben. You're in trouble of some sort, and that's when a man needs a friend!"

Man! I'm glad he took me for a man; I didn't feel like a man. I could still feel Rodolfo Fierro's hands on me, touching me, sliding along my flesh, stroking me when he made me put an arm into the striped silk shirt.

"Well," I sighed, "all right, Mr. McFall. It's your decision, and I hope you'll never be sorry on my account. But I'm grateful—I want you to know that!"

Together we went into the La Mexicanita restaurant. Some of the Villistas, temporarily at a loose end, were playing dominoes at a table. Rifle across his knees, the corporal sat outside on a broken sofa. Inside, the proprietor was trying to clean up the wreckage of the night before. Behind the counter was a frightened lady making coffee in a tin pot over an alcohol stove.

"Dos cafés, por favor," I said. I still had my Sunday-school dime.

Mr. McFall nodded approval. "Your accent is getting better, laddie. After you wash up a little, you'll look like a real sport in those new clothes!"

The lady wouldn't take my dime, probably thinking we were Villistas and not used to paying for anything. When we came out, the corporal was waiting for me. He pointed down the street to the El Tigre bathhouse.

"I guess," I said, "I'll have a bath right now, Mr. McFall."

4

Anyway, after I ran away from that horrible scene in our front yard, my brother Cleary lying on the dirt like a dead coal from Mr. Rayford Ellis' blacksmith's forge, for three days I hid in the cottonwoods and willows along Murphy's Creek. The sun came up and seemed to follow me as it moved through the sky, illuminating me so I could be seen better in my hiding places. At night it was dark, not a soft welcome night in autumn but a night like the outer blackness someone got cast into. There was no peace for me; I was damned, forever damned. With no food, and only water from the creek, I got a little crazy after a while. I heard voices talking, accusing voices;

> There he is, in the bushes!
> Where? Oh, I see him!
> The mark of Cain is on him. How it glows in the dark!

Grandpa's face loomed up out of the night, huge in size, his white mustache ending in long barbs and the hard blue eyes like the searchlight of No. 76 as she came down the tracks every night. Grandpa pointed a finger at me that was long as a bamboo fishing pole.

The devil has took possession of this child! The devil has worked his will through this child to destroy, to burn . . . yes, to kill, kill Cleary Wilkerson!

I bolted through bushes and brambles, falling over rocks and tripping in underbrush, my heart pounding. The voices followed me; I couldn't get away from them. Gasping for breath, I burst out on the hillside above the railroad tracks.

The tracks glinted in the moonshine, dwindling away toward El Paso, a pair of silver scissors. The railroad! Mr. Ballew! Maybe I could talk to him, tell him how it was.

Dawn wasn't far away. As the eastern sky showed pink and yellow and green against streaks of gray, I think I finally slept, the pursuing voices stilled at last. When I woke it was day. Cramped and hungry, I sat on a fallen log peering through a screen of bushes at Mr. Ballew's shanty below, trying to work up courage to leave my hiding place and go down.

On the other hand, maybe I could somehow sneak into McNary and talk to Mr. Dinwiddie, the schoolteacher. But he lived at the Ballard house, with Prue Ballard, and I would not dare have her see me—a wretched, dirty, hungry boy who was guilty of arson *and* murder.

Still, I had to talk to somebody or go crazy. The sun slid higher in the sky. Bugs began to crawl over me, itching me. In a rustling of dry leaves a rattler slithered toward me, then coiled as I moved. Trembling with decision, I finally slid down the deep cut, landing in cinders, and stood for a moment trying to brush off my church clothes, which had suffered badly. One pocket of the coat was ripped where I had caught it on a branch. For some reason my necktie had disappeared. My jeans had a rip in the knee, and the copper-toed boots were dirty and scuffed. My soul was also in bad repair. I cannot describe in words how alone I was that August morning, standing on the railroad tracks; all that comes back to me now is the feeling. The mixed special would be along soon, eastbound. Maybe I'd just stand there and let it grind me up in its maw.

Mr. Ballew was outside on his bench, sunning himself while he ate bacon and eggs from a tin plate. At first he didn't notice me. I came nearer, smelling bacon and eggs and willing to do anything to get a bite to eat. Then I thought: Suppose Mr. Ballew knows all about what happened, and will turn me in to the sheriff over at the county seat? He was always talking about being such a poor man. Maybe there was a reward out for me.

Just then I heard the mixed special chuffing its way

along the creek. McNary was a flag stop. Mr. Ballew picked up his flag. It appeared there was a McNary passenger for Austin or someplace east.

Then, in surprise and agony, I saw the passenger. It was Mr. Dinwiddie, carrying a leather suitcase. He and Mr. Ballew were talking loud over the hiss of steam from the waiting special, and I could hear some of their words.

"Anyone seen the Wilkerson boy?" Mr. Ballew asked.

I didn't hear all of Mr. Dinwiddie's reply, but he shook his head and looked down at the ground. "Promise . . . sorry . . . future . . ."

My heart burst. Mr. Dinwiddie was one of my two best friends. Now he was leaving for Austin and his sweetheart and college and I couldn't even say good-bye to him. I watched as he swung up on the step, carrying his suitcase, nodding his head in farewell to Mr. Ballew. The conductor looked at his watch, waved to the engineer in his cab, and climbed up after Mr. Dinwiddie. As the special passed, I saw my teacher through the windows walking down the aisle. It was funny; the train was going so slow before it picked up speed that with him walking back in the car he and I were together for an instant. Together—then the mixed special reached the downgrade east of McNary and vanished in a cloud of smoke and steam, blowing for the grade crossing on the Soda Springs road.

"Ben! Ben Wilkerson!"

It was Mr. Ballew calling; he had finally seen me. If I thought he would turn me in to the Hudspeth County sheriff, it was too late to worry about. Slowly, dragging my boots in the cinders, I approached the shanty.

"Ben, boy! Come here!"

I stood in front of him, torn, bedraggled, full of thistles, hangdog. Mr. Ballew took his time stuffing cut plug into his pipe with a gnarled thumb.

"In trouble, eh?"

"Yes, sir."

"Burned down a house, I hear. Committed arson on your brother!"

"I didn't mean to."

He puffed for a while, spectacles reflecting the morning sun so I couldn't see his eyes. What was he thinking?

"A lot of harm is did by people who didn't mean to, Ben."

I scuffed a copper toe in the cinders. "Yes, sir."

"Boy, you look like a nickel's worth of cat meat! You been hiding out?"

Swaying on my feet from hunger and lack of sleep, I nodded. Mr. Ballew jabbed at me with the stem of the pipe.

"I ain't going to give you away, boy! You're safe with me." The sounder in the shack began its clatter and Mr. Ballew heaved to a storklike stance and reached for his crutch. "There's KT calling me. You sit down here and eat the rest of them bacon and eggs."

Gratefully I sat on the bench and wolfed down the food, hardly stopping to chew. There wasn't much, and it was only greasy bacon and burned eggs, but nothing ever tasted more like ambrosia. After I'd scraped the tin plate clean I thought for a minute it was all going to come back up. Getting to my feet, I walked around for a little bit, breathing the fresh morning air. The stuff finally settled down in my stomach with only a little gurgling.

Mr. Ballew hopped out of the shanty. "Et it all, I see."

"Yes, sir. I thank you."

He stared at me thoughtfully. "Bleary-eyed! Guess you ain't slept much."

"No," I admitted. "Only a little here and there in the woods." His bulky image began to waver in my eyes, getting dim and then bright, the outlines disappearing into fuzzy growths like fur. I think I swayed a little, because he reached out and steadied me.

"Go in the shanty and rest a mite in my bunk. Boy, you're dead on your feet! Go, now!"

Tottering into the shack, I fell facedown on a soiled quilt, my feet hanging over the edge. I doubt if I moved for hours. I didn't dream; I was too tired for that. When I drifted back to consciousness it was dark. For a long time I lay there wondering what I was doing in the strange blackness that smelled of greasy old clothes, fried bacon, and a sharp acrid odor that was like . . . like battery acid! Suddenly I remembered, in awful detail. The burning house, Cleary's pitiful body, Grandpa's glass-hard eyes, *Beelzebub . . . Beelzebub . . . Beelzebub!* Groggily I sat up, rubbing my eyes, sick to my stomach. I couldn't stay here—they would find me. But what really made me scramble out of bed was the voices. Two voices; one was Mr. Ballew and the other was Grandpa!

"Well," Mr. Ballew was saying, "I ain't saying I seen him and I ain't saying I ain't, Mr. Johnson. Ah . . . what's the boy been up to now?"

Grandpa was real mad. "You know damned well, Tom Ballew, what he's been up to! The whole town knows! They probably know all the way to El Paso! He's went and put up some damn-fool kind of wire in the sky and it drawed lightning the other night and burned up my house and cremated my pore grandson Cleary Wilkerson and. . ."

I didn't wait to hear any more. The window in the back wall of the shanty was stuck; I heaved on it but it wouldn't come. Sweating and chilling all at the same time, I jerked it. Something broke, and it slid up. I scrambled through the window and dropped into the cinders outside, praying they hadn't heard me. As I fled down the tracks in the moonlit night, I could still hear Grandpa Johnson arguing with Mr. Ballew.

"Goddammit all, if you know where the boy is . . ."

Blindly I ran, stumbling on the ties, chest heaving, panic-struck. Behind me the voices grew fainter, then disappeared. Tripping over a switch-point in the darkness, I fell, feeling a sudden knife-edge pain in my ribs. My face scratched and studded with cinders, I crawled into a culvert and lay there panting. Scared to death, friendless, alone, I cringed under the culvert as if it would shield me from Grandpa's wrath—and God's. Maybe I slept a little, I don't remember, but I started again in terror when old No. 76, the evening freight, thundered over my head, relentlessly on time.

After it had passed by in a whirlwind of dust and steam and coal smoke I tried to hang myself with a piece of moldy rope I found under the culvert. That broke, as I have said, dropping me on some rocks that further bruised my battered knees. What to do now? Holding the end of the rope, I stared at it, melancholy. One thing was surely clear. If I couldn't hang myself right now, I had better light a shuck out of Hudspeth County before the sheriff took up my trail with bloodhounds.

I clambered painfully up the bank and headed west in moonlight, following the railroad tracks toward Sierra Blanca and Fabens and Ysleta, towns I had heard of but never been to. At first I ran, hoping to get away from McNary as fast as I could. Then I realized I had better slow down; I was dizzy and a little confused, and didn't want to fall again. My side hurt like the dickens and my knees throbbed with a dull aching, like a bad tooth. Finally I settled down to a reasonable pace, taking the moon and the dark and the rough ties and slippery rails all into consideration. At least I wasn't hampered by any luggage—except, maybe, my mouth-organ, the dead frog in the tin box I'd been preparing to lure Prue Ballard, the dime Ma had given me for Sunday school, and my barlow knife.

It's about sixty miles from McNary to El Paso but it took me a month to get there. That's because I zigged and zagged a lot, trying to cover my tracks, and my side that hurt so bad slowed me some, too. Also, I was broke and had to beg for odd jobs to cover expenses. Not that my expenses were too great—I slept in willows along the river, under culverts, and in ranch outbuildings with cats and goats and sheep and I don't know what all. Some of the people I met up with were kind and considerate; others told me to be off. One old man let go a shotgun blast right over my head when all I wanted was to cut some hay for him.

In Sierra Blanca I had my first decent meal for a long time. An old lady with a front porch full of cats saw me trudging by in the dust and called out.

"Yes, ma'am?" I said.

"Come in, boy, and have a glass of buttermilk!"

Grateful, I sat on the front porch and had some cookies,

too. She was a widow, all alone, and her place was awful run-down.

"I notice, ma'am," I said, "that this corner of the porch is sagging." It was true; as she rocked, the old chair kept sliding to one side. "Let me find a chunk of firewood and kind of shore it up."

I cut some weeds for her too, ground corn to feed the chickens, and painted the front door. The door ended up an ugly outhouse brown but it was all the paint she had.

When I left she insisted on giving me a quarter. I said no but she wouldn't hear of it.

"For you're a runaway boy, I'm sure," she said, "and probably ain't got a cent in them tore-up jeans! I know, because my boy Carl run away when he was your age and I ain't seen him since." She started to cry so I thanked her quick and went back to the El Paso road. Women crying bother me a lot. Yet I wished Ma had cried more for her troubles and not drunk so much of that Nervina stuff.

I gave Fort Hancock a wide berth; there were soldiers there. For all I knew, a soldier was likely as a sheriff to discover me and put me in irons in the guardhouse till the sheriff could come. At Fabens I took a job pumping the bellows in a blacksmith's shop. Back in McNary I used to work for Mr. Rayford Ellis in his shop, so I knew a little about the trade. I passed through Ysleta and had enough money to buy a straw hat and a meal of *carne asada* and beans and tortillas. But a Mexican in the Flor de Jalisco restaurant kept looking at me kind of funny. I decided he was measuring me for a jail cell, so I got out of there quick. Maybe he was an undersheriff or something in Ysleta.

Very late in October I got to El Paso. The nights were turning chill. With what was left of money from the blacksmith I bought a Mexican *sarape* and squatted in the plaza, like all the other Mexicans. With that shock of uncut hair, bleached almost white, and blue eyes, I guess no one would take me for a Mexican, but by pulling the *sarape* over me and hunkering down against a sun-warmed adobe wall, I figured I was inconspicuous.

In 1913 El Paso couldn't have been much of a place

compared to Chicago or New York. Still, to me it was a metropolis. They had trolleys and automobiles and stores with lots of goods in them; pots and pans, fancy chinaware, men's clothing, wheelbarrows, hardware, bright ribbons and laces, chocolate candies, washbasins and books and glass inkstands. Screwing up my courage, I strolled along Stanton Street, hungry as all get-out, the Sunday-school dime still in my pocket. I didn't intend to spend it because somehow it seemed to be a talisman, a bond to home and Ma and the once-safe-and-secure hideaway in the loft with my precious telegraph instruments, although all that by now was destroyed.

Sitting under a chinaberry tree in the plaza, a man played a Mexican-sounding song on a violin. A vendor in a straw hat ornamented with tassels was selling cornhusk-wrapped *tamales* from a big lard can carried by a rope over his shoulder.

"*Tamales, señor?*"

I was starved, but the Sunday-school dime was sacred.

"No, sir," I said. "I . . . I haven't got any money."

Showing a lot of white teeth, he shrugged. Digging through the crumpled newspapers keeping the *tamales* warm, he handed me one.

"But I haven't got any money!"

"Take!" He shrugged. "You hongry, *muchacho*!"

I took. "Yes, I'm hungry," I admitted. Remembering that Mexicans were very religious, I added, "God bless you, sir."

He thanked me and wandered away through the plaza, yelling "*Tamales! Tamales frescos! Quién quiere tamales sabrositos?*"

I still had my mouth-organ. After downing the *tamal*, I cooled off my mouth with a drink from a pump in the plaza and sidled over to the old man with the violin. He was playing a song I knew, "The Cowboy's Lament." Cleary wasn't any cowboy, but he used to sing it real good when he got drunk:

As I walked out in the streets of Laredo,
As I walked out in Laredo one day . . .

The white-haired old man in his threadbare suit thanked a businessman who dropped a nickel in his hat.

I saw a young cowboy all dressed in white linen,
White linen, white linen, as cold as the clay.

Very softly I started to play on my mouth-organ, even trying a little harmony. Cleary always said I had a tin ear but I think I did pretty good. A roustabout in muddy boots passed by and dropped a dime in the hat. Music seemed to be a good business in El Paso. I played on, daring to add a few flourishes and trills. The elderly violinist finally put down his bow.

"You know music, sir?"

That "sir" set me up pretty good. "A little, I guess."

He put out a hand that had little veins running all over it like creek branches. "George McFall, late of Memphis, Tennessee, and Leith, Scotland, where the distinguished family of McFall still lives."

For a moment I pondered telling him a false name, maybe like D'Artagnan Crockett. But his sharp eyes were on me and I hemmed and hawed a little bit, then blurted out, "Ben Wilkerson . . . sir."

"Glad to meet you, Mr. Wilkerson." He wiped his forehead with a pocket handkerchief—it was hot in the plaza for almost November. He stared for a moment at the smoke from the American Smelting and Refining plant north of the city, pursing his lips like he was thinking. Then he said, "Will you reach down and hand me that hat, please? My back is a little arthritic."

I did so. Counting the coins one by one, he put them in a pocket. "I saw you wolfing down that Mexican confection, whatever it's called."

"A *tamal*. Don't they have them in Memphis?"

"Tamils," he mused, "spelled with an I, are inhabitants of the island of Ceylon in the Indian Ocean. I believe Tamils do not come in lard pails. But a *tamal* is apparently something quite different. I am new here, you see, Mr. Wilkerson, and not yet acquainted with the local diet."

I was fascinated by the way he talked. "They're meat

and stuff with cornmeal and all wrapped round with a cornhusk,'' I explained. There had been a lady in McNary who sold *tamales*.

"I see." He got to his feet and it seemed like every one of his old joints was creaking and complaining. "Mr. Wilkerson, would you care to join me as my musical partner? You play a pretty good harmonica. With the two of us in company, the bystanders may be more favorably inclined to anoint my hat. What do you say, eh?" He peered at me, pulling at his bushy white eyebrows.

All I owned was a *sarape*, my frog in a matchbox, my barlow knife, the Sunday-school dime—and my mouth-organ; I'd never heard it called a "harmonica." But like any healthy boy I was already hungry again, and didn't know where my next meal was coming from. I'd be a musician.

"Yes, sir," I agreed. "I'd be obliged to you if you'd take me on."

That was how I met my friend Mr. George McFall. But even together we didn't make more than enough to buy beans and tortillas. The citizens of El Paso, Mr. McFall explained, were not very cultured, and he didn't have time at his age, he said, to educate them. He knew some Spanish, and so he proposed we go to Mexico and gather up some of the gold he'd heard was laying around in the creeks and rivers.

Well, that's how we got to Mexico. As far as I know, that gold is still lying around in the creeks and rivers of Chihuahua. And we get more than we bargained for; here we were, mixed up in a Mexican revolution, and I'd got to be the virtual prisoner of an evil man called Rodolfo Fierro, "Villa's Butcher." Julio, which I learned was the name of the skinny pockmarked man assigned to guard me, followed me everyplace; I don't think he ever slept. Every time I looked around, he was there, beady eyes fastened on me and a carbine held loose in the crook of his arm. Mr. McFall, who refused to leave me in my trouble, and I were unwilling members of General Villa's División del Norte, the "Division of the North" as it came to be called after the big victory at Ciudad Juárez.

Somehow it appeared I had taken the eye of Rodolfo Fierro. God knows I never considered myself pretty! Ma and Cleary and Grandpa—they certainly never remarked on my beauty. In fact, Cleary usually called me a snot-nosed little bastard, and certainly Prue Ballard wasn't overwhelmed. Sometimes I sprouted a crop of pimples on my chin, and I always thought I looked a little like a rabbit, the way my two front teeth stuck out. Now I had a dread of what might come. Mr. McFall was worried too, remembering what Mr. Tom Mix had said on the coal train.

"Somehow or other we've got to get out of here."

"How?" I asked, with little hope.

"I don't know. But I've got a fertile imagination and I'll think of something. I won't have that Fierro beast ruining a youthful innocence!"

I wasn't all that innocent, of course, but I didn't let on. Still, I remembered something from the Bible, Grandpa Johnson's big Bible. *Go and sin no more.* That was the ticket, all right. *Sin no more!*

"All right," I agreed. "Tell me if you figure anything out."

His clothes were pretty raggedy too. But he had taken advantage of the looted shops and now had a pair of white pants, a pin-striped vest with a gold watch and chain, and a green-and-white-striped *sarape*, making quite a colorful picture. "There is a minor matter of ethics involved," he admitted. "Still, it's not exactly stealing, you understand, Ben. The stuff was just lying around in the streets, and probably no one could know what belonged to whom."

"Yes, sir," I agreed.

"Be of stout heart, Ben," he said, and walked off to join a beckoning string band which wanted him for first violin. Mr. McFall was very popular with the Villistas. The band gathered around a fountain with no water in it and started practicing "Adelita." In my memories of the revolution that song always stirs up emotion. "Adelita" was everywhere. I never found out who Adelita was, but she seemed to be the sweetheart of the revolution. The Villistas sang "Adelita," they played "Adelita" on guitars and cornets, they hummed "Adelita," they ate and drank and slept "Adelita." Of course, at the time I didn't know enough Spanish to catch all the words, but eventually they became a part of me, as they became a part of every veteran of the División del Norte, and anathema to President Huerta and his soldiers. In translation, the song goes something like this:

> I'm a soldier and my nation calls me
> To fight in the fields of strife.
> Adelita, Adelita of my soul,
> For the love of God do not forget me!

There was another verse that had a saucy swing to it; they loved to roar it out:

> If Adelita left me for another
> I would chase her endlessly.
> In a warship if she went by ocean,
> In a military train on land.

In a kind of limbo, I sat on an adobe wall and watched the activity around me, Julio, my pockmarked guard, squatting at my feet. Feeling lonely, I tried to talk to him, but he didn't understand English and my Spanish was still pretty bad, though I had picked up a lot since I joined the Villistas. There was nothing to do but watch the bustling activity all around me.

In the city hall there were a lot of coming and going. Staff officers of the División del Norte hurried in and out. There was a great reading of maps spread out on tables in the autumn sunshine. Once General Villa himself came out on a balcony, a cup of coffee in his hand, and took the cheers of the *soldados*. At Cuitla, the place where the rebels had captured Mr. McFall and me, the general had been dressed kind of rough-and-ready in a worn and shiny serge suit with a huge leather belt around his ample stomach, a Texas hat, and shabby leather boots. Now he had on a neat uniform with a carefully tailored tunic and a visored military cap. With the victory at Ciudad Juárez the Villistas had changed from a raggle-taggle bunch of guerrillas to an organized army dressed almost like real soldiers.

I took a chunk of *panoche* candy from my sack and offered it to Julio, but he shook his head. I was munching it myself when someone slapped me on the back. I turned; it was Mr. Wickwire, the El Paso *Morning Times* correspondent.

"Ben, wasn't it? Ben something-or-other?"

"Yes, sir," I said. "Ben Wilkerson."

He had a plaid cap on backward, like Mr. Barney Oldfield the race driver, and sounded excited. "Oh, what a story I have to tell!" he said. Then, "By the way, I didn't recognize you, Ben, in all that finery. Where's your friend—McFall, was it?"

I pointed out Mr. McFall, sawing away at "Adelita" by the dry fountain.

"Well!" Mr. Wickwire said. "I'm glad you two survived the battle!"

I wanted to tell him about Rodolfo Fierro and all the rest of my troubles but he started first and there was no stopping him.

"Do you know what's in this book, Ben?" he asked, holding up his reporter's notebook as if it was a national treasure. Not waiting for me to answer, he went on, "This book contains an exclusive interview with General Villa himself! Think of that! Soon as I get to a telephone it'll be on all the national wire services! Do you know where there's a telephone that's working? Everything in the city is out of order!" For a minute he lost his train of thought. Looking down at Julio, he asked me, "Who is this ruffian?" When I started to tell him, he hurried on. "The whole world wants to know about the picturesque Pancho Villa—the 'Centaur of the North,' I'm going to call him!"

Finally I got a word in. "I don't know what's going on around here, Mr. Wickwire. All Mr. McFall and I wanted was to find some gold, and now I'm in bad trouble. You see, it's like this—"

He interrupted me. "What a story! This ragtag bunch of

rebels is becoming a national force and President Huerta is tottering on his throne!"

I didn't know presidents had thrones and tried to say so just to get my oar in, but he hurried on.

"There are great things happening here, my boy! Things I don't entirely understand, but you may be sure I'll find out. I'm a bloodhound when it comes to news! General Hugh Scott is here, and Henry Wilson too—he came with Scott."

I remembered the two bigwigs crossing the Stanton Street bridge.

"Wilson is President Wilson's ambassador to Mexico." His eyes shone behind the iron-rimmed spectacles. "Something big is going on, Ben, and I'm curious as a cat! Those two—Scott and Wilson—are important people. Where did you say the telephone was, the one that is working?"

I didn't know of any telephone, and said so. "Listen, Mr. Wickwire, I want to tell you about—"

"General Villa laid it on thick for them," he went on, not hearing me. "Such kowtowing and by-your-leave and *encantado* to meet you! Old Pancho even gave a state dinner for them. I'm not much of an eater—just looking at all that food gave me indigestion. They had oysters brought in from Guaymas, Campeche shrimp, red snapper from Vera Cruz—*huachinango*, you know. There were turkeys, roast kid, suckling pigs—and rivers of champagne. *French* champagne! I tell, you, Ben, no one lays out a dinner like that unless they're expecting to get something out of it!"

He went charging off in all directions, looking for a telephone. Kind of stunned by his rapid-fire delivery, I never even got to ask him for advice as to how to get out of my fix. Maybe, if I could get to this Ambassador Wilson . . .

"Hola, amigo!"

It was old Glass Eye; Ojo Parado, the man who had given me the pistol on the coal train. I had lost the pistol; probably left it under the bandstand the night before. Who should Ojo Parado have in tow but the *soldaderita* Valentina! From Ojo Parado's quick Spanish I finally figured out that Valentina had been looking for me.

"*Su novia!*" he guffawed, slapping me on the back. I knew that meant "sweetheart." Well, I wasn't her sweetheart. I wasn't *anyone's* sweetheart except—I had that queasy feeling in my stomach—Rodolfo Fierro's.

"*Gracias,*" I said, a little flustered. No, that wasn't it. *Encantado*, I remembered; I'd heard people use that to a lady. Of course, Valentina wasn't a lady, only a child.

"*Encantado,*" I murmured.

"*Señor,*" she murmured, eyes downcast.

I'll have to admit she looked pretty nice this morning. Apparently she'd had a good bath and the long blue-black hair was caught back with a red ribbon. When she finally looked shyly up at me, the non-Mexican blue eyes were large and moist. Someone—probably her friend old Victoria—had dressed her in style. I'm not much on women's clothes but these were pretty elegant—a white frock belted so tight at the waist that it made her hips and . . . well, chest poke out quite a bit. She had on white stockings and black patent-leather sandals with cross-straps.

Ojo Parado and my guard Julio were squatting together at the base of a wall rolling cigarettes. That left me with no recourse but to entertain Valentina.

"*Buenos días,*" I remarked, for lack of anything better to say.

Those cornflower-blue eyes were disconcerting. Trying hard to think of something in the way of conversation, all I could remember was *chingado*, the dirty word everyone used like it was only "Aw shucks!" No, *chingado* would hardly do.

"*Qué día lindo!*" I said for a starter. That meant "What a nice day!"

Unaccountably the blue eyes suddenly filled with tears. Before I knew what was happening, she reached down and grabbed my hand and kissed it.

"Here, here!" I objected, embarrassed. I turned to Ojo Parado. "She's kissing my hand!"

He took the wet cigarette out of his mustache. "She . . . she . . ." Frowning with the effort at English, he finally managed, "She thank. Valentina thank. Thank for save her life."

"Well," I said, "*I* think she doesn't owe me anything! I was as scared as she was!"

Ojo Parado's leathery brow wrinkled.

"Nothing," I said. "Just forget it."

Ojo Parado ground out his cigarette on the stone wall. "She love you, *yo pienso.*"

I didn't care what he *pienso-ed*—thought. Still, a feather of breeze came from the river, bringing me that flowerlike scent of Valentina's hair; it made me uncomfortable.

"Tell her to go away," I recommended to Ojo Parado.

Disappointed, he shrugged and spoke to Valentina. She looked hurt, though I certainly didn't mean to hurt her. Ojo Parado wandered away with Valentina in tow again. Julio, the guard, got up, stretching cramped legs, and looked at me.

"All right, you bastard," I agreed. "We'll take a little walk." He didn't understand English.

What a mess! Fierro wanting me, Valentina "loving" me, a gloomy record of arson and murder behind me—it's no wonder I was confused and repentant and anxious and puzzled, and fearful all at the same time. It was a heavy load for a thirteen . . . no, a fourteen-year-old boy to bear. I felt in my pocket for the Sunday-school dime. Maybe there was enough power in that religious dime to carry me through the rough times I knew were coming.

We hadn't gone but a few steps when someone called me. "Benjamin! Benjamin!" Only it wasn't "Benjamin"—it was kind of like "Ben-ha-*meen*," the way they pronounced it in Mexican. Long-nosed and high-domed Colonel Aguirre came up to me and said, "You go with me to telegraph office, eh?" He had a piece of paper in his hand. "Send message for the general."

"*Bueno,*" I said. That, I had found, was a very useful word in Mexico. It means "Good, satisfactory, agreed." In Mexico you can say *bueno* anytime and it will fit. Most Mexicans are so anxious to please, so anxious not to offend, that they will say *bueno* to almost anything, maybe even, "Would you like me to shoot you in the leg?"

In the Ciudad Juárez telegraph office were a lot of typewriters and clacking sounders and the clicking of brass telegraph keys and cigarette smoke and clerks in black sateen sleeve guards. There was a Villista guard watching everyone with enough guns and bandoliers on him to sink a battleship; he kind of came to a slouching attention when the colonel came in. The manager of the office hustled over, bowing so low he scuttled like a crab, washing his hands in the air. Colonel Aguirre spoke sternly to him and he led us over to a telegraph position with a sign above it that said "Ciudad de México." Colonel Aguirre handed me the paper and said, "Send quick, eh, Benjamin?"

I sent quick. Translated, I found later, it read like this:

TO DON VICTORIANO HUERTA, PRESIDENTIAL PALACE, CIUDAD DE MÉXICO. YOU ARE A SON OF A BITCH. (signed) FRANCISCO VILLA, COMMANDING GENERAL, DIVISION OF THE NORTH.

Rodolfo Fierro came to the telegraph office, then, looking for me. I guess he had just been promoted to assistant general or something because he had on a new uniform with gold shoulder boards ornamented with so many stars it looked like a comic strip in the El Paso *Morning Times* where someone gets hit on the head and sees a lot of stars. He and Colonel Aguirre glowered at each other for a while and jawed in machine-gun Spanish too fast for me to follow. Later I found they were deadly enemies. Generals changed fast in the División del Norte; when Aguirre had been a captain he tried to get Major Fierro shot because of his excesses. But Villa intervened, needing Fierro's bloody nature in the revolution.

Anyway, Fierro dragged me after him to the city hall, where General Villa and his staff had set up headquarters. "You no talk Aguirre." His squinched-up face was mad. "Aguirre is bastard!"

"Bueno," I said politely. I had no intention of not ever talking to Colonel Aguirre. He and a young Mexican reporter from *Excelsior* named Berlanga who had talked kindly to me, and a few others, were the only people I trusted.

"Donde . . . ?" I started. "Where's . . . ?"

"You see, *muchacho*."

The city hall was full of generals; I never knew an army needed so many generals. They ran around waving maps, scribbling on papers they handed to runners, drinking whiskey and rum and beer looted from city warehouses, and arguing with each other. When Fierro came in they were quiet, watching him warily; everyone was afraid of Rodolfo Fierro. There came to be a common saying in the División del Norte; "*Pícale! Qué allí viene Fierro!*" It meant, "Hurry up! Here comes Fierro!"

We went up a grand staircase and across a balcony to a suite of rooms I suppose the mayor had recently occupied. Fierro opened the door and went in. A guard tried to bar his way but he pushed the man aside. He knocked at a green door with a fancy design on it that probably was the seal of the city.

"*Pásele*," a voice answered. It was Colonel Aguirre.

Fierro's face became prunelike, if that was possible. Colonel Aguirre was General Villa's private secretary and didn't intend to be outranked by anybody. He must have come up a back staircase and beat Fierro and me. Now Aguirre stood, pleased as a cat that ate the canary, at General Villa's side.

Respectfully Fierro saluted. If there was anybody *he* was afraid of, it was Pancho Villa! Slumped in an armchair, the general sat at a big desk with the remains of a plate of fried chicken in green sauce and an empty beer glass dotted with foam. A hand-rolled cigarette hung from his thick lips. Through the rising smoke his eyes were half-closed, heavy-lidded. Waving Fierro aside, he muttered something to Colonel Aguirre, who translated for him.

"General say you are one of the true heroes of the Battle of Ciudad Juárez."

My tongue stuck to the roof of my mouth but I managed a squeaky, "*Bueno. Gracias.*"

"The general want reward you, *muchacho* Benjamin."

Not trusting my voice, I bobbed my head in acknowledgment.

"He want to gift you for services, Benjamin, telegraph

for him." In response to a nod from General Villa, the colonel took a paper sack from a drawer of the desk and handed it to me. "From general."

With shaking fingers I fumbled into the sack. Within was a beautiful small automatic pistol of Spanish make. The grips were ivory, decorated with carved horses rearing, hooves in the air. Someone else's name—Vicente Gómez Ybarra—was engraved on it. I always wondered who Vicente Gómez Ybarra was and what happened to him. I suppose the pistol had been taken from a local gun shop for presentation to me, a true hero of the Battle of Ciudad Juárez. Still, it was a personal gift from the Centaur of the North, and gave me some small importance in my own right.

"I . . . I thank the general," I stammered, forgetting any Spanish I knew.

General Villa laughed, the high-pitched laugh that sounded odd from such a big man. Tossing his cigarette on the carpeted floor, he stomped on it and came toward me, chuckling, with his pigeon-toed gait that made him look like a duck walking. Clapping me on the back, he spoke while Colonel Aguirre continued to translate.

"You to learn Spanish quick, *muchacho!* It is a beautiful sound, not like those damn English words! And remember—never dishonor the pistol, for it was give you by General Villa himself as remembrance of you hero."

The brown face was kind; the cat-green eyes changed to a warmer cast. It was almost as if General Francisco Villa was a kindly uncle giving a nephew counsel. Suddenly I wanted to blurt out my case to him, to tell him I feared Rodolfo Fierro, that Mr. McFall and I only wanted to get across the river and go back home, that I was only thirteen—no, fourteen—and wanted to see Ma and even Grandpa, no matter what awaited me in McNary, Hudspeth County, Texas. But Rodolfo Fierro acted quickly. Bowing to the general, he took my elbow and hurried me out the door, along the balcony, and down into the street, where he turned me over to Julio, the pockmarked guard.

"*Más tarde,*" he said to me, grinning. "*Más tarde, muchacho!*"

I knew it meant *later*. Later! What was going to happen later? I was afraid I knew. But now I had a pistol. If he tried to do . . . anything to me, I would kill him. Still, no one had supplied me with any bullets, and I figured Fierro would want to keep it that way.

— 5 —

The word was that Federal troops from Chihuahua City, under General Orozco, who had managed to elude Villa at Ciudad Juárez, were now returning toward Ciudad Juárez. General Villa sent out thousands of his troops, well-clothed and equipped from the Ciudad Juárez warehouses, to the south of the city, forming a battle line twelve miles long across the sandy wastes. Fortunately for me, he also dispatched Rodolfo Fierro with a train and a lot of wrecking equipment to destroy what was left of the Central Railroad so Federal troops couldn't use any of it to reach Ciudad Juárez.

As the general's official telegrapher, I was entitled to room in the Hotel Buena Vista, though the only good view from it was of the railroad yards. I invited Mr. McFall to share it with me. We dined well at the Restaurante San Ignacio, eating mostly Mexican food—corn, beans, chilis, roast pork, and young goat, *cabrito*—with beer for Mr. McFall and a glass of milk for me.

While he was in Ciudad Juárez General Villa tried hard to improve things. You had to give him credit for acting like a civic-minded victor. He assigned some of his own troops to police duty and put others to work running the telephone system, the electric plant, bakeries, and mills, and forbade the sale of liquor. He also started his own system of currency. Colonel Aguirre took over a local printing plant and made up thousands of pesos of what were called "bilimbiques," paper money. As an important person, at least to the general, I had a pocketful of the notes, and paid our bills at the San Ignacio with a flourish, leaving lavish tips. I was becoming very sophisticated.

Good Lord! When I look back on those days I wonder how a fourteen-year-old boy from McNary, Texas, with hardly a dime to his name could have turned so *bravo*, so cocky! There was only one cloud on my horizon: Rodolfo Fierro. But when I started taking cognac after my meals I almost forgot him.

Sophisticated or not, I did not comprehend Mexican politics. All I knew was that Grandpa Johnson was a Democrat, and Democrat didn't signify in Mexico. Mr. Wickwire explained things to me, though. Even though I was on call to go to the telegraph office and send messages for the general, day or night, I still had a lot of time. When Mr. Wickwire came back from the battlefield, saying he was through with getting shot at, he slept awhile in my bed. I brought beans and roast pork from the San Ignacio to refresh him, along with a bottle of his favorite beer.

"I guess," remarked Mr. McFall, watching the reporter eat, "you weren't as tired as you looked, sir."

Mr. Wickwire scooped up the last of the beans with his knife. "I can always eat, seems like!"

Mr. McFall put a hand on his stomach and let out a small puff of gas. "Excuse me—beans lie heavy on my stomach."

Seizing the opportunity, I said, "Sir, I've got to admit I don't understand exactly what's going on in Mexico. I never knew much about Texas politics and I sure can't handle what goes on in Mexico. It seems there is General Villa and this man Huerta and someone—Zapato—down south somewheres." Then I remembered that *zapato* meant "shoe," and added lamely, "Zapata, I guess."

Mr. Wickwire laid down his knife and put on his spectacles. Going to the window overlooking the railroad yards, he listened. When a passing locomotive stopped its chuffing you could hear cannon way off in the south.

"Still going on!" he muttered. "It's Katy bar the door and the devil take the hindmost!" Turning to me, he wiped his mouth with a handkerchief that was dirty and looked like it had a spot or two of blood on it. Seeing me stare at it, he said, "Got creased a little in the big toe near Sierra Blanca—nothing important. What was that you asked, Ben?"

"About Mexican politics, Mr. Wickwire. I just wanted to know what—"

"Ah! Mexican politics, eh?" He sat down again, started to put on his leather puttees. "A puzzle, to be sure! But maybe I can lay it out this way. Old Porfirio Díaz ruled this country for twenty years like it was his own private property. Then the people rebelled under Francisco Madero and threw him out. Madero was a good sort—kind and gentle and earnest, always trying to do the right thing. That's the kind that gets shot in Mexico, and that's what happened to Madero. Then an Indian named Huerta took over the presidency. Huerta is a scoundrel, so Villa and Venustiano Carranza and Emiliano Zapata all rose up against him. But each one has got his own army and each one wants to be top dog so they can't get together and that's why things are all *chingado*, for sure."

I knew that word, all right.

"Magnificent!" Mr. McFall commented. "I never heard such a concise assessment of the situation!"

I was watching Mr. Wickwire. His eyes started to close, and he slumped against the headboard of my bed, puttees still not laced.

"Sir?" I said.

His head fell on his chest and he started to snore.

"Mr. Wickwire!" I shook him by the shoulder.

"Maybe we'd best let him sleep," Mr. McFall suggested. "The poor old fellow is exhausted."

Mr. Wickwire seemed younger than Mr. McFall, but I let that pass.

"No," I decided. "When he came in he said something about renting a car and getting back to the battle. It's important to him." I shook him again. "Mr. Wickwire! Wake up!"

Blinking, looking dazed, he came to, looking around.

"Now, Carranza, you see, doesn't like Villa at all, and Zapata has little use for—"

"You'd better rent your car and go south again, like you

said," I told him, helping him get out of bed. When he started for the door, kind of unsteady, I reminded him to lace up his puttees. "It's almost sundown."

He took a deep breath, almost a sigh, and thanked me. "No rest for the wicked, I guess! What the hell is an old man like me doing sashaying around Mexico covering a dirty little war? I ought to be setting on my front porch in El Paso in a rocker with a shawl around my shoulders!" Then he grinned a tired grin and wobbled to his feet, reaching for his ragged plaid cap.

"Don't tell me! I know why. It's the story, the goddamned story! I could never resist a good story. When I get to hell I suppose I'll try for an exclusive interview with Old Nick himself! Well . . ." He clapped me on the back. "Thanks for the bunk and beans, my boy." He shook hands with Mr. McFall. Then, as he took out his wallet, his face fell. "Good Lord! I'm about broke!"

I took a handful of bilimbique notes from a vase and handed them to him. "Here. I've got a lot of these."

He took them and stuffed them into the pocket of the stained and ragged military coat he wore, with "CORRESPONDENT" stitched on the front. "Ben, you're a good story too! Thirteen years old and—"

"Fourteen!"

"All right, then, fourteen, and already Pancho Villa's fair-haired boy! When I get a little time I'm going to write you up as a feature story for the *Morning Times*!" Shaking hands all around, he tottered out.

Maybe it wouldn't be so bad being General Villa's favorite boy, but I sure didn't want to play that role for Rodolfo Fierro! Mr. McFall must have seen the worried look on my face as I closed the window against the smoky winter chill.

"I know what you're thinking, laddie. Now, don't plague yourself with worries! I've got a plan."

Someone knocked at the door. I knew who it was— Julio, the guard. I don't think he ever slept. He was on me day and night, following me to the San Ignacio, to the telegraph office, back to the hotel, even to the toilet.

"I guess he's restless," I said. "Julio wants to go for a walk."

"All right," Mr. McFall said. "I've got a little business to attend to myself." He picked up his battered old violin. As he put on his coat I asked him, "How is the Scottish Guards Band of Northern Mexico coming along?"

He was a prize, Mr. McFall. Already he'd located a few *soldados* who could play instruments, along with some civilian musicians. With looted band instruments he'd organized them, even found some old uniforms, and now he had his own band.

"Well," he said, "a Mexican playing the cornet sounds like a runaway noon whistle at the shirt factory, and the drums have a tropical beat to them that I've got to correct. But all in all, they do a pretty passable job on 'Loch Lomond.' By Bobby Burns's birthday in January we should be ready for our first concert in the plaza, although a couple of good pipers would surely add to the ensemble."

"Pipers? You mean bagpipers? People who play the bagpipes?" I'd heard a man play the bagpipes at a picnic the McCrackens once invited us to, and I wasn't anxious to hear another one.

"Of course, my boy! A band without a piper is a sorry thing!"

He went on to tell me about once hearing the famous, he said, Seaforth Highlanders Pipe Band.

"Laddie, they played 'Amazing Grace' and it was magnificent! Ah, the grand music of the pipes! Even playing a blackamoor song, a slave song from your American South, it brought tears to my eyes!"

I surely didn't want to hurt his feelings, but I couldn't help saying, "Why, Mr. McFall, I imagine it would have brought tears to my eyes too, and maybe a sob or two!" Sometimes we sang "Amazing Grace" in church at McNary, and I shuddered to think of a bagpiper skreeling the melody to shreds. But what I said went right over Mr. McFall's head. He was really a pretty innocent old man, for all his knowledge.

"Yes," he said absently, staring far away. "I wish you could have been there too, Ben."

Just then a runner came to tell me to hurry to the telegraph office. Villa's generals at the front were sending back a lot of messages about the battle, which they claimed they were winning, and wanted them put on the wire to the United States newspapers. The rest of the operators had mostly gone home—they never seemed very interested in their jobs because after General Villa had won Ciudad Juárez their salaries were in arrears—and I was just about the only one there; me and Julio, that is, him sitting on a stool like a skinny tomcat, carbine across his knees.

Mexicans ate supper late, and I too had got into the custom, feeling I needed at least a little snack before I went to bed. With Julio stalking me through the gas-lit streets, I stopped in the Panadería La Luz for some of those fancy Mexican cookies and a cup of coffee. Mexican cookies look very fine but if you don't eat them right away, fresh out of the oven, they're like cardboard with icing. I found that out when I tried to keep a sack of them in my hotel room for emergencies. Grandma Johnson always used butter for shortening, but the Mexicans used lard—*manteca*—and maybe that was what made the difference. Anyway, who was there, in the bakery, but the girl Valentina!

She was mixing bread dough in a big copper bowl, using a wooden paddle longer than her. Her bosom friend, old Victoria, was decorating a wedding cake, I guess it was. The Panadería La Luz was busy; bread came to be in such short supply in Ciudad Juárez that the mixed crews of *soldados* and civilians worked twenty-four hours a day. I bought Julio a roll and coffee but he didn't thank me, just sopped the roll in his coffee and kept a wary eye on me.

"Ah, Benjamin!" Old Victoria dropped the cloth cone she was using to decorate the cake and came around, wiping hands on her apron, to embrace me. Pressing her warty nose against my cheek, she beckoned to Valentina. "Come here, my heart, my life!" She was awful fond of Valentina, and of me too, for some reason.

Shyly Valentina came, hair done up in a white rag and her cheeks pink from the heat of the ovens in the bakery.

She wouldn't even look at me till Victoria took her by the chin and lifted Valentina's face to mine.

"Benjamin is here, *niña*! Benjamin, *el señor americano, el señor guapo*!"

Maybe right here I'd better stop to explain something. There is one thing about learning a new language. If you're picked up by the scruff of the neck and flung down in a new country, you learn fast. With what I'd found out from Mr. McFall and the Spanish I was forced to learn from being set down hard in Ciudad Juárez, I'd already learned a lot of the lingo. Oh, I wasn't any expert, for sure! Later on, of course, I'd get pretty fluent, but for now I could at least pick up the meaning and say what I needed to say. So to spare translating everything in this book from Spanish to English or back again, I'll explain that from here on I'm mostly talking Spanish—except, of course, when I was speaking to Mr. McFall or Mr. Wickwire or a few others I came across.

That evening I tried to pretend I had my eye on some of the pastries in the glass case, but it was no good; Victoria wouldn't let me alone. "Here! You're hungry, eh?" Taking a fresh-baked loaf, round and brown and crusty and hot, she pulled it apart and slathered butter on it from the big icebox in the rear of the bakery. "Eat!" she commanded. "A growing boy must eat!"

Well, it *was* good! Mostly the Mexicans preferred tortillas made from cornmeal. It was a common sight in the early morning to see housewives hurrying home from the *tortillería*—the tortilla foundry—with a napkin-covered basket of them for papa's breakfast. Still, I guess I had forgotten what real bread tasted like. I bolted that bread, and she spread me some more, grinning. That bread made me think of McNary and home and Grandma before her brains turned mushy, and my eyes misted up. *Home*! Home seemed far away and unattainable. Victoria didn't notice, I guess; no one noticed but Valentina. She came close to me, a wondering look in her blue eyes, and touched my hand. It was the smallest, most fleeting touch, but it had a powerful effect on me. It had been a long time since any female had been that understanding with me, and in spite of myself I started to bawl for real. Red-faced, blubbering, I bolted from the Panadería La Luz like the devil himself was after me. Julio didn't catch up with me till I was sitting on the bed in my room at the Hotel Buena Vista, staring out, red-eyed, at the locomotives switching cars below.

Goddamned fool! I said bitterly to myself. What's the matter with you?

These days people often speak of "role models" for their children. Well, I never had a role model. Maybe that's why I went through so much. When I was a little baby, Pa died at the sulfur mine. Grandpa Johnson always scared me. My brother Cleary never liked me. Mr. Dinwiddie, my beloved teacher, left me when I needed him most. Mr. Ballew, the railroad telegrapher, was hardly a fit role model for anyone. No, I didn't have any model to guide me; I was just a bewildered kid trying to be a man, tossed about on the crest of a bloody revolution in a strange country, trying desperately to "find myself," as they say now.

Julio was surly, and swore at me. For a minute I had escaped him, and he was afraid of what Rodolfo Fierro would do to him if he let me get away. Instead of camping outside my door, he came inside, glowering, and squatted on the floor at the foot of my bed, gun across his knees. When I went to sleep that night the last thing I remembered was the dark blob at the foot of my bed.

South of the city the battle went on, ebbing and flowing as the more-or-less evenly matched Federales and Villistas poked and probed at each other. At the telegraph office I was busy trying to keep up with the flow of dispatches. I was getting very professional at the key, even exchanging a little banter from time to time with the operators on the other end of the line. My "fist," as operators called it, was pretty good—fast and smooth and accurate. In the United States at that time there were many boy telegraphers like me. It is a shame that such opportunities no longer exist; it was an excellent chance for young men to embark on a healthy and well-paid career. In Mexico that winter I certainly did not see it as *my* ultimate career. I enjoyed the work, however, thinking back to my fictitious Benjamin D'Artagnan Wilkerson South Texas and Mexico Railroad. And at least the employment gave me surcease from the coming return of El Carnicero, Rodolfo Fierro. With the revolution taking so many twists and turns, who knew anyway what would happen tomorrow? Maybe *chingado*—who knew? Or maybe not.

Sometimes General Villa himself, when he came briefly away from the front, would visit the Ciudad Juárez telegraph office to have Colonel Aguirre read dispatches from the battle. It was odd; in the midst of a war, the Mexican telegraph system continued to function. There was even a line intact to Chihuahua City, the stronghold of the Federales. Occasionally I was required to send insults to the commander of President Huerta's garrison there, receiving in return a choice collection of Spanish cusswords. I did not understand many of them, but Villa chuckled when I read them off. *Cabrón,* that all-purpose epithet, was the least of them.

The general always came surrounded with an entourage. The streets were lined with people anxious to get a look at "the Centaur of the North." He brought along Colonel Aguirre, a few generals of brigade like Urbina and Banda, and always the pleasant young correspondent for *Excelsior*, David Berlanga. Berlanga was a nice young man but often critical and outspoken in the reports he filed to his newspaper. The general would clump inside in his pigeon-toed way, his kinky reddish hair cut, now that he was near a barber, and the thick brown mustache neatly trimmed. Never would he allow the barber to use bay rum. To him, scents of any kind were odious. The worst word he could use to describe an opponent was *perfumado*, a "perfumed" person. Good men, he believed, smelled only of hard work and sweat.

"*Bueno,*" he would say to me after he had heard the dispatches. "*Bueno, hombre!*" The "*hombre*" pleased me; "man," it meant. General Villa considered me a man! I would have died for him then, though later he and I had our differences.

Even then, as a matter of fact, I did not care for what was going on. Some of the Villistas had got the nickname of Los Dorados. It meant, "The Gilded Ones," and with good reason. As the campaign dragged on and funds began to dwindle, the Dorados robbed the Ciudad Juárez churches of their gold and silver, even tearing down and burning the ornamented wooden altars to recover the gold leaf. Grandpa made me fear God, even if I didn't understand much of the Bible. The Mexican priests were Catholics, and while Grandpa did not hold with Rome, I had a certain reverence, if not fear, for any God, Catholic or otherwise. I was uncomfortable with the looting of churches, even Catholic churches. Mr. Wickwire, on one of his visits from the front, explained that the Mexican church had come out for President Huerta. That was why General Villa allowed such depredations, he thought.

Sitting on the edge of my bed, Mr. Wickwire told Mr. McFall and me the latest news from the front.

"Villa," he said, "is conducting a brilliant campaign. He has Felipe Ángeles with him now, you see. Ángeles deserted from Huerta and came over to Villa because he admired Villa and was disgusted with that bullet-headed little Indian, Huerta. Ángeles is a top-flight military man, an honor graduate of Chapultepec. He probably knows more about the uses of artillery than any man in Mexico."

A thought had been in the back of my mind. Mr. Wickwire went home to El Paso once in a while, when, as he said, he got tired of being shot at. Why couldn't he take my case to the U.S. marshal there and have the U.S. government demand the return of a fourteen-year-old boy held captive in Ciudad Juárez? So, backing and filling a whole lot, I asked Mr. Wickwire about the possibilities.

"I don't know," he said. "Homesick, are you, Ben? Well, next time I'm in El Paso I'll see what I can do, but I doubt if old Pancho would let you go anyway." His eyes blinked wearily as he sank back on my bed. "Besides, my boy, for all practical purposes you're a soldier in a foreign army, and they'd say you'd forsworn allegiance to the United States."

"But I didn't mean to!"

He shrugged again, and his voice drifted into a mumble. Mr. McFall and I would always put a pillow under his head and throw a blanket over him. Each time I saw him he seemed to look more wrinkled and frail. But frail or not, he would not be denied the story. I sent a lot of his dispatches to El Paso for him. They were models—terse, factual, and informative.

This time he woke after an hour or so and sat up, holding to the brass bedpost for support. "You know," he mused, "there's a war going on in Europe. And in the States there are wheels within wheels." Polishing the spectacles I brought him, he went to the window and looked out at the steam and smoke in the railroad yards.

Mr. McFall knew all about the European war. It seems someone killed a king or someone, and the French and the Germans were fighting about it, though I didn't know exactly why.

"What do you mean, wheels within wheels?" Mr. McFall asked. "It's a provocative expression, but I don't catch your drift, sir."

Mr. Wickwire got to his feet, adjusting his leather puttees.

"A reporter," he said, "a good reporter, I mean, *senses* a story! He may be wrong, of course—I've been wrong a lot of times—but I think I may be on to a big one this time."

Curious, I said, "Tell us, then."

Rising, he slung the kit bag over his shoulder and shook his head. "No, not now, anyway! I hate like hell to be wrong. But I can say this: sooner or later, look for the United States to be drawn into this revolution. And when it happens, look behind the headlines!"

Mr. McFall was puzzled, and so was I.

"I've said too much already," Mr. Wickwire grumbled. "Maybe I'm a damned fool. Jesus, I don't know!" As always, he shook hands. As time went on and he got more and more close calls, I was afraid I'd never see him again. I believe he sensed that, because he gave me a kind of embarrassed fist in the chest and murmured, "I'll be back soon, fellows. You know: a bad penny . . ." Quickly he went out the door. A moment later his rented automobile tooled away in the dust of Avenida López.

Other interesting things happened. Some I saw, some Mr. McFall saw, others we only heard about. But there was no mistaking the herds of Mexican cattle driven across the international bridge to El Paso to be sold by an agent of the general's—a Mr. Samuel Ravel. It was no secret that Villa's raiders were stealing cattle from rich *hacendados* in Chihuahua and selling them to finance his operations. Villa explained they were a kind of tax levied to build a new and fair government in his beloved Mexico. The ranchers were scared of Villa and his men and put up with it. There wasn't much else they could do, but one of them had had enough, as I describe below.

I was visiting gun shops in the city, hoping to find .25-caliber bullets for my pistol against the return of Rodolfo Fierro, when a gentleman rode up on a handsome roan and barked, "You there—you look like you could speak English! Where can I find General Villa's headquarters?"

Either there were no .25-caliber bullets in Ciudad Juárez or Fierro had passed the word not to sell me any. That was possible; I had got to be a well-known figure in the city. Still, .25 caliber, I heard, was not a common bore among the Mexicans. They preferred .45 caliber, something that would blow a hole the size of a dinner plate in a man.

"It's down the street there, sir," I said, pointing. "In the city hall, the big building with the pillars in front, although maybe he won't be there. He drives back and forth to Sierra Grande every day—for the battle, you know."

The rider had an air of authority about him. For a minute I thought he was one of the victimized *hacendados*. He was certainly dressed like one: yellow boots, riding breeches, an imported cloth jacket with a scarf around his weathered neck, and wearing a Texas-style hat. He stared at me for a minute, reining in the curvetting roan.

"What the hell are you doing here in this dog's-meat place? Boy, you ought to be home doing sums and grammar!"

He had a curious way of talking, like through his nose, and I didn't like him.

"I'm not a boy, and you're no gentleman, to repay courtesy with talk like that!"

He laughed in the same hard barking way. "Ah, you're right, you know! Forgot my manners!" He tipped his hat and cantered off toward the city hall, street vendors moving quickly to get out of his way. They knew rank when they saw it; it had been built into them by centuries of oppression.

That man was William Benton, an expatriate Englishman who raised cattle at his Rancho Los Remedios down around Lucero, on the big lake called Lago Toronto. I don't know what happened at the city hall but I was on my way to the telegraph office an hour or so later when he came galloping by in a cloud of dust. Chickens, chili vendors, small children, mamas in *rebozos*—all scurried to get out of his way. An old man, knocked sprawling, rose to shaky knees, supporting himself on his cane and shrilling curses. I had only an instant to see William Benton's face, contorted in anger. He whipped the mare as he wheeled her around the corner so hard she almost slid on her haunches. Then he was gone, galloping southward, leaving a whirlwind of Chihuahua dust. Villa must have failed to convince him of the necessity of the tax. More, much more, was to come of the feud between the general and William Benton. Even England was to come into the argument, but that was later.

"Well, that's over," Mr. McFall said the next day when I came on him in Avenida López. "The Federales have been routed and are falling back on Chihuahua City."

"How do you know?" I asked.

"Henry Wickwire just rode across the bridge to go to the *Morning Times* with his copy. He stopped and told me."

"I . . . I suppose that means Fierro will be coming back."

"Of course. Rumor has it that he led a critical charge against the Federales and finally broke their back, although General Orozco, that fleet-footed man, got away again."

"What about your plan that you mentioned?" I asked. I

hadn't heard anything yet from Mr. Wickwire about the marshal at El Paso, and I was getting desperate.

Mr. McFall was getting up in years and was sometimes forgetful. For a minute he pulled at his eyebrows, thinking. Then he said, "Ah, yes! I know what you mean, laddie. Don't think I haven't been pondering a lot how to deliver you from that awful man!" Kneeling, he picked up a splinter from a packing case to draw a design in the dust. "Here's the bridge to El Paso, you see. Now, listen carefully."

I squatted beside him and listened.

"A lot of the people in my Scottish Guards Band of Northern Mexico don't like Fierro either, and would do anything to fix his clock, as they say. So here's what I've come up with."

I had a sinking feeling he'd forgotten all about helping me, and was just making something up.

"After the troops come back, flushed with victory, I'm going to assemble my band for a concert! We'll march down Avenida Juárez and turn right at the Stanton Street bridge."

"Right? Turn *right*? That's the way to El Paso!"

"Of course, Ben! Let's say that I, as the leader, made a mistake and took the wrong turn."

"But—"

"Just a minute, now. There will be a new trombone player in the band. I've already got a trombone for you."

"I can't play the trombone!"

He got creakily to his feet. "Who cares? The trombone man I've got now can't either! You'll be wearing a band uniform, and we'll cut that long hair of yours and stuff it under a uniform cap. In the general confusion that ensues, you can scoot across the bridge and be saved. What do you think of that?"

The whole thing took me aback. "I don't know," I muttered. "It sounds crazy to me." Still, I hadn't much choice.

"Well," Mr. McFall said, "sometimes crazy things work best. There is the element of surprise, you know! Napoleon used it very effectively at the battle of Marengo,

I think it was." He put a hand on my shoulder. "Trust me, my boy! I've even got a string of firecrackers to add to the general confusion!"

I was still doubtful. "What about that damned Julio that sticks to me like mucilage?"

Mr. McFall pondered. Then he said, "Well, no plan is perfect, of course. I'll have to work on that."

It seemed he was making up the whole thing as he went along. Still and all, he said he had a uniform for me, and a trombone, and firecrackers.

He must have been thinking about the trombone too because he said, "There's one thing, Ben. When you're safely across the river, manage somehow to get the trombone back to me. Mail it or whatever. We're short of trombones in the band."

I was astonished. "You're not coming with me?"

A little embarrassed, he shook his head. "I've got great hopes for my band! Oh, sometimes they sound like a bunch of cats with their tails tied together and flung over a wash line, but they mean well, and I've got them playing a fairly decent rendition of 'Coming Thro' the Rye.' "

"All right," I said, resigned to anything. "But there isn't much time. Rodolfo Fierro will be back here any day now."

Being in a strange land with strange people and a strange language, at first I didn't notice the Christmas season was near. But gradually it began to seep in on me. There were religious parades, especially one called Las Posadas, or "The Inns." It had something to do with Joseph and Mary and the baby Jesus. The parade went from one inn or hotel to another to find shelter for Mary and the baby Jesus that was coming, and no one had room for them. The long procession would sing beautiful songs and when they stopped at the hotels the proprietor would come out according to ritual and say there was no room and then the procession would move on, still singing. I tried some of those tunes on my mouth-organ but they didn't sound much like what the people sang; that was really moving and solemn and impressive.

Christmas! Last Christmas in McNary I got the mouthorgan and an orange and a sack of hard candies and a pair of wool socks. Now here I was, all alone except for my friend Mr. McFall, and no one would give me a present this Christmas. No one except . . .

It happened this way. On a December night, very cold and bleak and windy, practically no one in the streets except a few late passersby wrapped in *sarapes,* someone knocked on my door. With all that was on my mind—scared and nervous and sad—I called out. "Who is it?"

There came a muffled reply I couldn't understand, though it sounded like a woman's voice. Taking out the little pistol the general had given me, I held it at the ready. No bullets were in it, of course—I hadn't been able to get any yet—but maybe it would scare someone.

"Come in!" I called.

Well, it was Valentina, old Victoria's favorite. She was breathing hard from the cold and her cheeks were red and her eyes sparkled. Muffled in a fur-trimmed coat with a shawl around her head, she looked strange and bulky.

"Feliz Navidad!" she cried. *"Feliz Navidad,* Benjamin!"

Standing shyly on the threshold, she held out a package wrapped in tissue paper and bound with red ribbon, with a big pink flower on it made from crepe paper.

"Merry Christmas!" she repeated.

Remembering my manners, I took the gift and stood aside. "Thank you," I muttered, thinking at the same time it was probably wrong to have a pretty young lady in your room, especially at night.

Bobbing her head in acknowledgment, she hurried in. "Who is that man on the landing?" she asked, taking off the kerchief and letting her hair fall down over her shoulders. "Is that Julio?"

"Yes," I said sourly. "But . . . I mean . . . you brought me a present?"

She shook out her hair, laughing, and it swirled around her face in a blue-black cloud. "Yes. For Christmas!"

"I . . . I thank you."

Shrugging off the rest of the bulky stuff, she stood happy in the lamplight, smiling at me. "You are surprised?"

"Yes," I admitted. "I . . . I didn't
"I have my good old Victoria! You
"That's true."
"Open the box, then!"

The cardboard box was filled with little Christmas cookies—pink and green and yellow. Some were decorated with tiny bells and others with paper images of the Virgin and Child pasted on. Picking out a chocolate cookie with swirls of green icing, I handed it to her. "Here—you have one too!"

Taking it between dainty fingers, she bit it with small white teeth. "You scared me with that gun, you know!"

Belatedly I discovered I still had the small pistol stuck in the waistband of my trousers. I put it on the bed. "I'm sorry, but you needn't have worried. I haven't got any bullets for it."

Sitting on the bed, Valentina crossed her legs in their short leather boots—high-heeled, they were, and very elegant. I don't doubt they were fine Italian imports looted from some expensive shop. Too, she wore a silk frock with lots of lace around the waist and hem and collar; it also looked expensive. Old Victoria dressed her in style. Then, too, there was that mysterious and compelling scent about her; not perfume, but something else. The flood of blue-black hair, maybe? I didn't know. Remembering the scared tearstained face of the small *soldadera* under the bandstand, I marveled at the change and sought to say something suitable. I never learned to talk to Prue Ballard, either; I always got tongue-tied and red in the face. But Valentina was cheerful and friendly, chattering in that bright female way, and gradually I was put at ease or something near it.

"I am always excited at Christmas! Of course, at the convent it was always solemn, with a lot of singing of sacred songs, but I remember when I was *very* small, before the convent, our house was lit bright with candles, and a pig was roasted. Oh, everything smelled so good!"

"Where was that?" I asked.

She frowned; a shadow crossed her face. "I think it was

101

rrero. It was so long ago. My mother . . ." She
off, and began to cry.

"Look here!" I said in alarm. "I didn't mean to make you cry!" Female tears have always distressed me.

She shook her head, and wiped her eyes with a lacy handkerchief she took from a sleeve. "I'm sorry, Benjamin. It was just that . . . that . . ." Squaring her shoulders and putting the handkerchief away, she went on, chin up.

"You see, my mother died when I was little, and I was put in the Convent of the Blood of the Savior and I missed my mother and the good times and now I hardly remember them and it is all so sad." She sighed, shook her head.

"Well," I said practically, "how does a convent kind of girl come to be here fighting, carrying a gun, for the Villistas?"

"I ran away."

I always thought convents had high walls and the nuns or whatever they were didn't countenance any nonsense; they certainly didn't want anyone to run away.

"You see," she said, "I never really knew my father. But I heard—you see, the girls always have ways of finding out things—the girls told me they had heard he was an officer in the army—one of those who left that hateful President Huerta and went to join up with General Villa and the revolution. I am sure he was a fine man, and that was what I would have expected of my father. So I ran away. I made a rope out of sheets and some of my girlfriends helped me and I got over the wall and ran away to join the revolution!"

She had a lot of pluck, I'll say that. "Well," I said, picking up the gun and idly spinning the cylinder, "I hope you find him." I thought of my own father, dead in that accident at the sulfur mine. But of course, girls needed fathers more than boys did. *I* would get along, somehow.

"What was your father's name, then?" I asked.

She shook her head, and the blue-black hair glistened with light, like when Mr. Dinwiddie used to let us look through the glass prism he had on his desk. "I don't know. I don't even remember my mother's name, I was so small. And at the convent they called me Valentina Robles, but that was not my real name, I am sure."

"But didn't your father ever visit you in the convent? I mean . . . why didn't you ask him?"

She stammered, and her face became a little flushed. "I . . . I am beginning to believe I was not meant to know who my father was." Quickly she changed the subject. "You say you do not have bullets for your gun, Señor Benjamin?"

"No," I sighed. "It seems to be an odd caliber."

"Well," she said, "you had better get some soon. I am only a simple convent girl, but I have learned a lot since I joined the revolution. Some of the *soldaderas*, dedicated as they are, will still shoot their own comrades if they think they have been insulted."

"Well, how does a *soldaderita* protect herself?"

At the knock on the door, she rose. "Now I must go!"

"No," I begged. "Please! Wait a minute!" I didn't want her to go. Knowing I was no fit companion for a girl with all my sordid past, I still longed to have her sit on the bed and talk to me. Putting the pistol in my pocket, I touched her arm. "Please!"

"But—"

"Please, just a minute!"

The knocker was Mr. McFall, nose red from cold. Slapping his arms against his lean chest, he said, "I declare, it can be colder in Mexico than it was in Albany, New York, where I once spent a winter!" Noticing Valentina, he stopped short and took off his band cap with its gold braid, bowing; I suspect he had found a bottle of Scotch whiskey somewhere. "I'm sorry, Ben! Didn't know you were entertaining a lady. Ma'am, your servant!"

"I'm not entertaining anyone," I said testily. "It's just Valentina! You know, Victoria's little friend? She brought me a Christmas present." I offered him a cookie.

Mr. McFall shook his head, a kind of funny look on his wrinkled face. "*Tempus fugit*, eh, Ben? No, thank you. Just had a snack at the coffee shop. Well, I must be going!"

"Where? At this time of night?" After all, he slept here too.

He looked mysterious. "Oh, I've got some business to attend to. I'll leave you two young people alone!"

His manner annoyed me, trying to make something out of a casual visit from a friend. "Well," I said, "all right, but Valentina's about to leave, anyhow!"

Kind of grinning, he went out, closing the door softly after him, calling after him, "I'll be back in a while, Ben! Don't wait up for me!" I could have killed him, embarrassing me that way! *Old fool*! I thought. Why did grown-ups think they knew it all? Anyway, she was only a child.

Below, in the railyards, was more steaming and chuffing—ringing of bells, men shouting, the occasional crack of a rifle. Going to the window, still embarrassed, and not wanting to face Valentina, I looked out. In the glare of electric arc lights, trains were rumbling in from the south, couplers clanging and *soldados* hanging from the windows, cheering and firing guns into the air. Trucks trundled down Avenida Juárez filled with noisy and jubilant troops of the Division of the North. Vendors ran alongside, offering cold beer and ices, roast meats and pastries, crying their wares against the hubbub. From somewhere, this late at night, Mr. McFall had gathered up a few members of his Scottish Guards Band; they were marching around tootling, and sounded awful, although in the general racket they couldn't be heard very well and that was a good thing. As seemed to be the practice in Mexico, the smallest man was carrying the biggest instrument—the big Mexican bass fiddle.

In the icy blue glare of the arc lights the general's dusty old Dodge automobile tooled along. He was standing in the back seat, waving his hat as Colonel Aguirre drove. When the Dodge stopped at the rail crossing the general jumped down and a bunch of Villistas hoisted him on their shoulders and carried him along, singing a song I grew to know better, in various versions, in later years:

With Huerta's whiskers
I'll make a new hatband

For the sombrero
Of my general—Pancho Villa!

Later on, the words would change a little. When General Villa and Venustiano Carranza fell out for good, the Villistas would sing about Carranza's whiskers.

Wondering, Valentina came to join me at the window while we watched the spectacle. I didn't see Rodolfo Fierro but Garibaldi the fop was there in his forest-green hat and fancy uniform; also Felipe Ángeles, the Chapultepec artilleryman, along with Generals Urbina, Banda, and a few others. All of them except Garibaldi looked dusty and battle-worn. It had been a great victory on the plains south of the city.

Maybe I lost my balance, maybe she did and I tried to hold her—I don't know. But tight in each other's arms we fell onto the bed. My mind was a whirlwind of confused feelings and images: wires shining bright in morning sun, old Victoria's wart, the magazine *Electric World*, the dead telegrapher outside the little shack at Cuitla, old Mr. McFall pulling at his eyebrows and saying, "Let's go to Mexico and find gold." Grandpa Johnson's fierce mustache and cold blue eyes, Mr. Dinwiddie leaving my life on the mixed special for Austin, Prue Ballard's chestnut curls lying softly on her damp brow, the decaying frog in its matchbox, a box of Christmas cookies, Mr. Ballew, the telegrapher, my Sunday-school dime . . .

"Valentina!" I muttered desperately. "Oh, Valentina!" The soft compliant body for a moment struggled against my weight and I am afraid I only embraced her tighter, my lips seeking hers.

"No!" she protested. "Please, Benjamin!"

Driven by an impulse that was Prue Ballard multiplied by a hundred—or maybe a thousand—I couldn't help myself.

"Valentina!" I panted. "Ah, Valentina! I . . . I—"

I don't know what I was about to say because suddenly she bit my ear and threw me off her with amazing strength. Stupidly I lay on the bed, staring at her, one hand fondling my mistreated ear. "Look!" I said finally. "Blood! Dammit, you *bit* me!"

Coolly she rearranged her elegant clothing, disheveled in our short tussle.

"You have only yourself to blame, you know, Benjamin! What kind of a woman do you think I am?"

Ruefully I got to my feet. "A damned strong one!"

"You should not have treated me so."

I swallowed hard. "But . . . well, don't you . . . I mean, don't you have any . . . well, *feeling* for me, Valentina?"

Her tone was frosty. "If you mean I should apologize for biting you—"

"No, no! Of course not! But I mean . . . well . . ." I stammered, my face red. "Don't you like me?"

She put on her coat. "As a friend, Benjamin, of course I like you! But there can be nothing else between us now. There are too many things that must come first. I have to find my father. And of course I must keep in mind my duties as a fighter in the revolution until that great day when our General Villa is recognized as the rightful President of Mexico."

I am afraid I said something rather snide.

"Then they will have to look for you under some bandstand, the way I found you that first night!" My only apology is that I was frustrated, angry, and embarrassed.

She shrugged, imprisoned the lustrous hair in a colorful shawl. "That was my first experience, as you well know, Benjamin. Next time I intend to do better. I am learning to shoot well, and I will kill Huerta soldiers as well as the next man—or woman! Victoria tells me my aim is improving. She, as you perhaps do not know, has already killed many of our country's enemies—one, she said, with a shovel when she had no more bullets."

"I see," I muttered. "Well . . ."

Unaccountably she danced close to me in those elegant boots and gave me a quick peck on the cheek. "Do not be too discouraged, Benjamin! Someday, when this war is over and we have won . . ."

Then she was gone, closing the door quickly after her.

Drawing a deep breath, I sat down on the bed again, feeling a little dizzy. What an amazing child . . . or girl

. . . or female . . . or maybe woman—whatever word fit best! And I did not doubt she would shoot me if I stood in the way of the revolution.

Outside, the shots and raucous cries and gunfire grew louder against the background of hissing steam and clanking couplers and train whistles. As I watched from the window, I heard a click from behind me. Turning, I made out a dark figure in the doorway. Julio, my guard? Mr. McFall, returning?

It was neither of these. Rodolfo Fierro, the Butcher, thumbs hooked in his pistol belt, legs in worn and dirty boots spread wide, stood there. He wasn't wearing his usual carnation—they must have been hard to find in the battlefields south of the city—but the bells on his spurs tinkled as he strode across the room, tossing his hat on the bed Valentina what's-her-name and I had lately occupied to my sorrow.

"Well," he said. "Again we meet, Benjamin—after too long an absence. Come here and greet your friend, *chamaco*."

— 6 —

Now, so many years later, I look back on those times and have trouble believing that I am related to that boy, that *muchacho lindo* with his shock of blond hair, his dead frog in a box, his bravura experiences, the load of guilt about so many things. It is almost as if I am reading an adventure story laced with purple psychological streaks. Who was he? Where did he come from? What a strange creature! Of course, no man can ever be but one boy, himself, and his remembrances of the creature he was cannot be generally applied. Every boy, I suspect, is a wildly different amalgam. As I shuffle about the patio of my house in Parral, near where the general died, I am unable to sleep for wondering.

Old Magdalena, faithful as a dog, comes out into the moonlight wrapping a robe about her.

"*Señor*, is anything wrong?"

The scent of jasmine is heavy in the silver moonlight. From somewhere in Parral itself, two or three kilometers distant, a dog howls. He is answered at once by a chorus of yips from the coyotes hunting in the low hills that ring the town.

"No," I say with a mixture of annoyance and affection. "No, Magdalena! I couldn't sleep, and came out to take the fresh air."

She is still unsatisfied. "*Señor*, your medicine—"

"I have stopped taking medicines, Magdalena. The medicines cause me not to sleep, I think."

She is horrified. "But Dr. Velásquez . . ."

Fuck Dr. Velásquez. But I do not say it this time

because I know she will be again shocked at the obscenity. She is a good and faithful woman, a friend devoted to my welfare, and I do not want to shock her again.

"I will be all right." Taking her elbow, I lead her toward the wing where she and Concepción, the cook, sleep. Concepción is much younger and a hard worker, with a compact ponylike body and endless vitality. When I need what a man needs—even a sick old man like me—it is Concepción who comforts me, not Magdalena.

"You are sure?" she asks, picking up the hem of her robe to clear the step into the house.

I nod. "Now go to bed, and don't worry!"

Reluctantly she goes, and I am left to pace the cool flagstones of the patio, listen to the splashing of the fountain, the call of a nightbird. Why am I unable to sleep? I am still thinking of that night when Rodolfo Fierro, weary and fatigued from battle, confronted me in my room at the Hotel Buena Vista, where I had been living like a young lord. Mr. Tom Mix's words came back to me; dread seeped into my chest and paralyzed my brain.

When I stood stock-still, unable to move, he stepped forward again, holding out his hand; then he paused, sniffing the air.

"*Por Dios*! It seems to me I smell a woman here, Benjamin!" For a moment he scowled, looked uncertain. Then he shrugged, took from his pocket a gaily wrapped package, and held it out to me.

"For you, Benjamin!" When I hesitated, heart in my throat, he pushed it into my hand. "Here! Take! It is a present I hope will put us on better terms. You see, there is no need for you to fear me, boy! I am your good friend!"

Not knowing what else to do, I unwrapped the package with trembling fingers. My throat was dry and I had trouble with the string. Finally I worked it off and opened the box.

"Spurs!" Fierro said proudly. "Silver spurs—the same pattern as mine! And I have got you a fine little horse to ride, too, Benjamin! She is named Pinta."

I was still struck dumb, and could only gaze fixedly

down at the glittering spurs, afraid to raise my eyes to his. What was going to happen to me? I wanted to cry out, to scream, to escape, but my legs seemed made of India rubber and would hardly support me. Slowly I slumped on the bed.

"Now, Benjamin!" Scaling his dusty sombrero into a corner, he sat beside me, fondling my hand. "My boy, I will have to teach you manners. I am from a good family in Spain, you know, in Aragon, and there we put great weight on courtesy." When he patted my hand again, I withdrew it. He only inched closer to me, pressing a lean thigh against mine. "Come now, Benjamin! I am weary of fighting, and need some recreation! Do not be coy with me!" His voice took on an edge. "Dammit, boy, do not reject me so! I can show you delights you have never imagined! Come here, now!"

I think I shrieked out in panic, panic of the unknown, panic at the thought of being somehow violated. I knew nothing of the details of Rodolfo Fierro's vice, but I knew it was wrong, and that I was in deadly danger—not of injury or death, but of some unspecified but horrible degradation.

"No!" I cried. "Please, no!"

He clapped a hand over my mouth and threw me down on the bed. *"Merde!"* he spat between clenched teeth. "Stop your damned caterwauling or I'll—"

I bit his hand as successfully as Valentina had lately bitten my ear. "No! Leave me alone! I won't!"

Sucking his injured hand, staring at me with baleful eyes, he said *"Merde!"* again. Later I found out that the word meant "shit" in French. The French had occupied Mexico back during our War Between the States and the Mexican people envied them their stylish ways. Even today, a lot of high-class Mexican people speak French when they are out in society. Right then I didn't know what the word meant, but I was quite sure it was not a compliment.

Breathing hard, I scrambled away from him, suddenly aware of the fact that I had the small Spanish pistol still in my pocket. Of course, there were no bullets in it, but maybe Fierro didn't know that. Drawing it out, I pointed it at him. I remember even now how my voice squeaked and broke when I said, "Don't touch me, goddammit! Stay away from me or I'll shoot!"

Telling it now, it sounds like a badly produced melodrama on some provincial stage. What happened next made it even more melodramatic. Mr. McFall burst in, red-faced and a little unsteady on his feet. He had brushed aside the watchdog, pockmarked Julio, and had the battered violin and bow under his arm. Pointing the bow at Rodolfo Fierro, he screeched like the ancient owl he resembled.

"Sir, stand back! Don't touch that boy on peril of . . . peril of . . ." He frowned, hiccuped, not quite able to get his thoughts in order. "Anyway . . ."

Fierro regarded him coldly. He crossed his arms, looked beyond Mr. McFall to where Julio was staring at the confrontation. "You damned ignorant brute, why did you let the old man into the room! Have I not told you—"

"He . . . he just . . ." Julio stammered, and then broke off, terror in his eyes. After all, this was Rodolfo Fierro, the Butcher, and we were all in trouble—Julio too.

"You are a troublesome old fool," Fierro said to Mr. McFall. "Once I was about to make an end of you, and circumstances prevented. I should have shot you then and there and removed a meddling old woman." He drew the heavy revolver that sagged from the pistol belt around his lean waist.

Raising my bulletless Spanish pistol, I drew a bead on him. "He is my friend," I quavered, "and I'll shoot you if you hurt Mr. McFall!"

Hearing all the commotion, other people had come up the stairway and were peering into the room. As soon as they saw Rodolfo Fierro, most of them scurried away, not wanting to become involved, as the saying goes nowadays. But some remained; one was my old friend Ojo Parado, glass eye intense. Ojo Parado was afraid of no one but God, he always said. Fierro slipped the revolver back into the worn holster.

"This is getting to be ridiculous!" he complained. "I

111

am disappointed, but the atmosphere has been destroyed anyway." He strolled negligently toward the door. Julio shrank back, terror-struck at his dereliction; he knew Fierro would deal with him later. Mr. McFall, however, stood his ground, glowering under his tufted white cotton brows at the Butcher.

"And as for you," Fierro said, "McFall or whatever your name is, you will learn that to interfere in my affairs is a thing not many men have done. Those that have done so greatly regretted it—that is to say, in that last clear moment which precedes death!"

It was said quietly, deliberately, but with a chill in the voice that would have turned Murphy's Creek, so far away in Hudspeth County, into instant ice in a Texas August.

At the door, everyone had fled but Ojo Parado. Fierro turned to me.

"As for you, Benjamin, we are still friends, and I have asked that you be assigned to my brigade. The little mare Pinta is yours whenever you wish to claim her, and I hope you will be gentle with the new spurs. One should at least try to be gentle with those one loves." Almost as an afterthought, he added, "Oh, by the way, *chamaco!* There is no firing pin in that little pistol. Knowing your passionate nature, which I prize much as I prize spirit in a horse, I had it removed."

He closed the door; the clinking of his spurs on the stairway died into silence. I took a deep breath and faced Mr. McFall.

"You are a damned fool!" I cried. "And drunk into the bargain! Do you know what Fierro will do to you? Do you remember all those Federales he killed going over the wall after the battle? I . . . I almost think I'd rather have had him do . . ." I swallowed hard. ". . . do whatever he was going to do with me than put you in such danger!"

Sagging onto my bed, he fumbled in a pocket and brought out a small glass bottle with a cork in it. He had sobered a great deal in the last few minutes.

"Now, Ben," he wheezed, "I *really* need a drink!"
Gurgling down a mouthful or two, he handed the bottle to

me. "I don't approve of youthful drinking, but I see you're quite shaken up too. Why don't you—?"

I pushed the bottle away and threw my arms around him.

"I thank you," I said. "I thank you, Mr. McFall, for what you did for me. That was foolhardy, but very brave!"

He patted my hand. "When you get as old as me, Benjamin, it doesn't take much to be brave. After all, what would my worthless old carcass bring?" He corked the bottle with a smack of his hand. "Anyway, that was mostly what they call Dutch courage, I believe—came out of a bottle!"

Nevertheless, I knew I could never repay him. I even forgave him sitting on the riverbank playing old Scottish tunes on his violin while I slaved in the mud, vainly looking for the loose gold he told me was lying around all over Mexico.

In my dotage at Parral, old and weary and sick, I am thinking of how David Berlanga died. Such a young man, though at the time he was much older than me. Curly black hair showing tufts where his shirt loosened at the neck, white teeth in geometrical line, a brilliant mind that foresaw the need for honesty in Mexican politics, even in the midst of revolution. I did not see Berlanga die. Old Ojo Parado was there and told me about it.

"*Qué lástima*! It was murder, I say—plain murder! And all because he wrote that the general was wrong in stealing cattle!"

We were getting ready to move out of Ciudad Juárez for Chihuahua City. That was what we thought at the time, though it turned out later that the Federales had taken refuge in Ojinaga, northeast of the city, across the border from the Presidio where General Pershing commanded. Anyway, Ojo Parado went on: "It is the first time I ever saw Fierro nervous at killing a man!"

I knew and liked David Berlanga and was shocked to hear of his death—and at Fierro's hand. "But why. . . ?"

"Ah!" Ojo Parado shook his grizzled head. "The general is very sensitive about bad things written concerning him. I don't think he wanted Berlanga killed, but you know Fierro!"

I did indeed know Rodolfo Fierro.

"All El Carnicero needed was to know that the general was miffed at Berlanga's writings to *Excelsior* in Mexico City. That did it. He took Berlanga over to the adobe-walled compound where they keep sheep for shearing. No one was there but the two of them, though I was upstairs in the city hall, waiting for my medal, and saw what happened below."

He had a medal too, old Ojo Parado. Everyone had a medal after the battle of Ciudad Juárez. In fact Julio, my guard, unbent enough to show me his. Colonel Aguirre must have scoured every pawnshop in Ciudad Juárez to get medals for everyone. Julio's said "Perfect Attendance for One Year Sunday School. Parsons Memorial M.E. Church, Phoenix, Arizona." I almost laughed in his face but restrained myself to a small snicker. Come to think of it, I got a kind of medal too. Probably at General Villa's request, the colonel had a local jeweler make up one with a multicolored ribbon that said, "Telegrafista de la Primera Clase de la Revolución." On the other side were incised some straggly marks meant, I guess, to suggest electrical sparks.

"He told young Berlanga he was to die," Ojo Parado went on. "Berlanga did not even quarrel with that. Maybe he knew it was coming. At any rate, Berlanga took a cigar from his pocket and lit it. The sun was shining, and his shadow made a dark blot on the wall. Some sheep wool stuck to the leg of his trousers and he brushed it off. Then, with arms folded, he said to Fierro, 'When you are ready, *cabrón.*' He was smoking like a man on holiday when Fierro's bullet hit him in the head. He stood still for a moment. Then the cigar dropped out of his mouth and he fell back in the bloody dust."

At the music of a bugle, the troops were assembling. Someone yelled at Ojo Parado, "Hey, old man, saddle up!"

"Fuck you!" Ojo Parado yelled back. He turned back to me. "I tell you, Fierro was shaken by that young man's way to die! He walked over to the body and just looked down at it. Once he touched it with his toe and it did not move. I saw Fierro's face. It was pale, with a nervous twitch. After that, Ángel Domínguez saw him in El Globo, where he likes to take a morning whiskey. But he took only coffee and sat for a long time staring at the cup, which he hardly touched. Then he got up and walked away and no one has seen him until early this morning, when he came out to assemble his brigade."

That was how David Berlanga died. So much blood, Mexico! I wondered how many gallons, how many rivers full to the banks, how many red desert floods would contain it! What is it a man has in him—six quarts or so? Multiply that by Francisco Madero and Emiliano Zapata and all the other people who died to bring liberty to poor Mexico, and it is . . . well, arithmetic was never my skill.

The next morning I was sitting in my hotel room examining the small pistol, and observing that the firing pin had indeed been removed. Mr. McFall was searching in a bureau drawer for a piece of band music.

"Now, where in Hades is that tuba score? Ben, have you seen it?"

I didn't know anything about music generally, let alone a missing tuba score, and he went on searching, mumbling to himself. "Although why I bother, I don't know! That idiot Tomás Nadal generally goes his own way with his tuba, score or no score!"

I put the little pistol back together. The firing pin, I knew, was just a short metal rod less than an inch long; a good blacksmith like Mr. Rayford Ellis could make one in a snap. I would have to find a good Mexican blacksmith.

Mr. McFall seemed to have located the missing tuba part. Going to the daylighted window to examine it more closely, he stared down below.

"There he is, Ben—our Pancho, driving up in his Dodge automobile! Listen to the people cheer!" He turned to me. "Doroteo Arango from Durango—do you remember my little rhyme? Oh, how far this remarkable peasant has come, and on what a sea of blood has he sailed!" He came at me again. "Are you sure you're all right, Ben? The troops are assembling, you know. Are you ready to go? I hear you're assigned to Fierro's brigade now. I asked to bring my Scottish Guards Band along with Fierro too, so I'd be traveling with you in case I . . . in case you . . . well, needed a little companionship."

"Yes," I said again. "I'm all right, Mr. McFall." To reassure him, I got to my feet and began packing things in my bedroll like a good soldier is supposed to do. "You go now and round up your band. I'll be along soon." I guess he'd already forgotten about helping me escape.

As I closed the door of my room in the Buena Vista (the old hotel is long gone now, and there is an office building on the site) I stood for a moment in the hallway, bedroll across my shoulder, and looked back at the door of number seven, its peeling green paint and tarnished brass doorknob. I had narrowly escaped Fierro.

"Hurry up, laddie!" Mr. McFall called up the stairway. "The column is pulling out!"

I had thought it over for a long time, but finally put the silver spurs in my bedroll, along with the little Spanish pistol. It had no firing pin, thanks to Rodolfo Fierro, but maybe I could find someone who could fix it.

When I reached the street I took that damned Sunday-school dime out of my pocket and flung it as far away as I could. Sunday school obviously hadn't done me the least bit of good, anyway! The box with the dead frog I threw away also; I would hardly need it anymore. Now all I had left from home was my barlow knife and my mouth-organ; harmonica, that is.

Colonel Aguirre walked up to me where I was trying to repair a broken strap on my bedroll. It was cold that morning, and his long nose was red and steaming. The colonel could never get a hat big enough for his head, and the Stetson he wore wobbled on his big dome.

"How are you, Benjamin?"

"Very well," I answered politely. "And you, sir?"

He wrapped his arms about him against the cold. "Well enough, I suppose! But I miss my wife and children at home in Guanajuato, this Christmas season." He looked over to where Rodolfo Fierro was assembling members of his brigade. Wiping his steaming nose with a handkerchief, he nodded toward Fierro, who was haranguing his troops, rushing about, shoving them into some semblance of order, and swearing a great deal.

"You are to march with Fierro, I hear."

"Yes, sir."

"Well, good luck, Benjamin." He turned on his heel, stuffing the handkerchief into a pocket, then wheeled and came back.

"Fierro, now . . ."

"Sir?"

"Ah . . . has that scoundrel been bothering you, my boy?"

I was noncommittal. "Bothering me?"

"I mean . . ." He broke off, and just looked at me. The colonel was a very decent man, and I always respected him. Later, almost blind, he became subsecretary of war in a kind of rump government in San Luis Potosí. That government quickly fell, and Colonel Aguirre died bravely before a firing squad. "Well, you know that bastard has a reputation for liking young boys! That is to say . . . you know . . ." He was embarrassed to speak of such things, and that will show you the kind of man he was.

"Yes, sir," I said. "I understand." What else could I say? I could not tell an outright lie to this good man, so I made a great pretense of punching new holes in the strap around my bedroll and mumbled something about not having any problems. *No problems*! Good God! I was made up of problems. No bone, no flesh, no sinew—nothing but problems!

"If you like," he insisted, "I will speak to General Villa and have you ride with me. The general is still very annoyed with Fierro for having killed young David Berlanga."

"No, sir," I said. "Please don't make any trouble about . . . it."

He shrugged. "Very well. But if he should ever . . . that is to say . . . make advances toward you, you are to tell me immediately. Do you understand, Benjamin?"

"Yes, sir," I said. That was hardly a lie; I *did* understand. But I had no intention of running scared to Colonel Aguirre; anyway, he seemed very naive.

"You had better go now," he concluded. "I see Fierro is motioning to you."

Rodolfo Fierro had a reputation for being brutal with his men, but this morning he was cordial to me, like we were old companions instead of master and intended paramour.

"Look here, boy! Do you see this beautiful little mare?"

She was indeed beautiful. I didn't know much about horses except Grandpa Johnson had a big plowhorse named Babe and I used to ride on her back when I was little. Later, when times got hard in West Texas, he had to sell Babe, and bought a mule, which was cheaper. But no one, expert or not, could miss the quality of this animal. She was only fourteen hands high at the shoulder, but shortcoupled and powerful in her haunches. The saying among Texas cowhands would be ". . . a lot of bottom to her," meaning reserve strength.

"You see? She likes you. Her name is Pinta."

She *was* painted, too—mostly white with a lot of brown and black splotches. While I rubbed her velvety nose, she searched my pockets for sugar. Not finding any, she gave a little whinny and tossed her head so that the thick feathery mane flew in the air, and pawed the dirt as if anxious to be off with me on her back.

"Yes," I admitted. "She is beautiful."

Rodolfo Fierro's smile was often the prelude to a bloody incident. Ojo Parado said Fierro always smiled when he killed people. But this morning he seemed actually pleasant—one could almost say relaxed and serene.

"Then she is yours," Fierro said. "Take her and enjoy her, *chamaco*!"

I did not know what to say at this unexpected generosity. Though the División del Norte had what seemed to me a lot of horses, most of them had been burned out by strenuous campaigning. Some had been ridden so hard and so long that the blankets stuck to their backs like raw scabs. Even though Villa ransacked the Ciudad Juárez stables to get fresh mounts, and sent an agent across the river to El Paso to buy more, there were still not enough. Aside from horses, the army was, in general, well-equipped as it started out on the march to Chihuahua City. An efficient commissary had been set up to dish out nourishing meals, a staff of doctors and trained nurses with plenty of medicines and bandages was available, and there were long lines of automobiles and trucks loaded with food, water, and other supplies. The whole organization now looked so powerful that a lot of Ciudad Juárez citizens joined up, feeling Pancho Villa could not be denied the presidency of Mexico, and that there would soon be rich booty for them. But the few enlistees compounded the horseflesh problem. Most of the recruits would have to march with packs, loaded down with guns and ammunition. I thought I would be one of these, but now I had my own mount. Still, the División del Norte was marching south, away from the Rio Grande, and with it my hopes for an easy escape. I shrugged; at least I didn't have to worry about Mr. McFall's crazy plan to pass me off as a trombone player.

Fierro looked over to where Colonel Aguirre was trying to get the wagons organized into a train.

"As for that *fantoche* Aguirre, stay away from him. He is a nosy old woman! I do not want you to talk to him anymore."

Colonel Aguirre said Fierro was a *bribón*, a scoundrel. Fierro called Colonel Aguirre a *fantoche*, a nincompoop. I decided to stay out of that disagreement, and busied myself loading my stuff on the mare Pinta. I made up my mind there was no use crying over spilt milk. I would just get on Pinta and ride in style toward Chihuahua, distinguishing myself there, not by telegraphic skill, but by some uncommon kind of valor.

General Villa rode up and down in the crisp dawn on his big mare Siete Leguas, as always a magnificent figure. His staff was now efficient and well-organized; Villa himself had little to do but slap a back here, a rump there, call out words of encouragement, point sometimes to someone struggling with a fractious team, and help would come running. A lot of the revolutionary songs said they would die for Pancho Villa. Well, dying is a pretty serious business, but I do know they admired him, trusted him, and leapt to his commands. Incidentally, he didn't drink at all, not then. Later, after many reverses, he took to *sotol*, a fiery peasant drink made from fermented cactus, and eventually graduated to *anís*, the deadly licorice-flavored liqueur. But now he could say to interviewers, "I do not drink! Think what a terrible person I would be if I drank!"

At last everything was ready for the assault on Chihuahua City. The long train moved out. I rode near Fierro, and was surprised to find that Julio, my pockmarked guard, was no longer with me. I suppose Fierro thought he had me in his possession now and did not need to fear me escaping. Maybe he was right; I wasn't sure.

Though the dawn had been frosty, by the time we reached a canyon with a spring called Aguas Dulces, the sun bore down hard. Turning in the saddle, I looked back. The División del Norte was scattered for miles, like a file of ants crawling across the plain. Whirling dust devils rose from the wheels of wagons and trucks, veiling the column in what looked like smoke. At the spring, the toiling marchers were held back until the horses had drunk their fill, muddying the clear waters. There were a lot of men but few horses; horses were more important than men.

With Pinta grazing beside me on the scanty grass around the waterhole, I saw Valentina. Now she was again the *soldaderita*, trudging along with old Victoria, shoulders bowed under the weight of the pack and heavy Mauser rifle. When she knelt at the pool to fill her canteen I saw something green sticking out of her pack; I figured it was the lacy frock she had worn when she came to my room with my Christmas present. Her pack appeared so heavy and awkward that I guess she carried in it the rest of the female finery she had worn—the imported leather boots and the other female fripperies. For now, she wore *huaraches* like the rest. I thought fleetingly of inviting her to ride Pinta for a while, but I abandoned that idea as soon as it struck me. My bitten ear was still sore. She would just have to be another ant in the long column of marchers.

While Fierro was smoking an Egyptian cigarette and talking to another officer at the spring, Mr. McFall hurried up. "Are you all right, Ben?"

"Yes," I reassured him. "Fine as frog hair!"

"You have your own horse now, I see."

"A present from Rodolfo Fierro."

"Look here, Ben!" He tugged at an eyebrow. "I have evolved a new plan to get you out of the clutches of that evil man Rodolfo Fierro!"

I hope it wasn't as crazy as the one where I was to play trombone in the Scottish Guards Band of Northern Mexico. "Oh?" I said.

Mr. McFall looked around and saw Fierro nearby, scowling at us. Putting a quick hand on my shoulder, he whispered, "Just don't worry, laddie! I'll have you out of Fierro's clutches before you know it!" Then he scuttled away to rejoin the musicians of his band, who were collapsed on the grass, tootling and plunking weakly on their instruments. I guess it was a version of "Adelita," but it was so off-key and dispirited it sounded more like a dirge, a badly rendered dirge.

General Villa had been riding Siete Leguas at the head of the column. But in the afternoon he got into an automobile with Rodolfo Fierro, Colonel Aguirre at the wheel, and drove away in the sandy wastes, a band of horsemen galloping after the car. No one knew where they were going or what it was all about. As in any army, there is always a lot of grumbling and speculation as to what the brass is up to. However, an army that does not grumble and guess is an unhealthy army.

I remember well that first night. The army was camped in a wide canyon with steep sides. Through the grassy bottom, good pasture, ran a stream of clear water. A haze of blue-gray cooking smoke lay heavy over the valley as *frijoles* and tortillas were heated. From the slight rise where I squatted with Pinta, eating a chunk of burned beef from one of the steers driven along in the rear guard, I took pleasure in the orange wink of small fires scattered along the valley—the singing, the laughter, the peacefulness of the scene.

Old Ojo Parado, seeing me at ease, came up and squatted, offering me a warm tortilla. *"Qué piensas?"* he asked. "What are you thinking, *amigo*?"

"Wondering. Wondering about all these men, the *campesinos*. They all come from so far—Chiapas, Quintana Roo, Jalisco, Oaxaca . . ."

"I am from Oaxaca," Ojo Parado said proudly.

"Why do they come so far—why do they do brave things and bleed and die and lie in unmarked graves?" I had gotten pretty fair in a flowery way of speaking Spanish; not that I did not make ridiculous mistakes, and still do. But people caught my meaning and few poked fun at me anymore.

"For freedom," Ojo Parado said, rolling a cornhusk cigarette. He offered the first puff to me. I breathed in some of the harsh smoke and almost strangled—managing, however, to thank him politely.

"For *la libertad*," Ojo Parado continued. "Freedom is a great lady. She must be fought for and won by the spilling of blood. That is her price."

I liked this simple old man from Oaxaca. Sharing my beef, he told me about life in Oaxaca, far to the south in Mexico, almost to Guatemala. In the half-light of the moon, about all I could see of him was the occasional glow of the cigarette.

"There was no liberty in Oaxaca except for the rich *hacendados*. They lived in their big houses and had parties and sent their children to private schools in the U.S. or Europe." He paused. "I have heard of Europe but do not know where it is. Is it near Texas, *amigo*?"

I explained as best I could where Europe was situated.

"You have been there, *amigo*?"

"Oh, no!" I told him. "It is too far away. Besides, it costs a lot of money, and my family had no money."

He shrugged. "I have heard all *gringos* are rich."

"Well, *we* weren't!"

He went on with his story. "The *hacendados* bought up land from the Indians for a few pesos, a bottle of *aguardiente*, or whatever. A poor man might get drunk and then they would coax him to make a mark on a piece of paper. Or if the *hacendado* wanted a certain piece of land and the owner would not sell, the man might have an 'accident'—*tu sabes?* The widow would have to sell the land for almost nothing to put bread in the mouths of her children. So then the people had no source of firewood, charcoal, corn for tortillas, wood for house posts. There was nothing left for a man or a woman to do but go to work in the tobacco or *henequén* fields. I tell you, *hombre*, it was hard work! From early to late, in rain or cold or sun so bright and hot it hit you in the head like a club! And always there was the *capataz*, the foreman. *Hombre*, do you note this eye?" I could hardly see his face but by squinting I saw him point to his glass eye. "Do you know how I lost this eye?"

"No," I said. "An accident?"

He laughed, a laugh with no joy in it. "It was said that my *hacendado* owned a million hectares of land. His *capataz principal* was a man called Bojorquez, a Spaniard. When Bojorquez thought we were not working hard enough for our two *reales* a day, he would get busy with his whip. That, *amigo*, is how my eye went! The lash of the whip caught my eye and *zzzzt!* No more eye!"

He drew hard on the cigarette. "I did not lose my eye lightly, I tell you! Señor Terraza had to get another *capataz* and I ran away from the house of my poor father and sainted mother. Someday, perhaps, I will go back to Oaxaca and see what happened to them. By now they are very old or maybe dead. Anyway, I will bring flowers for their graves and say a prayer over the place where they lie." Stretching, he got up, dug the smoldering butt into the sand with the toe of his boot, saying, "Well, it is time to get some sleep. I hear we are to move again at midnight. *Buenas noches*, Benjamin."

"*Buenas noches, amigo,*" I said. "May you sleep well and dream about the *capataz* Bojorquez twisting on a spit in hell!"

I didn't rest much that night. Asleep on my blanket, Pinta grazing dew-wet grass beside me, I had an awful dream. A mustachioed *capataz* beat me with a whip. As I lay bloody and defeated in a field of *henequén*—that was hemp, to make rope and calking for boats and things—the *capataz* pounced on me. But the face was not that of Ojo Parado's *capataz*. It was the face of Rodolfo Fierro. I screamed out, and sat up in a cold sweat.

"Who's there?" I called out in panic. Near me I could sense, rather than see, a presence. Except for the occasional call of a sentry or a drumming of hooves when a courier came galloping in with a message, the camp was quiet.

"Who's there?" I called again. In fear I took out my barlow knife, realizing I had no weapon like the others—a carbine or rifle; all I had was a little popgun of a pistol with no firing pin or ammunition.

"Señor?" It was a small voice from behind a stand of agave growing tall and ghostlike at the edge of the pool.

"Who is it? Come out!"

Pinta moved next to me and rubbed her nose against my cheek. I pushed her away.

"Benjamin?"

It was Valentina, small and quiet in the night. Hesitantly she came closer to sit beside me on the grass. Laying down her Mauser rifle, she said, "I . . . I heard you cry out."

"You mean you've been there all the time, watching me? Go away, please! I need to sleep some more. They are moving out at dawn!"

I could not see her face in the dark but her voice was hurt. "But, Benjamin, I need to talk to you and you to me! Please, Benjamin!"

I was being cruel, needlessly cruel. After the encounter in my hotel room with Fierro I realized I was jumpy and nervous. After all, it had been a near thing. Not to give in too easily, I muttered, "You bit me!" I fondled my injured ear. "Look there! It's all red and splotchy-looking!"

Settling beside me, she giggled, a delightful sound. Prue Ballard had giggled that way, back in McNary, back in Mr. Dinwiddie's schoolroom.

"I hear you bit that Fierro's hand, too, when he tried to seduce you last night!"

I was astonished. "How do you know about that?" I was ashamed a female should even know about such things, and my face got red and I started to stammer, as I still do when I am ill-at-ease. "You . . . you weren't even there!"

She laughed again, squirmed closer to me, laying aside her carbine. "In the convent, news traveled fast—we girls knew everything as soon as it happened. It made the sisters furious. In the army, it seems, news travels fast also."

It was pleasant, lying there in the night, Valentina near me, her breath sweet and moist in my ear. I rolled over and tried to put my arm around her. Snatching up that damned hard cold carbine, she thrust it quickly between us.

"Do not get any ideas, Benjamin! I am a soldier now, and there is no time for this foolishment!"

"Foolishment?" I howled, sitting up. "Dammit all, why is love of a man for a woman foolishment, I'd like to know!"

She tried to placate me but my feelings were hurt. Prue Ballard had started my loins tingling in the first place. Now a little snip called Valentina was tingling them again, and just teasing me, which was not fair. A young man . . . boy—whatever I was—is sensitive about things like that. Indeed, I had had little love at home; this new kind of love looked like a fair substitute. But I had been repulsed again!

"Please, Benjamin! I . . . I want to be your good friend, you know that. But there is a revolution to be won, and I must find my father and—"

"To hell with the revolution!" I protested. "After all, life is supposed to go on even during a revolution, isn't it?"

I guess she saw I was in a snit. Picking up the carbine, she stood above me for a moment, looking down. Then she put a finger to her lips in the starshine, touched my own tenderly, and skipped away, a truly amazing and delightful female who turned me into spineless jelly.

Scrambling to my feet, I called, "Valentina! Wait!"

She was gone into the night.

"I was going to let you ride Pinta in the morning!" I wailed. "Come back!"

The moon was down and a chill was in the air. It was

shortly before dawn, although the sky still sparkled with cold-looking fiery stars. She was gone.

"*Eh, amigo?*"

At the gruff voice I whirled. It was old Ojo Parado, grinning at me.

"Love, *amigo*," he said, "is a damned rocky road."

"I don't give a damn about love," I said fiercely. Seeing signs of activity at the staff tent, where a huge bonfire had been lit, I asked, "What's going on, anyway?"

Ojo Parado pointed. In the light of a kerosene lantern General Villa and a group of officers huddled over a map. There was a flurry of bugle calls, racing of engines, hurried movement.

"It seems that General Orozco and his Federales did not go to Chihuahua City, as our General Villa thought. Instead, the old rascal has fled to Ojinaga."

"Where is Ojinaga, *por favor*?"

"Ojinaga is on the river about two hundred kilometers that way." He pointed.

Throwing the dregs out of his tin cup of coffee, he added, "It is across the river from the Presidio. Maybe that *carajo* Orozco thinks he will surrender his whole army to General Pershing, who commands at the Presidio. That way he thinks he can escape the vengeance of our General Villa. But Villa is a tiger! He might just cross the river and take back Orozco and his army!"

I did not know then what *carajo* meant. Mexican Spanish has a lot of rich and colorful epithets. *Carajo* meant "prick."

"*Gracias, amigo*," I said, and started to saddle up Pinta. She was in a playful mood and nipped at me as I tried to tighten the cinch. Deep in my unhappy mood, I kicked her and she reluctantly sucked in her belly.

"I'm sorry!" I said in her ear. "Please excuse me!"

All over the valley the División del Norte was getting ready to move. I did not know the count of troops then, but Mr. Wickwire joined Villa that morning after a period of convalescence from an infection of a bullet wound in his calf. The last time I saw him I noticed the puckered ridge on his leather puttee, where a bullet must have hit.

Well, it had. Now he got about with a crutch and a rented Locomobile auto. He told me that Villa now had more than five thousand men.

"And more coming," he said, sitting at the wheel of the dusty car he had driven from El Paso. "By the way, I talked to a poor man working a field near Villa Ahumada and he took me over to a crack in the land. Maybe it was caused by an earthquake—I don't know. Listen, this is priceless! He picked up a pebble and threw it in. I heard the pebble bouncing down and down as it dropped. It seemed it would never stop falling. 'You see,' he said, 'that is how it is with our revolution. It keeps going and going, gathering speed as it goes. Soon it goes so fast that no one can stop it. That is the day we will have our freedom—that glorious day!' "

When he turned the key on, the magneto started to buzz. "I've got to be going."

"Good luck," I said. "I'll probably see you in Ojinaga."

Leaning forward, as he raced the motor, shouting above the noise. "I hear you're marching with that rascal Fierro!" Fortunately I didn't have to answer him. He was a poor driver, and when he pushed on the pedal with the engine racing the Locomobile came to life. It went bouncing across the desert toward Ojinaga, slewing this way and that, Mr. Wickwire, cap on backward, trying hard to hold a steady course.

"Good luck," I said again, watching him go. Driving that way, he needed it.

— 7 —

Two days later I saw my first flying machine. Also, I shot my first man, although he didn't know it at the time. I mean he didn't know *I* did it.

As the above explanation is becoming complicated, I'd better start from the beginning. For a day or two there had been heavy rains and the wagons and trucks bogged down in a patch of swampy land underlaid with quicksand. That swampy land, or a patch somewhat like it, led—much later—to the final solution of my problems, but that's not what I'm talking about right now. While they were digging out the wagons and trying to get things organized again, there wasn't much else going on. If we didn't reach Ojinaga in a hurry, Orozco would have time to organize the city's defenses and General Villa would have a hard time of it. Still, it was fate, and there wasn't much to be done except to bear up under it.

As usual, there was a lot of grumbling at the slow progress. One of the chief grumblers was the dandy Garibaldi; he argued with the general about almost everything. If he hadn't been a foreigner and the grandson of the Great Liberator of Italy, General Villa would have had him in front of a firing squad every morning. Garibaldi's dissatisfaction infected others, too. Finally, without the general's approval, Garibaldi and some of his followers planned to ride out toward Ojinaga on the pretext they were scouting for advance patrols of Federales.

Idle hands make mischief; Grandma Johnson always said that when I was loafing around the house. Garibaldi got together several of his pals. I think everyone knew about his plan and wanted to go along, everyone but General Villa and his staff. Huddled under a mesquite, rain dripping on my head, I was bored too. When I heard about the proposed scouting party I wanted to go along.

"All right," Garibaldi agreed. "Where's your fucking gun?"

Sheepishly I admitted I didn't have one. He looked exasperated. Going away, in a few minutes he returned with a beautiful English fowling piece, walnut stock handsomely carved and the barrel engraved with fancy scrollwork.

"Here!" he said, tossing it to me along with the box of shells. "And take good care of it, mind! I just borrowed it for a little while."

Take good care of it? It was the first real gun I had ever handled, one of the famous Greener guns made in England, and I would guard it with my life! I didn't know where he got it, but being Garibaldi, he probably picked it up when the owner wasn't looking. At least this gun had a firing pin!

Fierro was in a tent conferring with the general when I sneaked out of camp to a meeting place in a stand of giant saguaro. Garibaldi, duded up in his tan velvet suit and his hat pinned up on one side by a giant brass medallion, sat on a big bay and told everyone we were going to distinguish ourselves on a perfectly planned raid. When we came back we would all get some more medals.

Riding behind a long sandy ridge so we couldn't be seen, we headed northeast in the general direction of Ojinaga. Oh, but I felt good! The rain stopped, sun broke through the scudding clouds, steam drifted up from the wet backs of the horses. Someone started to sing "Adelita" and I joined in with my mouth-organ, which seemed to make me part of the gang. Garibaldi didn't ride ahead; he was no fool. He ordered others to the point and flanks while he himself stayed safely within the main body.

It is good when men ride together. Maybe it's a throwback to an ancient time when men hunted in packs, dinosaurs or whatever, to feed the family. Anyway, noon came without any sight of the Federales. We stopped to eat cheese and soda crackers and drink water from a brackish pool. Everyone lay around in the sun and gossiped or dozed or puffed cigarettes. It was fascinating to hear their soldier talk.

"Ay, our general! What a prick he must have! He is like a prize bull!"

That was true; I remembered him pissing in the sand at Cuitla. The general was proud, however, to insist he never took advantage of women. In a way, I suppose, that was true. He always married them before a frightened priest before going to bed with them. Villa preferred Indian women, I learned from the gossip; "women with dusty Indian skin and breasts hard as rocks!" His current wife was one Otilia Meraz, somewhere in Chihuahua with two of his children, but it was common knowledge that he had several other "wives" scattered about in Chihuahua.

About medals, they showed each other their own, doing a little bragging. Someone mentioned what was apparently a *real* medal, given only for extraordinary bravery on the battlefield. A man snickered.

"There is this one thing! You've got to be killed three times before they will consider you for it!" It was called the Cross of Military Merit.

A man with a guitar mentioned that "Jesusita in Chihuahua" was the general's favorite song. Squatting in the scanty shade of a greasewood, he tried to pick it out on his guitar. He grinned. "I intend to stand near the general's tent each evening and play it for him. Then he will give me another medal!" As soon as I could figure out which way his chords were going, I joined in with my mouthorgan and the rest sang the chorus.

Garibaldi stood on a little rise scanning the desert with his fieldglasses and looking brave and commanding, though he didn't fool anybody. Fierro was outspoken in his opinion of Italians, saying, "They are good for nothing but fast movements toward the rear!" As Garibaldi stood on the rise like he was posing for a monument, one of the men lifted a finger and said, "What is that noise?"

We stopped our music. The queer metallic drone seemed to come from somewhere north of us. Nervous, I picked up my shotgun and made sure there was buckshot in each chamber. "I hear it!" I cried. "It sounds like a motor of some kind!"

"Perhaps so," the guitar player said, laying down the instrument. "Not an automobile engine, I think! Maybe . . ."

We all scrambled up. Garibaldi was too busy being monumental and apparently didn't hear the buzzing. Covered in the stand of greasewood, we all huddled together and checked the magazines of our weapons. The sound grew louder, like a giant bumblebee. Obliged to look brave, I poked my head through the vile-smelling bushes and stared at what I saw: a flying machine—an aeroplane! By this time Garibaldi saw it too. The big awkward bird hummed toward us at no more than fifty feet above the ground. Garibaldi tumbled down the slope toward us, slipping and falling, and dived into the cover of the bushes.

"Shoot!" he squalled. "*Todos*! Everybody shoot!"

He was sure the aeroplane, a thing of wire and canvas and whirling propeller, was a spy for the Federales holed up in Ojinaga. Maybe it was—no one knew for sure. The only marking on it was the number seven on the underside of the wing.

"Shoot!" Garibaldi begged, practically foaming at the mouth. "Shoot quick!"

As the apparition grew larger and larger, coming toward us, no one shot. They were simple peasants, and the sight awed them. I was junior to everybody and the rest only stared, mouths gaping. Garibaldi was tugging at his pistol, trying to get it free of the holster. Furious, he burst into a torrent of Italian and fell over backward.

The thing was almost directly over us, ready to drop its bombs or whatever. A goggled figure at the steering wheel, way out front, peered down at us. Garibaldi had got his pistol tangled in the strap for his fieldglasses and was swearing in Italian. When the goggled pilot raised his hand, I was sure he was reaching for the lever to let a bomb drop. Pointing the Greener at the diabolical machine hovering over us like a giant grasshopper, I pulled both triggers at once.

WHAM WHAM WHAM wham wham wham! The thunderous

report went echoing across the desert, to be returned in a reflection from a rocky ridge nearby. My ears rang. The force of the blast knocked me backward on top of Garibaldi and buried his bearded face in the sand. WHAM WHAM wham wham . . . wham . . . wham . . .

For a moment the big bird seemed to stagger in midair; then it fell off on one wing, fought the air as it looped around, almost brushing the rocky ridge, and limped back the way it had come, disappearing in the distance.

Spitting sand, Garibaldi sat up and beamed at me. "You are a fine fellow!" he said. "I think you hit that thing!" Turning to the rest of the band, still staring vacantly at the ridge over which the aeroplane had disappeared, he scolded them, "Oafs, dolts, pricks, dumbheads, fools!" As I have said, Spanish is a language rich in epithets.

To make a long story short, that was the end of the unauthorized scouting party. Learning of the escapade, Villa fell out for good with Garibaldi, calling him a damned *filibustero*. Garibaldi rode away mad, saying that General Villa did not know how to manage blowing his nose, let alone running a revolution, and recommended that the general study the campaigns of his grandfather.

Finally they got the column under way again by throwing out a lot of captured booty and combining teams on the remaining wagons. Some clever Villista thought of letting a little air out of the high-pressure tires on the trucks, and after that they went through sand much better. Stripped down now to the essentials such as food and water and ammunition, the train started rolling again toward Ojinaga with the sun low in the west. We had lost a day, in effect.

Just before the bugle for the advance sounded, Rodolfo Fierro found me saddling up Pinta. I don't know where in the desert he found a fresh flower for his buttonhole, but there it was, dew-wet and fragrant.

"You left without my permission!" he growled. "Never do that again! Do you hear me, Benjamin?" When he came toward me, raising his riding crop as if to strike me, I pulled the English shotgun from the boot and held it casually across my arm. Fierro stopped, looked at me, looked at the shotgun. "Where did you get that Greener?"

I broke the action in such a way that he could see the shiny brass ends of the shells tucked neatly in their chambers. "A man gave it to me."

He frowned, pulled at his lip. "That prick Aguirre?"

"No."

"Then who?"

I didn't answer him, only closed the breech with a loud click.

"Benjamin, I do not like for you to carry a gun, you know that!"

"Everybody else has a gun! Some have two, maybe three."

"You are not everybody else."

"Well, I've got to protect myself, don't I?"

"I am your protector. You don't need anything else, no one else either!" He changed tactics. "I see you have no spurs on your boots. Where are those fine silver spurs I gave you, and why are you not wearing them?"

They were still rolled in my pack, I told him. Fierro was getting madder and madder at the way I was acting, though I rather enjoyed baiting him, being the young fool that I was. Still, I knew I shouldn't push him too far. To placate him, I said, "I'll get them out and wear them, I promise!"

Still upset, he pulled at his long blond beard, now bleached by the sun almost white. In a way he looked like Don Quixote, a Spanish man I once read about in a book Mr. Dinwiddie loaned me. In a way it was surprising that General Villa was so close to Fierro, Fierro being a Spaniard, a descendant of the conquistadors who so cruelly oppressed Mexico. General Villa said he hated all *gachupines*, as the Mexicans called Spaniards. Even today there is in Mexico great dislike of Spaniards. There is a funny story about the Spanish Civil War in 1937. A Mexican came to a government office to inquire if it was legal for him to go to Spain and fight. The official asked him which side he intended to fight on. The man shrugged. "I don't care, just so I can kill *gachupines!*"

The Spanish, General Villa said, brought only the Catholic religion and death to the Mexican people. Later, when Villa was high on the revolutionary wave, having success after success, he banned all Spaniards from Mexico, giving them ten days to leave the country. But to Villa, at least in this phase of the revolution, Rodolfo Fierro was a necessary Spaniard, I guess.

"See that you wear the spurs immediately!" Fierro barked. He turned and started to walk away, spurs tinkling, but them came back, pointing a long forefinger at me. "I do not like rebellious boys, *muchacho!* Remember that."

Late in the afternoon the long train of marchers, horsemen, wagons, and trucks was painfully crawling again toward Ojinaga. Villa himself, riding Siete Leguas, rode along the column, urging haste. "For you know," he called out, "we must get to Ojinaga before that cocksucker Orozco has a chance to cross the river and jump into General Pershing's arms!"

I sat easily on Pinta, feeling good that I had been brave enough to show some spirit toward Rodolfo Fierro. In the west, wings tipped with gold from the setting sun, a hawk wheeled restlessly. But from somewhere ahead a crackle of musketry broke out. There was a whistling sound overhead, sending the watchful hawk fleeing. A shell burst in the middle of the wagon train, scattering rifles and cartridge chests and broken wheels sky-high. That was the beginning of the Battle of Ojinaga, a battle which General Villa always claimed he won in sixty-five minutes. Mr. McFall said he would estimate by his gold watch one hour and twenty-three minutes. He set a great store by that watch, wrapping it in an old sock at night. To me, however, dodging from bush to bush and dragging the shotgun, which was too short-range to do anything in a battle like this, the engagement seemed to last several hours.

As Villa had predicted, the cowardly General Orozco had fled across the Rio Grande to the protection of General Pershing at the Presidio, taking most of his troops with him. When we arrived at Ojinaga, General Pershing sent a message to Villa, praising him for letting Orozco's army escape, thus "avoiding needless bloodshed." The general was furious, and tore the message into shreds. "Letting that prick escape?" He got red in the face. "Letting Orozco escape? Jesus Christ, what a miserable joke!"

That summer we took Chihuahua City in an easy victory. It began to look like the United States, realizing Villa's growing success, might be thinking about swinging to his side, abandoning the Huerta gang in Mexico City.

With Chihuahua free of his enemies, General Villa marched triumphantly into Chihuahua City. There were a lot of civic problems, and again the general did his best to solve them. He issued a blizzard of special orders: no one was allowed to loot, to take money or anything valuable from the inhabitants, to requisition horses or any kind of property without a written order, or to molest any woman without her consent. Again, as in Ciudad Juárez, he assigned his own troops to police duty and put them to work restoring the waterworks, the electric plant, and the telephone system, all of which the fleeing Orozco had purposely damaged so that the pursuing Villistas would not have the use of them. The general also set prices for bread and meat, and banned the sale of liquor. Quickly he turned from warrior to knowledgeable civic official. Even the Huerta diehards in the city had to acknowledge his ability and cooperation.

Always a lot of hangers-on surrounded him. He basked in their praise, but kept a cool head. Munitions salesmen from other countries pestered him, foreign emissaries wanted to confer with him, local politicos demanded to see him, reporters (including Mr. Wickwire) besieged him, women wanted to sleep with him, to bear a child of the Great Patriot.

Mr. Wickwire had finally wrecked his rented Locomobile auto three miles from Ojinaga. "That's the third one," he told me gloomily. "The editor of the *Morning Times* said I had to pay for any more after the third one." Limping around on his crutch, he winced. "That long walk into Ojinaba made my piles worse too, dammit! Ah, it's hard to get old, Benjamin!" Then he grinned and said something I didn't quite understand, although now, at this late date, I understand, having the same trouble. "The fact is, Benjamin, my boy, it *doesn't* get hard anymore! That's the tragedy of old age. Don't ever get old, Benjamin, boy. It ain't worth it! Die young, I say! That was where I made *my* mistake!''

There was another man in Chihuahua City trying to sell the general something—a Scotsman named Donald Stuart. My first knowledge of Stuart came one morning when I rode out on Pinta to take the morning air of a peaceful Sunday. Somehow the Greener had vanished. Wary for any rascally Orozco snipers, I came on a grassy patch crowning a high plateau a mile or so from town. Pockmarked Julio was once again assigned to watch me. After my little spat with Fierro, I guess Fierro thought that with me turning sassy he'd better have someone keep an eye on me. Julio and I both stared at the strange sight. There, sitting like a hatching bird while a man worked on it, was a flying machine—*the* flying machine, I could tell from the number seven on its wing.

Cautiously I rode over, Julio following, and slid out of the saddle, throwing Pinta's reins over her head; she quickly started to pull up tufts of grass with her strong teeth.

"Good morning, sir," I said to the grizzled mechanic in his grease-stained overalls.

The engine was mounted behind, so the propeller could push the thing through the air. Before answering, the man undid a long chain that linked the wooden propeller to the engine and jumped down on the ground. Still, he didn't answer me, only started to hammer a link of the chain on a small anvil.

"Nice morning," I ventured, "if it doesn't rain."

The mechanic was a stocky man, pretty hairy, with a wild look in his eye. Mumbling something, he went on with his hammering, pounding the link as if he was mad at it, talking under his breath all the time.

"I guess this is an aeroplane," I offered.

Leaving off his hammering, he looked at me as if I was a loony. Then he erupted in the broadest Scots brogue I ever heard—to this day. Mr. McFall wasn't even in it.

"Aye, it is, ye ken! A goddamned cranky gasoline-swilling hog that couldn't fly a straight line if he set her on

136

rails! Oh, damn!" He sucked his finger where he had hit it with his hammer.

For a minute, I didn't take his meaning. Then I began to sort things out from the rich brogue. He didn't like his aeroplane.

"Well, she sure looks pretty," I said, stroking the taut canvas of the wing.

"So do a lot of females," the Scotsman grumbled, "but they're heartless bitches all the same!"

He dipped a square of canvas in a bucket. Finding a spot peppered with small holes in the wing, he plastered the sticky canvas over the area and smoothed it with a brush. I had a sudden sinking feeling.

"Ah . . . do birds fly into the wings sometimes and make these holes?" I pointed. "Peck holes in the wings, then?" I wanted information but wasn't at all sure I'd like it when I got it.

He snarled at me and went on hammering the chain harder, viciously. "Aye, birds, ye ken! Birds with shotguns, that lays doggo in the bushes and shoots holes in my *Maggie May*." That was the name of his flying machine, painted on a board wired to a strut.

"Someone shot at you, did they?" I cleared my throat, which seemed to be somewhat constricted. "Why would they do that, Mr. . . . Mr. . . ."

"I'm Stuart," he growled. "Donald Stuart, kin to the Highland tribe of Stuarts, and dangerous when I get riled, like I am right now!" Unhooking his bib overalls, he indignantly showed me a collection of welts along his stringy thigh. "Buckshot, they used! Buckshot! See there . . . here, too! Blasted my ass, too—d'ye see?" He pulled down his underpants to show me a peppering of small black holes there also.

I gulped; I had been a better shot than I knew.

"Broke some control wires, they did! I had to steer her back to the landing field practically with my teeth, and my teeth ain't too damned good! All I wanted was to inquire the way to Ojinaga! I figured maybe I could get in to see General Villa again and argue him into renting *Maggie*

May! But the damned villains *shot* at me! I swear I'll kill them all if I find out who they were!"

It seems Stuart was another of the hangers-on who were trying to sell General Villa things or services. Stuart said that once in Ciudad Juárez he got in to see Colonel Aguirre and convinced the colonel that his aeroplane would be a valuable service to the revolution by reconnoitering in advance for the Division of the North in the other battles that would soon come. Villa had been nearly persuaded but changed his mind when Mr. Stuart demanded a colonelcy in the division, along with a monthly rental fee of one thousand dollars in gold. Colonel Aguirre told me all about it later.

"No sirve!" Villa finally decided. "It won't work! A man needs to keep his feet on the ground, the good earth of Chihuahua, from which he gathers strength! I need no birds to win battles, anyway." So Donald Stuart had been barred from further visits to the Ciudad Juárez city hall, and he was mad about it.

"Aeroplanes are the thing of the future in conducting wars, ye ken, young man! Any scout can see that! Well . . ." He broke off, wiping his hands with a skein of waste. "You can't blame a man for trying. When I have *Maggie May* in good shape again I'll go into town and see if I can get direct to the general. Last time I had him almost convinced till the matter of money came up. There wasn't much profit for me in the deal; *Maggie May* swills gasoline like she had the thirst of a camel!"

Not to press my luck, I left him ranting and slipped away, Julio following. I don't think Mr. Donald Stuart even knew I had left, and that was the way I preferred it. I didn't want him to find out that Benjamin Wilkerson was the one who shot holes in his flying machine, and in him too.

After we took Chihuahua City, General Villa met with the rebel leader from the south—Emiliano Zapata—who traveled with his staff all the way from Oaxaca to make joint plans with Villa. Originally Zapata came from Ayala, the rich sugarcane-growing area of Oaxaca. He, like old Ojo Parado, had a great hatred of the rich *hacendados* who had stolen the land from the Indians. Zapata started his own war in Oaxaca by capturing the local garrison of Federales, cutting telephone and telegraph wires, blowing up trains, and taking towns almost at will with his army of landless peasants. I only saw him that once, but fire burned in his black Indian eyes, his flat Indian face, a fire that would never gutter out until land was won back for his people or death cut him down. He was a small man in poor clothes, leather sandals, and a straw hat too big for him that tended to slip down over his eyes. To me he looked like pretty small potatoes for history to take note of, but I was wrong.

In history books, this conference is held to have accomplished nothing. Villa held the north, Zapata the south, and Venustiano Carranza the middle of Mexico; they each looked on these territories as their own kingdoms, and the meeting changed nothing in that respect, but I think Emiliano Zapata got some good ideas for larger-scale actions from the crack artillerist Felipe Ángeles. Ángeles had been working for days with Villa, teaching him military expressions to use on the ragged Zapatistas, how to remain a gentleman while arguing, the proper tone of voice to use—courteous, but not too familiar. Villa was a good pupil, and probably impressed Emiliano Zapata. Still, they never came to any agreement; they were both too proud to concede anything. The Zapatistas soon went back to Oaxaca with their own ideas about allies.

I mentioned Felipe Ángeles. He and the brother officers he brought to the revolution were fine fellows, and well-respected by Villa. They were trim, well-educated men, very clean, precise in manner, in comparison with the rough-and-tough Villistas. I did not, however, hold with the Chapultepec custom of sleeping in cloth face masks to preserve the shape of their mustaches. Still, I had only the first peach fuzz of down on my chin. If I ever grew a mustache perhaps I would turn out to be as vain.

Not having much success with Emiliano Zapata, the general tried his wiles on his rival Carranza, giving a correspondent from the New York *Times* a somewhat slippery interview:

I have no ambition to be president of the Republic if our cause wins. They say that my victories at Chihuahua City and Ojinaga have attracted attention to me. I do not have the least desire to take over the role of Señor Carranza, who I recognize as the supreme chief of our cause. In case Señor Carranza becomes president I will continue giving him my aid and obeying his orders. As proof of my loyalty I declare myself ready to abandon the country should he order me to do so. I have always been in perfect agreement with Señor Carranza. I have never had any personal ambitions.

And so on and so on, for several hundred words. I do not think that Villa was intentionally duplicitous; he was too simple a man for that. Instead, someone on his staff had probably put those words in his mouth.

Having captured Chihuahua City and established a Villista government, Villa turned his attention to the city of Torreón, two hundred miles to the south, which Huerta's Federales still occupied. Chihuahua City bustled with activity as the Division of the North prepared for the march to Torreón. I was grateful because Rodolfo Fierro was kept busy night and day with staff meetings at the city hall. The general's status after his impressive victories at Ciudad Juárez and Ojinaga was such that several more guerrilla leaders joined up with him—Tomás Urbina, Maclovio Herrera, and others.

Prowling among the men, Villa whipped the troops into shape, exhorting them, inspecting equipment, squinting down the barrels of rifles and carbines, making sure each man had the specified quota of ammunition. Instead of eating at the hotels or the staff officers' mess, he would take a tortilla from a soldier and scoop up a few beans, gnaw chunks of beef from a campfire, and suck a few deep puffs from a trooper's cornhusk cigarette. Dr. Raschman, his personal physician, advised the general against such practices, insisting that he eat more fruits and vegetables. But Villa only laughed. "I am not fancy enough to munch on rabbit vegetables like the *perfumados* do! The food of the men is my food also!"

I have mentioned William Benton, the feisty little Englishman whom Villa scornfully called "the English gamecock." After Villa had taken Chihuahua City, Benton again galloped into town spoiling for a fight. The Villistas, he said, were cutting his fences at Los Remedios and stealing his cattle; he demanded satisfaction. I myself do not know exactly what later happened to William Benton, but there is no doubt that the general was exasperated and angry at Benton's clamoring. However, old Victoria of the wart was a kind of a clearing house for gossip. She told it about that she had reliable information as to how and why William Benton finally disappeared from Chihuahua, and Mr. McFall relayed it to me.

"This is Victoria's story, laddie. She says that Mr. Benton accused the general of being a thief and a robber! Of course, no one can talk to Villa that way! He tried to keep his temper but Señor Benton raved on and on. Finally the general had had enough insults. He told the Englishman it was all a misunderstanding, that the cattle raids would stop. Then, according to Victoria, he got up and gave Benton an embrace, which was the signal to that bastard—Victoria's words—Rodolfo Fierro, who was standing in a corner of the general's room. When Benton left, somewhat satisfied, Fierro had him seized and taken down to Samayaluca. Three men from Fierro's brigade—she didn't know who they were—made him dig his own grave at Samayaluca. Fierro told them Benton was a shit . . ." Mr. McFall cleared his throat. "Victoria's words, you remember, Benjamin—"

"Yes, yes," I said, becoming impatient. "I remember. Go on!"

"Fierro told the three men not even to waste a bullet on Mr. Benton. So they beat him to death with a club, wrapped him in an expensive Persian rug, and soaked it with gasoline. When the Englishman didn't burn up completely, they shoveled what was left into the grave and covered it up without a marker. Victoria said, 'Poor Mr. Benton, going to his death without a priest!'"

In the revolutionary tide that was sweeping across Mexico, one more killing would not have been important except that William Benton was a British citizen in good standing and had important friends, both in the U.S. and in England. Through the American State Department the British demanded satisfaction—an apology and heavy indemnities. The affair caused a lot of trouble for General Villa, reflecting unfavorably as it did on the revolutionary movement. On the other hand, the incident might have been said to help Villa to some extent; the Benton affair made him an international figure, leaving Emiliano Zapata and Venustiano Carranza in the shadows of the revolution. Now Villa *was* the revolution. Zapata and, especially, Carranza were jealous.

"So that," Mr. McFall concluded, "is how poor Mr. William Benton died, and I, for one, am satisfied that it is the truth."

He had a bolt of plaid-looking material and was busy cutting it up, squatting tailor-fashion on my bed.

"Whatever are you doing?" I asked.

He held up something crudely stitched together. "A kilt—a good Scottish device to replace the more commonly worn trousers."

To me it looked like a lady's skirt. "What do you intend to do with it?"

Standing up, he stuck his legs in their cotton pants through it and pulled it up around his waist. "There! How does it look, eh?"

It still looked like a female skirt to me and I said so. He was disgusted.

"Heroic Scots have worn the kilt into battle after battle, laddie, led on by the sweet music of the pipes and their own indomitable bravery!" He made a small adjustment to the way the thing hung. "Lord, I wish I had a piper! My band needs a good piper! Of course, I do the best I can by skreeling on my fiddle, but it's not the same!"

"So that's what you bought with the money I gave you!" I protested. "That material!"

"Well, perhaps you could advance me a bit more, then? I have a *señora* on Paseo Largo who is willing to sew up all of them if I can buy a wee bit more material and also pay her a small stipend in advance."

I was puzzled. "What the hell is this all about?" I had gotten to be somewhat profane in my career as a revolutionary, not yet having learned that a loud mouth does not necessarily indicate maturity.

Mr. McFall became uneasy, looking at me from the corner of his eye as he sat down and went to sewing again.

"Ah . . . well, there is the Scottish Guards Band, you know, Ben. Of Northern Mexico."

"Of course I know!"

"Well, truthfully, they don't look like Scotsmen! They're all dark-skinned and speak Spanish. I just thought that if I could get them into kilts, they might be a mite more convincing. So, through your generosity, I'm going to outfit them all with kilts—the national garment of brave Scotsmen!" He held up a swatch of the material to the light. "Of course, Señor Tomás Nadal, who plays the tuba, is rather large and I'll need correspondingly more material, but—"

I couldn't help laughing. The idea of that ragtag band of off-key musicians dressed in kilts struck my funnybone. Mr. McFall was hurt.

"You don't think it's a good idea, Ben? After all, in our concerts in the plaza I think we'd create a more favorable impression if we all dressed somewhat alike."

"I guess it's all right," I said, trying hard to muffle my giggling. "But have you sounded out the musicians yet? I mean . . . about wearing *kilts*?"

He shook his head. "Not yet, but I have lots of influence with them. They all want to improve their musicianship, and I hold daily classes of instruction. I'm sure I can convince them!"

I'd been enjoying myself lately, with plenty of bilimbiques and the run of the town, except, of course, that Julio was always with me like a leech. Sometimes I thought I had evaded him, but when I paused for breath, having hurried around the block and dodged through a few back streets, the pockmarked scrawny little man would be waiting. I think that was where my good Greener shotgun went, too: Julio probably stole it from me on orders from Rodolfo

143

Fierro. And I still hadn't got a firing pin for that handsome little Spanish pistol that General Villa gave me.

One day I came on Ojo Parado sitting in the Alameda, the park where grew the poplar trees that gave the square its name. He was feeding scraps of tortilla to a mangy hound which slunk away when I approached. Julio lurked in the bushes behind us.

"A man needs a dog," Ojo Parado sighed. "When a man is as old as I am, most of his friends are dead. That is when he particularly needs a dog."

He seemed very depressed, and I tried to cheer him up.

"I don't know how old you are, amigo, but you will live a long time yet. You will see!"

He sighed again, and spat. "There is too much youth around here; young people like you and that Valentina girl you are infatuated with. *That* is what makes me feel old! Now, if I were to go to a home for the aged and mentally scanty, I would probably be more comfortable there."

I had to laugh. The picture of this old desperado sitting in a rocking chair on the veranda of an old folks' home, perhaps with a shawl around his shoulders, was one too many for me. Ojo Parado hooted.

"You do not know what it is to be old, you foolish boy! Why, look! You have only milkweed fuzz on your chin!"

That annoyed me. "There is more coming," I protested. "Every day I see more! Soon I will have to buy a razor and a brush and soap!"

"That Valentina," he murmured.

"Eh? What about Valentina?"

"Have you seen her since Ojinaga?"

"No. Why should I? She is nothing to me!"

He ogled me, glass eye spinning furiously, and dug me in the ribs. "Don't give me that shit, *amigo!* You are in love with her! And I must say, she is not a bad piece, with all that fine hair and blue eyes and a fat little bottom!"

I became angry. "That is no way to talk! You should show women more respect! But what about Valentina, anyway?"

He shrugged. "Sweet female she may be, but I tell you at Ojinaga she was a small tigress! Colonel Aguirre is thinking about mentioning her in dispatches. It will make a good story in the newspapers, you know—'Little Valentina, the fighting *muchachita*, who has dedicated her life to the glorious revolution!' "

"What do you mean?" I asked, thinking of the tear-stained and dirty child whom I encountered under the bandstand at Ciudad Juárez in my own baptism of fire. "Whatever has she done now?"

"She has killed her man, that girl! One of Orozco's Federales came at her with his bayonet, and she shot him right through the head! Oh, I tell you, she was magnificent, charging about the place and singing 'Adelita' at the top of her voice and being tough and foul-mouthed along with it all! Jesus Christ! She is one real tough little rooster—or should I say fighting pullet?"

I was amazed. Valentina? Sweet, soft, desirable Valentina? It didn't sound like her at all.

"Do you know where she is?"

Ojo Parado guffawed, licked a few crumbs from his fingers. "Lovers always know the whereabouts of the other one! It is some kind of scent they leave, I think, like dogs!"

I shook my head. "Old man, you have a dirty mind! Dogs, indeed! Scents! Go to the devil!"

I found her sitting in the shade of a cottonwood tree in the plaza, cleaning her carbine.

"Well," I said, sitting beside her, "what is this I hear about you? Mentioned in dispatches? A tigress at Ojinaga? Shot your man, did you? I would not have believed it."

Suddenly she burst into tears and threw down the carbine. "I don't want to talk about it!"

"But it is nothing to be ashamed of, for heaven's sake! You were very brave!"

She turned tear-filled eyes to me, her face woebegone. "I wish they would not make so much of it! Even Victoria, my good old friend—she bought me a sack of peppermint candy to celebrate! But, Benjamin, he was so *young*! I . . . I . . ."

With no thought other than to comfort her, I tried to put my arm around her. She pushed me away.

"Well," I said, "I only wanted to—"

"Don't you understand?" She took off the tattered straw hat and brushed back the flood of blue-black hair that spilled into the sunlight. An old man with a tray of gewgaws came by and paused before us but I waved him away. "He was only a child, you see, probably not any older than me! I don't think he really wanted to kill me with his bayonet, but in war I guess one cannot stop to think about such things. Anyway, I aimed my carbine at him. Even then, I thought maybe I should just shoot him in the shoulder or something. But my carbine went off and the bullet hit him in the head!"

I could not help but remember Valentina that night in Ciudad Juárez when she brought me my Christmas present; Valentina, young and beautiful and innocent in her lacy green dress and Italian boots, the very essence of femininity.

"I see," I murmured. "Yes, I see. I understand, Valentina, I truly do."

"It seemed seconds—long seconds—that he stood there, a kind of surprised look on his face. Blood . . ." She shuddered, turned her face away from me. "Blood ran down his face and into his mouth. Then his eyes went dead and he slid down, still holding his rifle. Benjamin, I wanted to pray for him, pray for that boy, but there wasn't time! There was so much noise and yelling and smoke and shooting all around me that all I could do was run after the rest, where they were driving the Federales back across the river." Again she took a deep shuddering sigh. "After we won, and your friend Mr. Wickwire asked me a lot of questions and wrote in his little book, I went back to where that dead boy was—maybe to pray over him . . . I don't know. But I couldn't find him."

"Now, look here!" I said severely. "You must not let your mind dwell on such things, Valentina! You were very brave, and will be mentioned in dispatches. How do you think the people will ever get rid of that scoundrel Huerta unless soldiers like you are brave and kill those who stand in the way of liberty?"

She traced a figure in the dust with her finger. I noticed that her finger was dirty, and her small feet in their leather *huaraches* badly needed washing too. Which was Valentina—the elegant small creature in my hotel room that night, or the "real tough" little *soldaderita* that Ojo Parado had so praised? I was confused.

"Well," she said, wiping her eyes with the fringed hem of her *sarape*, "I suppose you are right. But if I knew wars were like this I would probably never have run away from the convent to find my father."

I looked at the figure she had scrawled in the dust—a small crucifix.

"How will you ever find your father? You haven't seen him for a long time. You don't even know what he looks like! You don't even know his name, do you? After all, you were only a small child when he left you at the convent, and after that you said he just sent money!"

"I will know him! I *know* I will know him! And someday I will find him! Listen, Benjamin, he may be right here in Chihuahua City, planning the attack on Torreón I hear General Villa will soon make!"

I could sit and listen to Valentina talk all day. My own Spanish, as I have said, was fluent and not very fancy. But Valentina's (maybe from the convent school) was what they called Castilian—a smooth, rhythmic flowing kind of music, like a cello playing Bach. Of course, at that time I didn't know anyone named Bach, although there was an old German shoemaker in McNary named Bachmeister. Since then, however, I have learned to enjoy good music and have a very fine record player at my home in Parral.

"Now," she said suddenly, "go away, Benjamin! You are taking my mind off the revolution! I have to keep this carbine very clean or my sergeant will say bad things to me."

I was miffed at my sudden dismissal. "Well, that's a fine way to talk to an old friend. I didn't realize I was bothering you! After all, I suppose a military hero or heroine or whatever doesn't have much time to sit around just talking!"

"I didn't mean—"

"I know what you mean!" I snapped, and got up. Over my shoulder I called back a very snide remark; I don't know what made me do it. My only excuse was that I was in love, whether I knew it or not, and lovers are sometimes easily provoked and say things they regret.

"And wash your hands and feet, while you're at it. They are very dirty!"

Night and day, staff meetings went on at the Hotel Corona, which General Villa had taken over as headquarters. The Federales under General Medina Barrón were defending the city, and Mr. Wickwire told me he thought Torreón would prove a tough nut to crack. I started to get my gear ready for the march to Torreón, Mr. McFall not having come up yet with his latest plan for me to escape the clutches of Rodolfo Fierro. He came to my room, and I was going to ask him about his plan, but he looked so dispirited that I didn't.

"You try to do something for people and they won't let you," he complained, sagging onto the bed. "Oh, the ingrates!"

I had been asleep, having troubled dreams, and only stirred a little. Hands locked behind my head, I stared at a crack in the ceiling. "What's the matter?"

He held up a kilt. "They refuse to wear them!"

Rolling over, I sat up on the edge of the bed, yawning. For a minute I didn't remember the business of the kilts.

"There was general dissatisfaction! I tried to tell them about the long history of the Scottish warriors but they wouldn't even listen! They said no man wore skirts!" Staring at the kilt mournfully, he picked at it with his fingers. "The tuba player—Nadal, the fat one—tried to shoot me! Fortunately, he missed."

Any other time I would have broken into a giggle. But with Valentina on my mind I was kind of moonstruck, and didn't say anything.

"Well . . ." He tossed the kilt away. "I must remember Robert the Bruce and the spider in the cave where he was hiding. You remember, Benjamin, he watched the spider try to span his web across to a bush and keep at it till he won out. That's what I need right now—inspiration!" He got up smartly for such an old man, dusting his hands.

"Well, that's that!" Laying a finger alongside his nose, he broke off, staring at me. "Goodness gracious! In all this kilt business I forgot about getting you out of this dangerous Mexico and back to the States!"

I wasn't sure I wanted to hear about another crazy plan. Too, there was Valentina to think about. I was mad at her right now but I knew that would pass.

"Now, listen, Ben! Listen carefully. Have you got any money?"

I nodded. "There is a big wad of bilimbiques stuffed in that jar on the bureau."

Rubbing his lip, he looked doubtful. "No, he wouldn't take those. Says they're not even good for wiping his whatever, and I daresay he's right!"

I was intrigued. "Whatever are you talking about, Mr. McFall?"

In his excitement he hurried about the room, pulling down the shade, putting it up again, taking a copy of the Mexico City *Excelsior* from the table, folding it carefully, and then laying it down very absently. "You mind that Scotsman Stuart, the one who has the flying machine outside of town? The man that tried to convince General Villa to hire him and his flying machine?"

I nodded. "I went out there one day and talked to him."

"Well, I talked to him too, him being a fellow countryman. Of course he's a Highland Scot, from way up in the mountains at Inchnadamph, near Loch Shin. Those Highland people are bad-tempered and feisty, and generally pretty ignorant, although my own sainted mother had Highland kin. Besides, they are tight as a tattoo with a farthing." Taking out his gold watch, he looked at it. "Doesn't keep good time, really! It says five o'clock and I know that's not right, at least not for Chihuahua City. But someplace on the world's surface it must be five o'clock. It's all a matter of geography."

He was rambling again, and I urged him back.

"Well, Mr. Stuart is leaving shortly, he told me, flapping out of here to go back to El Paso. He said he couldn't get in to see the general. I'm sure he would take you if he were paid a suitable amount."

"Take me?" I was puzzled. "You mean, in that flying machine of his? No, thanks! That thing is made from beeswax and string! I wouldn't trust my life in that rickety thing!"

Like any young boy, or a youth approaching manhood, which I thought I was, the thought of going aloft in a flying machine would have seemed an incredible adventure, one to be joyously looked forward to. But my mind had a different set. What about Valentina? Now I *knew* I was in love with her—madly, crazily in love with her. The mere thought of going back to the States and leaving Valentina made my soul shrink within me, turn to a curdled something like a prune. "No, sir," I said emphatically. "I thank you for your kind consideration, Mr. McFall, but I guess I'll hang around for a while and see what happens!"

He sat down on the bed beside me and put a hand on my shoulder. "It's that girl, isn't it, laddie? The one called Valentina?"

"What if it is?" I asked, very rudely, now that I remember. He deserved better than that and I was instantly sorry.

"Yes," I admitted. "It's Valentina. It was just that I thought you didn't know. I . . . I'm in love with her, I suppose."

He started to laugh, then stopped suddenly. I knew it was because he didn't want me to think he was ragging me. Very gently he said, "Benjamin, I suppose everyone in the División del Norte knows about you and Valentina. Believe me, it's no secret! But let me try to put things in perspective for you, laddie. I'm much older than you, and know a lot of things that you may not. Of course, being old is no guarantee of wisdom, but maybe I can help you if you'll listen."

Contrite, I said, "Of course I'll listen, Mr. McFall. You're my very best friend—except Valentina, of course, but that's a different thing."

He took out his gold watch and looked at it. "Getting late. I have a rehearsal soon, although the more I rehearse them, the more sour notes they play. Well, that's my burden, I guess—the cross I must bear."

He was rambling again, and I had to steer him back on course. "About Mr. Stuart and his machine, now, and Valentina . . ."

"Ah, yes! Everyone knows about you and Valentina, as I have said. And everyone knows Rodolfo Fierro and his reputation. Right now Fierro is busy with staff work for Torreón, but once we take that city, the betting is that Fierro will have his way with you."

I felt a big lump in my throat, and when I spoke, my voice kind of squeaked, I guess. I knew it might be coming, but . . .

"His . . . his way with me?"

"Yes, laddie. You must get away as soon as you can. Believe me, Rodolfo Fierro is a terrible man, and will not be balked. You are in danger every moment you are in the División del Norte, believe me."

The lump got bigger. He was talking sense, no doubt about that. "But Valentina—"

"This bloody war will be over soon, one way or the other, Mr. Wickwire believes. He is very enigmatic at times, but I think he is right. If you escape now, there will be a time when you can come back to Chihuahua and be again with your beloved Valentina."

I was miserable. Leave Valentina—*my soul, my life*, as old Victoria called her little friend, her daughter, almost.

"It is best that way, believe me, laddie." He rose, looked at the watch again. "Like all those Highland tribes, Mr. Stuart loves his gold! They are crude and miserly people, Benjamin, not like the McFalls, but one must occasionally do business with the devil himself. This is a fine watch, and there are probably two or three ounces of fine gold in it. I will go to Mr. Stuart and see if I can bargain with him. I hear he has been disappointed in hiring out his aeroplane, anyway, and intends in the next few days to fly out of here and back to the border."

He was fond of that watch, with its engraved case and complicated works, even if it didn't keep good time.

"No," I said. "That watch means too much to you,

Mr. McFall. I can't let you do it! Maybe I can borrow some money from Ojo Parado or Victoria or someone—"

Good old Mr. McFall began to sound testy. I had never heard him that way. "Dammit all, Benjamin, there isn't time to lose! Stuart is low on funds, and I'll wager I can swing him to take you along as a passenger!"

A sudden thought came to me.

"I've seen that machine and I remember there are only two seats in it. Don't you want to go home too?"

He took a last look at the shiny watch and strung it again across his stomach, carefully adjusting the chain to the right drape.

"My home is across the water, laddie—a long way across the water. I doubt I'll ever seen bonnie Scotland again. Anyway, it doesn't matter. I'm happy here, with my little band of peculiar musicians."

"But you *could* go!" I insisted. *Lose Valentina, and my good friend Mr. McFall into the bargain*? It was too much. "Look! I could hang on to the wing some way, and you could ride in the passenger seat beside Mr. Stuart, and we could all three— "

"No!" Mr. McFall shook his head. "I doubt if the ridiculous thing would carry more than two people anyway. If I die it will be on the ground. I prefer it that way."

I sighed. "Well, if that's the way it has to be! Anyway, it's awful good of you. Someday I'll find a way to repay you."

If I'd known then how I would repay him for his kindness, I never would have done it. Still, no one knows the future. It's better that way, I believe.

"Fumadiddles!" he said, probably an old Scottish expression. "Nothing to it, my boy, nothing at all! Glad to do it!" He kneaded the bridge of his nose. "Of course, there are details to be worked out—like that blackguard Julio who's always lurking about."

"Don't mind, Julio," I said. "He's pretty persistent, but I'll work something out. Maybe get him drunk or something. That *pulque* liquor he likes is powerful."

"And it must be done quickly, laddie!" Mr. McFall reminded me. "Mr. Stuart plans to leave as soon as he finishes patching up his airplane after that gang of bandits fired on him."

"Yes," I said insincerely. "That . . . that was too bad."

"And it must be done before the army leaves for Torreón, that is clear! I hear from my informant that marching orders are already being drawn up at the city hall."

"Victoria?" I asked.

"Yes, that useful compendium of information—Victoria Wartnose. I don't mean that to sound unkind—she is really a remarkable old lady. It's just that the wart—"

"I know," I said. "But she is really a very nice and kind old lady."

"I suppose so," Mr. McFall said, "although I hear at Ciudad Juárez she cut an ear off a Federal who gave her trouble, and at Ojinaga—"

"War," I said, "is war, Mr. McFall." I didn't really know what else to say, but was not anxious to hear any more gruesome details. "Maybe you'd better take my little mare Pinta and ride out to see Mr. Stuart in that meadow and bargain with him while I try to come up with some way of hoodwinking that little bastard Julio." Hastily I amended my statement. Mr. McFall never liked for me to use bad language; he claimed it showed a lack of imagination. "My friend Julio, I mean. That is, I mean—"

"I will do that," he said, "immediately, but not on a horse. I have always been leery of horses ever since one bit me on the finger while I was trying to feed the dumb beast an apple core." At the door he turned and looked back at me. "Be of stout heart, laddie! Gold will prevail; it always works when nothing else does!"

When he left I felt cold and shivery. *Damned if I did and damned if I didn't!* I was in trouble both ways. So much might go wrong! That damned Fierro might have a break in his staff work and send for me, and I know what would happen then. But if I flew off to the border with Mr. Donald Stuart in his rickety machine, we might run out of gasoline and crash and I'd never see Valentina again! Even if I managed somehow to get back across the border and escape the claws of Rodolfo Fierro, what then?

I would be a fugitive from the Hudspeth County sheriff, wanted for arson and murder, along with leaving the state to avoid prosecution or however the lawyers would put it. *God*, I prayed for the first time in a long time, *if you're up there in the sky, look down into Chihuahua and help me*! I didn't know for sure if there was a God, but it wouldn't hurt to try. Certainly the *devil* was breathing down my neck, as Grandpa Johnson always claimed.

I waited a long time but there was no answer. Maybe God didn't have any jurisdiction south of the border.

8

Now that the División del Norte had met with such success in its latest campaigns, people began to lose their fear of Huerta and his Federales and flocked to the red-white-and-green banner of General Pancho Villa. By now he had a whole staff of telegraphers to handle all the traffic between his headquarters and the various other generals scattered around Chihuahua; it was necessary to coordinate the plans for the attack on the city of Torreón. The general still, however, relied on me for what he called "really important messages," saying he depended highly on my skill and accuracy.

"For, *chamaco*," he said, handing me the carefully lettered sheet of paper that Colonel Aguirre had prepared, "this dispatch is in *code*, you see. One missing or wrong letter could change the meaning altogether! I trust you, Benjamin."

I took the paper, folded it, and put it into the pocket of my English jacket, now somewhat worn and out at the elbows.

"Yes, sir. You can count on me, General."

He spoke to Colonel Aguirre, who was standing behind his chair.

"Is this not a good boy, Aguirre?"

"One of the best, sir."

The general laughed his high-pitched laugh and tousled my long-uncut hair. "Benjamin, you may even change my opinion about Texans. Maybe they are not all big-mouthed and ignorant fools!"

As I left, he called to me.

"Tell that crazy old man—what is his name? ah, yes, the Scotsman, McFall—tell him I enjoyed the concert his little band played before my balcony last night. I am no musician, and it seemed to me there were some wrong notes, but they played 'La Bomba' very well!"

"Yes, sir," I said. "I will tell him, General."

Colonel Aguirre followed me outside. "Benjamin, how is it with you these days, eh?"

I would kill my own snakes, with the help of Mr. McFall.

"Very well, sir," I said.

He unhooked the spectacles from his lean nose; sunlight sparkled on the lenses. Cleaning them absently, staring into the street below, where a vendor of colored ices was hawking his wares, he said, "Very well, eh? You are sure? I mean—"

"Nothing to worry about, sir," I said. "But I thank you for your interest."

Hooking the spectacles back on, he nodded and gave me a friendly small shove toward the telegraph office. "Hurry, now, Benjamin! Great things may hang on that message!"

I got the message off all right and received a proper acknowledgment from General Banda's operator at the far end of the wire. The other operators stared at me in an unfriendly way; I think they were jealous of my relationship with General Villa. *"Cabrón,"* I heard, and several interesting variations of *"chingar."* But I didn't care. I had other things on my mind. If I was going to escape Chihuahua City and Rodolfo Fierro in Mr. Stuart's flying machine, I would first have to find Valentina and make my farewells to her. I hoped she would feel as sad as I was, but she was such a variable girl since she had killed her first man that I was not sure but what she would take it all very lightly. She was dedicated to the revolution, not to me; that was obvious.

I couldn't find her. I asked about in her brigade but no one had seen her lately. Even old Victoria, busy drilling an awkward squad of female recruits, did not know where she was. In an irritable mood because of the ineptness of the volunteers, she only growled at me.

"Can't you see I am busy with these miserable females who don't know their left foot from their damned cunt? No, I haven't seen Valentina! Am I her guardian or something? Go away and leave me to these dumb animals! Cows, they are—fat-assed lame-brained cows!"

On my way back to the hotel I tried to think of a way to shake that damned Julio. He had followed me all the way to the general's quarters in the Hotel Corona, and even now was strolling casually a hundred feet or so behind me, whistling and ogling the pretty girls walking through the Alameda. When I went up the stairs and into my room, I heard him mount the stairs after me and and I knew he was squatting on the balcony outside my door, probably swigging *sotol*, the cheap native liquor, from the glass bottle that he kept in the hip pocket of his ragged pants.

Mr. McFall was waiting for me, sitting in the rocker, chin in his hands, looking pale and concerned.

"Benjamin," he said, "a worrisome thing happened to me last night. To me and my Scottish Guards Band of Northern Mexico, also. You see—"

I put a finger to my lips to shush him. "That little skunk Julio is right outside the door," I warned in a whisper. "Come over here." I motioned him toward the window, and opened it so that the the street noises would mask our conversation from Julio.

"Last night," Mr. McFall said in a low voice, "I think an attempt was made on my life."

"Someone . . . someone tried to kill you, you mean?"

I guess I spoke pretty loud in my surprise, because he shushed me. Actually, Julio couldn't have hard. Street noises in Mexico are ear-splitting: women under canvas shelters crying the merits of their vegetables and eggs, the fish vendor blowing a tin horn and holding up a sample, drunken *soldados* arguing and making wild passes toward each other while their companions gleefully egg them on, an occasional string of firecrackers, and always the pat-pat-pat of a thousand tortillas being made by thousands of women—it is the heartbeat, the basic rhythm of Mexico.

"That is exactly what I mean! After we gave the concert

157

for the general, I was not exactly satisfied with the band's performance so I called an extra rehearsal in the Alameda. Oh, they were rebellious, all right, but finally sat down and started to play! Then . . ." He broke off, swallowed hard. "A bunch of Fierro's roughnecks galloped through the park, drunk and shooting in all directions. That is, I *think* they were drunk, but maybe they weren't. Anyway, they shot up the place. We all dived for cover, and . . . and . . ." He held up his bandmaster's cap. There was indeed a hole in it. "I guess I flinched, where I was behind a tree, and the bullet missed my brain by no more than a half-inch!"

His voice rose, and I had to quiet him again.

"I don't think they were drunk, Benjamin. I think they were ordered to do it by that scoundrel Fierro, and in the confusion one man was told to shot me!" He tried a little shaky humor. "I know my band plays badly at times, but this was excessive, don't you think?"

I didn't laugh.

"You know Fierro has hated you ever since that night you stepped in and saved me at the hotel in Ciudad Juárez," I said.

He nodded. "I know," he said, poking his finger through the hole in his cap.

"Look here! You had better stop thinking about your band, Mr. McFall, and escape with me on Mr. Stuart's aeroplane. If you stay here, Fierro will have you killed at a later date." I told him about General Villa's good opinion of the Scottish Guards band of Northern Mexico and his face brightened momentarily. "That," I explained, "is probably why Fierro had to cook up this plan to kill you, so it would look like just a drunken brawl. But believe me, he never forgets, and he is a dangerous man! We've got to forget this business of me escaping in Mr. Stuart's flying machine, and you've got to stay out of it! You're a marked man, and it's too dangerous for you! Fierro knows you're my friend, and I'll bet he hopes that with you out of the way he can get at me."

Mr. McFall got up, somewhat shaky in the knees, and put on the bandmaster hat again.

"No, Benjamin! I will not let that ruffian dissuade me! That band is the most important thing in my life . . ." He swallowed hard, put a hand on my shoulder. "Next to you, laddie, that is. But my record in life has been poor. I have never really stuck to anything, moving from one job to another, one interest to another—teaching, lecturing, office work, looking for gold in Mexico . . ." He smiled ruefully. "No, Benjamin, I have been a drifter, an aimless drifter, all my life. Now, with my band, I have really got my teeth into something, and I do not intend to give it up! My musicians, except for that idiot Nadal, the tuba player, are really making excellent progress! Someday my Scottish Guards Band of Northern Mexico will be at the head of the column when General Villa marches into Mexico City! I believe that! And someday my band will be playing Bach and Brahms in the Zócalo in Mexico City at Sunday-afternoon concerts!"

"Foolishness!" I cried. "This is all foolishness, Mr. McFall! You are in danger, I tell you, and must—"

He interrupted me, eyes intense under the tufted wool eyebrows. "Fierro cannot daunt me! I am a Scot, laddie—a true Scot! You remember when I mentioned Robert the Bruce and the spider? This little band of mine is my first real chance at success and I am not about to abandon it! Think of it—an opportunity to turn ignorant itinerant street musicians into polished concert performers!"

His eyes got glassy with his dream and I knew there was no chance of talking him out of it. Besides, I didn't know what "itinerant" meant.

"All right," I sighed. "But at least let's forget this crazy business of me escaping! If you meddle in that, there's no doubt that Fierro will kill you himself, the way he did David Berlanga—just take you out and shoot you down in somebody's backyard!"

He drew himself up. "Next to the band, Benjamin, you are my chief concern!"

"But—"

"You will hear from me later, don't doubt it! I am a Scot, and a true Scotsman laughs at threats, sneers at danger, rushes into the thick of the fight!" Squaring his shoulders, he marched to the door, opened it, and shoved Julio aside with his foot. "Out of my way, you little sneak!" He clattered down the stairs so fast I was afraid he would fall and break his old bones. But he was a champion, I'll say that!

Still, I worried about him. I even forgot to worry about my own predicament.

Night and day, preparations went on for the campaign to take Torreón, which was now occupied by the Federales and heavily fortified. Thanks to the influence of Felipe Ángeles and the other regular-army officers who had abandoned the despotic President Huerta, this was to be no slam-bang hell-for-leather attack that had always been Villa's style, but a carefully planned campaign with methodical use of cavalry reconnaissance, artillery bombardment to soften the defenses of Torreón, feints at various strong points to divert the Federales, and then a careful drive against the city from three directions. Villa's old comrades—roughnecks like Tomás Urbina, Maclovio Herrera, Manual Banda—were loudly vocal about the Chapultepec officers interfering in the conduct of "their" war for freedom. Daily reports reached headquarters (I received most of them, since General Villa, realizing the importance of taking Torreón if his campaign were to maintain its momentum, called on me more and more for important messages) informing us of General Velasco's continuing efforts to strengthen the defenses of Torreón.

"My God!" Banda roared, stamping about the railroad car and flinging his bearlike arms wide in a gesture of disgust. "Why do we listen to these *maricones*, eh, Pancho? This is no way to fight a war—to dawdle over papers and write things down while that fucking bastard Velasco builds Torreón into a fucking castle! Let us get on our horses and go to war like men, real men, with balls—plenty of balls!"

The others agreed, crowding around General Villa and the neat pale-faced Felipe Ángeles, the table before him almost covered with books and papers.

Villa started to speak but Felipe Ángeles, usually deferent to Villa, spoke first. In a calm voice that nevertheless had icicles on it, he told them off.

"You are a bunch of ruffians, not fit to command the breweries where you seem to spend most of your time! Go ahead—ride your horses against General Velasco's trenches and barbed wire and enfilading cannon fire. Go ahead, damn you all, and see what happens!"

Pop-eyed at the usually quiet Ángeles' words, the roughnecks stared at him. More than one mouth dropped open. General Villa, amused, settled back in his chair at Ángeles' side, hands locked behind his head, grinning.

"Then you will die," Ángeles went relentlessly on, "and the revolution will be deprived of whatever minor skills you may have! But if you listen to me—"

Maclovio Herrera blustered for a moment. "Goddammit, Pancho, why do we have to listen to these fancy words? Why don't we fight the way we used to, the way we did at Ciudad Juárez?"

"Because," Ángeles said, "that is ineffectual against Refugio Velasco. I know him well—he was an artillery instructor at Chapultepec, and has studied warfare in France and in Italy. Refugio Velasco will cut you to ribbons and make garlands from the ribbons for his Federales to wear. No—to go successfully against Torreón and that old fox takes careful planning, believe me!"

The "ruffians" looked at each other with hangdog stares, and dusty boots shuffled uncertainly. "There, now, *hermanos*," the general said. That meant "brothers." "The text has been read to you from chapter something-or-other in the Holy Bible and you had damned well better remember it! Felipe Ángeles is our plans-and-operations officer for this new style of warfare, and if any of you gets out of line, I personally will cut off his thing with my jackknife!"

Grumbling, they filed out of the hotel and went down into the plaza, where I could see them sitting in the spring sunlight, smoking cigars and arguing.

I had not heard from Mr. McFall and his plan to get me out of this dangerous place and back to the States. From time to time I heard his Scottish Guards band playing in the plaza or near—not too near—the general's red caboose, but I was always tied up with telegraph messages to be received or sent. Still, fear controlled my mind. If nothing else untoward happened, how about the irascible Mr. Donald Stuart somehow finding out that I was the one who had shot holes in his aeroplane and in addition punctured his Scotch hide? I would be lucky, then, to escape with my skin intact, let alone escape across the border. And in addition to everything else, I still had not located Valentina; I would *not* leave Chihuahua City without saying good-bye to her! After all, if I was going to return to Chihuahua someday—soon, I hoped—it would hardly do to fly away without a proper farewell. My mind was such a welter that I could hardly keep my dots and dashes straight. Colonel Aguirre noticed. Holding a dispatch I had just taken down from General Urbina, who had preceded the main body toward Torreón as a scouting force, he said to me, "Benjamin, there are a few errors in this copy, I believe. I know Urbina is an unlettered man, but some of this message hardly makes sense!"

The general strolled over to the colonel's desk, scowling. In accord with the new tactics planned with Felipe Ángeles, he had gotten rid of his soiled and dusty blue serge suit, the striped shirt without a collar, and now looked like a Chapultepec dandy himself in a carefully fitted military tunic with brass buttons and a visored cap with a high crown ornamented by several feet, it seemed, of gold braid.

"*Eh, chamaco?* Are you shirking your duties?"

"N-no . . . no, sir." I faltered. "I mean I . . . well, sometimes I make mistakes, I guess!"

He seized me by the shoulder in a way he had never used before.

"Listen, Benjamin! Listen to me! In this campaign against Torreón it is not permitted to make mistakes! A man who makes mistakes will *die*, you understand! I may have to kill him myself to prevent any more mistakes! Do you understand me, Benjamin?"

I swallowed hard. My tongue got thick and my throat constricted. I couldn't speak. I guess my face told of my contrition.

"Well, then . . ." He gave me a rough shove and shambled away, head bowed and hands locked behind his back, once more, apparently, in the deep thought which was part of his new military posture. Before, I don't believe he ever thought that hard; he just stormed a town and took it by force. Thought had always played second fiddle to sheer force, momentum, violence.

Colonel Aguirre spoke to me in a low voice. "Benjamin, something is troubling you, keeping your mind diverted from our proper business. What is it?"

Still mute, I could only shake my head.

"Is it that girl—Valentina, was that not her name?"

Refusing to meet his spectacles eyes, I muttered, "No!"

"Well, something is troubling you! You are a favorite of the general—I have never seen him so taken by a *gringo*—but I must warn you that he is nevertheless a man of violent temperament and can be very cruel. I would advise you, Benjamin, to keep your mind on this business of Torreón. You have been acting strangely of late!"

"I know," I admitted. "I will try to do better, Colonel. You can trust me."

Trust me? I did not trust myself. Harried and nervous about my telegraphic duties, worried about Rodolfo Fierro and his plans for me when he found time, apprehensive about Mr. McFall's ideas for my aerial escape, lonesome for Valentina and seeking her to explain and say good-bye, I was like a boiling pot with a tight lid, ready to explode— and each day made things worse. Would I prevail? Or would General Villa, losing patience, dispose of me as callously as he had dispatched others with whom he had lost patience? As they said in Texas, I was running out my string.

One night, despite the flood of telegraphic messages, I managed to catch a couple of hours' sleep at the hotel. As usual, the pock-faced Julio was squatting on the landing outside my door, carbine across his knees. I think he slept

163

too, although I wasn't sure. Anyway, I heard him growl at someone on the landing. Then Mr. McFall hurried in, nervously wiping his bald dome with a handkerchief.

Speaking in a whisper, he said, "Well, it's all settled, Benjamin! I have made the necessary arrangements. That old scoundrel has agreed for my gold watch and some extra cash I managed to dredge up to take you with him when he departs for El Paso tomorrow morning."

"Tomorrow morning?"

He sat down wearily on the bed. "Yes, tomorrow morning! He has finished the repairs on his flying machine and says he doesn't want to linger in Chihuahua City any longer—afraid of further damage to his airship, I guess. There *have* been rumors of General Velasco's spies in the city. He fears they may think his aeroplane is to be used in the coming attack on Torreón and might seek to damage it."

"But tomorrow?"

"Why not tomorrow? Laddie, it is now or never! You must go!"

I had been thinking about Valentina. But that had gotten me into trouble with the general, and I concluded that I must forget about Valentina—at least for now—much as it upset me to do so. "All right. Tomorrow."

Mr. McFall rubbed his chin, thoughtful. "How are we going to handle that blackguard Julio, now? He clings to you like a leech!"

I knew, I certainly knew. Julio was Rodolfo Fierro's insurance, you could say. But maybe it was because Julio and I had been together so long that I detected a small and welcome change in his attitude, an attitude I soon disrupted. Several times he had spoken longingly about his family in Michoacán—his *esposa*, Amalia, and his five, or was it six, children? Knowing Julio's fondness for strong drink, especially the high-voltage *pulque*, brewed from the heart of the cactuslike *maguey* plant and fermented in one day to make a sour milky-white liquid that burned the throat like fire, I figured a liter of that stuff ought to slow him down a lot.

Donald Stuart, Mr. McFall told me, was to leave in midmorning, the time having something to do with heat and the lift of the wings and the wind and other factors which I didn't pretend to understand. That next morning there was brilliant sunshine and a fresh smell to the air of Chihuahua. Already more troops had left on the march to Torreón, including the horse-drawn artillery units under the command of Felipe Ángeles. Julio sat companionably in my room, sipping a tin cup of the *pulque* I had bought for him. To lull any suspicions he might have, I took a glass myself. It was horrible and I could hardly get it down. Julio, to my satisfaction, swilled cup after cup, and soon became loquacious.

"*Ay*, it is hard to be away from one's wife and family, especially on days of the *fiestas!*" He poured himself another cup. "We are a very close family, you see. To make our family close like that, I used to beat my wife once a week, and the children whenever I saw them. There is nothing like authority, you see, to make a family close!"

Pouring another cup, he nodded toward the half-empty bottle. "You too, Benjamin! Drink! This is good stuff!"

I took a little more, beginning to feel a bit tipsy myself. This would never do! I managed to dump most of it into a potted plant near the window, half-expecting to see it wither completely. Julio did not seem to notice. He poured himself another cup, this time so full that some slopped on the table and a lot of flies came and dabbled in it.

"Unity, that is it," Julio said comfortably. "A man's family should be united!"

Good Lord! He had taken well over half the bottle and showed no signs of becoming drunk! Not only that, he rambled on and on, and it was very boring. In a little while the bottle would be empty and the loquacious Julio would still be upright in his chair, telling me much more than I wanted to know about his family in Michoacán. And Donald Stuart was preparing to leave in midmorning! Already it was nine; I heard the slow tolling of the San Gerónimo church bells and began to get excited. What to do?

With Julio maundering on and on, staring out the window while he talked, I finally managed to sneak behind him. He and I reached for the *pulque* at the same time. There was still enough in the bottle to make it a satisfactory bludgeon. While he stared, puzzled, starting to complain about my preemption of the bottle, I hit him smartly over the head. The bottle broke, sprinkling both of us with *pulque*.

For a moment I was afraid the liquor had somehow protected him from blows on the head. Julio continued to stare at me. Then his eyes glazed, his mustache drooped forlornly, and he toppled off the chair. I hadn't planned this very well in advance. Looking around, all I could find to tie him up was the soiled window curtains. Quickly I ripped them into strips, bound his hands and dirty feet, stuffed a yard or so into his mouth and tied it in place with a swatch of the flimsy material. I finished by pulling up the carpet, rolling him in it like an Indian papoose, and crisscrossing the whole package with what was left of the curtains. Eyes closed, a beatific smile on his pockmarked face, Julio seemed unconcerned about the whole thing.

Quickly I went out the window, over the slanting roof, dropped to the ground, and hurried to the stables, slinking down alleyways and peering around corners lest I be seen by someone who knew me and might demand an accounting. Pinta greeted me with a joyous whicker. Saddling her in less time than I'd ever taken, I tossed the astonished livery-stable man a handful of bilimbique notes.

"Just going for an early-morning ride," I explained.

He was curious. "*Caramba*! You stink of *pulque* this morning! And where's that scoundrel Julio that usually goes about with you?"

"He's sleeping," I told him. That was no lie. "He didn't want to be waked." Maybe *that* was a lie but I didn't care. Fierro would probably have Julio's liver and lights for letting me get away, but that was Julio's problem.

Riding a roundabout course through the back streets and dirt lanes of the city to throw off any pursuers, I reined up short when someone dodged from a courtyard directly into my path. Pinta, startled, bucked and reared and nearly threw me.

"*Vete!*" I snarled. "Dammit, get out of the way! You could have been trampled!"

It was Valentina! She clung to Pinta's mane and pulled herself—and me—into the courtyard, a dusty and unkempt place high with weeds. Apparently the owner had abandoned the property.

"Benjamin!" Her voice was excited. "I have been running after you for a kilometer! I must talk with you."

I slipped down from Pinta and threw the reins over her head; she started to crop the scanty grass. "And I you, Valentina! I have looked for you too. I've got to tell you that I—"

"No! Wait! There is something very important, and I do not know what to do!"

"What's the matter, then?" I sat beside her on a crumbling remnant of wall. "You look worried."

"Oh, Benjamin, I am!" She clasped her hands together in what was almost a prayerful gesture. "Father Eusebio is in Chihuahua City. I saw him!"

"Who?"

"Father Eusebio, I said!"

"Listen, Valentina! Listen! Slow down and stop wringing your hands and start at the beginning. Who is Father Eusebio?"

She did calm down a little then. Swallowing hard, she said, "He is a kind of inspector of convents for the church in Chihuahua. He used to come to the convent sometimes. The girls were supposed to talk to him and tell him any complaints. But we were all too scared after he had Rosalita Cazares punished for 'telling lies about the sisters,' as he said."

"All right," I said, "but please hurry and get on with it." Already the sun was climbing higher and I might miss Mr. Stuart's departure. In fact, so far I hadn't been able to get a word in edgewise to say good-bye to her.

"Yes, Benjamin. Anyway, Father Eusebio is here, in Chihuahua City, and I know the church has sent him here to find me and bring me back to that horrible convent!" She began to cry. "Oh, Benjamin, what shall I do? If he finds me . . ."

I patted her shoulder gingerly, knowing how she was about my passion for her. "Well, I should think you would get away from the city before he finds you!" Then a thought came to me, a brilliant stroke of creative thinking. I had tried to induce Mr. McFall to come with me on Donald Stuart's aeroplane and failed. But maybe Valentina could come with me, riding in the passenger seat while I clung somehow to the struts and wires of the wing. Of course, I didn't know if it was practical, of even if the grouchy old Stuart would go for it without another gold watch or something. But it was worth a try.

"Come with me!" I blurted.

She sniffled a little, and rubbed her nose with the back of her hand. "Come with you? Where?"

Quickly I told her the story. "And we must go quickly!" I said, hearing a church bell start its tolling again. "Mr. Stuart's aeroplane will be leaving in an hour or less and he is a mile or more away." I pointed. "Over that hill, on a flat grassy meadow."

"You . . . you are going away, then? Back to the United States?"

"I've got to," I said.

"But why? Why now?"

I couldn't speak to her about Rodolfo Fierro and his ugly plans for me; it was too awful to speak of it to a girl, even one who by this time knew how different from a convent the life of a revolution is.

"There is no time to talk of that. It is necessary, that is all I can say now." It was certainly a risky gamble, but had possibilities for both of us. "Will you come?"

Slowly she slid off the wall, rubbing at her eyes with the sleeve of her white *manta* jacket. That scene is etched in my memory. She stood small and erect, tearstains on her face, eyes dark pools in the shade of the big straw hat.

"No. I cannot go, Benjamin! I am a soldier of the revolution. What kind of a soldier would I be, then, to run away from the struggle? No, I must remain here until we have won freedom for our people!"

"Goddammit all!" I protested. "Have you thought of what will happen to you if that Father What's-his-name finds you? He'll take you back to the convent and you'll probably get whipped and made to eat bread and water!"

She had a faraway look in her eyes, a sort of quiet desperation. "They were cruel there. I used to hope my father would come riding up on a white horse and take me away. Sister Catarina was the worst. They made us take baths in a lot of rusty tubs. We couldn't take off all our clothes, but had to wear a scratchy kind of robe and wash ourselves under that—for modesty, I guess. Sister Catarina would watch us. She would walk up and down in that dingy old place with a switch, and when some of us joked and giggled, she would beat us."

I was getting impatient. Another bell struck the quarter-hour. Hungry for her, I tried to put my arms around her but she pushed me away.

"No, Benjamin! Now is not the time for that! Please, it is hard enough for me to have you go away!"

Angry at wanting her and being always denied, my temper rising, I protested, "Valentina, you are a fool! A big fool! We may never seen each other again, and it's all your fault! I love you, Valentina, and the damned revolution keeps getting in the way!"

We broke up in a quarrel, which I know now was all my fault.

"I am not a fool! I am a soldier, and I must go where the fighting is! It is all very well for you to run away, but this is *my* country, my *tierra*, and I will stay here and fight for freedom as long as there is breath in my body!"

Angry, I climbed up on Pinta and jerked her head around cruelly with the reins.

"Go on, then!" I shouted. "Go kill some more Federales! Put a lot of notches on your gun! Be a fierce fighter instead of the gentle and beautiful female I love! You are a little minx, do you know what? A damned scheming minx!"

I didn't know what a minx was, actually. Not only that,

169

I didn't know the Spanish for "minx" so had to use the English word.

"What? You said . . . what? I am a *meenx*? What, pray tell, is a *meenx*?"

I gathered from the way my brother Cleary had called the McCracken girl a minx that it meant some kind of troublemaking person. Cleary tried to spark Mary Lou McCracken but she would have none of him, so he called her a little minx.

"I haven't got time to explain!" I howled, wheeling Pinta around with a needlessly vicious whipping of the reins.

Furious and contrite all at the same time, a heavy burden to bear, I galloped blindly out of the shabby courtyard. But in the pounding of Pinta's hooves I heard her cry after me.

"Benjamin!"

It was a heartrending sound, and it tore my wounded heart in two. Suddenly ashamed of myself, I brought Pinta around in such a tight turn that my gentle little pony sat on her haunches, seeming amazed. I had been needlessly cruel to two females in the course of a minute, and I knew that was no good. That morning, leaving Valentina, I think I grew up. I was already fourteen and close to being fifteen, but still, I think I grew up, *really* grew up, that morning.

Kneeing the trembling Pinta back to where Valentina still stood, the back of her hand to her mouth and tears streaming from those so un-Mexican blue eyes, I fumbled in my pocket and handed her my precious barlow knife. That and my mouth-organ were all that remained of McNary, in Hudspeth County, Texas.

"Here," I muttered.

Puzzled, wiping her eyes with a sleeve, she took it.

"It's my good knife," I explained. "It's . . . well, it's kind of like a ring, do you see? Keep it and . . . and . . ." I was near crying myself. "Remember me, Valentina."

I bent down from the saddle—Pinta was only about fourteen hands high at the shoulder—and kissed her hard on the lips. Then I kneed Pinta around and dug my heels into her ribs. Startled, the little mare fled the courtyard and carried me toward the open country beyond, where Mr. Stuart and his flying machine still awaited me, I hoped. Well, she had made up her mind and that was that! Father Eusebio or whatever his name was would probably find her and drag her back to that dreadful convent where they whipped and maltreated young girls—and I didn't even remember the name of the place or where it was!

Grandma Johnson, before her brains softened, used to say, "Ben, it's no use crying over spilt milk." That old saying didn't comfort me any.

—— 9 ——

As I galloped toward the grassy meadow, the air was winy—crisp and bracing. In those days I didn't know anything about wine, but as I remember it now, the smell of it was like a good chilled white Bordeaux. A sprinkle of rain had fallen the night before. There is nothing like the herbal scent of fresh-washed desert shrubs. Pinta caracoled and acted foolish and I had to jerk on the reins to quiet her down.

At the grass landing field Mr. Donald Stuart waited, Mr. McFall's gold watch and chain prominent on his greasy overalls. "Well, you're late enough!" he grumbled, walking around the aeroplane for a final inspection, hanging on the wings, listening to the plink of wires as he pulled on them and let them snap back.

"I'm sorry," I apologized, tying Pinta to a bush. "There . . . well, there were complications."

He squinted at the road to town. "Did ye get away clean, then?"

"Clean as a whistle!" I bragged. "Oh, there was a little problem when I had to . . . well, restrain Julio, but I think I handled it well. It should be another hour or more before anyone finds him and begins to wonder where I've gone."

Mr. Stuart tugged at the big wooden propeller and the engine hiccuped. He hung on it again, and a few times more.

"All right, laddie, just so ye don't get me in trouble. Those damned greasers are homicidal. If ye'll just turn that nickel-plated switch now . . ."

I turned it. Nothing happened. He spun the propeller

again. The little engine caught and began to fire in a cloud of castor-oil-smelling smoke.

Mr. Stuart climbed into the seat beside me and clutched the throttle with a greasy fist. "So ye got well away, did ye?"

"Yes!" I yelled back against the roar of the engine.

He jerked his head. "Well, look back there, then, ye bare-chinned gossoon!"

Horsemen were galloping out from the town. Over the clamor of the roaring, clicking engine I could hear shots. The horsemen were too far away for bullets to reach but they were coming fast.

"Maybe," I conceded, "I didn't do so well, after all. Still, I don't understand how that damned Julio—"

Mr. Stuart's aeroplane began a slow rumble across the grass. "An aeroplane," he shouted, pulling goggles down over his eyes, "has advantages over horses, laddie! They don't need hay, they don't shit and pee all over the place, and they're about thirty miles an hour faster. Don't worry! Those fools haven't got a chance!"

The aeroplane rumbled faster and faster across the bumpy earth. Looking back, I probably turned pale. The pursuers had good horses and were gaining on us.

"Can't you go faster?" I screamed at Mr. Stuart, hanging to a strut with my eyes watering and my hair streaming out straight. I could hardly catch my breath.

He grinned a greasy grin. "Ye see that canyon dead ahead, do ye?"

I remembered that canyon. I had ridden Pinta along it. It was very deep, and full of needly cactus. The canyon was coming fast toward us. Something whizzed by my ear and Mr. Stuart swore.

"Oh, the bastards! They're shooting at my aeroplane again!"

Peering down through the pedals that worked back and forth as Mr. Stuart steered, I saw with a catch in my throat that Pinta had pulled loose from her tether and was galloping madly below us, dragging the bush I had tied her to. Poor Pinta—I loved that little horse!

Another bullet tore through the wing fabric just over my

head and the rip began to widen, assisted by the wind. The blue fog surrounding Mr. Stuart was either oil smoke or profanity. I didn't know which. He cried curses, Scottish curses, I think, because I couldn't understand them. Horrified, I saw us bouncing swiftly toward the bushes lining the edge of the canyon.

"Doesn't this thing fly?" I shrieked in panic.

Mr. Stuart's face was grim and joyous. "She does that, laddie!" Pulling back on the wheel, he jammed the throttle full on. The roar of the engine climbed to a scream and the choking blue smoke enveloped us. At the very edge of the canyon Mr. Stuart's aeroplane seemed to pause for a moment, like a cat contemplating a dangerous jump. Then a gust of wind caught us and we dropped off the edge, a drop that made my stomach flop over. I almost lost the *chorizo* and beans I had eaten for breakfast.

In midair, not far above the cactus-studded bottom of the canyon, the aeroplane struggled to gain altitude. "Get up, get *up*, ye doxy!" Mr. Stuart yelled, tugging back on the wheel so hard I was scared something would break. "Dammit, get up, *Maggie May!*"

Slowly the big bird flapped her wings and began to rise. We cleared the far edge of the canyon with inches to spare. In fact, the wheels caught a cactus and it dangled from the running gear. Mr. Stuart beamed.

"It's great fun, isn't it, my boy?"

If I had been pale before, I was now white as a sheet. "Fun?"

He laughed as his aeroplane began to gain altitude above the flat desert land. "Flying, I mean! Oh, there's always a surprise or two!"

I looked back. The horsemen had stopped at the edge of the canyon. There was a volley of rifle shots; I could see puffs of powder smoke, though the pursuers were too far away to hear, or for their bullets to reach. I looked up at the tear in the canvas wing, right in front of the gasoline tank. Already the tear seemed a foot longer.

"Yes," I agreed shakily. "There *are* surprises, all right!"

I didn't know if I could stand many more surprises. But I was glad to get away from Chihuahua City, from Julio the guard, who must have twisted like an eel to get out of my wrappings, from Rodolfo Fierro, Villa's Butcher, from Mexico in general. The danger of pursuers gone, I found aeroplaning exciting. We must have been doing thirty or forty miles an hour! Below us on the desert floor our shadow followed us, shrinking and expanding and taking on weird shapes as it crossed *barrancas*, sped up hillsides, and spooked wandering deer, coyotes, and wild turkeys. Holding tight to the strut, not completely trusting my canvas belt, I yelled in Mr. Stuart's ear, "This *is* fun!"

"Aye, laddie!" he yelled back. "We're bloody angels, we are, flying high in God's heaven!"

At this rate we would be in El Paso before dark. It seemed a miracle. In one angelic flight my life had taken a sharp right turn, a turn back to a world where I knew my way around, where there were standards, where people worked hard and went to church of a Sunday and lived a good settled life. Well, maybe it would take two angelic flights, or maybe three; Mr. Stuart said he would have to land somewhere and fill the gasoline tank from the cans strapped to the wooden struts. One flight, two, maybe three—I didn't care! I had a wild feeling of joy.

No more than fifty feet above the ground, we passed over a small lake. Waterbirds rose in panic at the sound of the engine.

"I'm going to set her down on that flat place alongside the lake," Mr. Stuart explained. "I'll top off the tank, and maybe that will get us to El Paso." Carefully he wheeled the aeroplane around, leaning out to observe the ground. "Hang on, laddie—it may be a bumpy landing!"

I gripped the strut beside my head. Above me the rip in the wing widened as the turn put new strains on it. "Do you think—?" I started, wanting to call his attention to the rip. But holding to that patched strut, I was conscious the strut was beginning to flex in my grip. Slowly, inexorably, it bent, taking on a dog-leg appearance, accompanied by a creaking sound.

"Mr. Stuart!" I cried in alarm. "Mr. Stuart! Should . . . should this be doing . . . this?"

He was busy with the wheel and throttle. "Close your

trap, boy!" he yelled. "Don't ye see I've got my hands full?"

He finished the turn to go upwind and his aeroplane sagged back into a normal conformation. I breathed a sigh of relief, but my relief was short-lived. As we headed into the wind the rip in the canvas came totally apart. A long flap of fabric trailed us. Holding the wheel steady, Mr. Stuart looked back at the tail flapping in the wind.

"Jesus Christ!" he cried.

As we both watched, horrified, more canvas came loose. In seconds almost the whole upper wing was bare of fabric, showing the spars and braces and wires. *Maggie May* slewed to the right, having lost lift on that side. At the same moment the strut I was gripping bent farther, sounding a pistollike crack.

"Hold tight!" Mr. Stuart yelled, fighting the wheel and trying to trim the airplane.

It was no use. The flying machine wheeled in a tighter and tighter turn, wires and struts and spars creaking and groaning. The desert floor came toward us in a mad spiral and I closed my eyes, terror-struck. *Lord Jesus, God, whatever you're called—save me!*

Struggling with the wheel, trying to straighten the crazy spin, Mr. Stuart called on the deities too, though not in supplication—more in anger. "Goddamned fucking cocksucking Jesus Christ hell and damnation! Oh, Christ!"

We hit the desert floor next to the lake like a Fourth of July pinwheel, scattering a great cloud of dust. Pieces of the airplane flew in all directions. Something hit my right arm, numbing it. Something else caromed off my forehead and dazed me. For a moment there was silence. Then the gasoline tank atop the wing tipped drunkenly and fell down, setting off sparks as metal ground against metal.

"Mr. Stuart!" I cried. "Are you all right?"

Swearing all the while, he was struggling to get out of his safety belt. Drenched in gasoline, he looked piteously at me, a mute cry for help. My arm trailing, I tried to reach his hand so as to pull him free. But then the leaking gasoline bloomed into a great ball of fire and smoke, blowing me clear out of the airplane into the mud at the edge of the lake. I lay there dazed, burned, and gasping for breath.

"Wait a minute!" I yelled. "Wait! I'm coming!"

I don't know who or what I was demanding to wait. Maybe it was directed at the roaring flames that licked at the remaining canvas and swallowed up the outline of Mr. Stuart, vainly trying to free himself. Against the crackling of the flames I heard his scream.

"Wait a minute!" I insisted, and tried to get up. When I put weight on my right arm, it collapsed under me and I fell back into the mud. *That arm is no good*, I thought. Staggering up again, I stumbled over to *Maggie May*, shielding my face against the heat. "Mr. Stuart! I'm coming! Wait!"

I was dizzy, and again fell. Struggling up, aware of blood pouring into my eyes, I tried to reach him but flames drove me back. A pillar of black smoke, lit red and yellow and orange at the bottom, towered into the sky.

"Mr. Stuart!"

In the inferno that was the cockpit I could barely make out his body. It was frozen, unmoving, one hand still on the wheel, the other on the buckled of the jammed canvas belt. As I watched, sick and horrified, his form dwindled. Still frozen in that casual pattern, as if he were thinking, it blackened. A flood of gasoline had spilled out. Ignited, it stitched fiery trails across the sand in grotesque patterns, licking at my boots. Well, not my boots; somehow I had lost one boot, and my tweed jacket was smoking from a peppering of tiny sparks.

Struck dumb, I collapsed, seeing the licking flames finally gutter out, leaving a mass of red-hot tubes and wires and twisted metal. Mr. Stuart still sat in his seat, not quite a skeleton, and certainly not a body. Mr. Stuart looked like a black African doll. Retching, I fell down in the mud.

I don't know how long I lay there, sick and exhausted, chilled in the black mud as the sun climbed higher. At the sound of hooves I looked up stupidly. Pinta trotted over and nuzzled me. She must have followed the airplane the whole way.

"I thank you, lady," I said, and pulled myself up by her mane. There were more hoofbeats in the desert sand, and indistinct forms rode up on indistinct mounts. Holding to Pinta's mane, I squinted, trying to make out things in the blinding sun.

"The little bastard!" I heard Julio the guard say in exasperation. "Hit me on the head and tied me up! Look at this bump! Fierro will roast me on a spit!"

Someone put an arm under mine and pulled me toward a hummock of grass. "'Here, *chamaco!* Sit down—you're hurt." It was old Ojo Parado, and his touch was gentle.

"Let me at him!" Julio begged. "I'll hurt him for good, I will! Tricky little bastard! Forcing *pulque* down my gullet and then trying to bash my brains out!"

"Shut up," Ojo Parado said in a voice that was calm enough, but no-nonsense. "See, the lad's arm is broken, and he's covered with blood from that cut on his forehead! Dip this rag in the lake and bring it to me. And stop your fucking bellyaching!"

Lying on the grass, Ojo Parado squatting beside me and bathing my forehead—arm broken, cut and bruised, and still horror-struck at the way Mr. Donald Stuart had died— all I could think of was *chingado, chingado, chingado*! Fucked again! I wanted to cry but couldn't; tears wouldn't come. There was nothing but a horrible feeling of confusion, bafflement, loss. Maybe I couldn't cry because all the tears inside me had dried up. I would never cry again, in fact, until . . . But that came later, years later, in a little house on Calle Fuente in Torreón.

"Try sitting up," Ojo Parado advised, getting an arm under me. Vomit was all over my shirt, and I brushed at it with my good hand. "I . . . I'm a mess," I apologized.

"*No importa*," Ojo Parado said. "It doesn't matter! Rest this way for a few minutes. Then we have to take you back."

Julio and a couple of other men were poking in the remains of the wrecked machine. One of them was fascinated by Mr. Stuart. He stood stock-still, shocked, crossing his chest with his hand and muttering, "*Dios mío, Dios mío, Dios mío!*" The rascal must have seen a lot of blood and violence and death in his time, but that mute black doll undid him.

Julio, poking about with a stick, let out a cry of triumph. Hurrying over, he showed Ojo Parado a lump of gold—blackened but undeniably gold—studded with small wheels and cogs and springs. It was the remains of Mr. McFall's gold watch, melted into a blob.

"Give me that, please!" I begged.

Julio shook his head and bit the lump. "No, this is gold! *Real* gold! I can get a lot of money for this! Not bilimbiques, but real money!"

"Give it to him!" Ojo Parado ordered.

"Not on your life! It's mine!"

The old man's glass eye rotated erratically. Drawing his pistol, he pointed it a Julio's crotch. "Give it to the boy, quick, or do you want me to shoot your balls off?"

Grumbling, Julio handed it over. It was warm in my hand. I grasped it hard, as if to draw warmth from it, comfort, maybe even an understanding of what had happened.

"Make him get on his feet now!" Julio sulked. "We've got a long way to go!"

"Do you think you can ride your little mare?" Ojo Parado asked.

Shakily I got to my feet, wincing with pain and not sure I could stand upright. "I . . . I guess so."

They escorted me back to Chihuahua City, Julio and Ojo Parado riding beside me, one on each side, to catch me if I fell from the saddle. We reached the city without incident. Lord! There was no incident left in me by that time! People—street vendors, merchants, ladies fresh from the *tortillería*, soldiers—all stared at me, at my burned clothes and sooty face. Even Pinta seemed put off at the tattered scarecrow on her back, smelling of smoke and blood and gasoline. Weak from my injuries, my knees turning to jelly, Ojo Parado helped me off Pinta.

"*Amigo*, I will take care of your little horse." He turned me over to Julio, who snapped, "Up the stairway, you little bastard! Remember, I keep well in mind that bump on the head you gave me this morning!"

Fierro sat behind his carved desk, appearing agitated, tapping on the polished wood with a fingernail. Julio, probably fearing retribution for his failure to guard me properly, shoved me forward and quickly closed the door after him.

"So! You have come back again, eh, you little prick!"

I tried to speak, but couldn't. All I could do was to stand there swaying, staring at the pattern of the carpet, which swam giddily before my eyes, swirling arabesques of garrish design. Fierro rose suddenly from his chair, cigarette dangling from his lips, and grabbed my arm, twisting it.

"Have you touched her, you little swine? Have you done anything to her? You were seen, you know! I find you have been seen many times with her!"

I didn't know what he was talking about. Touched who? Seen with who? He twisted my bad arm harder and I nearly fainted. Lightnings of pain, red-hot pain, lanced my arm. I tried to pull away from his grasp but things started to go black—a clinging velvety blackness. I had only enough consciousness to mutter, "Please! My arm! It's broken, I think!"

His lips curled. "You arm? *Merde!* What do I care for your fucking arm? I ask you again, young Texas pig— have you touched her? Have you violated her? By Christ, if you have . . ."

He broke off as I dropped to my knees, the room reeling about me. I fell over and lay there, only half-conscious, until he took water from a basin and threw it in my face.

"Get up, you sniveling little bastard! Arm broken, eh? I'll see that every bone in your body is broken, one at a time, if you don't tell the truth! Admit it now! Tell me, dammit! You fucked her, didn't you?"

I couldn't get up. I couldn't think. I couldn't do anything but lie there groaning, good arm across my eyes. Contemptuously he kicked me, and I was already in such pain that the blow didn't even count.

"Get up, damn you!"

Wearily I shook my head. "I . . . I can't."

He was disgusted. "Have I not always treated you well?

I always spoke well of you to the general, and made opportunities for you. I have . . . I have kept a special place in my heart for you, Benjamin!" He seemed almost to weep, that fiendish man, that butcher. "Now you have tricked me, ruined the thing that was most precious to me in my life, the good thing I intended to speak of that day when I come before the Lord! I could shoot you as you lie groveling on the floor there! I am El Carnicero, you know that!" Fiercely he strode about the room, puffing hard on the cigarette. Finally he called to Julio, who appeared at the doorway, very nervous.

"Take this little whelp to a safe room and summon Dr. Raschman to tend him." Fierro fixed Julio with his terrible eye. "And keep him well, do you understand me? I will deal with him later—and with you also, you careless fool!"

"*Sí, sí sí!*" Julio stammered, and came to drag me to the door. By that time I think I had fainted completely. The last thing I remembered was fragments of Fierro's tirade. *Have you touched her? Have you done anything to her? You were seen, you know!* I tried to make sense out of his words but it was too great an effort. My mind melted into the blackness and that was all there was.

Julio was hardly less gentle with me than Fierro had been. As he shoved me ahead of him, I caught a last glance of Rodolfo Fierro. Again he sat at his desk, but this time his head was pillowed on his arms. I could have sworn he wept.

Julio pointed to an unmade bed in a small room with only a single high window, and that barred. "There! Lie down now, and don't move from that bed! I will go fetch Dr. Raschman."

Gratefully I collapsed on the stinking sheets. Someone had recently used that bed with a woman. No matter—I was too tired to care. Running my hand gingerly over the bad arm, I could feel a place under the skin where the broken ends were poking up. Jesus Christ, but it hurt! The skin was already turning red and blotchy-looking. I only half-heard a key turn in the lock. Then I passed out again.

After a blank eternity, I heard a voice. "Wake, boy. Wake up!"

Opening my eyes, I stared, wondering for a moment where I was, who I was. In my mind's eye I saw that black African doll in the twisted remains of the flying machine, and cried out in terror.

"That's all right, now," the voice soothed. "You are all right, boy."

I sank back on the pillow, trying to focus my eyes. Gradually a kindly bearded face swam into view.

"Dr. Raschman," I whispered. It was the general's personal physician.

"Yes," Dr. Raschman said. "Let me take a look at you, now. Don't move. I will move you when necessary." Gently he touched my arm. "Hmmmmmm! We must see about that soon." With a basin and a rag he sponged off my forehead. "Deep cut there . . . deep cuts, actually. We will need stitches." Expertly he examined me, pushing gently here, probing there, lifting me a little and letting me sag back in the bed.

"Hmmm," he said again. "In an aeroplane, eh? My boy, you are lucky to be alive. I understand the pilot burned."

"Yes," I said in a choked voice.

"Well, first of all, we must set that arm." Taking a small bottle from his black valise, he poured liquid onto a piece of gauze. "'Now, this can be very painful, so I want you to breathe into this chloroform for a while. That will take the edge off the pain."

Trusting him, I did so. He was no different from old Doc Birkett in McNary except that he spoke Spanish. He asked me to count, and I did. *One, two, three, four*—the room darkened, everything started to go out of focus. *Five, six, seven, eight, nine . . .*

I was falling into a deep dark chasm but I wasn't afraid. Actually, I wasn't falling; it was more like floating.

Light, deliciously light . . .

I didn't wake until dawn the next day. Dr. Raschman sat beside me in a gray light filtering through the barred window. A pile of melted wax was all that was left of a candle. The erratic electric plant had probably failed again; Villa's people were soldiers, not electricians.

"Slept well, did you?"

"Yes, sir," I whispered. My arm was splinted and my forehead heavy with bandages. My body smelled of some kind of aromatic salve he had put on the burned places and my face felt strange and puffy. Gingerly I felt a cheek.

"It will be all right," Dr. Raschman assured me, rising and yawning. "The swelling will soon go down." Putting on his long black coat, he picked up the bag. ""I will send someone to bring you a little beef broth. Later I will find a person to stay with you and help attend to your natural needs."

I tried to thank him but my throat got thick and I couldn't swallow; all I could do was make an ungracious strangling sound.

"That is all right, boy. You have been a good patient!" After a pat on my shoulder, he went to the door. I slept again, a long dreamless sleep. Was it part of the dream that Dr. Raschman muttered something about Fierro as he closed the door?

At that stage of my life I was a healthy young animal, I guess, like most boys. But even healthy young animals can sicken and die. That is what I did for the next few days; not die, of course, or I would not be telling all these things. But I was sick, sick almost unto death. I felt like my brains had turned to cornmeal mush, like Grandma Johnson's brains. I like cornmeal mush with butter and salt and pepper and maybe a few chiles stirred into it to hotten it up a little. I do not care for it, however, between my ears.

My broken arm became infected and Dr. Raschman spoke grimly of amputation. The cuts on my forehead turned yellow and green and smelled bad. The burns, too, sloughed off bad skin and refused to heal. I faded in and out of consciousness and had terrible dreams. *We were falling, the flying machine twisting in that crazy spiral, and the ground came up faster and faster and I could see rocks we were going to fall on and a coiled snake and Mr. Ballew was down there, perched on his one leg and laugh-*

ing, and Ma slapped me and told me to go to bed and she was taking Dr. Miles's Nervina out of a spoon big as a shovel and—

"No!" I screamed. I tried to get up but a gentle hand pushed me back on the pillow.

"It was a dream," I babbled. "A bad dream!"

"Yes," a soft voice said. "I know. Now sleep, Benjamin."

Whose voice? Familiar—a woman's voice . . .

Dr. Raschman spoke. "Well, I do not know—"

"Please, Señor Doctor! I am well-known as a *curandera*, a healer who knows all about certain herbs and plants. I am also a *bruja*—a witch—but a good witch. I can help him, I know I can! Please!"

Dr. Raschman's voice was uncertain. "It is not wise—from a professional standpoint, that is. I should be laughed at by my fellow practitioners. But I suppose—"

"Thank you, Señor Doctor! Thank you!"

Through pain-deadened eyes I saw the woman embrace the doctor and hurry away.

"Who?" I murmured. "Who . . . woman . . . ?"

Dr. Raschman bent over me. "You have a breath like a camel, Benjamin! I must give you something to clean out your stomach."

Against my wishes he gave me a spoonful of thick greenish liquid and water to wash it down with. I started to doze again.

Who . . . woman . . . ?

I vomited, I shit, I pissed. They were always trying to keep me clean, washing me, changing my nightshirt—where did my nightshirt come from? Anyway, there were several of them, women moving silently about the room, sitting by my bed, one with her arm around my shoulders as the other tried to feed me beef tea and soup and mashed fruits.

"Eat!" the familiar voice insisted. "Eat, Benjamin, or I swear I will put you over my old knees and spank you for the stubborn little boy you are!"

Victoria! It was old Victoria, Valentina's fierce elderly friend, the one who took such pleasure in dressing her in those fine looted clothes, the one who reputedly cut ears off Federales she had killed in battle. Tough, kindhearted old Victoria!

"All right," I whispered in a husk of a voice. "I . . . I will try."

It was morning; I had lost track of time. Sunlight slanted in through the barred window and I put a hand over my eyes. Then the moment of consciousness passed and I started to babble about a bad dream and again blacked out. The fragrance of ground herbs was the last thing I remembered, and again I dreamed terrible dreams. A beast chased me through a green jungle, baying like a hound, mewing like a cat, jabbering like a monkey. Finally, spent, I lay under a tree. But the nameless thing jumped into the tree and sat there looking at me, licking its chops. It was a kind of cat-dog-lion-tiger thing, and its mustache was neatly trimmed like Rodolfo Fierro's. It was Fierro! He pounced on me and—

Good old Victoria was there again; she was always there. When did she sleep? Perhaps she dozed in the rocker near my bed, but was always at my side when I called. "I am grateful to you," I murmured, "and to all the good ladies who came to help me."

"I know, Benjamin." She stroked my forehead; the bandages were gone. "Dr. Raschman says you could not be killed with an ax. It is his way, I think, of saying you are better."

Well, I *did* get better, and was convinced that old Victoria's herbs did the job. Dr. Raschman was surprised, and said he would ask Victoria how to compound some of her medicines, though I think he was a little embarrassed at being outdone by a *bruja*. My arm began to knit, although to this day it seems a little weak and perhaps misshapen. The cuts on my forehead healed and left a few scars. The burns began to turn a healthy pink and itched, a good sign according to Dr. Raschman.

"You have had visitors, Benjamin," Victoria said one day while she was washing my face.

"Visitors?" I feared it was Rodolfo Fierro.

"Mr. McFall, the leader of the band. And Mr. Wickwire, that funny little man in the leather puttees. But you were always asleep, and it was not good for you to be waked." When a knock sounded at the door, she laid down the basin and cloth and went to open it. Julio sat there with the rifle across his knees.

The caller was Mr. McFall. I tried to get up to shake his hand, but he only stood at a distance, not looking well at all.

"Ben," he said. "Ah, Ben! You are getting well, I think. The last time I came, you looked like warmed-over death. I came several times, you know."

"Yes," I said, beginning to choke up. "I know." With my good arm I beckoned him to come closer. Reluctantly, I thought, he sat in the chair next to my bed, avoiding my eye. When he pulled at his eyebrows in that way he had, I knew something was wrong. There was something strange in his attitude, in his manner, in his . . . face. I squinted hard, my eyes still a little puffy. What looked like bruised patches were on his cheeks, and one eye was darkened. He had limped into the room, also.

"I . . . I have a confession to make to you, Benjamin," he said, looking into the gold-braided bandleader's cap on his lap. He was ill-at-ease, distracted; he was not the cheerful Mr. McFall I had known.

"Confession? What do you mean?"

"Well, I . . ." He hesitated. "I am trying to think of a way to avoid losing your friendship, Benjamin, but I am afraid there is no way."

"You will always be my friend!"

"Not after . . . not after you . . ." He turned away and I saw a healing scar on the back of his head, a ragged thing showing through the thin gray hair. "Well, there is nothing to do but explain."

"Yes. What do you mean?"

He looked at Victoria washing things in a basin. "I am so ashamed." He nodded toward her. "Do you think she could . . . well, go away while I . . . I . . ."

Victoria nodded, slipped out the door, and soon I heard her talking to Julio. Mexican people are very *simpático*—sensitive to the feelings of others.

"It is like this," Mr. McFall started, staring into his

cap. He looked very old and frail, much older and more frail than I remembered. "The hotel clerk discovered Julio bound and gagged shortly after you left, I guess. Anyway, he rushed to tell Fierro, and Fierro had me brought to his room in the hotel."

I felt sick, suspecting what was coming.

"Fierro, of course, knew that you and I . . . were . . . good friends. He asked me to tell him where you had gone, laddie, but I refused." Mr. McFall swallowed hard, and his old Adam's apple bobbed up and down in the lean throat. "So they . . . he . . ." His voice broke; angrily he wiped away a tear that was running down his nose. "Fierro said he didn't want to dirty his hands on me. He brought in Julio to torture me! Julio burned me with cigarettes while that fiend Fierro watched. He put a cord around my neck . . ." Mr. McFall's veined hand touched a red welt on his throat. "He poured water down my gullet till I almost drowned. That was when I . . . I . . ." He looked piteously at me. "They got it out of me, Ben, where you'd gone! They sent a patrol out right away to catch you before Mr. Stuart's flying machine could leave for El Paso." Shaking his head, he ran bony fingers through the thinning hair. "I am not a young man, Ben, in either body or spirit. I try hard, and fancy I do some things quite well. But I could not withstand the torture. I told them where you were." He started to cry. "God, I am so ashamed!"

"You needn't be," I said. I tried hard to get up, to walk over to him and put my arm around the trembling shoulders, but my legs just weren't up to it. The melted gold watch was on the table beside me; I picked it up and handed it to him.

"What . . . what is this, Ben?"

"Your gold watch. It melted in the fire and one of the men was poking around in the cinders with a stick and found it."

His smile was wry. "I daresay it won't keep good time anymore, not that it ever did."

"Listen," I said. "Listen, Mr. McFall! No matter what happened, you are my true friend. You should not blame yourself for what happened—I mean, what they forced you

187

to do. I don't care who hears this—Valentina or the general or Rodolfo Fierro himself! I respect you and wish you were my true father, so I could be a son as true to you as you were to me!"

His eyes were wet again, and he rubbed them with a fist. Putting on the dingy bandleader's cap, he slipped the blob of gold into his pocket. "I am ever so grateful to you, Ben, for how you took this! Of course, you did not escape as we had planned, but let us look at the good side. If they had not known where you were, you might have died out there on the desert. At least you were brought back to receive proper medical treatment." He sighed, shook his head. "But I am still ashamed of what I did, laddie! Maybe I can make it up to you sometime. Maybe I—"

"Listen," I said. "Listen, Mr. McFall! Anyone would be proud to have such a friend as you! You do not need to make anything up to me. It was fate, that's all! You did your best, and don't need to apologize to anyone, let alone me, who am in your debt for so many things."

His face still looked troubled. "You mentioned Valentina several times in your delirium, Ben."

"Valentina? What about Valentina?"

"I am afraid there is more bad news, Benjamin. Valentina has found her father."

"Her father? Who . . . ? Who is her father?"

He took a long breath, not looking at me. "Valentina is Rodolfo Fierro's daughter!"

I could not believe my ears. Sitting bolt upright in bed and biting my lip at the pain it caused in my bad arm, I stared at him.

"No! Not Fierro! Why, that's impossible! Are you joking? Because if you are—"

Slowly, sadly, he shook his head. "It is true. According to rumors about Fierro's brigade, she is the daughter he put in a convent years ago, for safekeeping, I guess. But she escaped and came to find her father, who was said to be a high officer in Villa's División del Norte. A kind of bloodhound—a Father Eusebio, whom I would not like to meet in a dark alleyway—traced her here and turned her over to her father."

I swallowed hard. For a moment it seemed I couldn't breathe. Then, dizzy and confused, I fell back on my pillow again. "Valentina! Daughter of that perverted *bastard*! How can it be? She is sweet, she is lovely, she is—" I broke off, and maybe I began to weep a little bit, distraught and shocked as I was.

Old Victoria bustled in then, carrying a tray. When she saw me and glanced at Mr. McFall, she was cross.

"What have you been doing to my patient, eh, Señor McFall? He looks like a ghost!"

I *was* a ghost, a disembodied spirit, with no Valentina. My head swam with the realization of what had happened. Valentina—my Valentina—the Butcher's daughter? It couldn't be!

"Yes, it is true," Victoria said, bathing my forehead with a damp cloth. "It is said that General Fierro was married to a highborn Spanish lady. She died giving birth to a second child. Since then he has kept the girl in a convent somewhere, and she escaped to find her father." She shuddered. "Oh, that fox-faced Father Eusebio!" Hurriedly she crossed herself. "He is the devil himself, I believe! He is small, like a ferret, and has small and very bright eyes, like a ferret, too! He is the one who smelled out her trail to our División del Norte."

Flat on my bed, eyes closed in pain and sorrow, I asked, "Where is she now—Valentina?"

"No one knows for sure," Mr. McFall said. "But Father Eusebio took her away in an automobile with a driver from Fierro's brigade. I suspect she is by now safely locked up someplace where she cannot escape again."

After Mr. McFall left, Victoria and I sat together for a long time. I managed to get down some chicken *mole*, chicken smothered in a sauce of many spices, a dark rich sauce that had chocolate in it, of all things! Usually I favored it, but now could only pick at it.

"Eat!" Victoria urged. "How are you going to get well when you eat like a mouse? Eat, I tell you!"

I shook my head. I did not want to eat ever again. That way I would waste away and die; I looked forward to it.

"Don't think you are the only one saddened by the loss

of our Valentina," Victoria said. "I loved her too. She was like a granddaughter to me, who have no other relatives now." Unaccountably she began to weep, great racking sobs that shook her ample bosom. This tough battle-hardened old woman wept, and I was the one to comfort her.

"We have both lost," I said.

Angrily she pushed my hand away. "I should not weep like that! What do I care about anything anymore! The revolution goes on, and there is fighting, much fighting, to do before we put our Pancho in the Presidential Palace!" She blew her nose hard, dabbed at her eyes with the hem of her skirt, and rose.

"I will leave you alone now, Benjamin. I have things to do. But I will be back soon."

For a long time I lay in the darkened room with only a candle end burning smokily. Finally it guttered out. The electric plant had gone bad again.

That night I did not sleep well. Valentina gone, perhaps forever . . . Mr. McFall in trouble . . . I couldn't do anything about Valentina, so I tried to forget that. But it was not like Rodolfo Fierro to let poor Mr. McFall off with only a beating. Fierro had shot many men for lesser offenses, or for no offense at all.

I was still awake, although groggy, when the rosy light of a Chihuahua dawn showed through the barred window of my jail.

10

The great battle for Torreón was at hand. By now most of Villa's troops had left Chihuahua City. Except for a company or so, the streets were empty of soldiers. With Julio squatting outside my door and looking in every once in a while to see I had not sawed the bars off the window, I read *Excelsior* and *Universal*, Mexico City newspapers several weeks old. The European war Mr. Wickwire had told me about was still going on. The Huerta-approved line was that Mexico might send troops in support of the Allies, though President Huerta obviously had his hands full with Pancho Villa and Emiliano Zapata and was a pretty devious character, anyway; you couldn't put much stock in anything he said.

Mr. McFall came to my room to say good-bye.

"But where are you going?" I asked, surprised.

He shrugged. "God knows! All *I* have found out is that Rodolfo Fierro sent word back from Torreón that he wants my Scottish Guards Band to come and play."

"But aren't a lot of them just civilians?"

He shook his head. "In this bloody war, Ben, there are no civilians."

It was true. When General Villa first took Chihuahua City his firing squads executed a lot of civilians who Villa or Fierro or somebody thought had supported the Federales. From my barred window I often heard the shouted commands; "*Listos! Apunten! Fuego!*"—then a volley of rifle fire and more bodies hauled to the city dump and burned "for sanitary purposes," according to Dr. Raschman.

"Well . . ." Mr. McFall sighed and got up, looking very tired. "I may not see you again, Ben, so—"

"That's not true!" I objected. "Listen, Mr. McFall! As soon as my arm heals, as soon as I get out of this cast and can travel, I'll be in Torreón too. Fierro sent word that as soon as Dr. Raschman approves, I am to go to Torreón with Julio."

He smiled a wan smile. "Well, boy, come quickly or it may be too late."

"What do you mean?" I asked.

Refusing to say any more, he shook hands and went out the door. Julio, in spite of Rodolfo Fierro's orders, had begun to let me have visitors, though he always locked the door until they were ready to come out again. It was a kindness I appreciated, but Julio made one thing clear.

"I still remember that clout on the head you gave me, *chico*! Someday I will pay you back for that. *Ay*, my skull rang like a church bell for a week!"

I had another visitor—Mr. Wickwire, the reporter for the *Morning Times*. On his way back to El Paso for an editorial conference with the publishers of his paper, he stopped in Chihuahua City.

"Well," he said, "you don't look too bad, Ben!"

"I'm healing," I agreed.

"Had an aeroplane accident, I hear."

"Sure did."

"San Francisco *Bulletin* man beat me on that story. Well, you can't win 'em all!" He sprawled in a chair and I noticed a small burned hole in his shirt. He saw me looking and said, "Bullet hole. Came pretty close to my gizzard, but only scratched me. Sometimes I feel like a duck in a shooting gallery."

He dozed off again, the tired old man, and I let him sleep. After a while he came to.

"What's the news from Torreón?" I asked.

He yawned, stretched, put his cap on backward. "Can of worms! Villa bragged he could take Torreón *'con puro fusil,'* you know—with just a rifle. Even with Felipe Ángeles planning the strategy for Villa, the División del Norte has been thrown back time after time. I'm no military expert, you understand, but it's not hard to see what's happening. General Velasco has set up a lot of strong points around the city and they all cover each other with enfilading fire. It's like a chain, you see. If Villa could break one link and get inside, he could roll up General Velasco like a rug. But that's the problem! Villa's troops can't break that first link. And until Villa breaks that link, old Huerta—El Chacal, they are starting to call him, 'The Jackal'—is safe on his throne in Mexico City." Wearily Mr. Wickwire got up, seeming to totter almost. I wondered if the leather puttees were the only thing giving support to his thin shanks. "Got to go now, and rent another car."

I could not help kidding him a little. "How many is that, now?"

He bristled. "Those were all accidents! Could have happened to anybody, dammit!" Then he grinned. "*Morning Times* treasurer says I've got to have a driver from now on." With an airy wave of his hand, he teeter-tottered out the door. I looked out the window a moment later and saw him sprawled in the back seat of a Willys touring car while a straw-hatted *mozo* drove. Maybe someday Henry Wickwire would have a story written about him; he deserved it.

The next day Dr. Raschman gave me a pretty good inspection but wouldn't take off the cast. "Young bones heal fast," he said, "but not that fast. Anyway, if it's all right with Julio, you can walk about the streets a little bit."

That elated me. A gun shop could replace the missing firing pin in my little Spanish pistol. There were a lot of pistols and revolvers about; I could easily have stolen a good one. But I had made up my mind to kill Rodolfo Fierro with that particular pistol, the one General Villa himself had given me. It seemed more appropriate, more just, that way.

General Villa set up his headquarters at a hacienda near Bermejillo, south of Torreón. So far, the campaign against the Federales, well dug in around Torreón itself, had been indecisive. General Velasco had joined forces with the respected regular army of General Medina Barrón, and together they had organized an almost impenetrable defense of the city. A succession of strong points supported each other with enfilading fire, backed up by a huge steel water tower which they had drained and cut loopholes in by acetylene torches.

Technically, General Villa had the superior forces—nine brigades of infantry and cavalry in addition to two regiments of artillery under the command of General Felipe Ángeles, the Chapultepec honors graduate. But attack after attack did not get us anywhere. The Torreón defenses caused high casualties among the Villista forces hurled against them. For a while the attacks stopped while Villa and Felipe Ángeles and the brigade commanders, including Rodolfo Fierro, tried to think of a new approach. I was grateful that Fierro was too occupied to bother with me.

It was about this time that I met a young reporter for a New York magazine called the *Metropolitan*. John Reed was tall and fair, slender, with the kind of pug-nosed face that the Mexicans call *chatito*, meaning sort of like a kitten. He rushed all over, excited, interviewing people right and left and making notes. He even said he was going to do a story about me, which I was not too happy about, fearing that somehow it might put the U.S. authorities on my trail for the murder and arson I was guilty of.

Of all people, Reed was a great favorite of Tomás Urbina, one of the toughest and most profane of Villa's generals. Urbina, whom Reed nicknamed "The Lion of Durango," was a real roughneck. I never liked or trusted Urbina but he and John Reed got along just fine. The U.S. newspapers were criticizing General Villa as a crude and reckless man, speaking more and more of Venustiano Carranza as a better choice for the presidency. Urbina got John Reed to take down his defense of Villa for the *Metropolitan*. Urbina said, "General Villa is a true patriot! He has no designs on the presidency. When we are victorious over the evil forces which confront us, the general will withdraw from politics and become a simple citizen of the new Mexico. He has told me so himself."

Of course, Urbina never talked in such a polished and fluent way. Normally, every word he spoke was followed by some variation of *chingar*. But I guess John Reed cleaned up his message; certainly he had to leave out all the *chingar*.

Many of Villa's officers did not like John Reed, seeing him as a symbol of an oppressive and changeable U.S. government. Urbina, however, quickly shut up Reed's critics. "That's enough!" he cried, brandishing his revolver. "This *compañero* comes thousands of miles to tell his people the real truth about our fight for freedom! He goes into battle without a gun, so he's braver than all of you are because you have pistols and rifles to defend yourselves! Shut up and don't sneer at him anymore or you'll feel my displeasure!"

Of course, I have cleaned up Urbina's words too.

A lot of crazy things happen during a war—at least, this war, which is the only one I really know much about. I guess wars are craziness raised to the nth degree. I know no better example of craziness than what happened at the siege of Torreón. The incident shows also a side of the Mexican character that makes things even crazier.

I was loafing in the telegraph office when General Villa himself clumped in, followed by Felipe Ángeles, our new chief of artillery. Again, the general was a long way from being the best-dressed man. He prowled around for a while, hands in pockets, wearing a dirty shirt without a collar and a badly worn and shiny brown suit. He and General Ángeles conferred for a few minutes with the head telegrapher, who didn't like me in his station but couldn't do anything about it. They finally found a telephone line to Torreón, a line unaccountably intact after Ángeles' shelling of the city. I could hear only snatches of the conversation but later I read a full account in a book called *Heroic Mexico* by a man named Johnson, like Grandpa. That book, to my mind, is the best account of the revolution ever written, though Ben Wilkerson isn't in it.

The operator rang up military headquarters in Torreón and got General Velasco, commander of the Federal forces, on the line. General Villa, drinking coffee, motioned to Felipe Ángeles to speak to Velasco. The book reports the entire conversation. I can vouch for what I heard at the other end.

"Good afternoon, Señor General Ángeles."

"Good afternoon, Señor General," said Ángeles.

"Have you taken Bermejillo already?"

"Yes, Señor General."

"I congratulate you."

"Thank you, Señor General," Ángeles said.

"Were there many casualties?"

"Hardly any, Señor General. That is why I am calling you. You will save the lives of many Mexicans by bringing your useless resistance to an end and surrendering the places you occupy."

Johnson says that General Velasco then left the line and turned over the instrument to a Colonel Solorzano, who declared that it would be the revolutionists who surrendered. General Villa, impatient, got on the telephone.

"Who is speaking?" Colonel Solorzano asked.

"Francisco Villa, *señor*."

"Francisco Villa?"

"Yes, *señor*. Francisco Villa. Your servant."

"Fine, because we are coming for you in just a moment."

"Come on, *señores*," General Villa invited. "You will be welcome."

"Good! Fix supper!"

"We'll have something warm for you." Villa grinned.

"We'll be there!"

"Good, *señor*—but if that's too much trouble, we'll come and get you. We traveled a long way just for the pleasure of seeing you, and we are tired of looking for you everywhere."

"Are there many of you?" Solorzano asked.

"Not so many, *señor*. Just a couple of regiments of artillery and ten thousand men."

In the midst of all the blood and death in the sands of Chihuahua, a polite, almost jocular conversation, including an invitation to supper, between the chiefs of the two opposing armies! *Gringos* will never understand Mexico. I am not sure Mexicans themselves do.

That spring I had plenty of time to myself. Colonel

Aguirre from time to time gave me dispatches to Carranza and Zapata, which he regarded as too important to be left to the regular railroad telegraphers. "Accuracy is very important," he instructed me. "And secrecy too, Benjamin." For a while he watched me at the key in the small *jacal* that was the Bermejillo station; then he clapped me on the back and said, "Good! Very good! General Villa can always trust you, *hombre!* He says you are his lucky piece, that he has not lost a battle since that day at Cuitla when you sent messages to Ciudad Juárez for him!" Well, that set me up, of course.

I had plenty of time to ride Pinta. Julio had brought her along with his own walleyed and fractious mount in one of the boxcars. The hills around Bermejillo were lush and green from winter rains. I enjoyed the wind in my face and the fresh smell of growing things, even though controlling Pinta was a little hard with my arm still in the cast. Finding Dr. Raschman at one of the brigade headquarters tending the wounded, I asked him about it.

"Busy now, Benjamin," he said. "Too busy! Look at all this blood, the guts, the broken bones! As your General Sherman once said, 'War is hell!' No, come to me after we take Torreón."

Disappointed, I wandered off on Pinta with Julio close behind me. We both flinched when an unexploded artillery round from Torreón whistled over our heads and dug up a clod of earth in the hillside just beyond us without exploding. In fact, we often heard short rounds while we were riding, and occasionally a spent bullet would fall near us. Infantry and cavalry charges against Torreón went on night and day, and artillery boomed deafeningly in daytime and lit up the skies at night. Riding south of Bermejillo, we came on a small Indian village. On a ridge stood a line of Indians in colorful *sarapes*, watching the battle from a distance. Julio galloped up to warn of the danger they were in.

"But, *señor!*" the head man protested, "this is where we always stand when there is a battle for Torreón!" It was a simple but profound statement; Torreón had over the years been fought for many times.

Too, I looked for Mr. Wickwire, the *Morning Times* reporter, but did not find him; I hoped he had not received his last bullet. Even if that had not happened, he was an old man, tired and infirm; natural causes could have carried him off by now. And Mr. McFall—in the distance I heard the Scottish Guards Band of Northern Mexico tootling off-tune and galloped over to General Villa's headquarters. There they were, the barely talented musicians, mangling "Camptown Races." On a wooden crate stood Mr. McFall, his own attempt at a Scottish kilt draped around his waist while he waved his violin bow that few of the musicians paid attention to. When the band had staggered through the song, I went up to him.

"Benjamin!" He pumped my hand. "So we meet again, eh, laddie?"

"Your band," I remarked, "seems to have lost some of its players, Gutiérrez, for instance? The skinny man that played the trombone?"

His face was sad. "Fierro took several of my musicians and put rifles in their hands to attack that strong point over there." He pointed with the stick at a hillock wreathed in smoke. "We lost Gutiérrez and Paco Ramírez and others. Now there are only a handful of us left."

I went quickly away when Rodolfo Fierro came out of the half-wrecked adobe headquarters building. He looked cross and tired and dirty, angrily flinging away a cigarette as if something had gone wrong in brigade headquarters.

Now I come to something completely horrible, something I can never forget. It is burned into my soul like a cattle brand, but it never fades, as does a brand when hair at last grows over it. No, nothing has grown over this brand, and never will.

It came about like this. After several fruitless charges against the fortifications of Torreón, one led by General Villa himself, he and Felipe Ángeles and the various brigade commanders had a long conference. Rodolfo Fierro, after a lot of arguing, won out with his idea of how to breach the deadly circle of strong points. All this I heard from my good friend Ojo Parado, who was a great gossip.

"But what is his idea?" I asked. "This great idea of Fierro's?"

He shook his head and rolled the glass eye at me. "*Quién sabe*? That is kept a great secret. But I have heard it involves Señor McFall and his band of musicians."

"Mr. McFall and his band? How in the world . . . ?"

"That is all I know, *amigo*."

I hastened to find Mr. McFall. He was as puzzled as I was, and both of us had a presentiment of something bad. "If you find out anything more," he said, "I hope you will let me know at once, Ben."

"Of course," I agreed.

We found out about it all too soon. Late that afternoon Mr. McFall was summoned to the headquarters of Rodolfo Fierro's Ninth Brigade. Later I came on him sitting on an empty ammunition box, violin across his knees. The sun was setting and the air cold and biting.

"You ought to put on a *sarape*," I advised. "You will catch your death of cold sitting out here."

He looked up, tragedy in his eyes. "To die of cold might be better."

I didn't get his meaning. "Better? Better than what?"

"Better that to be spitted on a bayonet."

I sat down beside him. "Whatever are you talking about?" I thought his trials and tribulations with the Scottish Guards Band might have unhinged his mind. It could certainly happen.

Shaking his head, he fumbled at the long eyebrows, now drooping over tired eyes. "You haven't heard?"

"Heard what, for heaven's sake?"

He gestured with his violin bow toward the strong point of the Federales which Villa's soldiers were beginning to call Loma de Muerte, the Hill of Death. Already Fierro's brigade had lost more than fifty men trying to take it and thus break the iron chain around Torreón. "My Scottish Guards Band is supposed to take that hill."

"What?" My mouth dropped open.

"Well, not exactly *take* it! But the band is essential to Fierro's plan, approved by General Villa, and to take place as soon as it is good and dark." His voice had died away to little more than a husky whisper, and he took out a handkerchief and blew his nose hard. Beginning again, he said, "It was all decided this afternoon. Fierro, I am told, spoke to General Villa about the element of surprise in warfare. Well, my band is Fierro's idea of surprise. When it is full dark, we are to march toward Torreón by the Nazareno road."

I knew that road. The Nazareno road, shell-pocked for miles, was covered by artillery night and day.

"We are to create a diversion," Fierro said. Joking, though it was a deadly joke, he said my band would create a diversion anywhere. But the purpose of this move was to distract the Federales while the Ninth Brigade slips up on the . . . what do they call it? . . . . ah, yes—the Hill of Death."

"But that's murder!" I cried. "You will all be killed!"

Mr. McFall nodded. "Probably so."

"But . . . but . . ."

"Fierro said the musicians could draw rifles and ammunition from our stores to defend themselves, if they liked. But can a musician shoot with a rifle while he is playing his trombone, eh?"

"How can he do this?" I cried. "You know as well as I do, Mr. McFall, that this is plain murder! And the reason is—"

"I know the reason as well as you do, Ben," he interrupted. Then, trying a little humor, he said, "Fierro is obviously not a music lover. He can no longer stand our sour emanations."

"Don't joke about this!" I protested. "Fierro has been planning something like this ever since you made that bargain with Mr. Donald Stuart and tried to help me escape to El Paso! That sticks in Fierro's craw!"

Mr. McFall shrugged. "Oh, he had an audience when he told me the plan! There were a lot of his staff officers there, and much talk about how we should be happy to risk our lives in the service of the revolution. And make no mistake about it—Fierro will have some of his ruffians detached to make sure we march on time and don't run away, which I am tempted to do, even if it means abandoning my musicians and my plans for them!" He rubbed fingers over the polished wood of his violin, slowly, lovingly. "I had thought to give a gala concert when General Villa took Mexico City, but—"

"Well," I said, "Fierro can't get away with this! I'll see to that!"

"What can you do? No, I will sit here until time to go, and think about Leith and our old house and Mother in the kitchen running up a batch of scones, hot, with churned butter and . . ."

I left and hurried to Rodolfo Fierro's tent. A sentry tried to bar my way but I pushed him aside. Fierro, lying on a cot, had a bottle of imported Scotch whiskey on the table beside him, and was reading *Universal* by lamplight.

"What the hell do you want, you little bastard?"

I was hot. "I want to know why you intend to murder poor old Mr. McFall, who never did any harm to anybody!"

He shrugged, turned back to his newspaper. "He is a meddling old fart who always turned you against me!"

"Listen!" I said. "He is my friend, and I'll go to General Villa and—"

He stood up, folding the paper. "You will go to nobody, you conniving fool! The general has already approved my plan. And as for you, I should have killed you too, at Cuitla, that first day. *Ay*, if I had known then how you would dishonor my daughter, my Valentina, who has been the only sweet and good thing in my life—"

I was reckless. "Has she learned, then, what a vile and evil man her father is?"

He struck me across the face and I reeled back from the blow. It drew blood, too, from my teeth being mashed against the inside of my cheek. I tasted the sticky salty blood, and spat. Maybe a tooth had gone.

"I would have disposed of you a long time ago, Benjamin, if you had not by some trickery become the general's favorite! Even now I must put up with you because it would be awkward to account for you to Pancho! But hear me now! If it should come about that my daughter is pregnant by you, nothing will stand in my way! I will crunch you under my heel like a cockroach, a dirty cockroach, a shit-eating scuttling Texas cockroach! Do you hear me?"

He called to the sentry, one of his damned sneaky Yaqui scouts. "León, take this boy out of my tent and give him a kick in the butt, too!"

León grabbed me by the scruff of the neck and dragged me outside. He was lean, almost skinny, like the others of his tribe, but amazing strength was in those slender brown arms. Laughing, he hurled me down the hill on which sat Fierro's tent. The mocking sound followed me as I staggered away, sick at heart. My mouth was still bleeding.

Dizzy and confused, I sat on a pile of old railroad ties, wondering what to do. In the distance I heard the Scottish Guards Band of Northern Mexico, the few that were left, anyway, dispiritedly attacking "Jesusita en Chihuahua," the general's favorite song. I took out my mouth-organ, just about the last thing I had left from my boyhood in Hudspeth County, Texas, and played softly along with them. Julio had lost track of me for once, and when I heard him squalling my name, angry, I decided what to do.

That awful night on the Nazareno road, my broken arm still in its itching cast, I shot my first man—with deadly intent, that is. Of course, I had peppered Donald Stuart with my Greener shotgun, but my intent was only against his flying machine. This night, however, I truly shot a man—a simple-looking man who was probably an unwilling conscript. It was different from Mr. Stuart because this time the man knew I had shot him but *I* didn't; I always said wars were crazy!

At sundown the sky was like a bloodstained canopy to match the ground over which the two armies fought. As darkness fell, the ruddy explosions of artillery shells took the place of the failing sun. Nervously the remnants of the Scottish Guards Band of Northern Mexico gathered along the Nazareno road, herded into column by a couple of Rodolfo Fierro's plug-uglies. A rind of moon was in the western sky. In the pale light filtering through the leaves of the cottonwoods Mr. McFall's face was ghost-pale as he

202

moved about in that ridiculous kilt he insisted on wearing. He came up short when he saw me.

"Ben! Ben Wilkerson! What are you doing here?"

I held up my mouth-organ. "You're short of musicians, I see. I've come along to fill in."

He was agitated. "No, no! I forbid it, Ben! Save yourself! There's no reason to—"

"Move back!" One of Fierro's ruffians gave Mr. McFall a shove. "And keep your men in line, Señor Músico!"

We were all ghosts in the night, or soon to be, anyway. Mr. McFall's musicians in their white *manta* shirts and pants milled around, talking nervously in low tones. There was a lot of crossing themselves. From time to time one or another of them would look at Fierro's men as if calculating the chances of running away, but a menacing gesture with a rifle rapidly changed their minds.

"I can't allow it!" Mr. McFall cried. He called to one of the plug-uglies but I quickly put a hand over his mouth.

"Don't! I'd rather be with you at whatever end we're due for."

"But—"

A red star shell curved up into the sky, the signal for the advance on the Hill of Death to be led by the Scottish Guards Band.

"*Apúrense, músicos.*" One of Fierro's men grinned. "Get going! You will all be heroes soon. Think of that, eh?"

In the red-spattered half-light Mr. McFall felt for my hand. A tear rolled down his cheek. "Then I guess this is it, Ben, old comrade!"

I swallowed a big lump in my throat. "I guess so. But I want you to know I've been proud to know you, Mr. McFall, and count you as my friend!"

"Get along there!" A rifle butt hit me in the small of the back. In the darkness I guess none of Fierro's men recognized me, thinking I was just another of the *músicos*. My back pains me in that spot till this day, although it is only one of the many *achaques*, the word Mexicans use to cover all the pains and illnesses, the aches and indispositions of old age.

As we moved unwillingly forward, Mr. McFall muttered, "Lord! I wish we had a proper piper!"

Atop the Hill of Death was the huge metal water tower, bulking gray and ominous in the night. Rifle fire already sparked from it in anticipation of the attack by General Villa. The orange-yellow spurts looked like a jeweled necklace around the huge iron cylinder. Bullets clipped leaves from the cottonwoods that lined the Nazareno road. We all cringed, only to be hazed forward again by Fierro's men.

"*Apúrense, cabrones!* Play, play! *Más alto*! Louder, louder!"

Mr. McFall started to saw on his violin as we came out from under the shelter of the cottonwoods onto the stark sandy plain that gradually sloped upward to the iron monster on the hill. Fat Nadal, puffing halfheartedly into his tuba, broke off as a bullet tore a raged hole in the battered brass bell of the instrument. "*Aieee!*" he quavered, staggering forward as one of Fierro's roughnecks shoved him.

Battered by repeated blows from gun butts, the band started an off-key rendition of "Adelita."

"Louder!" Fierro's men shouted. "More noise, *hombres!* They must know that an army of *músicos* is about to attack them!" Safe in the ditch alongside the road, they jeered and laughed, made fun of the sorry band.

Warm sand crunching under our boots, we plodded upward, steadily upward, trying not to look at the iron death machine crowning the hill. The off-key rendition of "Adelita" wailed a kind of dirge in the bullet-laced air:

> I'm a soldier and my nation calls me
> To fight in the fields of strife.
> Adelita, Adelita of my soul!
> For the love of God do not forget me!

Things—bullets—whistled above my ears thick as honeybees around a hive. Flinching, Mr. McFall and I trudged on, him skreeling on his violin and me blowing "Adelita" into my mouth-organ. Whether from panic or the difficult footing in the sand, I didn't know, but I was short of breath. Looking behind, I was horrified to see several crumpled white forms flung on the sand. Nadal's tuba stuck up beside him like a monument while he twisted in agony. The skinny trombone player bent in the middle like a jointed toy and sank to his knees, trying to prop himself up with the instrument.

"Don't look back, laddie!" Mr. McFall gritted between his teeth. "Keep going, Ben! Look, there is the white rocket! That means Fierro's brigade is starting to attack from the other side! That should take some of the pressure off us!"

Now it seemed there were only a handful of us—the drummer, staggering along and sounding out a slow and funereal beat, a gangling trumpet player, tootling valiantly with his eyes tightly closed against the bulletry, Mr. McFall, and me; I guess that was all that was left of the dozen or so benighted *músicos*. The rest had been shot down, either by Federal bullets or, more likely, by Fierro's men when they hesitated. By now, however, the bastards had deserted us to join their own brigade. We were alone, terribly alone, like bugs under a descending flyswatter.

> If Adelita left me for another
> I would pursue her endlessly,
> In a warship if she went by ocean,
> In a military train on land.

That was how "Adelita" went, all right. But what was Mr. McFall playing? I couldn't follow him with my mouthorgan. Now that Fierro's men had abandoned us, it was time to cut and run, dodge across the road into the ditch, and maybe save ourselves. I tugged at his arm, suddenly realizing what he was playing—"The Campbells Are Coming," the old Scottish war song.

Ignoring my pulling at him, he marched steadily on. "By God!" he cried. "I'll not go to my death with a foreign song in my ears! No, goddammit all, I'm a Scot, and I'll die like a Scot!"

I had never heard him swear before and it was the last time, too. Though Fierro's attack was already swarming up the hill to the west of us, myriads of white-clad *soldados* kneeling to fire, only to dash forward again, the fusillade from the deadly water tower seemed still to direct most of its energy on what was left of the Scottish Guards Band of Northern Mexico.

"Mr. McFall!" I tried again, grabbing at him. "Leave off, dammit! We can get away now!" It was hard, because I had to hold the mouth-organ in my mouth with my teeth while tugging at him with my good hand. The broken arm, still in its cast, dangled at my side. Just then a bullet hit the cast and tore off a chunk, raising a cloud of white powder that made me sneeze. While I was searching the ground for the mouth-organ that had dropped out of my teeth, I heard Mr. McFall make a kind of wheeze or gasp.

"What . . . what is it?" I asked, getting painfully to my knees. "Are you hit?"

"Nae mind," he muttered, unaccountably speaking a broad Scots brogue I had never heard him use, something that reminded me eerily of the black doll in the burning aeroplane—Mr. Donald Stuart, the Highland pilot. "Nae-thing to worrit aboot, lad."

"But you . . ."

He staggered; his knees went out from under him. Slowly, very slowly, he sat down in the sand. By what seemed a tremendous effort, he carefully laid down his violin, placing the bow across it.

"You're hit!" I squatted beside him. "Where are you hit?"

Slowly he fell back. I got my arm under his head, trying to hold him up. "Oh, Mr. McFall! Where . . . where . . . ?"

"In the side, laddie," he muttered. Blood began to fill his mouth, dripping a dark stain in the sand. "Only a scratch, I'm sure, but ye ken it will do, it will do! As Mercutio said in *Romeo and Juliet*." Blood soaked into the white shirt, made sodden the threadbare vest across which once swung the precious gold watch and chain.

I looked wildly around. What to do? Now there was little fire at us. Fierro's brigade had reached the water tower and were dug in around it, rising to fire and then dropping down behind the little hills of earth they dug with machetes.

"Ben . . ."

"Yes, sir."

"Not much time," he gasped. "Not much . . ." He spat blood, and I wiped his mouth with my sleeve. "Be true to yourself, laddie." He coughed hard, and for a moment was silent; his eyes, staring upward at the slice of moon, were galzed. "Be true, as Mr. Shakespeare said in another . . . another . . ." His head dropped over; he gasped again, a long rattling sound.

"Mr. McFall! Please! Don't . . . don't die!" He was all I had left. My cheeks were wet with tears; my hands, holding him, wet with blood.

With a tremendous effort he seemed to gather himself. Trembling, one hand rose to touch my cheek. "True," he murmured. "Always . . . true, laddie. Remember that—for me, an old sinner. Remember . . ." There was one last convulsion, and the life drained from him.

Only a few random bullets now seared the night over my head, but from the water tower the racket was deafening, echoing and reechoing in the night. Felipe Ángeles had started his bombardment. It looked like some of the shells were falling on our own men. Well, who cared? I mean, who cared about a few Mexican lives lost in the fight for freedom? They were only poor and ignorant men, and you can't make a revolution without men dying. Dizzy, spent with weariness and emotion, I stood up, trying to clean the blood from my hands by wiping them on my pants.

Mr. McFall was dead; I felt dead too. The dead seem so small, so calm, like children who do not yet know the hurts of life. Gently I picked up the battered violin and laid it across his chest. Then I stuck the bow in the sand beside him. I didn't know any appropriate thing to say but I remembered a Latin phrase Mr. Dinwiddie once told me about; things like that stick in my mind. The Romans used to say it about their great men when they died.

"*Ave!*" I said. "'*Ave atque vale!* Hail and farewell, Mr. McFall."

Finding a Krag rifle and a cartridge belt half-buried in the sand from a previous assault on the Hill of Death, I picked them up, shook the sand out of the rifle, and loaded it. *Chingado*! I thought. *Chingado* for good! What a useful, what a necessary and all-covering word! *Chingado*, Ben Wilkerson! I wanted to die right then, die beside my friend Mr. George McFall, born in Leith, Scotland, in 1857. But now no one was shooting at me. I would have to go up the Hill of Death and stand in front of that damned water tower to seek my end. *Chingado*!

— 11 —

As Dr. Velásquez and I talk in the patio of my house at Parral, burning moonlight floods the area. The moon of Mexico is like that, almost a secondary sun. This night the ancient white tower of the church at Parral seems to float in the velvety sky. Night birds sing, and there is the plash of water in the fountain with the cherubs. I live well at Parral, but it was not always so.

"I am not satisfied with your progress, Don Benjamin," Dr. Velásquez says, drawing deep on one of my Havana cigars. The coal glows red, then diminishes. "'Magdalena says you are very uncooperative about the medicines I prescribed."

I draw too on my cigar, which the doctor has forbidden. He looks at me with exasperation, and shrugs.

"Your medicines make me ill, Señor Doctor. Is that the way medicines are supposed to work?"

I like to joke with Velásquez; he is always so serious. Maximilián Velásquez is a good doctor. He was a surgeon to the Federal forces at Torreón, escaping after Villa took the place. But that was a long time ago; now we are friends, and do not talk of politics. Mexican politics often lead to loss of friendships, sometimes even the shedding of blood. I have seen too much of blood.

"You had best be careful!" Dr. Velásquez wags his finger. "Magdalena says you sometimes faint, and fall down! That is a bad sign!"

"My life has been lived under a bad sign," I say. "Anyway, to feel faint is nothing new to me. I have described to you what happened to me after Torreón, after my friend Mr. McFall was killed. I remember feeling faint, then I slipped into a kind of daze. I could see, feel, hear—all those things. But for a week or more I was a walking ghost. All seemed to me distant and unreal. They say I talked nonsense and stared at things no one else could see. And I remembered nothing of what happened after Mr. McFall was killed. Doctor, tell me—was there a medicine for that strange thing that happened?"

He flicks ash from the good cigar and sips a whiskey and water Magdalena brought. "I do not know of such a medicine. This thing, Don Benjamin, happens inside the brain, where we physicians are not able to go. But I have heard of such things, and understand how they are caused. Sometimes, when the mind has been subjected to horrors it can no longer accommodate, there is within the brain a mechanism which simply turns it off, turns off the brain, until it can recover."

I nod. "That is a reasonable explanation."

"It takes a while, then, for the brain to rest and prepare itself for further impressions."

"About a week, in my case."

"Yes. And, being at that time a young boy, it is likely that the horrors you saw were more vivid than they would be to a grown man—an experienced soldier, for instance." He shook his head. "Old soldiers! They have seen so much blood that the brain is permanently turned off, it seems to me. They are not moved by it; it has no meaning to them. It is a pity!"

In the moonlight the tawny peaks that surround Parral are gentle and silvered but I do not mistake their changed appearance. They are cruel mountains; all the mountains in Mexico are cruel. So many of us died in that march up the Sierra de la Silla.

With a disapproving look Magdalena brings us more whiskey and water, then disappears into the house.

"Well," I say, "I was at that time certainly not an old soldier. Perhaps I was not even a soldier. But they said I was very brave. And I did not know that I had been brave until my friend Ojo Parado, with some help from the good

210

Colonel Aguirre, he of the kind face and crossed eyes, told me about it. And I could not believe it!''

After all these years I still want to talk about it, almost as if by talk I can lay phantoms to rest. While Dr. Velásquez nods over his whiskey I maunder on and on, remembering.

One morning I woke to the sound of a song outside a window in the Hotel Superba. Someone was playing a guitar and singing a love song:

> I am going to lose myself from thee,
> Exhausted with weeping;
> I am going sailing, sailing,
> By the shores of the sea.

A new morning had come, fresh-washed by the night mist. The sky was blue and gold—flame-trimmed white clouds over a brazen and lustrous desert, every bush standing out clear in the dawn, every sound clear and precise, every color remarkably vivid. I remember that in the street below, a funeral procession passed. A harpist, lugging his heavy instrument, played a waltz called "Recuerdos de Durango." Following him came four men carrying a canopy decorated with gold and silver tassels. On the canopy lay the body of a little girl with bare feet, brown hands crossed on her breast. A wreath of paper flowers was in her hair, and her lifeless form was heaped with them. And in the wake of the harpist's music and the silent mourners came the timeless *pat-pat-pat* of a woman making tortillas. My senses had recovered.

Below my balcony old Ojo Parado was strolling, chewing on a *tamal*, pulling along a balky hound with lop ears and a sad expression. He saw me and his wrinkled face lit up. "Benjamin—*chamaco!* Now you look well! *Gracias a Dios!*"

"Wait for me!" I called. "I'm coming down! I'm hungry!"

"'No, you wait there, *chamaco!* I'll come up!" Dragging the protesting hound, he disappeared. A moment later he clattered into the room.

"This dog," he said, "is a thoroughbred lion dog! After

the war I am going to hunt mountain lions with this dog and make a lot of money. Mountain lions kill sheep and cattle, you know, and ranchers will pay me money to rid their lands of the pests!"

The hound looked remarkably meek to be a lion dog. Ojo Parado tied him to my bedpost, saying, "He is very fierce and I must keep him under control at all times." Wheezing, he sat on my bed, saying, "Well, you have regained your senses, eh?"

"I think so. At least the world looks good to me this morning."

He shook his head. "*Qué caray*—you were brave! All the Ninth Brigade talks about it!"

I was embarrassed but didn't want to say anything; to admit, possibly, that I had gone loco.

"That water tower! You banged on it with your carbine till it rang like a church bell—and your poor arm still in a cast!"

Dim images floated in my mind: the great iron water tower, ringed by spurts of rifle fire . . .

"They followed you, cheering, and Emilio Guzmán threw an iron bomb into one of the rifle holes. *Jesús!* There was such an explosion! It killed a lot of the damned Federales, and those that were left were so dizzy that our machetes made short work of them!"

"I . . . I did that?"

Ojo Parado grinned a toothless grin. "Now you remember, eh? But I am sorry your Señor McFall was killed." His face became sober. "He was a good man, but not much of a musician!"

"He was the best," I said. "I . . . I will miss him." Almost, tears came, but I winked them back.

"You came on a rifle pit," Ojo Parado went on, "and when the damned Federal rose up, you shot him through the head with a carbine someone had dropped and went plunging and galloping up the hill, whinnying and screaming like a fierce Durango horse!"

I swallowed hard. "I killed someone? A . . . man?"

"A perfect bull's-eye!" Excited, he went on with his story while the lion dog looked at him with eager eyes. "I saw it all, *chamaco*, with my own eyes! As you stood above Señor McFall it looked like you were saying a prayer for him."

"I don't know any real prayers, I'm ashamed to say," I muttered.

"Then you ran up the hill toward that iron monster, shooting. Well, you know those heavy iron sheets shed bullets like a duck the rain! Those Federales made the air thick with their bullets and the Ninth Brigade was pinned down, as they say. But you came on, shooting and screaming insults at those bastards!" The hound raised beseeching eyes and he gave it the rest of his *tamal*. "And when the men saw you, so brave, General Villa said '*Compañeros*, let's not let that *gringo* boy shame the men of the División del Norte!' He raised his sword and we all ran up the hill following you."

I had killed my first man, then—intentionally, that is. I felt sick. He had probably been a poor peasant youth pressed into the army, and I had killed him.

"Now, *chamaco*, you are properly blooded! In Mexico, you know, a boy does not become a man until he has drawn the blood of an enemy!" He brushed his hands free of crumbs and said, "No more, Hércules," to the lion dog. Turning to me, he went on.

"When that bitch of an iron tower was taken, all the other strong points fell, one after the other. And there was rich looting to be had, also. I am sorry it is too late now for you to join us. But I have a fine cloth suit, three pairs of American shoes, a sack full of glass eyes I took from an optometrist's shop, and a German camera, although someone robbed all the film from the shelves before I could get any. This fine dog I took possession of also."

So I had been heroic at the battle of the water tower! I couldn't believe it; I was hardly a heroic person. But Colonel Aguirre later confirmed it all.

"General Villa," he said, "has taken note of your heroism in dispatches." Smiling broadly, he clapped me on the back. "There is to be a ceremony tomorrow in the general's private railroad car at three P.M. I am to bring you there, Benjamin. Wear your best clothing."

Dr. Raschman had taken off my plaster cast, and that arm looked wasted and crooked. He said it would gain strength and straighten out, but to this day it is weaker than the other. I was practically in rags. The English tweed coat was torn and dirty, I had lost a boot, my hair was long and uncut, and I was out of bilimbiques.

"Here," Colonel Aguirre said, handing me a wad of bills. "Dress yourself well, *hijo*, and get your hair cut, also!"

As Ojo Parado said, it was a great victory. But General Villa's great victories were usually attained by great losses also; I was shocked at the casualties on both sides. Colonel Aguirre, in charge of giving information to the press, estimated our losses at five hundred dead and perhaps fifteen hundred wounded. The losses of the Federales, he emphasized, were much more—as many as a thousand killed and twice that many wounded.

Disposing of the dead, both Villistas and Federales, was quickly undertaken to prevent the outbreak of disease. Many bodies were buried in shallow trenches, but that took too much time and labor. Thousands were thrown into abandoned mine shafts. Still more were stacked like cordwood onto railroad flatcars and hauled out into the desert, where they were dumped, a feast for buzzards and coyotes. Hundreds more were piled in ricks in the city plaza, doused with gasoline, and burned.

Freshly barbered, wearing a white manta coat and pants, new boots polished to brilliance, and a Jalisco sombrero on my shorn curls, I held my nose as I passed such a horrible bonfire and hurried into a church. Seeing all this carnage, I decided that maybe Valentina was right: maybe there was a God after all, a wrathful God who was fed up with man's wars. Maybe I had better "copper my bets," as the gamblers put it. Anyway, my experiences of the last few months had made me a good candidate for some kind of spiritual renewal. I needed someone, something, to lean on in time of crisis. I did not feel comfortable with Grandpa Johnson's fierce and vengeful God, hoping for something or someone more gentle and understanding. But I had to work with what there was. Maybe the Blessed Virgin?

A cloud of blue incense crawled out of the dark doorway of the church. Inside, I watched others dip fingers into a basin and cross themselves; I did likewise. Down front, all was a glitter of red and gold, lit by many candles. That area, I figured, was best left to the true believers. I, still not completely decided, would sit in the back, watch, listen, and wait for a revelation.

There was a hum of mumbled prayer, a sound like bees around a flower, a flower that might have been the figure of Christ in agony on the cross that was the centerpiece of the altar. People, mostly humble farmers, *pacíficos*, those who had taken no part on either side of the warring factions, came and went. A Villista officer sauntered in, looked thoughtfully at the sheen of gold leaf on the magnificent wooden altar, and departed.

It was warm in the church. In spite of my attention to God I began to feel drowsy; I found my mind wandering. McNary came again to mind in my reverie, in Hudspeth County, Texas, so far away and so long ago, *Prue Ballard, the golden girl, she of the chestnut curls in rich foliage, and the proud walk.* Starting, I looked around in alarm. Surely thoughts like these, impure thoughts, had no place in a holy temple. But no one had noticed.

Mr. McFall—where was he now? My lips moved soundlessly as I did my best to compose a prayer for his safety and ultimate rest in the arms of the Blessed Virgin or whatever. *Mr. McFall, here in this Mexican church I am thinking of you. I will never forget you. In the way of men, I loved you. You were a real and a precious father to me. And I will someday kill Rodolfo Fierro for what he did to you.* Again I looked around, sensible of guilt. Such murderous thoughts probably had no place here either.

Valentina—where was little Valentina now? In that damned convent, being scourged by cruel nuns, persecuted by that bloodhound of a Father Eusebio, aware now—cruelly aware—that her father was El Carnicero, Villa's Butcher, the vicious killer who had slain innocent young David Berlanga, who laughed as he shot Federal prisoners trying to scramble over that wall at Ciudad Juárez. I murmured a small prayer for Valentina. I wasn't sure it was in the right form for a Catholic church, but it was the best I could do. *Someday, Valentina, I will come to you in that convent and carry you away on my horse, just like the knights of old did in storybooks.*

Outside, the bright sun hurt my eyes. It took me a moment to make out Ojo Parado, squatting on the steps and smoking a cornhusk cigarette. The mangy "lion hound" sat dolefully at his feet, secured by a length of hemp rope to an iron grille.

"I saw you go in there. Did you find God in there, *chamaco?*"

I shrugged. "I don't know. But it is always a good idea to take advantage of anything that might work to one's benefit. I would pray to a witch doctor if I thought it would help."

He scratched the hound's ears. "Praying did not help our good old Victoria."

"What do you mean?"

He crushed the cigarette butt under a bare heel. "Why, you didn't know?"

After all I had been through, I was in a snappish mood. "Know what, dammit all?"

"That night you were so brave, one of Velasco's shells exploded in an old house where Victoria and some other women were cooking beans for the soldiers. She died quickly, thanks to God or whoever it is that takes care of such things."

I felt another upwelling of grief. Valentina gone, Mr. McFall dead at the attack on the water tower, good old Victoria killed. It was too much.

"Victoria prayed a lot," Ojo Parado said, untying the knot in the rope, "and she is dead. Your Valentina prayed a lot, and she might as well be dead. Myself, I never pray. I even doubt the existence of God. Yet, I am here." He clapped me on the shoulder. "And you are here, Benjamin! What does it all mean, eh?"

I didn't know.

Now, after Torreón, Villa was magnificently supplied. It was said he had over five million cartridges in warehouses at Ciudad Juárez. There was a huge supply of heavy weapons—some taken from the Federales, many purchased new in the United States by Samuel Ravel, Villa's agent in El Paso. Ravel also sold the cattle the general had taken on raids against the rich *hacendados*, but the agent was getting nervous at the pressure put on him by the U.S. State Department. Anyway, the División del Norte now had locomotives, rolling stock, a complete railway system with hundreds of cars for automobiles and artillery pieces, boxcars for the troops, and cattle cars for the thousands of horses. Spirited cavalry charges, often led by Rodolfo Fierro, were the hallmark of Villa's campaigns until Felipe Ángeles taught him the proper use of artillery, but horses were still important.

The many generals each had a private car, and there were well-equipped hospital cars complete with operating tables, surgeons, and a supply of bandages and medicines. Inside they were enameled a spotless white; on the outside they bore a large blue cross and a sign—"Servicio Sanitario." The general now commanded an army of over twelve thousand men, marching with well-made leather shoes instead of bare feet or worn *huaraches*. His staff had changed, too, for the better. Many of his officers were now regulars, graduates of Chapultepec, like Felipe Ángeles, who had deserted the Federal forces in disgust at the government's policies. Altogether, the División del Norte had become a magnificent fighting machine, more powerful than anything President Huerta could put in the field, and infinitely larger than the raggle-taggle band of Emiliano Zapata, still struggling for freedom in the mountains to the south.

A being so powerful as Francisco Villa could not help but attract a crowd of hangers-on. Every day his red caboose was besieged by newspaper reporters, soldiers of fortune, foreign emissaries anxious to make friends with the powerful man who might soon rule Mexico. Professional soldiers also came from European countries to join Villa. The usually pleasant Colonel Aguirre became fretful and impatient as he tried to sift out the gold from the dross. For instance, there was the case of Mr. Ambrose Bierce.

Bierce was an erect and powerfully built old man, more than seventy years old, with a curly white beard and penetrating blue eyes. He had worked for the Hearst newspapers but after a series of reverses he came to Mexico. Why? No one seemed to know. He did not appear to be in search of articles for Mr. Hearst, and after Colonel Aguirre approved, he was allowed to travel with General Villa's headquarters. Mr. Bierce had a biting wit and was almost vicious at times, spouting epigrams to cover every situation. I remember Colonel Aguirre telling Bierce that as soon as Huerta was overthrown, Mexico would have a democratic government, with a vote for everyone, rich or poor.

"The vote . . . Ah!" Bierce jeered. "Do you know, Colonel, what the vote represents? It is the instrument of a free man's power to make a fool of himself and wreck his country! That is all the vote means!"

Colonel Aguirre did not care much for Mr. Bierce. But the old man had a fund of bawdy jokes, and General Villa, for a time, at least, was fond of him as a sort of court jester.

Unfortunately, General Villa's victory at Torreón was accompanied by excesses which caused international concern. Although forbidden by División order, looting, abuse of foreign nationals, and unprovoked murders were commonplace. To escape execution, many rich and well-connected ranchers, businessmen, clergy, and government officials were forced to pay heavy ransoms to Villa. It was later said that over more than a quarter-million pesos were thus extorted. Villa's cavalry stabled their mounts on the lower floors of government buildings, fine homes, even in churches, trampling manure into parquetry floors. Leon J. Canova, a special agent for the U.S. government, was appalled at what was going on and wrote highly critical though sometimes misinformed dispatches to President Woodrow Wilson. To some extent, these excesses were the seed that eventually led to Villa's downfall, though that came much later.

The general's caboose was elegant. Chintz curtains hung at the windows. On the walls were tacked a lot of showy posters showing ladies in theatrical poses with very little clothing. There was a portrait of Rodolfo Fierro, of whom it was said that Francisco Villa loved him like a brother, and a portrait of Venustiano Carranza, now Villa's reluctant ally but soon to part company with him. Inside, the caboose was divided by a partition into two rooms. One room was the kitchen, presided over by Fong, General Villa's beloved Chinese cook. The other room was a combined bedroom/staff conference room where most of the general's business was conducted. Two double-width bunks folded up against the wall in the daytime. General Villa and Felipe Ángeles slept on one; the other was occupied by Dr. Raschman and at times by Fierro. This afternoon there was little space left for the generals and staff officers who crowded the room, along with photographers, reporters, and moving-picture men. Seeing the cameras made me think of Mr. Tom Mix and his caution to me. Where are you now, Mr. Mix? You were surely right. *Stay away from Fierro—he likes young boys*! Too, he had said, "Stick with Villa, kid! He's a great man, and you can get more gold that way than grubbing in a fucking creek!" He seemed to have been right on both counts, and while I hadn't amassed any great stock of gold, I had a lot of bilimbique notes anyway.

I was pretty uneasy in that assemblage of decorated generals, diplomatic representatives, and the press, but Colonel Aguirre pushed me forward. "Here, sir, is the *gringo* boy you asked to see."

General Villa sat on the edge of his bunk in his underwear. Scrubbing his short-cut hair with his knuckles, he yawned and blinked, scratched an armpit while an orderly brought a basin and razor to shave the stubble on his chin and trim the brushy mustache.

"*El gringuito, eh*?" He yawned, stretching hairy thick arms. "Our little hero, *verdad*?"

"Yes, sir," Colonel Aguirre said.

I saw Rodolfo Fierro at a grimy, smoky window of the caboose, elbow on the sill, watching me with what might have been pride. Mr. Wickwire, too, notebook in hand and pencil poised, beamed at me.

"Well!" The general got up, waving away the barber, and scratched his behind. Bearlike, he shuffled over to me and put a fatherly hand on my head. "Benjamin, is it not?"

"Yes, sir."

I must say right here that with all the talk, even with the evidence that Francisco Villa was a cruel and vindictive man, he was always kind to me, a homeless waif. It was known that he had family and children all over Chihuahua; in fact, at Torreón he married still another "wife" without divorcing any of the others. But that was his business and did not concern me, who was an immoral person of another sort. Still, Mr. Leon Canova vented his disapproval of the general's ways in another shocked dispatch to President Wilson in Washington.

"Young man," General Villa said, taking a box and opening it, "you are a true hero of the revolution! By your brave deed in assaulting that shit-box of an iron tower on the hill, you probably helped to make our great victory possible!"

"Yes, sir," I mumbled, and then felt foolish. Was I agreeing that I was a hero?

The general went on, speaking the rude Spanish of the very poor. Felipe Ángeles, Colonel Aguirre, Rodolfo Fierro—all were careful to speak something very close to pure Castilian. Fierro, as I have said, frequently used a little French. But sometimes I had to struggle to make out what the general was saying because he used so many folk expressions and pure Indian words.

". . . this medal," he was saying, "which very few men attain or deserve."

He took out the medal, dangled it in his stubby fingers. It was *the* medal, the one they said you had to be killed three times before they would even consider you for it.

"Your services," the general went on, "in the cause of our great revolution, have been a great boon, *chamaco*. But you are now relieved of such duty, to serve as my personal runner at División headquarters. What do you think of that, eh, my little *gringo* telegrapher?"

I really don't think Fierro had been expecting that, having considered me his private property.

"And so . . ." He pinned the shiny medal with its colored ribbon to the white cotton of my shirt. Stepping back, he saluted me. "'It is heroes that win revolutions! You are a hero, Benjamin, and the Mexican people are in your debt!"

I was blinded by the flash things that went off in my face. Awkwardly I stuck out my hand and General Villa clasped it. "In the morning, come to me," he said. "I will instruct you in your new duties at that time."

Colonel Aguirre led me out on the back platform of the caboose while reporters and photographers tugged at me and demanded my time. I nodded to my friend Mr. Wickwire, indicating that I would see him privately later.

"This is a great experience for any man," Colonel Aguirre said. "I myself would be proud to have such a decoration, Benjamin. Wear it with pride, and never dishonor it!"

On my way back to the Hotel Superba the moving-picture men and photographers still dogged my steps, along with a worshipful gaggle of small boys and girls waving flags of the revolution. I fled, and they pursued me. Finally I reached the hotel, bolted through the lobby, and ran up three flights without waiting for the ancient wire-cage elevator. Somehow two or three reporters had gotten there ahead of me but I crashed past them into my room and bolted the door. Gasping for breath, I collapsed on the bed. After a while they went away, angry and frustrated. Shakily I got up and poured myself a glass of water from the *olla*. Then I took off my medal and laid it on the bureau. I was tired, very tired, and did not care too much for this business of being famous.

For a while I slept. Then, hearing a small knock at the door, I woke.

"Ben? This is Mr. Wickwire. Can I come in?"

Feeling light-headed after all that had happened, I shambled to the door and opened it. "Of course, Mr. Wickwire. I'm always glad to see *you*," I said.

With two crutches he hopped into the room. "Ah,

Benjamin, what a story! I just put it on the wire to the States! 'Texas Boy Decorated by Pancho Villa'!"

"What's the matter with your leg?" I asked.

Propping his crutches in a corner, he sagged into a chair. "Varicose veins, the doctors say. But I don't want to talk about that. I—"

"And your hand?" I had just noticed the bandage.

Ruefully he held it up. "I got too damn close to that iron water tower on the hill. One of Medina Barrón's bullets clipped off my little finger, neat as scissors could do."

I shook my head. "Mr. Wickwire, do you know what's going to happen to you down here?"

"What do you mean, Ben?"

"Bit by bit you're going to disappear, pieces of you flying this way and that. Finally someone will come along with a broom and dustpan and sweep up what's left and put it in the ashcan!"

He grinned. "Maybe so! I don't care, long as I get a good story out of it!"

I didn't drink, but a previous occupant of the room, probably a Federal officer, had left half a bottle of Scotch whiskey. In response to Mr. Wickwire's inquiring look, I got him a glass of water from the *olla* and he poured a stiff shot of whiskey into it.

"Ah!" He sighed comfortably. "I need relaxation, and Highland ambrosia satisfies that need!"

I sat down on the bed. "Things around here are going too fast for me. I need relaxation too."

He poured himself more Scotch, this time without water. "In trouble, are you, Ben?"

I shrugged. "I don't know. I suppose if you concede I just got a medal and General Villa likes me so much he wants me around as his runner, I'm in good shape. But I don't feel good about it, Mr. Wickwire. Look, this isn't real! I have a feeling I'm in some dumb kind of play and don't know my lines and all the other actors are just talking on and on while I'm trying hard to figure how I ever got up on the stage."

He sipped the Scotch, looking at me over the rim of the

glass with owlish eyes behind the iron-rimmed spectacles. I noticed one lens was cracked, and the other spotted with what might be droplets of blood.

"Interestingly put, Ben. Tell me about it."

"Well," I said, "no matter what happened, I'm just an ignorant country boy from Hudspeth County, Texas. All I ever wanted was to go fishing and play my mouth harp and swim in Murphy's Creek, down by the church. So what am I doing here, way down in Mexico, with a medal and General Villa putting his arm around me and saying I'm his runner?"

Looking thoughtful, he held up the bandaged hand and stared at it. "I know what you mean. I get the same feeling at times. By God, I ought to be setting on my front porch right now in a rocking chair, looking at the dahlias I planted and waiting for supper!"

"So what happened—to both of us, I mean?"

"I'm not sure about me, Ben, but I know about you."

"What do you mean?"

"It's easy. You're not a boy anymore, Ben Wilkerson. You're a man! You've grown up real fast. Oh, some take a long time to grow up. I guess I never did. That is to say, I'm in love with adventure. I've been so ever since I read about pirates and the Spanish Main and Mr. Stevenson's *Treasure Island*. So I never grew up, and have got to be chasing adventure till they sweep up what's left of me and dump me in the ashcan, as you say. But you, Ben—you did it different! You, like most boys, were probably in love with adventure too. But you grew up, grew up fast in this crazy revolution, and now you're a man, whether you wanted to be or not." He finished the Scotch, drank the few remaining drops directly out of the bottle, and laid it down with a purr like a cat.

"Welcome to man's estate, *hombre!*"

"I guess so," I sighed, "but I don't know if I can stand the pace." I told him what had happened to me after the battle, how I kind of left reality and went floating around for a week, out of my mind.

He nodded. "A fugue, doctors call it. It's to be expected when a young and impressionable person like you,

223

Ben, is subjected to something awful, like having that good Mr. McFall practically die in your arms." He yawned, stretched. "Mind if I lay down for a few minutes? I haven't had a good sleep for almost a week."

"Sure." I turned down the coverlet and helped him, with his bad hand and bad leg, to take off his boots.

"Clean sheets," he muttered. "I'll get 'em dirty!"

"Never mind that, Mr. Wickwire. Just get some rest. If you want, I can call Dr. Raschman to look at that hand."

Stretching out, he shook his head. "No, thanks. I heal fast. It's the one thing about my poor old body that works the way the instruction book says it should!"

I started to leave but he called me back. "Ben?"

"Yes, sir?"

"Maybe you remember that some time ago I told you the United States was going to get into this revolution?"

"Yes, sir, I remember."

"Well, it looks more and more like I was right."

"I haven't read any newspapers lately," I admitted.

"Well, things are getting to be a real can of worms! Carranza is jealous of Villa and Zapata both. He's trying to pull the carpet out from under both of them by holding back the supplies he'd agreed to furnish them—the stuff that comes in through Tampico. The European war is heating up too, and it looks like Germany is going to swallow up the whole continent unless they're stopped pretty quick. And there's no one can stop them but the U.S. And listen to this! I heard that Hugh Scott spent three hours with Villa yesterday—what do you think of that? Scott, you know, is chief of staff of the U.S. Army now!"

Frankly, I didn't know what to make of that. It was all too much for me, all the stuff that was going on. After all, I was only a simple soldier in the revolution. The men in the ranks never know what's going on. They just pick up their guns, slog wearily to the front, and get killed, still wondering what's going on.

Mr. Wickwire took off his spectacles and laid them on the bureau next to my medal. "Pretty thing, that medal," he mused.

Impatient, I said, "Tell me, then! What am I supposed to make of it?"

Laying back on the bed, he crossed hands over his lean belly. "'You're no dummy, Ben Wilkerson. If you can't see what's going on, I guess you're not growed-up enough yet, in spite of that medal! Like most people, you only know what's on top of the can of worms! Me, I'm old enough and suspicious enough to dig clear to the bottom of the slimy things and find what I call the Core of Truth."

I was on a routine of trying to clean up my bad language, trying never to swear or say *chingado* or anything like that, but now I was tempted, I was so irritated.

"All right, goddammit! Explain it to me!"

But he was asleep, or pretending to be. So I went out and found a gunsmith who put a firing pin in my little Spanish pistol. Paying for it, I had again that strange feeling of unreality, like a bad actor in a worse play. Here I was, getting my gun fixed so I could kill my tormentor, Rodolfo Fierro, and I was going about it casually, like I was buying a stick of peppermint candy at Mr. Hawley's store in McNary. How could I do such a thing? Well, Mr. Wickwire had said I was growing up, even though I apparently wasn't grown-up enough to understand all his vague hints about what was to come. Maybe I *had* already grown up. I had already murdered Cleary Johnson, my own brother, bone of my bone, flesh of my flesh, and they said that in my rage at the death of Mr. McFall I had shot a Federal infantryman right through the head, though I didn't remember that. Maybe I was getting used to murder. Was that—could it be—part of growing up? Right then I wasn't sure I wanted to grow up if that was part of it. I really didn't want to kill anybody.

— 12 —

It was obvious no progress could be made in unifying Mexico without agreement among Villa, Carranza, and Zapata. Each had his own army, his own politics, his own concept of the future Mexico. There was now danger of civil war, which could mean the ruin of a potentially great nation and its collapse into a ragged assembly of warring city-states. Venustiano Carranza, whatever might have been his other defects, at least saw the danger. After weeks of haggling, he finally arranged a conference to be held at Aguas Calientes among the leaders of the different parties.

In my new job as runner to General Villa's headquarters I had an inside view of the maneuvering for position, the covert side deals, the enmities. General Villa was aware of this.

"Benjamin," he said sternly, "I trust you, *chamaco*. You will hear and see many things during this meeting. But your lips must be sealed—*me entiendes*?"

"Yes, sir," I said. "I understand."

He drew a thick finger across his throat. "Otherwise—"

"I understand! Yes, sir!" I repeated.

I was glad Rodolfo Fierro was busy with plans for the coming convention, to be held in October. And I was now free of the watchful eye of Julio, my pockmarked jailer. I asked Ojo Parado if he had seen Julio lately. He had been trying out various glass eyes from the bagful he took from the oculist's shop, and now had a china-blue one, contrasting strangely with his own bloodshot brown one. The new eye rolled sidewise and he crossed himself.

"*No, señor.*" He was impressed by my new status at División headquarters. "I have not been to hell recently."

"What do you mean?"

"Why, General Fierro had Julio shot for not minding his business! Did he not lose you that night of the battle for the iron tower, and let you run away from him?"

"Oh!" I said.

"So he is in hell, where he has belonged all the time! He cheated me at cards, that Julio!"

The staff officers at División headquarters occasionally gave me typing to do. I pecked it out on an ancient Oliver typewriter like the one Ojo Parado tried to give me that time in Ciudad Juárez. Also, I still had some telegraphic duties; whenever the general had a dispatch he was anxious to have transmitted correctlly, he asked me to send it. These duties kept me busy and I had no time to grieve about Valentina—or Mr. McFall or Victoria, dead cooking beans.

Aguas Calientes is three hundred and fifty miles south of Torreón over a network of bad roads and worse railroad tracks, but everyone finally got there. General Villa's army of eleven thousand men encamped at Guadalupe, some hundred miles north of Aguas Calientes. Carranza's men were at Querétaro, south of Aguas Calientes, astride the main route to Mexico City as a precaution against any of the conferees who might decide to march on that place. Emiliano Zapata, distrustful of the whole thing, sent a delegation of twenty or so officers and civilian intellectuals, but refused to attend himself.

In Aguas Calientes the railroad yards were choked with locomotives, sleeping cars, and cabooses, temporary headquarters of the important figures. The city stretched in tension like a rubber band as men from the three groups swaggered around, loaded with pistols, cartridge-studded gunbelts, and tequila. A commission formed by representatives of each of the three factions closed all the cantinas but there was no shortage of liquor; each group had brought along boxcars full of it. Of course, Aguas Calientes had not enough hotels to house everyone. The wary commission billeted people with care, trying to keep hostile factions apart. When hotel rooms ran out, private homes were requisitioned. The people of Aguas Calientes were nervous, rushing to offer rooms to gentlemen like Colonel Aguirre and Felipe Ángeles, rather than be stuck with roughnecks like General Villa's favorite Tomás Urbina or known killers such as Rodolfo Fierro.

It was the first time I saw Venustiano Carranza, the man who badly wanted to be President of Mexico. He arrived at the Teatro Morelos, site of the convention, in a long shiny Protos limousine, accompanied by his military chief, General Obregón. I sat down front in the theater, alert for any summons from General Villa.

Carranza was a tall, big-bellied man, an aristocrat in bearing. He had all the characteristics of aristocracy except true nobility, I decided. He was elegantly tailored, and the chef at the Hotel Mercedes was hard put to deliver the epicurean foods and wines he demanded. Carranza always wore blue-tinted spectacles, and it was said he had weak eyes. Weak eyes or not, he was shrewd, seeing at once every opportunity to advance his own cause. In comparison with the blunt and forthright General Villa, he was diplomatic and soothing, even when pressing a point. His only sign of agitation or displeasure was rapid combing of his full white beard with clawed fingers. His opening address to the convention was as elegant and smooth as his personal bearing, asking that all consider the welfare of the state before their own personal ambitions.

In contrast, General Villa spoke crudely but passionately. Though smartly uniformed due to the efforts of Felipe Ángeles and Colonel Aguirre, and with his unruly hair slicked down, he was still the rude countryman from Durango. "You are going to hear sincere words spoken from the heart of an uncultured man," he said. "What I want to say to you is that Francisco Villa will not be an embarrassment to men of good conscience because he seeks nothing for himself. I want only that the destinies of my country be bright." It seemed to me this simple declaration had much more meaning than Carranza's oratory. Perhaps it did, but one should never underestimate the skulduggeries that can be perpetrated at a meeting among three passionate groups fighting for a common prize—Mexico.

The convention rapidly broke up in untoward incidents. Carranza had presented the convention with a special flag; that of Mexico, with MILITARY CONVENTION OF AGUAS CALIENTES printed in large letters across its face. One speaker took exception to what he considered desecration of the flag and grabbed it, shaking it and referring to it as a "rag." There were shouts from the floor: "Bastard! Crazy man! Let go of the flag!" A Zapatista speaker tried to smooth things over and was hooted from the floor. The Zapatistas, seeing their spokesman in danger, drew guns. For a moment, a battle was imminent in the Teatro Morelos. It was Venustiano Carranza who managed to restore order by his unruffled bearing.

There were more incidents. A Carrancista colonel complained he was set upon and attacked by Villa adherents. Soldiers, even those of high rank, protested there were not enough whores in Aguas Calientes, and fought over the few. The shortage was so acute that a special train was sent to Guadalajara to bring back a principal product of that city: *mercancia*, it was called; "merchandise"—prostitutes!

Though it was nearing the end of the rainy season, the rains hung on. Dark clouds hovered over the city; rain fell every day. The sky split open from horizon to horizon, thunder rattled windows like a fist, and water poured from the clouds thick as a flood. Pencil in hand, I sat in the red caboose, taking notes while big drops rattled like machine-gun fire on the roof. The general and Colonel Aguirre were discussing the progress of the convention without much enthusiasm.

"That prick Carranza!" the general growled. "A *perfumado*, if ever there was one! Carranza is like a snake, striking out of the tall grass with fancy words and elegant ways! I prefer men around me who smell of dust and sweat and blood. They are the real people of Mexico! They are the people to whom Mexico rightly belongs, not to fops and dandies! I spoke truth to the convention, *amigo!* But those others—pah!" He spat.

Villa, I was surprised to find, had a phenomenal memory; my respect for him continued to grow. Carranza had made a proposal to leave politics and turn the battle over to others, which the general considered only a ploy. Adopting a simpering manner to resemble Carranza, he quoted verbatim from Carranza's speech to the convention. "If the convention of Aguas Calientes believes my retirement would be the most effective means of restoring harmony among the revolutionary elements . . ." Again the general spat. "The fucking hypocrite!"

"Sir, you are right about Carranza," Colonel Aguirre agreed while rain crackled on the roof like bullets and winds rocked the caboose. "But I would also keep my eye on his military chief, General Obregón. Really, I think Obregón is the mainspring behind Carranza!" It was probably so. Álvaro Obregón turned out in time to be Francisco Villa's chief nemesis.

After much sparring and argument the convention produced a document signed by all three factions. In a complicated arrangement a provisional president was chosen—Eulalio Gutiérrez, an earnest heavyset man who did not appear to have political aspirations. The military commands of the three factions were made subordinate to the secretariat of war of the provisional government. I could not imagine any of the three factions being subordinate to anyone; the whole thing was ridiculous. In effect, it was a paper solution with no real force behind it, and it led to trouble later on.

The rains had finally ceased and the dry season was at hand. Winds from the east blew dust and grit over everything. Inky clouds hovered over the great extinct volcanoes of Popocatapetl and Iztaccihuatl. Dispossessed by the war, the poor *pacíficos*—farmers who did not know who was fighting whom, or why—gathered in rude shelters along the railroad tracks, reduced to miserable circumstances, forced to beg for food: a tortilla here, a handful of beans there. I spent most of my remaining bilimbique notes on food for them. They were strange people, mostly Indians with flat Oriental-looking faces, and they spoke little if any Spanish, using instead a queer guttural Indian tongue. Valentina told me., "One should always give to the poor." A stranger, Victoria claimed, might be God himself, come down to visit the earth and see what is happening with the people he created.

It made me feel good to give them food. I know Valentina would have approved. Anyway, I was spooning out beans from an earthen pot I had stolen from Fong, the general's Chinese cook, when there came an unexpected grinding of hooves in the cinders along the tracks. A rider reined his mount to a sliding halt.

"Ah, there you are, Señor Hero!"

I paused, spoon in midair while the hungry Indians, patient as always, waited.

"I am here, yes."

The horseman, colored pictures of Christ and the Virgin pinned to the front of his sombrero, grinned at me. Pepe Ruíz was a sergeant in the general's headquarters staff.

"You had better stay away from Fong! He says he will cut off your thieving hands with his cleaver for stealing those beans!"

I went back to spooning beans into waiting hands. I *mean* hands—most of the *pacíficos* had nothing else to receive the food.

"Surely you did not come all the way down here to warn me about Fong!"

He grinned again. Pepe Ruíz was the happiest man I ever knew, and he was never happier than in battle. He sang a lot and knew a lot of songs and could always cheer people up. One of them was especially funny, and always brought howls of laughter:

> Say farewell to my friends for me, Antonia.
> I am going to become an American!
> Oh, may the *gringos* allow me to pass
> And open a saloon on the other side of the river.

"*Verdad*! You are wanted in the general's red caboose right away. I think he has some messages he wants you to send for him over those copper wires in the sky." Pepe had always ben puzzled by the workings of the telegraph, and crossed himself whenever he came into the telegraph office.

"All right," I grumbled. "First I will get rid of the evidence—the beans, I mean." Fong, fat moon-faced Fong, could throw a cleaver with deadly aim; I once saw him chase a chicken for the general's dinner and beheaded it from a distance of several yards.

Pepe whirled away in a clatter of hooves and rising dust, slapping his Durango pony over the eyes with his holy hat to make it buck. Pepe always made a spectacle of riding.

When I knocked at the door of the general's caboose and was told to enter, I almost choked from the cigar smoke and fumes of liquor. The general rarely smoked or drank, to keep a clear head, he said. But Mr. Ambrose Bierce and Colonel Aguirre were making up for his abstinence, both puffing on imported Cuban cigars and drinking full tumblers of tequila.

General Villa had by this time a whole trunkful of uniforms. Busy trying them on, for the moment he waved me aside. Some of the newspaper correspondents, jokingly pointing out that as an important man he should abandon his usual costume of soiled shiny brown suit and collarless shirt, had taken up a collection and bought him a gaudy ill-fitting white duck uniform that made him look like a bandmaster. Now in his underwear, he put a hairy leg into the pants. "*Compañeros*, how do you like this one?"

Big as the general was, the uniform, tailored by ear, I think, was too large. The baggy pants flapped around his ankles as he paraded back and forth, and the white jacket hung around his barrel chest like a tent.

"Bravo!" Mr. Bierce cried, applauding. "And let us think also of colorful medals on your chest against that virgin and snowy background!"

The general shook his head. "I wear no medals, *amigo*. I don't want any medals!"

"Really, sir," Colonel Aguirre said, puffing smoke rings, "I think it is a little too much. The size, I mean, though the general effect is good."

"Now, look at this!" Rummaging in the bottom of the

trunk, the general brought out the blue serge uniform of a divisional commander of the Mexican Army, heavy with gold braid, gold frogging, and gold buttons. He managed to squirm into the pants but the back of the coat split when he flexed his heavy arms. Mr. Bierce whooped with laughter. Colonel Aguirre, unsteady of his feet, spread his booted legs wide and held up his tumbler of tequila, managing a clumsy salute.

"I believe it *is* a little tight," the general admitted. "I will have to capture a Division commander of the regular army who is more my size!"

They laughed together, all three, until tears came, and Mr. Bierce scribbled on his pad of paper, notes for the book he was going to write about General Villa and the revolution.

"What is this writing you are doing, *señor?*" the general asked.

Bierce shrugged. "Only a few lines to fix this scene in my mind, General."

The general scowled. "To fix my ridiculous appearance, eh?"

Bierce was a little annoyed. He drew hard on his cigar and then laid it down. "I have told you, sir, I intend to write a book about you and the fight for freedom!"

"And make me look like a fool?"

"No, sir. I only—"

"Have the world laugh at me because a uniform does not fit, eh? Is that what you have in mind?" In one of his sudden changes of mood the general snatched away the pad and ground it under his heel. "Señor Bierce, you are an amusing fellow. But you have leave to be here only with my permission, and that can be withdrawn at any time!"

Mr. Bierce was angry too. Colonel Aguirre tried to calm the general down but fuel was only added to the fire when Mr. Bierce protested the general's action.

"That was small of you, sir, to destroy my notes!"

Colonel Aguirre hurried between them. "Mr. Bierce, I think you had better leave. There is no point in—"

"I will not leave," Mr. Bierce said coldly, "until I have said certain things!"

I pressed farther back in my corner, wondering at how quickly the jovial atmosphere had changed. There were still cigars, there was still plenty of tequila, but there was also murderous passion in the caboose. For a time General Villa had been amused by Mr. Bierce, laughing hard at his japeries, but lately it was rumored the general had begun to tire of him.

"Make yourself clear, then," General Villa snapped. Even in his underwear he was impressive; most men would not dare to cross him. But Mr. Bierce was very angry, blunt in words and stinging in his sarcasm.

"I came down here," he said, "with a good opinion of you, General. But I must admit my sentiments are changing. Sir, you are only a freebooter!"

Colonel Aguirre drew in his breath sharply. General Villa smiled, a quiet and dangerous smile.

"I do not know this term," he said, "but it is offensive to me, having come from your mouth, Señor Bierce."

"Is it not a fact that your men pillage the lands of defenseless ranchers, stealing cattle, assaulting their women, frightening children?"

"Go on, sir."

I was frightened, and drew still farther back in the corner.

"You caused to be murdered the Englishman William Benton, did you not, when he protested your stealing his cattle?"

"Make your case, then!"

Mr. Bierce did not see the door open. Rodolfo Fierro entered, closing the door silently behind him.

"Is it not true that the British government is demanding reparations for the murder of one of its citizens?"

Fierro looked inquiringly at his chief and fingered the butt of the revolver at his waist.

"And now," Mr. Bierce continued, "I have it on good authority that Mr. Benton's wife, domiciled in El Paso, was visited by a cowardly night prowler and strangled to prevent her making further requests to the State Department to avenge her husband's brutal killing. Sir, is that true? Did not one of your henchmen strangle Mrs. William Benton in her bed?"

General Villa sat on the edge of his bunk and drew on the dingy serge pants. Casually he fastened the shirt at the neck, fumbling for a moment at the collar button.

"Is that all, Señor Bierce?"

Mr. Bierce's face was red with anger as he bent to pick up the scattered notes. "I should think it a plateful, General! When will you eat it?"

I was surprised and shocked when General Villa laughed a hearty laugh. Tightening the belt around his ample waist, he clapped Mr. Bierce on the back. "Let us not argue, *señor!* A revolution cannot be made with half-measures! And here is our good friend Rodolfo. *Amigo*, what news do you bring?"

Fierro stalked out of the shadows, spurs jingling. "None, sir. It is only that I heard harsh words being spoken, and was anxious to—"

"Only a little disagreement, Rodolfo, nothing serious. Mr. Bierce has just completed an analysis of my part in the revolution. It was nothing."

"But—"

The general put bearlike arms around Mr. Bierce, who I think was as startled as anyone, and gave him a warm embrace. I think that over Mr. Bierce's shoulder the general must have passed a signal to Fierro.

"And now," he said, "Colonel Aguirre and I have papers to examine—a matter of an error in the payrolls, it appears. Mr. Bierce, will you excuse us?"

"Yes," Fierro said. "Come along with me, Mr. Bierce. I have some excellent French cognac."

Mr. Bierce must have realized he had now gone too far. His ruddy face paled and his hand trembled as he attempted to put the crumpled pages of notes together. "I . . . I . . ."

"Do come along, will you?" Fierro said impatiently. "One of my *tropa* will get to that cognac before we do, *señor!*"

Mr. Bierce seemed dazed as Fierro led him out of the

general's caboose. That was the last time I ever saw Mr. Ambrose Bierce. It was the last time most people saw him. His fate remained uncertain; he just disappeared. Later, much later, I heard how he died from one of Fierro's Ninth Brigade, and it is as good an explanation as any. Fierro had a ritual way of disposing of people he didn't like and it seems that Mr. Bierce died the same way Mr. Benton, the Englishman, did. Old Pablo Urrutia, on his deathbed, told me that Fierro sent him and three other men of the Ninth Brigade to take Mr. Bierce down to Samayaluca and kill him. Pablo said they made Mr. Bierce dig his own grave and then they clubbed him to death; Fierro said Bierce wasn't worth a bullet. "He wiggled a little for a while," Pable whispered to me, voice sounding like an old cornhusk in the wind, "but in mercy I finished him off with a shot through the head. Then we rolled him in a rug and doused it with gasoline and set it afire. He did not burn too well. After the flames went out, we dumped him in the grave and covered him with a little sand." Pablo's lungs were rotten; he coughed and closed his eyes. "The vultures flapped as we rode away and there wasn't much left of Señor Bierce. Yes, that is how he died. He was brave, that man, at the end. But no one insults our general without paying for it!"

I had known Pablo Urrutia for a long time and I believe that is how, and why, Mr. Ambrose Bierce died, much as did "The English Gamecock," William Benton. Well, the general believed that revolutions were not made with half-measures! Mrs. William Benton was causing a great deal of trouble for General Villa by keeping alive the murder of her husband. Newspaper reporters came often to her house in El Paso and there were many stories in the press about her activities. The Benton case, still unsolved so far as most people were concerned, turned many important figures against Villa and his so-called brutalities. England was still furious, and the world press carried articles criticizing the general. In fact, it was rumored the U.S. government was about to abandon any good opinion they may have had of Francisco Villa and deal instead with Venustiano

Carranza. From a revolutionary standpoint, however, I suppose something had to be done about Mrs. Benton.

After Mr. Bierce had been led away by Rodolfo Fierro, the general recovered his good humor. "There are you, Benjamin," he said. "Come here, *chamaco!*"

Slowly I came from the shadows in the corner, rather wary, as I remember. "Yes, sir?"

Colonel Aguirre had gone to sleep, booted feet propped on a table and head slumped on his chest. His spectacles had fallen off, and for a moment I had an idiotic thought. Were his eyes still crossed when they were closed?

"Here," the general said, tossing me a pamphlet. On the cover it said "The Rules of War as Established by the Geneva Convention." "Read this thing to me, Benjamin! Maybe you can make me understand it. My friend Hugh Scott gave it to me but I cannot make sense out of it!"

To Colonel Aguirre's snores I read the condensation of the complete "Rules of War," all the things having to do with humane treatment of prisoners, rights of the Red Cross on a field of battle, disposal of the dead, and other clauses. When I finished, the general crawled into his bunk, yawning, and pulled up a blanket.

"*Qué caray!* Who can make rules for a war? A war is what happens when someone does not pay attention to the rules, *verdad*?"

"*Verdad*," I agreed. It was a good point.

He burrowed into the blanket, a large lump, an indifferent lump. "Throw away that nonsense, Benjamin! It is not good for anything but to wipe one's ass. In war, who needs rules?"

A moment later he was snoring, sleeping peacefully with thousands of killings on his mind—rather, completely *out* of his mind. But when I opened the door to slip out he suddenly sat ramrod straight in bed, knuckling his close-cropped head and yawning.

"Did you fuck the girl—Fierro's little Valentina?"

Astonished, I could only gape.

"Tell me now, *chamaco*—be truthful! Did you soil Rodolfo's precious little dove?"

I stammered, I guess. "What . . . what do you mean?"

He scratched his armpit and yawned again. "You know very well, Benjamin, what I mean! That is why Rodolfo is so angry with you and has sworn to kill you if Father What's-his-name—you know, the ugly *padre* from the convent—reports that she has missed her period."

"No!" I blurted. "No, I didn't! I . . . I don't do things like that to women! Unless . . ." I swallowed hard. "Unless someday, after the war is over, I can marry her!"

He nodded. "I am glad to hear that, Benjamin! Maybe you learned that from me, and I am happy to set you on the right track. It is the honorable thing to do, to marry your women. You have learned morals in a very unlikely situation."

Lying back on his pillow, hands clasped behind his head, he seemed to doze for a moment. Then, as I was tiptoeing away, he called to me.

"If Rodolfo gives you any trouble, *chamaco*, let me know. He is a violent and unpredictable man, perhaps more so than me, old Pancho. But you are under my protection. I have made that clear to him."

As I climbed down the iron steps, I noticed that the sentry always outside his door had changed. Now it was Pepe, the ruffian with the colored religious pictures on his hat.

"He sleeps?" he asked me.

"Yes," I said. "He sleeps."

Pepe offered me half of his cold *tamal*. "Good!" he said. "Our general sleeps! There is peace only when he sleeps!" In the light filtering from the chintz-draped windows of the general's caboose, he looked at the watch on his wrist. "*Caramba!* I have another hour of this dreary duty yet to do!"

"That is a fine watch," I remarked.

He took it off to show it to me. It was indeed a fine watch, with a gold case and ghostly glowing green numbers. "Señor Juan Reed gave it to my *tropa* when we loaned him a horse and saddle. Of course, the horse was not ours to give. It was one of the many of that *hombre* at Los Remedios ranch."

"Mr. Benton? William Benton?"

"*Sí, señor.*" Carefully he put the watch back on a hairy wrist. "We all voted to give Señor Reed the horse, so we each get to wear this watch two hours each day."

I thought this was comical but did not crack a smile. "Wear it in good health, *amigo*," I said.

Preparations for the assault on the key city of Zacatecas took a long time. General Villa was impatient. A mad cavalry charge was his favorite tactic, but now Felipe Ángeles and Colonel Aguirre prevailed on him to use his forces more wisely and economically. The general had not understood the uses of artillery, and Felipe Ángeles, an expert in this field, daily pored over maps with him to lay out fields of fire. "For you must understand, General," he said, "that an enemy softened and terrified by an accurate bombardment will not offer much resistance to infantry!"

I thought it funny how Felipe Ángeles and Colonel Aguirre despaired of dressing the general in clothes befitting his status as commander of the largest and most powerful army in Mexico. This morning, for instance, the general walked around the caboose for a long time in dirty underwear, sipping coffee from a cracked mug. Then, still listening to Felipe Ángeles, he put on a heavy brown sweater with a roll collar, slipped pillarlike legs into shapeless and soiled khaki pants, and laced up heavy scuffed shoes that had seen better days, crowning the whole ensemble with an artilleryman's helmet. Felipe Ángeles looked at Colonel Aguirre and shrugged.

"Now, sir, let us consider the hill above the town," he sighed.

Torreón hummed with activity as preparations went on for perhaps the most important battle of the campaign, the taking of Zacatecas, key to Mexico City itself. Cavalry, wearing automobile goggles against the dust, galloped on foam-mouthed horses across the plain, forming and reforming, sweating in the sun. Under the tutelage of Captain Treston, the Canadian, machine-gun squads practiced the "three-mil tap" that allowed their fire to walk across a target with maximum effect. Artillerymen unlimbered, set up field guns, and tried to beat their own time in getting off a round. Doctors and nurses were not exempt; Dr. Raschman catechized them on surgical procedures. Daily the insides of the hospital cars were scrubbed with soap and water and carbolic acid. Most of the wounded from the Torreón battle had now been sent to base hospitals in Chihuahua City and Ciudad Juárez.

For a time no one in the red caboose seemed to need me, so Colonel Aguirre granted me eight hours' leave. The little mare Pinta that Fierro had given me somehow disappeared. I think someone stole her; in Fierro's brigade horses frequently changed ownership. So I went back to my friend Pepe Ruíz.

"I have no wristwatch to give you," I said, "but I would appreciate the loan of a horse and saddle to ride out into the desert for a few hours. The desert air refreshes, and I need refreshment, *amigo.*"

He was delighted to offer me his own mount, the tough-mouthed and fierce little Durango mare. "Take along a club," he advised. "If that bitch devil tries to bite you, hit her over the head! This is the way to make friends with her." He gestured to a friend nearby. "*Andale*, Pedro—it is again my time to wear the watch of the wrist!"

The mare was skittish but I talked gently to her, the way I had always done to Grandpa Johnson's mule, Jupiter, and she settled down, racking along at a good gait. We passed through a mile or so of low scrub, across a shallow muddy stream, and climbed a high mesa where I reined up and looked back at Torreón. It seemed a ghost city shimmering in the heat mirage, vapors of dirty brown rising where Villa's troops drilled and sweated. To many the view might have seemed sterile and desolate. But somehow, like a vine growing around a tree, Mexico had wound its way to my heart. Mexico was not Hudspeth County, Texas—it was Mexico, with an indefinable flavor that captivated me. How long this vine of Mexico had been growing in me, I didn't know. But Mexico was beginning to become my *tierra*, my country, with all the bad things that had happened to me there along with the good things. Even the heat, the stark forms of great barrel cactus and saguaro, the ground hostile with the spines of the nopal, the beavertail cactus, were now familiar and comforting.

In a way, the nopal characterized the people of Mexico. This fearsome needle-studded plant was a welcome item of diet to the humble farmers. They knocked off the spines, skinned the paddlelike leaves, and ate *nopalitos*, the young tender growth, fried in lard. Hostility capitalized on and made friendly; that was Mexico.

As I passed through a scorched riverbed filled with hot sand, the great bowl of the desert seemed a platter rolled up at the edges to meet the eye-hurting blue of the Durango sky. General Villa, I remembered, told me he was born nearby, in Durango, in the little town of San Juan del Río. In the hazy blue distance I could see the jagged slopes of the Sierra de la Silla and the Sierra del Gamón where he had once hunted deer and wild boar.

The little mare shied suddenly and I reined up, seeing beneath her hooves a rattlesnake—*cascabel*, the Mexicans called it. Remembering the little Spanish pistol in my pocket, I snatched it out and with a lucky snap shot blew the head off the rattler. Watching the wriggling remains, I thought of Rodolfo Fierro. Pantomiming, I snapped off several more shots, each aimed at his heart. The idea of killing Fierro did not arouse great passion in me anymore. I would do it, yes—but it had become an idea so firmly fixed in my mind, so strongly rooted in shame and desperation, that I took it now as a given. When circumstances were right, I would kill him, that was all. No more jingling spurs, no more bright red carnations in a buttonhole, no more El Carnicero!

After that I felt better. As we came to a small town a hawk swooped low, examining us, then soared aloft on strong pinions. I doffed my hat to him. "Señor Gavilán," I said, "good health to you, and good hunting this day."

An old woman gave me tortillas and *queso fresco*—the good fresh cheese of Mexico—and a gourd of cool water from a sweating *olla* that hung in the shade. I offered her fifty centavos, which she did not want to take. *A stranger might be God*, I thought. Tying the mare to a mesquite tree, I walked about for a while before returning to Torreón.

The color of the street was red, the rich red clay of Durango. The mesquite trees were thatched with hay and corn, the way the peasants stored winter feed for their animals. The town tumbled down an arroyo, roofs like stairsteps, with occasional palms and the red-purple of bougainvillea softening the harshness of the flat mud roofs. Roosters crowed, burros sobbed burro complaints, there was a rustle and crackle of dried cornstalks as someone shook feed out of a tree. Babies wailed in the *siesta* time; a woman sang an old song as she mashed corn in the stone trough women always had about them to make tortillas. *Whish, whish, whish*! Peace, rest, contentment!

Someday after the revolution, if fate and Rodolfo Fierro had not intervened, Valentina and I might have come to a tiny village like this. We would have a little patio where we could sit drinking coffee, eating fresh-sliced papaya, and loving each other on summer mornings. We would watch our children feeding the pigeons, playing with the cats; every household should have a cat. If papayas and tortillas ran short, we could live on love, I knew that, Valentina and I; love for each other, love for our children, love for the *tierra*, love for the cats, enough love to go around for all. We would welcome travelers to our table, and . . . Somber, I broke off. That had all been blasted by Rodolfo Fierro; I must not think about Valentina anymore. Still, I knew there would never be another woman for me.

On the way back, the dusty trail paralleled the railroad. For a time I reined up and watched Villa's repair train patching the track where the retreating Federales had ripped it up. The first car was a steel-encased monster on the front of which was mounted the great cannon Felipe Ángeles was so proud of, the one they called, *El Niño*—The Child. Next came an armored car filled with soldiers, then a car loaded with steel rails to replace the ones the fleeing Federales had torn up and twisted into grotesque shapes in still-smoldering fires. The train moved slowly while men sweated and strained, staggered under the weight of the iron rails, swung hammers and drove spikes with a musical *clang clang clang* ringing like church bells.

Later that afternoon I noticed a dusty and battered Willys touring car next to the track. Beside it stood a weary goggled figure in a linen duster and plaid cap. Three tires were flat, and cactus needles stuck in the punctured rubber. Steam floated from the radiator, and as the goggled figure leaned on a fender it fell off and tumbled down the hill. The goggled figure swore, picturesquely and in English.

"Mr. Wickwire!" I cried, spurring the mare forward and dismounting in a cloud of dust. "How are you?"

For a moment he stared at me sourly. Then he took off the dirty goggles. "Ben! Ben Wilkerson! How are you, my boy?"

Each time, Mr. Wickwire looked a little older, a little more rackety, more desiccated and hard-used. Limping toward me, he pumped my hand. "Ben, am I glad to see you!" He turned to the car. "This devil's invention has a personality of its own! An ugly and resentful personality, I must say! I treated it kindly, gave it good water and gasoline filtered through a chamois skin as the man I bought it from told me. But the tires were obviously defective, and went flat one by one."

"Well," I said, "you can't run over cactuses and not have flat tires!"

He didn't seem to hear. Kicking a door panel, he went on. "I filled the radiator last night but . . ." Lifting the hood, he peered in. "Some kind of rubber hose seems to have come loose."

I looked. Rusty water was sprayed all over the red-hot engine.

"Did you put oil in it lately?" I asked.

"Oil? I don't recall. Do these brutes need oil too—besides gasoline and water?"

He was hopeless. I dropped the hood and locked it. "I'm afraid they do."

Sitting on a flat rock, he took a brown bottle from his satchel. Measuring carefully, he poured some into a spoon. Seeing my curious look, he said, "Liver. It's for my liver! Doctor says my liver is drying up. Maybe this stuff lubricates one's liver. I don't know. At any rate, it tastes horrible, something like castor oil mixed with goat's milk."

"Well," I asked, "what do you plan to do now?"

Corking the bottle, he put it away. "I don't know. Somehow I've got to reach Torreón and file my dispatches." He looked thoughtfully at the Durango mare. "How much do you want for the horse?"

I laughed at the thought of his goggles and linen duster on a cranky pony. "Have you ever ridden?"

"No, but I will if I have to. Of course, I can only give you an IOU for now. This Willys contraption I had to buy myself, and so I'm a little underfunded, you see." Taking a sheaf of notes from his pocket, he thumbed through them. "I've learned that the United States may be about to recognize Carranza as President of Mexico. It's an exclusive, and I have to get it on the wire fast!"

"That can't be true!" I protested. "Carranza? That big fake?"

"That's the way it appears. Ambassador Wilson figures Carranza is the most stable influence in Mexico, so they're going to go with him. The European war is heating up like a wood stove full of pine knots with the draft door open, and the U.S. doesn't want trouble in Mexico if they have to go to war with the Central Powers."

"But . . . Carranza!" I shook my head. "The people love Villa, you know that! He's a hero to them! They make up *corridos* and sing them about Villa—the 'Invincible General,' they call him!"

Mr. Wickwire shrugged. "That's true. But men aren't put in power because the people love them, Ben. They're put in power by a lot of international dickering and hornswoggling. President Wilson is a very proper man, and he's offended by Villa's cattle stealing, his wild ways, his executions. For example, there's the Benton affair. Britain's still yammering for satisfaction. And now I understand that other man . . . What's his name?"

"Ambrose Bierce, you mean?"

"Yes, that's him. He's turning up missing too, and the State Department's holding Villa responsible. No, old Pancho's getting to be *persona non grata* with the U.S. You can't just go around shooting important people!"

"Well," I said, "there's a cruel side to the general, no doubt about that. But he's a fine man, actually, and he's always been good to me. He's fighting for the people, too! Carranza's fighting to become President of Mexico. There's the difference!"

Mr. Wickwire put the notes back into a pocket of the dirty linen duster. "By the way, have you got anything to eat? I'm powerful hungry!"

I gave him a tortilla from the packet the old lady had made up for me. "For the road, *señor*," she said. "Go with God." For a while Mr. Wickwire chewed in silence. "My teeth are going too," he muttered. "Can't hardly chew anymore!" I gave him a drink of water from my canteen and he gulped it down, afterward apologizing for drinking so much. "Don't have to chew water," he said.

"That's all right. Torreón isn't far now. Another five kilometers, I'd say."

"You're getting to talk and act and look like a Mexican, Ben, except for that long blond hair and those blue eyes. Five kilometers, eh? How far is that in miles?"

"About three miles. Well, let's get on the mare! She's small but strong. I guess she'll carry double or that distance."

A weird figure in duster and plaid cap, he huffed on his goggles and wiped them with a sleeve while I tightened the mare's cinch, avoiding occasional baleful attempts to bite me.

"She's mean, is she, Ben?"

"You'll sit in back," I said. "She can't reach you there."

Approaching cautiously, he then drew back as if willing to call off the whole thing. "I never liked horses!"

"I don't particularly care for this one," I said, "but she's all we've got except shank's mare, as they say in Texas."

He continued to dally, making conversation. "By the way, why don't you wear that medal General Villa gave you, Ben?"

"I don't believe in medals," I said. "I guess it's in my room someplace."

"Not many people get that medal, my boy. You ought to wear it."

"Come on!" I said, exasperated, holding out my hand to give him a leg up. "It's getting late."

"All right, then." Holding the satchel like a shield, he sidled closer.

"By the way, I wrote up a story about you and the medal. Sold it to a French magazine for five hundred francs. That's about a hundred dollars!"

"Listen," I said, impatient, "I'm tired of hearing about that damned medal! It doesn't mean anything to me! I didn't even know what I was doing when I cut up that way!" Taking his hand, I drew him over to the mare, whose eyes rolled up white at the sight of something new to bite. "A lot of good men died in that fight. They died knowing full well they were going to die. *They* should get the medals instead of being rolled into a damned ditch and getting dirt in their dead faces!"

Mr. Wickwire stared at me. "All right. All right, Ben! I didn't know—"

"Hurry, now!" Finally I got him hoisted on the mare. To show her independence she had to skitter around a little bit. Mr. Wickwire, satchel in one hand, the other clutching my shoulder, was terrified. I whacked the mare on the nose with my fist and she settled down.

"Now," I said, swinging up, "let's get going."

On the way back to Torreón the mare was more cooperative, knowing she was headed for the stables. In late sunshine the desert glowed with a warm radiance. The light was yellow, and seemed thick as water. All round were the tall cactuses, shedding color like the corals in an ocean bed in a picture book Mr. Dinwiddie once loaned me. I knew again why men were willing to die for the opportunity to live here—in Mexico—free, and with dignity.

"Ben?"

The word brought me back from a reverie. "Yes, sir."

"You're a strange one."

I didn't say anything.

When we finally reached the telegraph office in the center of Torreón, I had to help him down.

"Take it easy, Ben!" he groaned. "Easy, now! I've got to do her slow and easy! Oh, my back!"

Gently as I could I finally got him on the ground, all rubber-legged and bent over. Gradually, like a creaking well-sweep, he straightened, rubbing his bottom with both hands. "Well, I thank you, Ben! If it wasn't for you and your little horse I'd be eating scorpions and drinking sand out there tonight."

At the door of the telegraph office I heard the old familiar song of the clacking brass keys, the relays, and sounders. "I'm glad to do it," I said. "If you're going to be in town for a while, Mr. Wickwire, I'm billeted at the Hotel Superba on Calle Siete."

Still rubbing his back, he paused, looked thoughtfully at me. "As I said, Ben, you're a strange one. You're honest, Ben—too honest for Mexico. It's a hard country. Beautiful, but hard! You'd best learn a little duplicity, my boy. It'll serve you well in this beautiful wicked country." He picked up the threadbare satchel and shook hands with me again.

"Well, *adiós, amigo!*"

I think it was all the Spanish he knew. I turned away, feeling a little sadness. I didn't know if I would ever see Mr. Wickwire again. He was so small and fragile-looking to be running around in Durango.

— 13 —

Speaking of learning Spanish, I was getting to be pretty fluent. When you're plunked down in a foreign country like I was it's sink or swim; either you learn the language fast or you're in for trouble. Of course, I was often in trouble anyway, but it wasn't caused by lack of the lingo. Some of my trouble was probably because with the brashness of youth I said too much, spoke when I ought to have been listening. Besides, there are a lot of linguistic booby traps in Spanish. For example, the word *madre* means "mother," of course. But for a reason I was too innocent to understand at the time, a man's mother was always referred to as *mamá*; the word *madre* had a connotation that would start a fight. I believe it had something to do with a common vulgar expression like *chingar su madre*, which is best left untranslated.

A woman going to a grocery store would never ask a clerk if he had *huevos*, the word for "eggs." If she did, the clerk would either burst out laughing or be somewhat embarrassed. *Huevos* was a slang word for "testicles." To avoid embarrassment, a lady would best ask for *blanquillos*, a subterfuge translatable as "those little white things."

This is a digression, I realize, but maybe it helps to give the flavor of the country. Anyway, Spanish, I found, was a beautiful language. When I managed once in a while to speak it with the lilt that Valentina used, it was like music.

John Reed was fluent in Spanish, though I never knew where he learned it. He was such a brilliant man that maybe he just picked it up; some people have what is called "language sense," and I think he had. One day he asked me, "Where is that sour-faced old man with the red nose? You know, the one that's always shooting his mouth off with all kinds of epigrams."

I wouldn't have known an epigram if one fell on me, but I knew who he meant. "Mr. Bierce?"

"Yes, that's it. I want to do a piece on him for my book. You know, local color."

I told him I hadn't seen Mr. Bierce lately, and that was true. At the time I didn't know the grisly details of Mr. Bierce's death at Samayaluca. Anyway, people always came and went around General Villa's headquarters. Of course, certain of them, like William Benton and Mr. Bierce, mostly went.

"I'm disappointed," Mr. Reed sighed, putting his notebook back in a pocket; he never went anywhere without that notebook. "Did you know, Benjamin, that he wrote a book? A sour and pessimistic thing called *The Devil's Dictionary*, loaded with rage and sarcasm. He must have led a very unhappy life."

I was impressed by anyone who wrote books. My old teacher, Mr. Dinwiddie, had instilled in me a reverence for books. I felt then that I had underestimated Mr. Bierce, but it turned out to be too late to do anything about it anyway. He was dead in Samayaluca.

These days I was kept very busy at División headquarters. There was great bustle and confusion as preparations for the assault on Zacatecas went forward. The unpredictable city electric plant failed most of the time and kerosene lamps burned smokily all night as staff officers pored over plans, poked stones and pieces of wood around on maps to simulate troop movements, argued tactics. On one point General Villa was adamant: the División del Norte must move quickly and silently before Zacatecas, then strike at night. "For," he said, "at night, three men are an army!"

He always listened politely to his staff officers. Then, having heard and considered, he would sweep away argument with a wave of his hand and make a decision graven in stone, like the Ten Commandments. After that, he was stubborn as a mule in a rainstorm; he would not budge. It was not a bad system because he had a natural feel for the battlefield. There was only one change in his established tactical ways—he was finally learning from the brilliant Felipe Ángeles the proper use of artillery.

After a long period of inactivity I was grateful for the action. In the first place it kept Rodolfo Fierro so busy that he had no time for me. He did not even seem to notice my presence at headquarters, where I was running messages to and fro, doing a bit of typing, and bringing coffee to the staff officers. Almost—I said almost—I had again a feeling of being sorry for him. Under the strain of the campaign he had lost weight, the long blond beard was straggly and untrimmed, and deep circles sagged under his bloodshot eyes. Still, the memory of what he had tried to make me burned in my mind and I steeled my heart. When a good time came I would kill him as casually as he had killed hundreds of others, but at a place and time of my own choosing so he would know and understand before he died. Now, as an old man, I am astonished at the cold resolve of that beardless boy. Still, the boy was a Texan, and Texans do not take insults lightly.

The Spanish pistol I kept always in my pocket, small and oiled and cleaned, deadly at short range. But for now, all I could do was scamper from División headquarters to the various brigades, carrying messages and exhausting myself in the process. A tired body means a tired mind, too weary to maintain passion.

The streets of Torreón boiled with activity as wagons and trucks loaded supplies for the campaign. Men cursed, fights broke out, the useful *soldaderas* cooked huge pots of beans in the plaza. A major with gout, legs wrapped in bandages so they looked like fat *tamales*, hobbled about giving orders no one paid attention to. Urchins from the city streets, pressed into service, giggled and skylarked as they poured black powder into corrugated iron bombs. Cavalry trotted through the streets, raising clouds of dust above which fluttered their red-white-and-green pennons. A woman roasting chestnuts for sale lifted a coal from a brazier with her bare fingers to light a cigarette. Men from the Brigada Hidalgo slaughtered a roaming cow at the steps of the church and with machetes hacked off chunks of bloody flesh while the beast was still twitching. One of the ruffians recognized me and shouted gleefully, tearing with his teeth at a dripping morsel.

"*Hola*, young hero! We of the Brigada Hidalgo are tough! We like our meat raw and our women strong!"

From what I overheard at División headquarters I managed to form a picture of what was going on. General Urbina was driving the Federales before him from the northwest. We—the División del Norte—were to come down on the government troops from the north. In the northeast, the army of Pablo González, one of Villa's trusted allies, was prepared to move south. These three powerful armies would sweep Huerta's troops before them, breaking them up into smaller units to be dealt with at leisure, while the main body of the combined rebel forces made the final drive on Mexico City itself.

In Zacatecas, General Luis Medina Barrón, another who always seemed to manage somehow to escape from lost cities, was again in command. Villa's spies reported that Medina Barrón had at the most only twelve thousand troops, with a dozen or so fieldpieces and perhaps a hundred machine guns. Still, Medina Barrón had prepared the city cleverly for defense. Our spies reported that funds extorted from the church and from wealthy merchants were used to purchase huge quantities of food which were stored in fortifications on the hilltops surrounding the town, from which could also be directed a withering fire on attackers. Horses, mules, grain, fodder, saddles—all were "requisitioned" from surrounding ranches and farms. Reinforcements under General Pascual Orozco, some four thousand men, had been promised by President Huerta to arrive from Aguas Calientes in time to supplement Medina Barrón's forces. That city, site of the convention, had been captured once again by the Federales in the crazy teeter-totter of war. On the steps of the great cathedral, it was told, the women of Zacatecas were kneeling daily to pray, lighting candles in supplication of victory.

Zacatecas was an old and rich silver town. At a mean elevation of two thousand meters or so, the climate was brisk and fresh. The city boasted fine residences and elaborate churches. The adjoining hills and uplands were honeycombed with silver mines which, after millions of ounces of silver had been taken out, still promised riches. Unfortunately, the streets were narrow cobblestoned passages, rising steeply, and so chocked with tile-roofed buildings that a great deal of hand-to-hand fighting would be necessary to take the place.

At Torreón I had already killed one man and I had no inclination to kill anyone else. I decided to confine my warrior role to hanging around División headquarters. That place, I suspected, was far enough back of the actual fighting so I would not be drawn into the fight. But in that I was mistaken. General Villa's headquarters before Zacatecas were in the middle of everything. Shrapnel from the Federal forces on the hills fell on us like rain just as soon as headquarters was set up in the dusk a few thousand meters from the base of the mountain called El Grillo, "The Grasshopper," although why a mountain should be called a grasshopper I didn't know.

I will never forget that sound of incoming shrapnel. I have tried to reproduce it, to give some idea of what it sounded like, but it took John Reed to do it justice in the book he later wrote, *Insurgent Mexico*. Crash . . . wheeee . . . a . . . a . . . a! High-explosive shells made a different sound: Boom . . . pieeuu! That evening we were mauled so brutally and so quickly that Colonel Aguirre rushed among us, spectacles coming off and dangling, to pass the word that the División was to move at once back to the cover of a grove of cottonwoods a few hundred meters to the rear.

Old Ojo Parado was unconcernedly sharpening his bayonet on a whetstone, from time to time testing the blade with a gnarled thumb. When he saw me departing hastily for the new position to the rear, he yelled, "*Hola, compañero!* Where do you go so fast, eh?"

Gasping for breath, I told him. He grinned a gap-toothed grin.

"*Mucho susto, eh?*"

"You're damned right!" I wheezed. "I'm scared to death, and you'd better be too! Come on!"

Another burst of shrapnel fell in the midst of the Brigada Hidalgo and several men were wounded. The air reeked of cordite, the foul-smelling explosive. Villa's wounded rarely cried out; they seemed to bear pain with tight-lipped stoicism, waiting patiently for someone to take them to the hospital trains in the rear.

"Come *on*!" I cried. "Let's get out of here before they blow us up! Do you want *two* glass eyes?"

Casually Ojo Parado fixed the gleaming bayonet to his rifle and strolled after me, as if on a Sunday walk with his children.

"If this is the day," he said, cigarette hanging loose from his lower lip and bobbing as he talked, "'then why worry? Worry does no good."

I scrambled through thick brush in a great hurry. Ojo Parado followed the trail of broken branches I left in my flight, still talking.

"And if this is not the day, then there is no reason to worry!"

He paused to watch the flight of a shell approaching us. When artillery fire is directed right at you from a distance, you can see the shell coming, screaming like a banshee, growing larger and larger. It hit in a pile of rocks between us. There was a gout of orange flame and an explosion that deafened me, seeming to drive my eardrums into my head. Murderous bits of metal flew this way and that, shredding the trees, spanging off rocks, and wheeing into the distance. A fountain of pebbles rose into the air and then rained down in a steady drizzle, like rain. Flat on my face, wondering if I had been killed, I covered my skull with my hands and waited for the last bit of rock to fall. When I staggered to my feet, my ears still ringing, I heard Ojo Parado's voice, very distant and far away.

"*Mucho susto*, eh, Benjamin?" He was squatting beside me, grinning, rolling a fresh bit of tobacco into a cornhusk. "That bastard of a shell clipped the cigarette right out of my mouth!"

I had risen too soon. A final fragment of rock dropped out of the sky and hit me on the shoulder. It must have weighed a good pound, and knocked me down again.

"Goddammit!" I yelled, staggering up again and rubbing my bruised shoulder. "Let's get the hell out of here before we both get killed!" I ran again toward the distant rise where the general's flag had just fluttered up on a hastily rigged staff, Ojo Parado following me, singing a bawdy song, rifle reversed over his shoulder; I think it was the one about the three whores, ending with a whoop of "Viva Pancho Villa!"

With the general's instinctive mastery of battlefield tactics and Felipe Ángeles' use of artillery, the defenders of Zacatecas had little chance. At dawn the next day, with borrowed fieldglasses I watched the assault on El Grillo. Our infantry had climbed halfway up the steep rocky slopes during the night, sometimes drawing enemy fire deliberately to locate hidden strongholds. The Federales had dug trenches but the flinty soil was so hard the trenches were only shallow scars, providing little protection. They had started to face the trenches with barbed wire but had been interrupted by the vanguard of Villa's troops. Great coils of the snaggy stuff lay all about, unrolled. By 1 P.M. or so the Ninth Brigade had swept the summit of El Grillo. Artillery pieces were close behind the foot soldiers, setting up where they could train their guns on the other hills.

A battery of Felipe Ángeles' artillery wheeled into position near División headquarters, ready to add its murderous fire to the guns now on El Grillo. I have read about the skill of Napoleon's artillerymen but doubt it surpassed the quickness, spirit, and accuracy of these ragged farmers turned cannoneers. As I watched, they ripped off the canvas cover and tilted up the cannon. The battery captain, who had probably never before adjusted anything more complex than a plow, took the telescopic sight from its plush-lined case and quickly screwed it on the breech. While he squinted through the sight and spun the polished brass crank of the raising mechanism, a corporal in a ragged shirt with homemade chevrons unlocked an ammunition chest where shells were racked in polished rows. Two men pulled out a shell; staggering under its weight, they propped it on the tailpiece while the gun captain, a spry little man with bare feet, white hair tucked under a gold-braided navy cap, adjusted the shrapnel timer. The shell was shoved into the maw of the piece, the breechblock crashed shut, and . . . CRA BOOM! The shell whined upward, a black dot growing smaller and smaller as it sped, until I could no longer locate it against the blue sky. Then came a flash of flame among the fortified Federales, accompanied by a great pillar of black smoke. The report of the explosion whispered back down the mountain, echoing and echoing among the rocky crags and gorges.

"*Olé!*" the gunners shouted, clapping each other on the back. "That was a good one! That will twist Medina Barrón's tail!"

As they slammed in another shell, the gun captain grinned at me and wagged an exultant salute. "That is how to do it, eh, *gringo?*"

"*Verdad!*" I called back. "That is indeed the way to do it!"

Pepe of the holy hat galloped out of the grove of trees to summon me to headquarters. "Quickly!" he said. "The Brigada Juárez has taken the road where the telegraph line runs to Zacatecas, and the general wants you to send a message to Medina Barrón, that prick!" Reining in his big horse close to me, he said, "Come up, *compañero*—we will ride double! There is a hurry!"

He reached down his hand to pull me into the saddle. At that moment the Federal battery found the range of the newly set-up fieldpiece I had been watching. Medina Barrón's gunners knew a few tricks too. A tremendous blast of hot air hit me, rolling me through the rocks to bring up against a stunted tree. The report of the explosion sounded curiously muted, I suppose because my ears had been damaged by the shock. A great ball of fire bloomed on the hillside, searing trees, igniting dry grass, curling the leaves of hardy bushes. My mouth, my ears, my eyes were filled with dust and dirt; I spat out leaves. As I lay propped against the stunted tree, reality gradually swam into my focus. The new battery was gone—completely evaporated except for splinters of ammunition chests, smoking remnants of brass, an iron-bound wheel, spokes broken, hanging from the limbs of a cottonwood tree. Pepe's big horse lay on its side, screaming, pink gut spilling from its stomach. Pepe, face scorched, manta shirt smoldering, crawled over and cut its throat. He lay back on the carcass, staring at me. Trying to speak, he could only gesture weakly. Then his arm dropped to his side. All that remained in him was that uncomprehending stare.

I had some burns and cuts but thought I could stand erect, walk. Overconfident, I fell down again, dizzy. On hands and knees I crawled over to Pepe.

"Are you hurt?" I asked, my voice a dusty croak. Then I realized Pepe was dead. Dazed, I passed a hand over my brow and found it wet with blood. Unbelievingly I looked at the wreckage of the battery. The gun captain was gone, the artillerymen had vanished. I shook my head, feeling my brains turn again to that cornmeal mush, unable to grasp the reality of their disappearance. Then I noticed a leather *huarache* here, with part of a foot in it—a burning straw sombrero—the barrel of the fieldpiece halfway down the hill with what looked like a twisted rag doll wrapped around it. I was sick. Doubling over, I retched.

After a while I remembered my assignment. Swaying, holding on to the branches of cottonwood trees for support, I made my way to Division headquarters, far back in the grove, behind a low ridge that gave them protection and concealment. Staff officers gathered under the cottonwoods, arguing over maps pinned to trees. From time to time a stray bullet ripped through the trees, clipping off a shower of leaves. Colonel Aguirre, his hand bandaged, stared at me in astonishment.

"Where have you been? I sent Pepe Ruíz after you and—"

"A shell," I said hoarsely, pointing. "It hit down there in that pile of rocks." My head still hurt from the explosion, and my shoulder, I thought, might be broken. Unsteady on my feet, giddy and disoriented, I would have fallen if he had not caught my arm.

"Oh! I am sorry, Benjamin. You mean that big one that just hit down the hill?"

I wiped fresh blood from my lips. "Yes, sir. The battery was . . . well, our battery just disappeared! And Pepe's horse . . ." I started to retch again.

"Here. Sit down." The colonel gestured and one of Villa's *soldados* quickly brought a folding canvas chair. The Division of the North never had such niceties unless they captured them from a defeated enemy. "Are you hurt? Tell me, please!"

I sagged gratefully into the chair, grateful especially for my escape from that shrapnel shell that had done so much damage otherwise. "No," I said. "I'm not hurt, I guess."

Colonel Aguirre unhooked his spectacles and huffed on them. Polishing them with his sleeve, he put them on again and examined me closely.

"Well, I guess you'll survive." He handed me a piece of paper with a scrawled message across it in pencil. "This is a telegraphic message to Medina Barrón that General Villa has just dictated. It demands that he surrender the city before any more brave men die."

I got to my feet, fighting off the giddiness. "But how can I send a message when—?"

"The Brigada Juárez is out there on our left flank, about five hundred yards distant, being held in reserve. They have cut their portable telegraph set into the Zacatecas line but don't have anyone who can send. Be off with you now, and stay out of the way of those cursed shrapnel shells!"

"Yes, sir," I said, and ran.

Colonel Aguirre called after me, his crossed eyes concerned, "Are you sure you're all right, Benjamin?"

Wavering in my course, I lifted my hand and waved to him as reassurance, at the same time trying to correct my erratic course toward the Brigada Juárez. As I ran I tried hard not to think of the vanished artillery battery, the spry little gun captain, the ragged soldiers who had capered about and cheered only moments ago. *Gone . . . all gone!* My brain was turning to mush again, and black smeary spots danced before my eyes, but I fought it off, gulping cold clear air into my lungs; I was still out of breath. Division headquarters, I had found, was no safer than any other place. I would be safer, I figured, with the Brigada Juárez than among General Villa and his staff.

Zacatecas was a great victory for the general. Demoralized by Felipe Ángeles' artillery, the government troops fled to the only defensive position left—the hill called La Bufa. I think that meant "snort," like a pig snorts, although I never knew why they called it that either. By four in the afternoon Villa's men, moving swiftly and fiercely, had taken La Bufa also, and the Federales retreated in a disorganized mob down into the narrow city streets, where they holed up in shops and houses, sniping at us.

Many of them tried to hide in the houses of the poor—the wealthy had fled Zacatecas at Villa's advance, locking their heavy oak doors in hope of returning when the fighting had stopped. But the Villistas prowled the alleys and byways, flushing the diehards out to be dispatched immediately with rifle fire. The city hall had been used by the government troops as an arsenal. To prevent the Villistas from capturing the huge stock of arms and ammunition, the Federales dynamited the building and there were more casualties, for the most part women and children.

Other Federales dynamited the state building, and when that was done they fled southward, trying to escape toward Guadalupe through a narrow canyon. Rodolfo Fierro anticipated them. He had ordered machine guns set up on the sides of the canyon, and as the unlucky government troops passed, the machine guns opened fire. They raked the fleeing horde until the pass was choked with bodies of the dead and dying. Zacatecas and its environs ran rivers of blood. It was estimated by foreign observers that between five thousand and eight thousand Federales died, and perhaps another two thousand were wounded. To be wounded, however, meant death. Villa's hospital trains were too busy with their own wounded to treat the hated Federales.

President Huerta was driven from office by the defeat at Zacatecas, and Venustiano Carranza's star rose accordingly, although he had had little to do with the Zacatecas victory. Foreign sentiment nevertheless was turning toward Carranza, seeing Villa as the great general he was, but judging Carranza to be better fitted for the statesmanship department. Too, the foreign observers were appalled at Villa's shedding of so much blood, the brutal executions without trial, his holding priests and bishops for ransom.

Leon J. Canova, the special agent for the U.S. State Department, sent more alarming dispatches to his employers. In a long, rambling, and characteristically inaccurate report he said what he saw in Zacatecas was ". . . like the sacking of Europe by the Moors . . . lust for blood . . . gluttony for loot . . . a fierce thirst for vengeance . . . a litany of crime." Such reports damaged General Villa's reputation, even in the midst of his great military victory. I remembered Mr. Wickwire's dour speculations about the general.

Although no one could predict General Villa's reaction in a given situation, he could be humane and understanding at times. I was at headquarters one day when a Federal officer disguised in peasant's clothing was brought before the general before being routinely shot. He claimed to be only a simple farmer but the general ordered him to show his hands.

"These are not an honest farmer's hands!" Villa snorted. "These are the hands of a fucking *perfumado!*"

The officer continued to insist he was only a poor farmer. The general pointed to some sacks of seed corn in a corner of the granary that was temporarily serving as his headquarters. "What is that," he asked, "in those bags?"

The frightened man gave up. "I am only an artist, Señor General, who was forced into the Federal army against my will! I paint pictures, I play the piano, I have never concerned myself with politics."

"Play the piano, eh?" A looted piano stood in the street outside, with several ruffians from Tomás Urbina's brigade trying to carry it away, although what they intended to do with it I don't know. The general ordered it to be brought into the granary and dusted off.

"Now," he said to the poor man, "play me something, for your life, you understand."

Shaking with fear, the prisoner played some classical piece, hitting a great many wrong notes.

"And what the fucking hell is *that*?" the general asked.

"A composition by the great Beethoven Señor General."

"I don't know anybody by that name. Play me something Mexican or I will have your balls nailed to a stump and push you over backward myself—do you hear me, *cabrón?*"

The terrified prisoner played the favorite revolution jingle called "Las Tres Pelonas." When he finished the general roared with laughter. Turning to some women who had been watching the impromptu concert with open mouths, he cried, "You ladies are to join the dance now!" He jumped into their midst, choosing the prettiest for his partner and capering about in clouds of dust that rose from the granary floor. At last he collapsed on a stack of feedsacks, weak from laughing, and dismissed the man. "You see," he said, "I am not such an ogre after all! Benjamin, go find me your reporter friend and tell him how merciful I can be, rendering always true justice!"

Still, Francisco Villa's eventual downfall has always seemed to me to date from the taking of Zacatecas. A British rancher who had a hacienda near Zacatecas put into words the widely held opinion. His holdings had been looted by both Federales and Villistas, and he said in an interview with a Chicago reporter that they ". . . killed my pigs, stole my horses, wrecked my house, cleaned out everything they could get their dirty hands on! And I am sure they didn't do all that because I was an Englishman; I know, because I have seen them rob their own countrymen equally!" General Villa did not deny the excesses, which usually took place in spite of his orders, saying only, "Well, the poor people are only paying back the foreign oppressors, Spanish and others also, for what they have suffered for centuries!"

I admired the general, God knows, but I must admit that his casual disregard for human life began to sow seeds of doubt in my young mind. It was of course true that the Mexican people had suffered much from the Spanish, the French, and the colonial policies of the "big brother" to the north—the United States. But there seemed to me, and to many others, no justification in paying blood for blood. When would it stop? Poor Mexico, drowning in blood!

Colonel Aguirre sent me back to Chihuahua City to pick up secret documents from the Villista general Maclovio Herrera, left in command there. I went on the train, now that the Villistas had repaired the track. As I had been thrilled by the passage of the mixed special through McNary every day in a magical cloud of smoke and steam, firebox glowing and whistle shrieking, so I enjoyed riding on the Mexican trains. Now I was actually on the train, instead of merely watching it pass with my mouth open in awe and admiration.

Mexican train schedules were never very reliable. After all, this was said to be the land of *mañana*. Too, there were still many places where temporary track had been laid, the rails wandering down into arroyos and through riverbeds to reach the other side. This, of course, meant a lot of delays, as the engineer had to throttle down the engine, an uncharacteristic action for a Mexican engineer. The cars were not in much better repair than the tracks. Plush seats had been damaged or torn out and oil lamps were sieved with bullet holes. Windows were smashed so that chilly air whistled through the cars, sending up a whirlwind of chicken feathers, grain dust, dried manure, and stuffing from the ruined seats. It worked, but it was really not much of an excuse for a railroad. Still, steam hissed in great plumes, sooty smoke mingled with cinders filled the drafty coaches with the wonderful railroad smell, and the Mexican whistle played a melodious and exotic tune almost continuously. I was happy, and made friends with everybody.

The passengers were a medley of Mexico—farmers with big straw hats, impassive Indians in blue workclothes and cowhide sandals, women in black shawls with babies on their laps. A cockfight was going on in my car. As we swayed and rocked along the rough roadbed, men squatted in the aisle, betting on a favorite bird and passing around a brown bottle of *sotol*, the cheap liquor of the country. A pale-faced officer with a smidgen of mustache looked disdainfully on these plebeian activities while holding on his lap a bamboo birdcage containing a meadowlark. Every time we stopped we were besieged by an army of peddlers hawking *tamales,* cigarettes, bottles of milk, sacks of pine nuts. It was glorious.

A blind old man sat beside me, beating time to the music on his thigh while a one-legged soldier played "Adelita" on a tin flute. Turning to me, he said, "*Señor,* I am Juan Gómez Ibarra. May I have the pleasure of knowing your name?"

His manners were courtly. Only a peasant, he might have been a courtier to the Spanish kings. All the old men of Mexico, I thought, had beautiful manners and an innate dignity.

"*Sí, señor,*" I said. "I am Benjamin Wilkerson, attached to the headquarters of General Villa."

"*Americano, verdad?*"

"*Verdad, señor.*"

"With your permission, *señor* . . ." His long brown fingers, stained even more brown from cigarettes, touched my face, tracing my features with the lightness of a feather. "You are very young to be so important a person. Still, many of the general's fighters are very young. All, young and old, must fight for our freedom." His finger touched the corner of my mouth, ran gently along my cheek, felt near my eye. "You are troubled, young man. Ah, much trouble for one so young!"

"That is true," I had to admit, a little surprised. He must have had eyes in his fingers. *Much trouble!* I thought. *Rodolfo Fierro, Valentina, my lost friend Mr. McFall, a house with locustwood pins burned down, not to mention the killing of my brother Cleary.* Much trouble, all right!

"But you will win out in the end. Trust me, young man! I see these things clearly even though I have no eyes." He smiled. "Sometimes the eye sees falsely. The eye of the mind sees clear and sharp!"

Startled, I jumped as our car passed a loping coyote and all the men rushed to the window, firing pistols at the beast and whooping with delight. Settling down again, I offered the old man a *tamal* from my greasy sack.

"No, thank you, young man," he said. "*Aprovéchelo!*

Enjoy it yourself! The old do not need a great deal of food. We live on memories."

At Chihuahua City I got off the train, walking between the flaring torches of fried-chicken stands, vendors of shoes, shirts, cigarettes, cigars, cheap jewelry. The city looked much the same. Drunken soldiers careened through the streets arm in arm with painted women. Automobiles honked and drivers swore as they tried to make passage through the crowded streets. From somewhere a church bell tolled the vespers. In the dusty plaza lovers wrapped in *sarapes* fumbled covertly at each other while guitars twanged and a barker screeched himself hoarse, attempting to sell his marvelous elixir for only one peso per bottle. This was Chihuahua City, where so many things had happened.

I am here, I thought, free, unencumbered. Chihuahua City is only a couple of hundred miles south of El Paso. With my important papers and telegrapher's badge I could probably get a ticket to Ciudad Juárez and swim across the river to El Paso. In a way it was an attractive idea, but I dropped it quickly. I loved Mexico, I loved Valentina, I loved *la gente*, the hardworking and gentle people of Mexico. Someday, perhaps, I would go back to Hudspeth County, but for now my heart was in Mexico. Anyway, what awaited me in McNary? Prosecution for murder, probably, and a hangman's noose!

It was late afternoon the next day when I returned to Zacatecas with the packet of papers under my arm. The trip back had been long and tedious and the papers were sealed with a great blob of red wax; I couldn't pass time by reading the documents. As the train clanked and banged to a stop alongside the end-to-end hospital cars, I swung down off the platform and stood for a moment watching the sunset. Mexican sunsets are spectacular. While it is the same sun that makes its daily passage over Hudspeth County, there it only sinks in the west with little fanfare. Here, the sun went down behind the distant purple mountains and for a moment a fan of clear light poured up into the sky, a light that seemed to quiver and pulsate. Then it was gone, but the vanished sun still painted the lower margins of clouds with a golden brush. For a split second I saw the "green flash" that Mr. McFall had once explained to me. The sharp edge of the mountains acted like a prism, he said, breaking the sun's waning light into primary colors, of which the green was the most evident. Thinking of poor Mr. McFall, I felt lonely. Perhaps, before I delivered the package of documents to División headquarters, I might stop and speak with some of the *soldaderas* laboring along the tracks. In the revolution the *soldaderas* were sent here and there to do all kinds of things: shoveling ballast between the rails, cleaning hotel rooms for the officers, doing laundry, grooming horses, and when required, fighting alongside their men.

They cheered me up a little with their jokes, their laughter, their poking fun at me and asking, with sly intent, if I had had a woman lately. Several of them offered me their services then and there, although I suppose they were joking. Still . . . maybe not. I wasn't sure. Anyway, I don't think the revolution would ever have succeeded without those valiant ladies whose hearts burned for freedom.

Opening the door of the caboose, I found no one there but Rodolfo Fierro. I make no bones about it; I was scared. I laid the papers on General Villa's bed and turned to flee.

"Where the hell have you been?" he demanded, seizing my arm. "Prancing around a lot lately, aren't you?"

"Take your hands off me, you bastard!" I yelled.

It sounds brave now, but I can tell you my unreliable voice squeaked up and down as I said it.

"Where have you been?" he insisted.

When I didn't answer, he slapped me across the face. "Little gamecock now, aren't you? I once had hopes for you, Benjamin, but all that is gone now!"

Fong, the Chinese cook, stuck his head out of the kitchen door, paled, and closed the door quickly.

"Fuck your damned hopes for me!" I cried, and when he came toward me again I pulled out the little Spanish pistol.

"Leave me alone! This pistol has a firing pin now, and

the clip is loaded! So help me, if you touch me again with your dirty hands, I'll . . . I'll . . ."

I might have killed Rodolfo Fierro then and there; I'm not sure. He smiled a wicked smile. Taking a cigarette from a pack, the Egyptian brand he favored, he lit it. Breathing the smoke in deep, he blew a wavering smoke ring, watching it twist and turn upward in the light of the kerosene lamp.

"You would shoot me, Benjamin? Really? What a silly idea! Shoot *me*?"

My finger tightened on the trigger.

"I will if you don't leave me alone!" With that pistol I had taken courage. I think he thought I *would* kill him.

He started to walk very slowly toward me, the cigarette dangling from his thin lips, the haughty Spanish face in shadow. But I could see his eyes; they shone like the eyes of a treed coon when someone turns a light on it.

"Don't!" I warned, my heart pounding.

The door slammed open and General Villa walked in, clumping in that bearlike gait, munching a soggy tortilla wrapped around some meat.

"Well!" He paused, deliberately finishing the tortilla and then wiping his hands on his soiled trousers. "What have we here, now? Mutiny in the ranks? My little telegrapher holding a pistol on Rodolfo Fierro?" He laughed his high-pitched laugh and flung a tattered sombrero across the room to light on his bed. "Really, it is too ridiculous!"

I put the pistol away. Fierro was silent, glaring at me like one of the treed coons I spoke of.

"I . . . we . . ." I faltered. I swallowed hard and tried again. "You see, sir, we were having an argument and—"

"And you have won it, for now, apparently!" the general chuckled, sagging onto the bed. He yelled for Fong to bring him coffee; while he drank he watched both of us with interest. "By God, Benjamin, you are not afraid to twist the panther's tail, eh? Threatening *Rodolfo Fierro*! I must tell you, not many men have done that and lived!"

Fierro watched me through narrowed lids. Every moment from now on, I would have to guard my rear, as the

Chapultepec officers always said in their instructions on military tactics.

The general got up, wiping his mustache with the back of a hand. "Benjamin, is that the packet from Chihuahua City?"

"Yes, sir," I said.

"Then you can go, *chamaco*."

Gratefully I left the caboose. The general was saying something to Fierro; the words died away as I crunched through the cinders and back to my room the the Hotel Mercedes. After the encounter with Fierro I couldn't sleep, however. I lay awake till dawn, watching the rising sun paint the faraway mountains. Was Valentina, my Valentina, standing at a barred window someplace, staring at the same early sun and thinking of me? I hoped so.

— 14 —

Dr. Velásquez is indignant. "Don Benjamin, how many times have I told you to rest, *amigo!* To spare yourself! Spend each afternoon in bed, where your heart does little work!" He calls Magdalena. "Woman, come here and help me get this contrary old man to bed! His heart sounds like a cheap clock that has been dropped on the floor too many times!"

I protest, but weakly. It is a fact that I do not feel well. My eyes do not focus properly, I am dizzy, and have little appetite for Concepción's superb *arroz con pollo*, Vera Cruz style. Ah, Vera Cruz! The women there are the most beautiful in the world. Still, my Valentina was from Guerrero.

Magdalena tucks a sheet around me. "What are you saying?" Dr. Velásquez asks, peering at his clinical thermometer.

"She did not come from Vera Cruz, but she might as well have," I insist, my voice small and husky.

"Who, then?"

"Why, Valentina, of course!"

He smiles, restores the thermometer to its leather case. "Your Valentina is immortal, Don Benjamin! I wish I might have the good luck to be so remembered someday."

"Probably not," I tease him. "At least not on your record as a physician!" I pull at his sleeve. "Listen, Velásquez, were you at Zacatecas in 1914? We drove the damned Federales out of Zacatecas like sheep before a pack of wolves—hungry wolves! And then, as was proper, the División del Norte enjoyed the fruits of victory!"

Dr. Velásquez shook his head. "You forget, Don Benjamin, that I was captured earlier. No, I was not at Zacatecas, lucky for me!"

At first the looting of Zacatecas was haphazard and random in nature. Later it became an organized activity that stripped the city clean. A long file of horse-drawn wagons stretched in the rain from the plaza to the railroad station, all loaded with furniture, clothing, rare paintings, statues, wine bottles, musical instruments, and birdcages. Over a half-million pesos of loot was taken from the homes of the wealthy. Horses and carriages, trucks, automobiles, motorcycles, bicycles—every kind of transportation was confiscated. Some of the well-to-do protested, and were shot at once. Others were forced to pay heavy ransom to avoid violence to themselves and their families. Headlines in the world press excoriated the Villista movement; Mr. Leon J. Canova had a field day.

General Villa groaned. Pacing about headquarters, he raised clenched fists above his head. "Aguirre," he protested, "why are my orders not obeyed? Why doesn't this crazy stuff stop? Does no one pay attention to my orders anymore? Does no one realize how we look to the world?" He swore until the room seemed almost blue with obscenities. "Maybe I will have to shoot every tenth man in my army to bring about order and discipline!"

Colonel Aguirre spread helpless hands. "General, the men are only poor peasants, as you know. They have never seen such wealth, so many good things! I have given orders for the execution of anyone caught looting, but the men called for the firing squads cannot be found; they are themselves looting!"

"But we were once true revolutionaries! Now the fucking newspapers describe us as brigands and robbers! It is not good, you know, Aguirre!"

Colonel Aguirre agreed. Shrugging, he said, "All armies have looted since the dawn of history. I have read where—" He broke off, startled. The general had drawn his pistol, charging out of the room with a wild look in his eye. Shooting into the air, he addressed a group of tough-looking cavalrymen gambling with dice on a blanket.

"If I, Francisco Villa, find one man—one man, I say—carrying away anything that does not belong to him, I will cut off his privates and stake the rest of him to a hill where the fire ants and the field mice and the vultures can have their fill of him! *Oyen, hombres!* Do you hear me?"

Sobered, they folded up the blanket and fled with General Villa shooting at their heels. Colonel Aguirre, standing beside me, shook his head.

"Benjamin," he said, "our general is a good man. At times, however, I have a feeling that this sacred revolution, so well and justifiably begun, is turning into a nightmare!"

It was true. Corpses had their teeth smashed with hammers so the gold could be pried out. Salvador Hernández, manager of the Calderón Theater, and widely known as a good man and friend of the poor, was shot backstage by a drunken *soldado* as a Villa general sat his horse among the orchestra seats watching the famous María Conesa in *The Girl of the Kisses*. Hernández' son was also murdered when he came to the rescue of his father. When the two bodies were found, the teeth were missing. The church of San Juan de Dios was despoiled of its gold and silver ornaments, along with a solid silver pedestal on which the image of the Virgin of Guadalupe had stood. No one was sure who had been responsible for these ugly incidents, but blood feuds broke out among several Villista factions, the rich booty traveling from one group to the other as they fought over the spoils.

Annoyed, the U.S. government finally was forced to recognize Venustiano Carranza as the head of the Mexican government. Whatever else could be said about him, Carranza at least gave the appearance of being a gentleman. Furthermore, he had the merchants, industrialists, bankers, and clergy with him, and the State Department apparently figured that he would be easier to deal with than the mercurial Pancho Villa.

Carranza's recognition was a great shock to the general. Before a gathering of his generals he paced back and forth like a wounded cougar.

"What have I done, *amigos?* I won a great battle for the

revolutionary cause! I forbade the sale of liquor. I issued orders that there was to be no more looting. I said no one was to be shot without my personal approval. I did everything a man could do, didn't I? And now they decide that Carranza, that old fart, is to rule Mexico! What is left for the true heroes of the revolution, eh? What recognition is to be given to the brave dead who perished in the cause of freedom while that old man in his fucking blue spectacles was sitting on his ass? Answer me that! Is that fair? Is that just? Is this the way to free the people? Is this the way to make a respected nation out of our beloved Mexico?"

No one spoke. No one dared. Finally the general dismissed them and sat slumped in a chair in his red caboose. I stood silently in a corner where the rays of the kerosene lamp did not reach. He knew I was there, however. With a sigh he picked up the woven horsehair lariat with which he often amused himself by doing tricks, and ran it through his fingers.

"Benjamin?"

"Yes, sir."

"You have that thing, that mouth-organ or whatever it is called. Play me music, *por favor, chamaco*."

It had been a long time since I had played it. After I lost Valentina, I did not want to hear music. No music compared with her.

"Sir, what would you like?"

"There is a *corrido* the people sing. Do you know it? The one about Pancho Villa riding his horse, Siete Leguas?"

"I know it, yes, sir."

"Play, then."

I did not remember all the words; it was one of those tricky off-rhythm things that I never did get the swing of. It went something like this:

> Our general has a great Durango horse.
> The enemies of the people fly in fear
> And the hooves of Siete Leguas run them down
> As our general leads us to freedom.

But I knew the music. Softly I began to blow the melody.

"Come closer, *chamaco*. I cannot hear you!"

Playing, I emerged from the shadows. Elbows on the table, the general stared somberly at the coils of the lariat, as if trying to find in the twisted strands an answer to the problems that plagued him. As I played, he began to talk to himself, almost silently at first, running a hand through his close-cropped reddish hair.

"I did not want anything for myself. The people can have me, have my body, for dog meat if that is what they decide. All I wanted was to get freedom for them, and then I would be glad to give up my gun and be a peaceful farmer." He rubbed weary eyes with his fingers. "I have always been an honorable man. I do not drink. I do not smoke. I do not chew tobacco. Any woman I have slept with I have married, with a priest, although I do not put much stock in priests. That is what the women wanted, though, and I obliged them. That is my way. I have always been kind to women."

He sighed again, shook his head. "I did not want power for myself. But I did not want Mexico to fall into the hands of that Carranza, that . . . that prick!"

Rising, he flailed about the caboose with the lariat, flicking it so that it cracked like a pistol shot. Frightened, I drew back.

"Well, I will not let him have his way, do you hear me? I will not let my mother, Mexico, fall into the hands of a conniving old fart who does not love her as I do!" The knotted end of the lariat snapped near my face, and I dropped the mouth-organ in panic.

"Ah, Benjamin!" Contrite, the general coiled the lariat and tossed it on the table. "I am sorry, *chamaco!*" He beckoned. "Come here."

Hands on knees, face intent, he asked me, "How do I seem to you, Benjamin? Am I that crazy man the *gringos* in Washington seem to think? Am I a rascal, a scoundrel, a troublemaker? Am I an honest man, trying to win a little bread for the people, a plot of land, an ox or a mule to plow with? What do you think?" Picking up the mouth-organ, he handed it to me. "Do not be afraid to talk. Much wisdom can come from the mouth of young people!"

Still frightened, I think my voice quavered. "Sir, I do not know much about politics. I am only a boy, I know. Someday this knowledge may come to me, but now all I know is that you have been a father to me, a father to his son, and that's enough for me."

I would swear that tears glistened in his eyes, in the hard brown eyes of Francisco Villa that could turn to cat's-eye green when angry. He gave me a huge hug, almost suffocating me in the bearlike embrace.

"*Ah, gracias, chamaco*! Thank you for that! Perhaps, a little bit, it gives me back some courage to do what I know I must do!" Releasing me, he cried, "Now go find me Colonel Aguirre, Rodolfo Fierro, Felipe Ángeles—all the rest! The fight begins again! We must plan our campaign well, lest Mother Mexico fall into disaster and ruin under that fucking Carranza!"

I scurried about, summoning the officers to General Villa's caboose. Colonel Aguirre, reading a volume of sonnets in his hotel room, laid it down and peered at me through cracked spectacles. "What mood is he in, Benjamin?"

"A fighting mood! He says he will not let Mother Mexico fall into the hands of that prick Carranza!"

He blew out a long breath and stood up. "Did you ever read Robert Browning, Benjamin?"

I had never heard of anyone named Browning, although there was a Mr. Catullus Brown who was some kind of an official with the sulfur company at McNary.

"Well, you must read him someday. In the meantime . . ." He worked his way into his tunic and buttoned it carefully. "Someday, perhaps, more people will read Browning and forget war."

In the rain-wet plaza was the usual confusion so characteristic of Mexico: peddlers of patent medicines hawking their wares under gaslight, a magician making an egg appear and disappear, sellers of *carnitas*, little chunks of broiled pork, colored juices, footwear, *sarapes*, pumpkin candy. An officious corporal with a squad of ragged infantrymen from Guerrero was searching for contraband, stopping passersby and ransacking them for looted jewelry, coins, firearms. A peasant lady with a big stomach stared uncomprehendingly at the corporal.

"Well, speak up, now!" he ordered. "What's the matter with you, woman? I asked you what you were hiding under your dress! What is it, now?"

Puzzled, the poor woman began to cry. "I don't know, and that is the truth, the Blessed Virgin help me! It's either a boy or a girl, but there is no telling until it comes out!"

The corporal's detail exploded into laughter, injuring his dignity. Red-faced, he marched his squad away at the double, mustache twitching.

That night there was much arguing back and forth in the red caboose, much haranguing, much stubbornness, a hot discussion that nearly came to blows. Colonel Aguirre, believing in a continuation of the campaign, argued that Villa's División del Norte, now well-provisioned and renewed in arms from the warehouses of Zacatecas, should swing south and east to capture Vera Cruz and thus deny Carranza the use of that seaport, where most of the Carrancista supplies came from. Rodolfo Fierro, on the other hand, was for a cavalry attack on Mexico City itself.

"Cut off the head of the Carrancista creature," he demanded, "and the rest of the body will die! That is the only way to do it!"

I guess it was the first time I had seen Colonel Aguirre get mad. He banged the table so hard with his hand that an inkwell jumped into the air. "Rodolfo, you are always for the stylish thing! It will make all the newspapers, I know, but if it fails—then what?"

"It will not fail!"

"Neither you nor any other person can guarantee success in this crazy world! If you fail, it will be the betrayal of the revolution! Are you saying that all we have fought for these many years is to be risked on a chance throw of the dice?"

"*Tímido!*" Fierro jeered. "Bookkeeper! We succeed always by surprising the enemy! My men are poor men, followers of the revolution, who fight for liberty in their own way! I tell you, not a man of my *brigada* would disagree with me!" He rose, hands planted flat on the table before him. "Aguirre, you are a coward, and I do not know why our general puts up with you and your old-maid ways!"

Colonel Aguirre's face became pale as death; his voice was flat and deadly. "No blustering scoundrel can call me a coward, *cabrón!* I invite you outside, where we can settle this argument with pistols!"

The general had been silent, turning his catlike gaze from one to the other as they spoke. Suddenly, characteristically Villa, he drew his pistol and fired a shot into the air—an unfortunate shot, really, because immediately a thin stream of rainwater splashed on the table between Aguirre and Fierro.

"Stop this foolish arguing, you idiots! Are we not in enough trouble without my staff carrying on their own little wars in front of my eyes? Let us get back to this fucking business with clear heads and no animosities!"

Sulkily Fierro sat down. Colonel Aguirre, voice tight and strained, said, "I apologize, General, for my anger in your presence."

Fierro, not to be outdone, mumbled some sort of apology. Hating him as I did, I still could understand how, and why, the general loved him like a brother. *Puro corazón*, the general often said of Fierro; "pure heart, all heart." While often rash, Fierro would storm the gates of hell itself if the general ordered him to do so. Very likely he would have brought off the raid on Mexico City too if bravery would win the day. But there is more to the science of war than bravery alone, as Colonel Aguirre knew.

"Sir," the colonel said after a pause, "I am still in favor of the move toward Vera Cruz. In the meantime, Emiliano Zapata and his troops can attack Obregón's rear and divert him."

Fierro snorted. "Zapata! He and his men are nothing but ignorant farmers! When has this ass Zapata won a battle, tell me! Oh, he has had an occasional skirmish with the government troops, but afterward they all go home to the cornfields. No, we can hardly depend on Zapata for anything!"

"Aguirre," the general said, tipping the table slightly to let the water drain off, "I have always valued your counsel. But this time I think you are wrong." He turned to Fierro. "You are wrong also, Rodolfo. I accept neither plan, since I have a plan of my own."

Expectant, they waited.

"I shall go after Obregón and his Federales at Celaya. He is Carranza's military chief, and when I defeat Obregón the potbellied old bastard will have no army to protect him. I shall go to Celaya and demolish Obregón—like this!" He slapped his hand down hard on the remaining water that lay on the table. A shower of drops flew into the air, into the faces of Colonel Aguirre, Rodolfo Fierro, and the rest of the staff, who had been sitting mute, not wanting to speak up while Fierro and Aguirre were squabbling.

"That is the way I shall defeat Obregón!" General Villa laughed a great bellow of a laugh while Fierro and Aguirre wiped their faces. "I shall hit hard and fast to scatter his troops like the way this water flew into the air! Do you hear me, *compañeros?* Get the men ready! We are off to Celaya!"

Colonel Aguirre, leaving the caboose, muttered something as he left. I believe it was *no hay remedio*—"it can't be helped."

The correspondent for a German newspaper—I think it was the *Allgemeine Zeitung* or something like that—had requested an interview with the general. I was kept for another hour or more, taking down notes as the general talked, so he could not be misquoted. Since the clamor about his bloodthirsty ways he was very careful as to what he said, realizing at last how the right word in the wrong place could give his enemies a chance to attack his policies. Chewing on a mesquite twig as a Texas rancher might munch a blade of grass, he stated his case to the reporter.

"At first I had respect for Señor Carranza, feeling that he represented well the cause for which all of us fought. I opened my heart to him, but I soon found out that he was not a friend but a rival. He would never look at me directly, as one man looks at another, but instead always looked away, talking in riddles about legislation and finances and how to organize a government. He has no blood in him, no *man*'s blood—nothing but ink, the ink bookkeepers use to scribble in their ledgers! Soon I found that Señor Carranza was only a clerk, a dry and dusty man who knew nothing of the struggles of the people of Mexico for land and justice. Señor Carranza wants only the presidency of Mexico, while I want only that my people win freedom and dignity. After that, there will be time to talk about who will be President.''

It was late when I walked through the streets of Torreón. Already the orders had been passed and there was a bustle of activity, even at midnight. Horses galloped this way and that, loaded wagons rumbled on the cobblestones, locomotives were getting up a head of steam. In the east a hunter's moon rose low and orange, adding its light to the flare of torches, the greenish-yellow sputtering of gasoline lanterns, the strings of small electric bulbs around the balconies of the hotels. I almost stumbled over Ojo Parado, busy making bombs in front of a shuttered shop while a gaggle of wide-eyed urchins watched.

"You see," he said, demonstrating, "it is only a matter of dynamite. One takes this stick of the fucking stuff and sews it, thus . . .'' He took up a heavy needle and a hank of waxed thread. "Thus, in this scrap of cowhide! When that is done, all that is necessary is to stick a fuse in one end, light it with a cigarette, and stick it up Carranza's backside to blow him to the hell he deserves for fucking up our country so!"

They all giggled and reached for the makings of bombs while I squatted beside the old man.

"*Hola*, Benjamin!" The wrinkled face split into a thousand cracks as he pumped my hand between his own two. "You see, we have here a class of apprentice bombmakers! But the fuses—I keep them here, in my shirt pocket, as you see. It is not good to give children dynamite fuses."

"I should think not," I agreed. "But have we no real bombs? I mean, bombs made in a factory?"

"These are real enough to blow your ass off!" Ojo Parado protested. "But I know what you mean, Benjamin." Pushing the straw hat far back on his grizzled locks and rolling a cigarette, he said, "I hear that the battle to take this city used up almost all the Division's ammunition. I hear also that when we march on Vera Cruz each man will have only twenty cartridges issued to him because there are no more. That old bastard Carranza has millions of cartridges that come to him on ships through Vera Cruz. So we must make do with less. That is why children make bombs by night, *amigo*." Drawing deep on the cigarette, he blew twin spirals of smoke out of his weathered nose. "Ay, sometimes I do not know if we are going to win after all!"

I guess everyone had heard about the shortage of ammunition and other necessities of war. Not knowing exactly what to say, I murmured, "Sometimes you think of Oaxaca, eh? Your land there, your wife, your children?"

For a long time he was silent, watching the children make their bombs. "Look, Marta! Draw the thread tighter, child!" He drew hard on the cigarette, so short by now it seemed it would burn his lip. From the smell I realized it was not tobacco but *macuche*, the dried weed people smoked when they were too poor to buy tobacco. "Yes, *hombre*. At times I think that way. But there is a war to fight. And I will stand with our general till a bayonet or bullet reaches my old heart! It is the least I can do for those children of mine in Oaxaca. And he who stands under a big tree gets the most shade, eh, *compañero*?" Slyly he dug me in the ribs. "The general offers much shade." Grinning, he ground out the cigarette. "Would it please you, Señor Important Man, to perhaps stop for a while and help my little people make bombs?"

I shook my head. "I do not know anything about making bombs. Anyway, I have a message for General Banda's brigade I am to deliver immediately. It seems the División del Norte is going to Celaya right away."

"Celaya?" Ojo Parado spat, and continued lacing a stick of dynamite in cowhide. "Why Celaya? The talk around is that we are going to Vera Cruz and cut off old Carranza's supplies!"

"Fierro's idea." I shrugged.

Ojo Parado spat again. "That fucking bastard! He will get us all killed. Celaya will be a hard nut to crack with the little ammunition we've got! We will have to kill Federales with our bare hands!"

"Perhaps so," I said. "I am no tactician, *amigo*. I just do what I am told."

The old man laid a hand on my arm. "And when you do it, Benjamin, take care to look behind you always."

"What do you mean by that?"

He went on with his stitching. "Keep an eye out always, *amigo*. Be like the little owl that lives in the desert; he can turn his head clear around and see everything. Be that owl, *amigo*."

It was still raining when I got to the Hotel Villano, where Banda was supposed to be. But an orderly told me he was at the Hotel Luxor, conferring with General Fierro. So I hurried over there, looking like a drowned rat, my *sarape* soaked and weighing about ten pounds, I figured. My boots squished as I walked, and my socks were cold and clammy.

Fierro always had the best suite in any town the Villistas took. The general preferred his red caboose, where he did not need to put on airs, although he often slept elsewhere so as not to be too ready a target for an assassin's bullet.

The parlor of Fierro's suite was ornate with velvet hangings, potted plants, a small porcelain Buddha with smoke from incense curling out of its mouth. When the sentry let me in, I handed General Banda the papers and waited for his reply, as I had been told to do. I was uncomfortable there; Rodolfo Fierro, seated at the table smoking a cigarette, stared fixedly at me. He was always a handsome devil, no doubt of that, with his elegant ways, the narrow ascetic Spanish face, the silky blond beard, the smell of expensive cologne always about him, even on the battlefield.

After scanning the papers, General Banda nodded. "Tell the general I will follow his orders," he told me, and went back to arguing with Rodolfo Fierro.

I got out of there in a hurry, believe me. I wanted nothing to do with Rodolfo Fierro. Outside, it was raining harder. Puddles formed in the streets, and streams of clear water gushed from drainpipes. Ojo Parado and his small band of bomb makers were gone, probably inside someplace to avoid wetting their products. Ojo Parado had predicted: *We will have to kill Federales with our bare hands*! Well, maybe it would be so. As little as I knew about such things, it seemed to me that Colonel Aguirre's plan to go to Vera Cruz was the better idea. Still, who paid attention to me, a lowly runner?

I splashed through the puddles on my way back to the railroad tracks. In spite of the drumming of the rain on my soggy sombrero, I had a vague feeling I was being followed. Several times I halted, spun around, and searched darkness for a sign of a pursuer. *Be that little owl*, Ojo Parado had said. *That little desert owl that can turn its head completely around*. But try as I would, I saw no one, heard nothing except the slanting sheets of rain, silver in the light from an occasional cantina, and the endless drumming of the downpour. It had turned into a cloudburst, and if it continued, it would be a hard job to move the División del Norte toward Celaya.

— 15 —

The march toward Celaya was under way. Most of the División del Norte had left Torreón, with the exception of a few headquarters troops and some of the wagons, trucks, and automobiles. For the time being, General Villa stayed in the red caboose, making some final decisions with Felipe Ángeles for artillery coverage for the final assault. I remained in Torreón also. Ángeles was to remain in Torreón, nursing an injured leg sustained when his horse fell on him, and hobbled about on crutches. If General Ángeles (now he was a general, to Rodolfo Fierro's disgust) had been able to go to Celaya, the star of General Villa might have risen to even greater heights. Ángeles was the only one, it seemed, who could dissuade the general from his favorite slam-bang hell-for-leather frontal assaults which resulted in the loss of so many men of the División del Norte. But Ángeles, it appeared, would not be at Celaya. His broken leg and weakness after the incident made General Villa decide to leave him in Torreón as general in charge of the conquered town.

Since most of the orders had been typed by me and carried to the various chiefs of brigade, there was little for me to do but stay close to the general, in case he needed me, and mope about for my lost Valentina. Oh, it was a grim time for me!

Rodolfo Fierro's brigade had left for Celaya to accomplish the necessary reconnaissance and I was glad he was gone. Next time we were near each other, it might come to a Texas showdown; I always carried the little presentation pistol.

"Benjamin!" I was in the red caboose thinking about Valentina and Colonel Aguirre eyed me sternly, holding in his hand another sheaf of papers. Wars run on paper, and the revolution was no exception. "*Chamaco*, did you not hear me call?"

I scrambled to my feet, very nervous.

"No, sir," I muttered. "I . . . I was just—"

"Daydreaming about that girl of yours, eh? But daydreaming in the revolution is forbidden, you know." He had been scowling, but when I looked so crestfallen, he relented.

"Well, you are young. Youth dreams dreams, I know that. When I was your age I dreamed also." He handed me a packet of maps and told me to take them to General Banda, whose brigade was to be the rear guard. "Keep them well, Benjamin. They are very important to our success at Celaya." He said "success" but I knew he had his doubts also.

"Before you go, have Fong give you a cup of strong black coffee. That should keep you from dozing. In the revolution, you know, sleeping on duty is a sure way to get shot!"

"Yes, sir," I murmured, hitching up my pants. I had grown taller by now but looked rather like a string bean, having trouble keeping my pants up even with a halter rope cinched about my middle. I had not really been dozing—just thinking—but I managed to dare the murderous Fong in his kitchen and drink a cup of the strong black stuff.

On my way I met Ojo Parado. He was standing before a looted clothing store admiring himself in the show window as I passed, while a frightened proprietor was making changes in the fit of his new uniform. In a hurry, I tried to avoid him, but I failed. Catching sight of me, he demanded that I come over and look at his new splendor.

"Look, *hombre*, do you not think this coat pinches a little in the back? Tell me honestly, now."

Actually, the whole outfit was a poor job of tailoring, but Ojo Parado was never a judge of fashion.

"Well," I said judicially, "I don't know about the back. That is to say . . . it looks all right to me."

The nervous proprietor looked relieved.

"Actually," I said, wanting to be gone, "it is a very dashing outfit, and you look well in it."

I turned to go, but thought of something.

"*Amigo*, do you know where Valentina has gone? I hear Fierro had her taken back to that cursed convent where she was so maltreated."

He grumbled, and twisted again to try to see the back of the coat. "How should I know? I do not meddle in Rodolfo Fierro's business. It is not healthy. Take another look at this coat, *amigo*. Do you think silver buttons on the sleeves, or gold?"

For the first time I noticed his new glass eye. It looked like solid gold, and had a diamond or some other jewel set in the pupil. I couldn't suppress a giggle.

Ojo Parado was immediately offended. "What the hell are you laughing about, you damned fool? Are you just jealous, that no one has given you permission to have a coat like this?"

The proprietor fled to the cover of his shop, not wanting to be involved in an argument with these strange roughnecks.

"No," I apologized. "I am . . . I am probably just a little giddy, with all the sleep I have missed lately. You know I attend the general night and day."

He was partially mollified, at least. Grumbling, he yelled for the proprietor. "Come out here, you big *cabrón*, and let out this back a little! I can hardly breathe, and when I get on a horse I will look like a sausage in too small a skin! Hurry, now, before I kick out that fancy glass window!"

After I had delivered the messages to the gruff General Banda, packing up his bedroll in the hotel, I wandered back to the red caboose, only to find that the general and his staff were packing things in two automobiles, getting ready to go to Celaya.

"There is room in the general's car for you too, Benjamin," Colonel Aguirre said, "if you will squeeze yourself down very small."

Somehow I managed, sitting on my bedroll, and we were off to Celaya, leaving Torreón behind in the rain.

General Obregón, Carranza's military chief, was a shrewd man, a master of tactics. Obregón had been a simple farmer in Huatabampo but he was a man of great intelligence, adaptable to the changing situations in warfare. He was largely self-educated and had a reputation of studying every military situation carefully before he acted. The plain of Celaya was broad and flat, planted in wheat and crisscrossed with irrigation ditches which could be used for trenches. Dug in among these makeshift trenches and further protected by rolls of barbed wire, Obregón's soldiers in their shabby white uniforms were well-trained and their morale was high. "All you have to do," Obregón was said to have told them, "is to stay down and wait for the bastards to come! Then you meet them with such a withering volley of rifle fire that they crumble like an old wall!"

He had stationed his artillery on the heights above the town; it was a formidable trap he prepared for the Villistas. Besides, the Villistas were short on ammunition, each man having been issued only eighteen rounds of cartridges. Villa had been confident they would take Celaya easily and he could then replenish his dwindling stores with Obregón's ammunition and supplies.

The attack failed miserably. General Villa had ten thousand men and the defenders of Celaya many less, but Obregón's defenses held. For a brief moment Villista cavalry reached the center of the city, but were driven out.

Seeing his tactics fail, General Villa ran about among the men shouting, "Hold fast, boys! We are not beaten! Form up, and go forward for liberty, for freedom!" A bullet split the crown of his Texas hat—he showed it to Colonel Aguirre later, cursing. "Better it had blown out my brains! They stoned us! I would prefer to be beaten by a Chinaman than by that *perfumado* Obregón!"

Every Carrancista was to him a *perfumado*. But the *perfumados* had held Celaya and beaten General Villa decisively. Obregón gave figures to the press of four thousand Villistas killed and wounded, more than eight thousand captured. General Villa denied these figures but they were probably correct. The once-invincible División del Norte had been cut to pieces in a single engagement. I suddenly remembered what old Mr. Wickwire told me that day so long ago, it seemed, when I found him and his ruined automobile in the desert south of Torreón. *Ambassador Wilson figures Carranza is the most stable influence in Mexico, so they're bound to go with him. The European war is heating up like a stove full of pine knots and the U.S. doesn't want trouble in Mexico if they have to go to war with the Central Powers.*

Certainly General Villa would rise again, as he had on so many occasions. After all, he had started the revolution with four men, three led horses, two pounds of sugar and coffee, and a pound of salt, as he was fond of telling. But I had a gnawing feeling that the battle of Celaya might be a turning point, something that would later be analyzed in history books.

Colonel Aguirre was pessimistic, too, as we rode back to Torreón in a railway car with mostly flat wheels; the general's railroad was also in bad shape. Chin in hand, he stared out the window as the car bumped along. "Ah, Benjamin, war is a chancy business! Sometimes it is the only way to get what you want, but at other times you are apt to lose what you have."

"I . . . I . . ." I didn't know quite how to put it. Still, he had always been kind to me, and reasonable. Finally I asked, "Do you . . . I mean . . . well, is this maybe the end of the revolution?"

"I didn't say that!" He was suddenly angry, peering at me through his thick spectacles, one eye boring into me and the other at an angle. "No one should say that, even speak such words!" He looked around at the staff officers in the car. Some were asleep, others were playing *conquién* with a greasy pack of cards. "Mind your tongue, *chamaco*, or it will get you a firing squad!"

He felt bad for other reasons. Obregón had herded many of Villa's officers into a goat pen with rock walls and killed them all in less than a minute with machine guns. Some of Colonel Aguirre's friends had been in that goat pen.

"I'm sorry," I said. "No, I believe in the revolution, and it has got to succeed!"

General Villa fell back on Torreón. Furious at defeat and still without the calm counsel of Felipe Ángeles, his artillery ineffective without Ángeles' leadership, he was like a mad bull stalking about the red caboose, muttering, unable to sleep. I would have to be careful with my wagging tongue.

I had come almost to revere this big awkward humble man from Durango who so loved his country, his *tierra*, and I hated Venustiano Carranza along with the best of them. Too, I had come to love his country, his Mexico. Texans in Hudspeth County took Mexicans lightly, contemptuously. Cleary and Grandpa Johnson and Mr. Rayford Ellis and Mr. Claude Teasdale always referred to them as "greasers." But to me the simple hardworking peasants with their inborn dignity and graciousness were fine people. It was an awakening for me, and I suddenly realized, too, that I was nearing my sixteenth birthday in that same Mexico.

In Mexico I was growing into man's estate. Although always slight in build, even now, I had become wiry and tough, hard-muscled, a good horseman. Somehow, I concluded, I had even developed a brain; I gave myself unstinted credit for logic, fairness, and other virtues, and my smattering of book learning caused me to be looked on with some respect.

I soon found out what Rodolfo Fierro's new absence meant. With General Villa's approval he made a mad cavalry attack on Mexico City itself, even riding into the plaza with his men. The idea had been to distract Obregón and his forces, but El Invicto, as the people had taken to calling Obregón, was too clever to be pulled away from Celaya.

Colonel Aguirre worried that the defeat at Celaya had unhinged the general's mind. Felipe Ángeles had once said that a major battlefield defeat could well be the end of the once-powerful División del Norte. He told this to General Villa in an effort to convince him to dispose his forces more carefully, to plan well in advance, to use artillery effectively. Now Ángeles hobbled about headquarters on his crutch, looking gloomy. The general did not even listen to him anymore, it was said. Instead, counting on a quick victory to recoup, the general led his weary and dispirited army to Aguas Calientes, where Obregón again defeated him. Short of ammunition and riddled with desertions, we marched to Zacatecas, where he had once scored a great victory, and were defeated again. Finally a beaten and discouraged remnant of the old División del Norte straggled back to Torreón.

It had been one of the bloodiest and most disastrous years in Mexico's long history. Actually, Villa and Carranza believed in about the same things: land for the peasants, schools, more doctors, all the good things. But Venustiano Carranza was determined to seize the presidency of Mexico for himself and his powerful patrons, and Francisco Villa was determined to stop him, though Villa himself had denied wanting the presidency.

More and more he kept himself secluded in the now famous red caboose, denying entrance to once-trusted officers. I sat for hours in the corner, watching him chew his fingers, spit into the coffee can, scratch his close-cropped head in bewilderment. I did not dare speak. The day before, General Delgado, who was Villa's finance officer, in charge of raising funds and printing the now almost worthless bilimbique notes, at last gained access to the caboose. He was an old friend of the general, one of the four men who had ridden across the Rio Grande to start the great revolution. Sadly he begged the general for permission to leave, to go back to his home and family in Monterrey.

"For," he said, "I am only a kind of accountant, sir. I am no use in pitched battles because of my rheumatism, and I am afraid I have also been a failure as your finance officer. You will understand—"

General Villa shook hands with him. "There is no need for explanation, old friend! Go, and find better luck than with this cursed army that wins no battles but continues to eat like a horse and wants their pay in silver!"

Delgado bowed, shuffled backward toward the door. Unfortunately for him, his coat caught on a nail someone had driven in the wall. There was a ripping sound, and a flood of gold coins poured from his pocket.

For a moment there was silence as the last coin tinkled to the floor. I held my breath. Delgado's face was pale and his mouth worked uncertainly. Quickly the general drew a revolver from his belt and shot Delgado through the head. A spout of brain flew out, wetting the wall—and me.

"Bastard!" Villa's face was purple with rage. "Double-dealing bastard! A failed finance officer, eh?" He looked down at the limp body, nudged it with his toe. "You were successful enough in your own finances, old friend!"

Hearing the shot, Villa's Dorados poured through the door. Taking Delgado by the heels, the general dragged him to the door and kicked the body out into the drizzling rain.

"Hang him in a tree!" he ordered. "Let the buzzards pick him clean!" Furious, trembling with rage, he turned on his heel, lay down on his bunk, and finally went into an uneasy sleep while the never-ending rain drummed on the roof of the caboose.

When I thought he was asleep I stole out of my corner, trying to wipe the sticky stuff from my shirt. My brain quaked with the sudden tide of violence. I looked down at my hands; brains, Colonel Delgado's last thoughts, perhaps. Shakily I mopped the floor with a wet rag and gathered the coins, stacking them in piles. There must have been thousands of pesos, worth several thousand dollars in the U.S. money. Delgado was cheating, I told myself, cheating the general and the División del Norte, cheating the people who fight so hard for freedom and justice. He, Delgado, had it coming, certainly. Still and all, I was stunned by what had happened. Violence and death came so quickly in this country. First, an old friend taking a courteous leave—then a limb rag doll on the floor, and human brains scattered about. Even the hard-bitten Dorados seemed uneasy as they bore away the corpse to hang in a tree, as the general ordered.

The battle of León went no better. General Villa, obsessed by his desire to smash Obregón and the Carrancistas, again refused to listen to advice from his worried staff. Colonel Aguirre, Felipe Ángeles, and others tried to persuade him to first regroup, reform, build up his meager supplies of arms and ammunition. But now he would listen to no one but Rodolfo Fierro, who urged him to strike hard and fast at León. Again, at León, the Villistas were soundly trounced.

The general had finally consented to the use of an aeroplane before León to perform reconnaissance duties, having heard that the Carrancistas had done so. Unfortunately, the aeroplane crashed and burned from ground rifle fire, bringing back unhappy memories of my own experience at Torreón. The recollection of that day still lingered in my mind, remembering good old Victoria tending me in my scorched and battered state.

There were other disasters. The general himself led a daring cavalry raid around Obregón's flank, cutting his supply lines. But his own horsemen were then stretched so thin that the Carrancistas broke through and drove Villa and his cavalrymen back. A stalemate ensued.

Hordes of green flies buzzed around the dead and wounded, rats gorged on corpses, everyone had lice, some as big as grains of rice, grains of rice with legs, that walked around. When the Carrancistas almost took the general and his staff, I had to run for it. Out of breath and scared, I lay behind a screen of chaparral and emptied the magazine of my little Spanish pistol at the fleeting figures galloping by. Finally Fierro's *brigada* rescued us. Riding up on his big horse, he scowled at me.

"Be careful with your life, Benjamin! When this war is over I intend to claim it for the shame you have done to my name!"

A stray shot hit the brim of his sombrero and turned it around, almost comically. He looked ruefully at the hole, then tossed the hat away, shouting, "Come on, boys!

Let's chase the bastards into the river!" He was a romantic figure, certainly, and his men adored him. I hated him. How could he so risk his life, anyway, with the knowledge that a stray bullet might send him quickly to hell, where he would be dealt with as he deserved?

Our cause suffered further damage. Unexpectedly, several Latin-American states also recognized Carranza: Bolivia, Brazil, Colombia, and Guatemala. A few days later the United States issued an order forbidding the shipment of supplies of any sort to "anti-Carrancista elements." It hardly mattered to Emiliano Zapata. He was contenting himself with light skirmishes and quick withdrawals, having no more value to the revolutionary cause than bee stings. But the embargo was catastrophic to the División del Norte.

Now Obregón and his army drew the noose tighter. Villa's once-proud army was crumbling away. Dozens of men deserted daily, going back to Quintana Roo or Sinaloa or wherever, to be with their families, plant crops, take up roles again as simple farmers, hoping no one would identify them as revoluntionaries. My old friend Ojo Parado stayed, however.

"I am too old a dog to change my ways." He shrugged. "When this great tree of a general falls, I suppose I will be crushed under the weight. But I am an old man. Who cares if I live or die?"

His proud uniform was stained and ragged and he looked tired as he squatted under a palo verde tree growing in a scorched riverbed filled with hot dry sand. We were on our way back to Torreón, that city and Ciudad Juárez the only places still in our hands. The desert south of Torreón, the desert where General Villa had once whipped General Velasco so soundly, shimmered in the noonday sun. The damnable rains, such an obstacle to an advancing army, had stopped. Vultures hovered over Spanish bayonets, sword plants, thickets of chaparral.

"I suppose," Ojo Parado murmured, "you do not have on you a crumb of tobacco, *amigo?*"

"You know I do not smoke, *hombre.*"

"A little *macuche*, then?"

"No one has even *macuche*, you know that."

Around us rested the remnants of the defeated División del Norte. Someone had put up a canvas fly and the general and his staff were examining maps and arguing under its shade. Even the general's horse, the famous Siete Leguas, looked thin and worn as she nibbled at a sprig of faded green poking through the sand. Our jaded horses were tied to mesquite bushes, and on each bush hung a man's only *sarape* and a few strips of drying meat. In the shade of a mesquite lay an indifferent coyote, tongue lolling out in the heat. Like lions waiting for us to weaken and die, the tawny mountains ringed the desert plain.

I took out my mouth-organ and began to play. That little instrument was all that was left of my brief life in McNary, Hudspeth County. All the rest was gone—even memories, at least sharp and clear memories. McNary had faded. I could hardly remember what Ma and Grandpa Johnson and my brother Cleary looked like. Even Prue Ballard; all I recalled was that she had long brown curls that had fascinated me, and one day she called my shoes "clodhoppers." *Valentina*, I thought again. Someday will I forget her too? No, I would never forget Valentina. There was an old song some of the men sang, called "Flor de Té," about a homeless little shepherd girl who was lost, who did not know where she came from or where she was going. I started to play the simple melody.

Ojo Parado listened in silence, chewing on a bit of brown grass. Amazingly, a tear trickled down his lined and wrinkled face, so like old and hard-used leather.

"I know that song."

The melody ended on a haunting minor note, long sustained.

"I had a lot of women," he said, "but there was one . . ."

I blew spit out of the mouth-organ, dropped it into my pocket. I guess I looked as bad and forlorn as Ojo Parado. "I also, *amigo*. There was one . . ."

Noticing the general emerging from under the tent fly, Ojo Parado got creakily to his feet. "You will find her again, Benjamin—I know." Wiping away a tear, he joked,

"In Oaxaca I had a small reputation as a *brujo* myself. I see things that will come to happen. Trust me!"

Brujo meant "sorcerer," a kind of male witch. I shook my head, climbing on my own horse, a sorry and spiteful animal named Relámpago—lightning. Relámpago had replaced my little lost Pinta. If real lightning was as slow as Relámpago, a man could see a thunderbolt coming and have plenty of time to amble away before it struck.

"I hope you are right," I said. "But I do not know."

Advance scouts of Obregón's victorious army pursued us. Although we turned and fought, they harassed us unmercifully. Many of our shrinking army were killed and wounded. I remembered dead Pepe Ruíz, the man of the picture hat, who had so proudly worn the wristwatch John Reed had given him. Now I saw one of Pepe's companions draped limply over a tub-sized barrel cactus. A stripling, chest heavy with empty cartridge belts, squatted nearby, holding up a lean brown wrist to admire the flash of the sun on John Reed's much-traveled wristwatch. Seeing me look at him, he shrugged, pointed to the dead man impaled on the cactus.

"What can time mean to him, eh?"

Gingerly I pulled the body free of the needles and laid the man on the sand. Looking at the placid face, I could not stand it. Carefully I turned him over, head resting on one outflung arm, so that he looked only asleep.

The stripling snickered. "He will not know the difference, up or down!"

"But I will!" I said. "Get along your fucking way, *carajo*!"

Laughing, pulling up his pants, he scurried away. Youth laughs at death; youth is indestructible. I was young too, but I couldn't laugh. Sixteen, was I, then? Almost. But in my heart I was a bitter old man. Valentina had softened me, made me want life and love and laughter, but Valentina was gone. I climbed back on my sorry mount and followed the staff toward a distant Torreón, a faint smudge on the northern horizon. I had come close, too close, to shooting that insolent youth with the wristwatch, a kind of memorial to Pepe and his sombrero with the pictures of the Baby

Jesus and the Blessed Virgin. As I rode I was appalled that I had even considered it. I guess I had been blooded, really blooded now, so that human life, even my own, meant little to me anymore.

Torreón had been the main seat of General Villa's power. Now Torreón was short of food, short of arms and ammunition, short of temper. The citizens were tired of the endless battles, the disruptions of the city power and water, the general's taxes, made heavier now because of his need for money to carry on the fight against Carranza. Before the remnants of his army the general finally made a speech from the balcony of the city hall:

"Old friends! Our struggle to recoup our losses has failed completely. This seems to be proof that the people support Carranza, though mistakenly. I am going back to the sierra with only my escort, to think about the country, to make plans, to get ready for a new fight against the usurper. Make sure of this: the people will get tired of Carranza and than I will rise again, more fiercely than before! In the meanwhile, do whatever you like, *compañeros*. I hope soon you will again hear my call to arms. Now I give you thanks and wish you happiness."

Of course, General Villa never talked that way; he was crude and unlettered. Felipe Ángeles, decent gentleman and expert artillerist, put the general's rough but sincere words into good form. One of my last duties as *telegrafista de la primera clase* was to send the text of this message to other towns where some Villistas were still holding out. It was a sad duty.

"*Qué caray!*" Ojo Parado was unhappy. "It is cold in the sierra! My old bones will freeze and break up there! I am from Oaxaca, where it is warm in winter. The sun shines and the birds sing. Who wants to go up into that fucking sierra?"

Of course it was all talk; Ojo Parado would follow his idol anywhere, and so would I. What did we have to lose?

The general and a few of his loyal officers began to prepare for the arduous march into the sierra. Colonel Aguirre came to me, brow furrowed and a worried look on his face.

"Listen to me, Benjamin."

"Yes, sir."

"The general has said that you are not to come with us to the sierra. He says you are only a boy, and can make much of yourself with your skills if you go back to the States. But Rodolfo Fierro intervened. He and I had an argument about it. Finally the general agreed; you are to come into the sierra with us." What with all the troubles, I think the colonel had taken to drink; his eyes were red and his hand trembled as he put it on my shoulder and looked around. "What I say is this: you can just disappear and make your way back to the border. Here!" He handed me some silver pesos. "That way is best for you, I think. Who knows if we will ever come down from the mountains?"

I thanked him, but refused. In the first place, I had cast my lot with General Villa for better or worse. If it was worse, as it appeared to be, then all the more reason for sticking with it. Too, I still had a forlorn hope that I would find Valentina.

"You are a good boy," Colonel Aguirre said, his crossed eyes understanding. He was a fine and gentle man. "I hope you find your beloved Valentina someday when this war is over."

The general's speech from the city-hall balcony seemed to have made an impact. It was reprinted in many newspapers, both U.S. and foreign, and it soon resulted in a message from Ambassador Wilson in Washington. He wanted the general to meet him and General Pershing, the new head of the U.S. Army, at El Paso as soon as possible. At first, General Villa only swore horribly and said he was done talking to *gringo* officers and diplomats. He especially disliked Ambassador Henry Lane Wilson. Wilson, whom I had seen only from a distance, was a nervous little man with pince-nez and a toupee, well known to be aligned with American mining interests in Mexico and distrusting any attempt to bring democracy to Mexico.

"They tell lies, nothing but lies!" he growled. "They say they will help you, then they cut off your supplies! What do I have to say to that damned old-maid busybody of a Wilson? Only this: go fuck yourself, old man!" But

Felipe Ángeles, always the cool head and now getting around at headquarters with a bad limp after his accident, finally talked him into it.

"Sir, what do you have to lose? Maybe they have changed their minds. Maybe they want your help in some matter. A thousand things are possible. You must go!"

The general sulked for a while, then decided he would go after all. No one invited me but I was so much a part of the furniture around headquarters that I just assumed I was to go also. And I did.

The railroad from Torreón to Ciudad Juárez was still running, although frequently interrupted by roving patrols of Carrancistas who were trying to tear it up so as to trap the Villistas in Torreón. Several times we fired from the car windows at fast-riding Carrancistas in their dirty white uniforms. They rode mockingly alongside our car, making obscene gestures, until the general snatched up a Krag rifle, one of the many that had once been given to him by the U.S., and shot one of them through the head.

"*Qué caray!*" he shouted. "Ángeles, I thought I had lost my eye! But now it has come back to me! Right through the head! That bastard will roast in hell tonight!"

He watched in satisfaction as the man's body, heel caught in the stirrup, dragged through the dust until one of his companions halted the horse and shook his fist at the on-speeding train.

"One less louse!" the general jeered, and slumped back in his seat again, hat tilted over his eyes. Instead of the greasy suit and shirt without a collar, Felipe Ángeles had persuaded him to dress for the meeting as an important person. Now he wore a loose Norfolk jacket and a Texas hat, with a ridiculous loud bow tie. He and Ángeles had argued over that polka-dotted bow tie but the general insisted on wearing it.

"I have seen pictures of important people in the States. They wear such things. If you are going to get me up as a damned *perfumado*, Felipe, I want to be in the latest fashion!"

Rodolfo Fierro was left behind to command in the general's absence. I was glad to be away from his continual scrutiny, and looked forward to seeing El Paso again, where Mr. McFall and I first met. Too, I yearned for a chocolate ice-cream cone; I had never run across any in my travels through Mexico.

An olive-drab touring car with general's flags waited for us at the river. We rode across in style with an enlisted chauffeur and a young shaved-headed lieutenant sitting in the back seat with General Villa and Colonel Aguirre. I sat on a little jump seat.

As we drove up Stanton Street and out on the dusty road toward Fort Bliss, I thought that Texas looked much the same. My leaving it hadn't been any great shock to the country's economy, customs, or appearance. Texas was still Texas—vast, spare, burned brown, littered with the shacks of small ranches where thin cattle stared as we rolled by. I didn't miss Texas anymore, but I sure wanted that ice-cream cone.

General Villa and Colonel Aguirre had lunch with General Pershing and Ambassador Wilson in Pershing's quarters, a rambling house with a wide veranda and even a green lawn where prisoners with a big P on their backs were planting shrubs and watering the grass under the eye of a burly line sergeant. No one had invited me to lunch, so I asked him if there was anything for me to eat.

Taking a wet cigar from his mouth, he spat. "You one of them greasers just drove in the general's Dodge autymobile?"

Annoyed and very bumptious, I said, "Sergeant Big Belly, your mouth is as big as that pot of yours! No, I'm not Mexican, though I came with General Villa as his private secretary. I'll ask you again. Where can I get something to eat?"

He grinned, stuck the sodden cigar back between his teeth. "My, ain't you the little firebrand! Guess I misspoke myself." He beckoned to a corporal lounging under a chinaberry tree. "Lou, keep an eye on these jailbirds, will you? This here gentleman and me are going home for a little chow."

Sergeant Mulcahy was really a nice man. Mrs. Mulcahy was nice too. She fried ham and made biscuits while

Mulcahy tried to pump me about what was happening in the general's quarters.

"I don't know anything," I said truthfully. "Thank you, ma'am—yes, I will have another couple of those biscuits. Remind me of the ones Grandma used to make back in McNary."

"Whatever are you doing, then, young man, traveling around with that awful Mexican bandit?"

"Begging your pardon, ma'am, but General Villa is only fighting for freedom for his people, just like Sam Houston and Stephen Austin did in Texas in 1846 when he beat old Santa Ana."

She thought about this, then said, "Well, maybe you're right. The world is so complicated anymore that a body can't tell *what's* going on!"

After a while I wandered over to the big house. An officious private took me to task. "No one ain't allowed to sashay around here while this here conference is going on. Stand back!" He took a little poke at me with his bayoneted rifle and I stepped back, not willing to press my luck a second time.

"All right, Sergeant," I said mildly. "But I'm part of General Villa's delegation, so is it all right if I just set down in that swing on the front porch and take a nap?"

That "Sergeant" got to him. "Well," he said, fingering his lip, "I guess that would be awright, if you don't make no noise or commotion or anything."

The porch swing had some nice cushions on it and I laid back and swung a little, my feet dangling and the swing making small creaking sounds. They sounded sad, in a way, and after a while that got to me. Being in the Mulcahys' place and eating home-cooked food made me sentimental, I guess. Though it was warm and sunny at Fort Bliss, the time must have been near Christmas; I had lost track of time. This year there would be no Christmas for me, no stocking with an orange, no cookies from Valentina, no Bible from Grandpa Johnson. No, Bibles were not for me anymore. I was a great sinner, forever outside the pale. God had lost track of me. God was made for good simple honest people, *la gente*, who would soon be winding their way through little towns and villages signing "Los Peregrinos," "The Pilgrims," and acting out the Christmas ceremony of Las Posadas, the touching search of Mary and Joseph for an inn.

Of course, I was across the border now and in the States. I could just chuck the whole thing and walk away, taking up a new life in the U.S. But there were two reasons I couldn't. First, I loved Valentina, was determined to keep looking for her, and she was certainly not to be found in the U.S. Second, I still believed in General Villa and what he was trying to do for the people he loved. Rough, uncouth, violent, and all the rest, he still was a great man, and I would not desert him. So there it was. El Paso was only a few miles distant and freedom beckoned, but I turned my face against her and dozed.

I don't know how long I slept but finally I came drifting back. Trying to remember where I was, I lay for a long time in the soft cushions. Then I became conscious of voices, angry voices, filtering through the closed parlor window with its chintz curtains. General Villa's high-pitched voice I knew well enough; he was angry about something, and there was a thud as if his fist slapped a table hard. Then came a soft murmur. That would be Colonel Aguirre, translating. I yawned, stretched my arms. A new sentry had come on and eyed me suspiciously. I gave him a hard stare and he walked on by. Then there were Anglo voices, though I could not make out any words. I guess that would be Pershing. Well, they were certainly wrangling about *something*!

After a while Colonel Aguirre came out on the porch, mopping his brow. He saw me and came over to sit in the swing.

"What's going on in there?" I asked imprudently. It was really none of my business.

"Ah, Benjamin! Such arguing!" He shook his head. "The general is furious."

"I gathered that, sir."

Folding the handkerchief, he tucked it back in his breeches pocket. "We did not expect them to make such an offer, really. It is something that will take discussion."

I waited for him to explain the offer but he didn't. Instead he got up, took a deep breath.

"Well, while they are drinking coffee and eating some little rolls, I must visit the bathroom. My kidneys are weak, you know."

I knew. Everyone knew about the colonel's weak kidneys. "Sir, how long will they be?" I asked.

He took off his spectacles, rubbing the white mark where they sat on the bridge of his long nose. "I am certain we will be here tomorrow as least, and perhaps longer. Are you getting along all right, Benjamin? Have you found food? You will probably need a place to sleep, also. Perhaps one of the enlisted men can—"

"I'll get along all right," I said. Suddenly I thought of old Mr. Wickwire. He lived in El Paso, at least when he wasn't rousting around Mexico, staggering from news story to news story. Maybe I could find his address and talk to Mrs. Wickwire, find where the old gentleman was and what he was doing. "Sir, would it be all right if I just went away for a while? I mean, I have friends in El Paso I'd like to see."

"Of course, Benjamin." He hooked the spectacles over his ears. "If the general asks for you I will tell him that I excused you for a while."

I probably scanted my thanks, and got out of there in a hurry. Mr Wickwire was about the only Anglo friend I had. If he hadn't yet perished foolishly someplace in Durango, I wanted to talk to him.

His number was in the El Paso telephone book. I wasn't used to the telephone—never used one before—but I turned the crank and a voice came out; the "operator," she was called. I gave her the number but she said, "That number has been disconnected for nonpayment of bill, sir."

Well, I had the house address. Maybe it wouldn't do any good because they had moved or something, but I thought I'd try it. A Mexican selling *tamales* from a lard can told me where 743 Houston Street was, so I walked there. It wasn't far.

It was a neat little cottage with a white picket fence and washing flapping in the backyard. I knocked at the door and an elderly woman opened it. She looked gray and haggard, and was wiping soapsuds from her hands.

"Yes, sir?"

She looked at me kind of funny and I don't blame her. I had on a Jalisco sombrero, a ragged cotton shirt, a dirty canvas coat, and my jeans were tucked into badly worn boots. I hadn't had a haircut for a long time, either, and a few wisps of blond beard were beginning to sprout on my chin. I was proud of those few.

Politely taking off my hat, I asked, "Ma'am, is this where Mr. Wickwire lives? The reporter for the El Paso *Morning Times*?"

"Who are you?" she wanted to know.

"Ma'am, my name is Benjamin Wilkerson. I knew Mr. Wickwire in Mexico. I'm here on business and—"

"Why didn't you say so?" She beamed, fussed at her hair, straightened her apron. "You're the Ben the mister talked about so much! Come in, come in!"

I followed her into the small parlor, smelling of furniture polish and old books, her talking all the time. "I ain't been able to dust much since the mister was took sick, but you'll have to pardon me!"

Anyway, he was alive. I hardly expected that, with all the chances he took.

"Sick, is he?" I asked.

Her face became grave. "Some kind of inflammation of the lungs he caught in Mexico. I told him, 'Stay out of that place or you'll catch your death,' but he'd never listen to me!"

Beckoning me to follow, she went heavily up the stairs. "I'll just see if he's awake." Turning the knob, she peered in. "Wickwire, you awake?"

"I am now!" a familiar voice protested. "Mildred, why in hell do you keep sticking your nose in here when I'm trying to take a nap! I swear, I—"

"Now, you just hold your tongue, Wickwire!" Mildred snapped. "There's a gentleman here to see you!"

He was small and fragile in the big brass bed. The tattered khaki jacket with "Correspondent" stenciled on it hung lifeless from a hat rack beside the plaid cap he always wore backward so he could see better with his field glasses. Quilt tucked up around his chin, he stared at me.

"Ben Wilkerson," I said, holding my hat in front of me. "How are you, Mr. Wickwire?"

For a moment he stared with watery eyes. Then he whooped with delight. It wasn't much of a whoop, kind of bubbling away as he started to cough. Anyway, he started to throw aside the quilt and get up, but Mrs. Wickwire pushed him back. "You know what Dr. Duggan told you!"

"That goddamned doctor! He's a horse doctor, I tell you! He doesn't know a light cold from the TB's!"

"Don't try to get up, Mr Wickwire," I urged. With a look at Mrs. Wickwire I said, "If it's all right, I'll just sit on this rocker here and talk for a little while."

She nodded. "Can I bring you some coffee, Mr. Wilkerson?"

"I'd like some too," Mr. Wickwire said.

"You know the doctor said—"

"Go away, Mildred!" Mr. Wickwire grumbled. "Ben and I have got a lot to talk about."

"Please, Mr. Wilkerson, don't tire him," she said, concern in her eyes. "He's weak, though he don't let on." She went out, closing the door after her.

Mr. Wickwire snorted. "Weak, am I? That's a good one! A little cold in the chest, that's all it is." Pulling pillows behind him, he sat up. "Now! What brings you to El Paso, Ben? Is there a story for the paper in it?"

He couldn't ever see anything except in terms of newspaper stories. I started to open my mouth but he beat me to it.

"Look here!" He showed me a pile of newspapers on a stand beside the bed. "I follow everything real close, even though I am stuck in bed for a little while." He held up a stack of papers. "New York *Times*, Denver *Post*, San Francisco *Call Bulletin*—I read 'em all to get a feel for things." Suddenly he stared at me. "That's why you're here, eh? I mean, probably with that old rascal Villa! Why, of course! President Wilson has recognized that booby Carranza and Villa is here so Pershing and Ambassador Wilson can simmer him down and get him to throw in with Carranza!"

"I guess you know more than I do," I admitted. "For a while I sat on the general's front porch at Fort Bliss, but I couldn't hear what was going on."

His eyes narrowed and he scratched his chin. "Didn't hear anything, eh?"

"No," I said truthfully, "but Colonel Aguirre came out on the front porch to take a little rest from all the arguing and said something about they never expected them to make such an offer. I don't know what that means."

"Offer?" Mr. Wickwire was excited. He grabbed a pad of notepaper and a pencil and started to scribble, muttering to himself. ". . . young man who is General Villa's clerk . . ." He broke off, stared at me. "Is that what you are? Villa's clerk?"

"I guess so. But don't put too much in it, Mr. Wickwire. I really don't know *what* they're doing in there, except that Colonel Aguirre—"

"Villa's adjutant?"

"Yes."

"Go on!" He scribbled some more.

"Well, he said things would take a lot of talking over, and they might be here awhile. Come to think of it, I guess General Villa was really mad! I couldn't make out any words, but he was pretty loud. It sounded like he was banging his fist on the table."

Mr. Wickwire put down the pad and leaned back in the pillows, grinning like a Chessie cat. Hands locked behind his head, he asked, "Ben, you remember me telling you that something odd might happen in Mexico soon?"

"Yes, sir. I remember."

He got into a fit of coughing and put a handkerchief to his mouth. It came away speckled with dots of blood. Staring at it, he said, "I saw a lot of blood in Mexico—too much blood. It didn't bother me that much. I used to work in a butcher shop on Midland Avenue before they took me on at the *Morning Times*. But I must say my own blood kind of bothers me."

"Look here," I said, gathering up my hat, "I'd best be

going, Mr. Wickwire. I don't want to tire you out. I'll stop and pay my respects to Mrs. Wickwire as I go out."

He grabbed my arm. "Stay awhile! Let me tell you something, Ben Wilkerson. You're in on history, history being made right now!" When I sat down reluctantly, he went on.

"You know what's happening in the European war?"

"No," I said. "To tell the truth, I haven't been around much where there were any newspapers!"

"Well, all hell is about to break loose! The Germans are rolling up western Europe like a carpet! See, it's all in the papers!" He held up the Boston *Globe*, rattled a few others. Coughing again, he smeared at his mouth with the back of his hand; his cheeks were flushed and he seemed to me to wheeze a little, but I couldn't stop him. "The Allies are losing ground in France and Belgium. Their big autumn offensive failed, and they lost over a quarter of a million men. The damned Huns are even using poison gas! Now, you *know* the U.S. can't just stand by and let the bastards overrun Europe!"

"I guess not," I said uncomfortably.

"Then there's the Zimmerman note. Our spies got a copy of it somehow. In it Zimmerman—he's the Boches' foreign minister—sent a note to Carranza asking for Mexico to attack the U.S.! In return, Mexico would get Texas and New Mexico and Arizona as the spoils of war if the Germans won, as they damn well seem to be doing!"

I thought he was crazy, but it turned out he was right as rain.

"So what do we do, eh? We haven't got a real army—nothing but a bunch of green recruits that don't know their ass from a penwiper. We've *got* to get into it, and soon!"

"I guess I follow you," I said, "but—"

"I don't wonder Villa pounded the table and got mad! It's only a guess, Ben Wilkerson, but I'm willing to lay this house on the line to prove it!" He coughed again, fumbled for the handkerchief. "The house is all Mildred and I have got, too. They even turned off our telephone." He swallowed hard and seemed to collapse into the high-piled pillows, but kept on, his voice not much more than a croak.

"Mark my words, Ben! That Pershing is smart, and that young Patton is too, and they probably put the idea into Ambassador Wilson's head! They're going to try to work some scheme where U.S. troops go into Mexico and chase Villa around Robin Hood's barn to give our green troops a workout. Blood them, you might say, so's when they're shipped to Europe they'll be veterans that know which end of a gun the bullets come out of!"

I was startled. "Why would you ever think that, Mr. Wickwire? You don't know General Villa. All he wants to do is beat Obregón and Carranza! Why, he hasn't got time to be a clay pigeon for General Pershing! And he's too proud to be made a fool of like that!"

Mr. Wickwire's voice was hollow as it came from the dark cave of pillows. "I'm tired, Ben, and can't talk a whole lot more. But let me tell you this. Villa's beat! Carranza is the new strong man of Mexico. There's not a chance Villa can overtake him now. So all that's to be seen is whether Villa will humble himself enough to take the bait. That's all he has left, believe me. He can go out a hero, running all around Durango and Chihuahua pulling Uncle Sam's tail! After it's over he can retire and be a senator or something in the Mexican Assembly or whatever they call it."

I got up, shaking my head. "You don't know General Villa, Mr. Wickwire. He'd never betray his cause." I was curious. "Have you told anyone down at the *Morning Times* about this . . . this theory?"

His voice was muffled. It was getting dark on a winter afternoon and I couldn't see his face.

"They think I'm crazy."

"You're not crazy," I said. "Maybe you're just a little feverish, Mr. Wickwire."

From somewhere under the blankets he put out a thin cold hand. "I'm that chilled, son. Will you ask Mildred to come up and lay another blanket on me?"

This time I knew I'd never see him again. Poor old man! He was a great one and he'd tempted death I don't know how many times just to get a story for his beloved *Morning Times*. I took his hand in mine, afraid if I shook it like men do he'd come all apart, a pile of old bones in the bed.

"I'll tell her," I agreed. "And I want to say something else, Mr. Wickwire. You're my best friend, and I always respected you. I'm glad to be your friend."

He didn't seem to hear me; maybe he was asleep. Tiptoeing to the door, I went out. Downstairs Mrs. Wickwire was lighting an Argand lamp that had a fancy hand-painted shade, while a coffeepot bubbled.

Anxious, she asked, "How is he?"

"Sleeping, I guess. Thank you, ma'am."

It was after six. The sky was clear with a crescent moon, a single bright star perched near one of the horns. After a cup of coffee I caught a ride back to Fort Bliss on an army truck. As it rumbled along I thought about Mr. Wickwire and what he had told me. I couldn't believe it, no matter how I stretched my imagination. It was a wild tale, probably only a kind of nightmare he had in his fever. General Villa could never be a party to such an underhanded business!

— 16 —

On the way back I sat in the swaying coach reading a copy of *Excelsior*, the Mexico City daily I bought in El Paso. Some of the Dorados played poker on the floor between the seats. In the other end of the car, bare feet propped on the seat opposite, General Villa was talking to Colonel Aguirre. He was still angry about something, and his sunburned face was more red than usual. I listened but couldn't make out anything because of the hubbub of the stud-poker game.

The European war was certainly going badly. The Germans were having success after success at places called Loos and Lens and Artois. The Russians, who were supposed to be our allies, had been badly whipped on the Eastern Front, whatever that was. German submarines were sinking French and British ships in the Atlantic and there was a battle in the U.S. Congress as to whether the U.S. should join in to keep Europe from becoming a German kingdom.

"What the fucking hell do they think I am?" the general bellowed.

Startled, I looked up from my newspaper. Irate, he strode up and down the worn carpeting of the coach, scattering the poker players, waving his hands in the air. He had changed back from his elegant clothes, wearing again the familiar shiny and stained brown suit, vest unbuttoned and with no collar. His broad peasant's feet tramped back and forth, toes seeming to curl in anger and frustration. Colonel Aguirre watched owlishly from the other end of the coach.

"Am I a leader, a man who has great dignity and a good cause? Or am I a damned puppet, to be jerked about and dangled from their fucking strings?" He turned to one of the poker players under his feet. "Tell me that!" He dragged the frightened man to his feet and shook him like a dog shakes a rat. "Tell me, you! Which am I, eh?"

His grip on the collar was so tight that the man could only roll his eyes and stammer.

"Bah!" Breathing hard, the general flung the man down. For a minute he stared at the cringing Dorado, then lumbered back to sit beside Colonel Aguirre, who usually had a way of cooling him down.

A puppet on a string? Jerked and dangled about? The words sounded like something old Mr. Wickwire might say. Still . . . I shook my head and went back to reading *Excelsior*. Ambassador Wilson and Pershing probably only asked the general to cooperate with Carranza. The way he felt about that "old bastard with his big belly and blue spectacles" had certainly been enough to set him off; it always was.

Back in Torreón it was raining again, a cold and icy winter rain turning to sleet. Festooned with a coating of ice, the telegraph wires sagged. Before long, some of them would break, and there would be a lot of confusion. Pulling my *sarape* around my shoulders and hunching my shoulders down, I crunched through the frozen cinders, following the general and Colonel Aguirre to the red caboose.

Alongside the tracks a huddle of poor women was heating tortillas on an iron plate over a scanty fire. A sheet of corrugated tin was propped over the fire to give them shelter. Cold, oppressed, with little food and less shelter, still they endured, with dignity. As I passed, one of the women, a *soldadera* whom I knew as Encarnación, tugged at my sleeve.

"*Señor*, come and have a warm tortilla."

I thanked her, saying "*Aprovéchela,*" the gracious way to express something like "No, but enjoy it yourself." But she insisted on tugging at my arm and urging me toward the shelter of the corrugated tin roof.

"Come, *señor!* Come, *por favor!*"

Reluctantly I squatted beside the fire. A young girl, head and body swathed in an old blanket, picked up a hot tortilla with a pair of sticks and handed it to me.

I nodded. "*Gracias, mujer.*"

The tortilla was warm, fragrant with the odor of corn. There is nothing like fresh tortillas patted into shape by loving Mexican hands and warmed over a wood fire. I remember Mr. Dinwiddie—oh, so long ago, and so far away—saying the baking of bread was a religious experience for some women. I could believe that of the tortilla.

Chewing on it, the delicious fragments slipping down my gullet, I stared at the young woman. Something began to stir in the recesses of my brain. There was nothing definite—yet—but I began to feel as if the moment was significant; the young girl, downturned face almost hidden by the worn and faded *sarape*, the other women, much older, grinning at me with hidden delight. I paused in my chewing, holding the half-eaten tortilla in one hand, blinking in the smoke to clear my eyes.

"Valentina!" I dropped the tortilla, sprang to my feet, unbelieving. "Valentina! My God! Where did you come from?"

Before she could answer, I grabbed her in my arms, squeezing her hard against my chest. My face was wet against hers as I kissed her.

"Oh, Valentina! I can't believe it! *Mi vida!*"

Giggling, joining hands, and dancing around us crying, "Valentina! Benjamin! Valentina! Benjamin!" the old women capered about while hail rattled on the tin roof. In the glow of the fire I pushed her back a little, holding her by both arms, the better to see her. Slowly she pulled aside the folds of her *sarape*; her hair shone in the glow. The blue eyes, now seeming a darker and more brilliant blue, were lovely and luminous, sending back the warmth of the blazing fire.

"It is a long time, Benjamin, but I have come back to you, have I not?"

"But . . . but how . . . ?"

The women had squatted again, beginning the *pat pat*

pat of shaping tortillas. Valentina and I were left to ourselves in the rear of the sheet-iron enclosure. We sat down on a pile of blankets, which was probably where the dispossessed *pacíficos* slept. I looked furtively around. Rodolfo Fierro had a long arm. Someone might already be spying on us, know that Valentina was here with me.

"How—?" I started again. But Valentina, my lovely Valentina, lovely even in the rough peasant clothes she wore, put a finger to my lips.

"*Corazón*, my heart, it is not easy for me to talk. I am too full here!" She put a hand to her breast.

I hugged her hard. The old ladies at the fire kept their heads firmly averted. This was lovers' business, they seemed to say, and no concern of theirs. I was grateful for that.

Down the tracks the general and Colonel Aguirre had already gone into the red caboose, glistening now under a coating of ice. A yellow light bloomed in the window. Fong, the cook, was probably already cooking up a mess of beans and chiles for the general.

"Well, then!" She brushed back a vagrant strand of hair and I caught a momentary scent of her hair, of her, of my Valentina. "It is a long story but I see you are tired, Benjamin, after your journey to Chihauhua City." She fumbled at her bosom and fingered the barlow knife I had given her, slung now from a gold chain around her throat.

"I . . . I . . ." She struggled for words. "It is hard to tell you, Benjamin, because no one will ever know what I felt when I found that General Fierro, Rodolfo Fierro himself, was my father!" For a moment she wept, then raised her head proudly. "But I will speak no more of that, except to say that when Father Eusebio took me back to the convent he gave orders for me to be kept in a locked room and fed only bread and water and made to pray seven times seven times each day for forgiveness from God. The sisters were very hard on me but I do not blame them too much because they were afraid of Father Eusebio too. Anyway, I— "

"Hush!" I said. From down the track I heard the familiar slam of the caboose door. Someone got off and boots crunched in the cinders. Who was it? I drew Valentina farther back with me into the sheet-iron shanty, as far as we could go without bumping heads. The old ladies continued their tortilla-patting and gossip. "We must be careful," I said. "Your father is very clever."

In the fire-streaked gloom her face was pale and sad. "He is my father no longer, Benjamin. I have no father, no mother—all I have is you!"

I took her in my arms, and she pressed tight against me. Lord, what a feeling! I loved Valentina. It was if we were on the moon or at the bottom of the sea—just the two of us, wrapped in each other's arms.

"How did you get away?"

"The girls helped me. Oh, Benjamin, I wish I could have helped them escape too! That convent is a bad place, but they would not leave! They said they had no place to go, but when I told them about my Benjamin, they helped me, at the risk of their own punishment when the sisters found out I was gone." She held up the barlow knife on its chain. "Sister Clemencia ran after me—it was night, you see, and I had climbed down on bedsheets the girls had knotted up for a rope. Sister Clemencia is very big and has long legs. She almost caught up with me on the road outside the convent. She grabbed my arm and threw me to the ground. But I had got that far, and was not to be denied my Benjamin." She opened the blade and stared at it. "Maybe it was an evil thing to do to someone who is married to Jesus, but I cut her hand with the knife you gave me and she sat down and started to scream."

"I think Jesus will forgive you," I said. I had never really thought much about Jesus. Even in church of a Sunday I just passed the time till the service was over, and thought instead how nice it would be to become invisible or something like that. "Yes, Jesus is on our side." He *must* be, because here were Valentina and I together again.

Valentina snuggled close to me while rain scratched monotonously on the tin roof. Inside, however, we were sheltered from the wind and rain, warmed by the fire—lying together in our own little nest, I guess, is what you could call it.

"Valentina," I said, my voice thick with passion, "I

love you so. I love you more than anyone or anything!" The blood raced through my veins, hot blood, warmed by love. "Do you love me?"

Her cheek was against mine; my hand had slipped down to the rough stuff of her skirt—gray coarse stuff, probably convent clothing.

"You know I do, Benjamin."

"Then . . ."

Awkwardly, I know, I dragged her down into the blankets and smothered her face with kisses. For a moment she struggled, her small solid body pressing hard against mine.

"Benjamin! Stop it! No, I don't mean that! Help me, Jesus!"

I held her harder.

"The revolution, Benjamin—"

My voice was hoarse. "Damn the revolution, Valentina! We are two people in love! This time may never come again. Father Eusebio may find you, I might die in battle—"

Her body went limp. "Oh, Benjamin, don't talk that way, please!" Her hand crept down between our bodies and pulled away the coarse skirt. "I am hot, Benjamin. I feel like I am burning. But I love you so! Now that I know who . . . what my father is, and Victoria gone, I have no one but you!"

"And I too," I muttered, feeling the soft womanly flesh of her inner thigh. Lord, it was soft and smooth as a rose petal! My hand trembled on that rose-petal thigh. "I have no one but you either, Valentina."

Vaguely I heard the old women chattering, heard the rain on the tin roof, heard a distant locomotive whistle and a string of pops from a distant firearm. Villa's men sometimes shot wildly, at the moon or stars or a streetlamp, just to work off high spirits.

"Oh Benjamin!" She sighed as my thing on a heavenly track of its own slid into her trembling body. "Benjamin! Benjamin!" Her voice raised in pitch, and I was afraid for a moment the old women would turn to watch us, and giggle or something. On the other hand, what the hell did *I* care? I was with Valentina again. We were reunited, Valentina and me. At the moment there was no one else on the spinning globe but me and my *novia*—"sweetheart." It was my first time, and Valentina's first time, and we were transported in ecstasy.

We both breathed deeply, and at last rested in each other's arms while the old ladies dutifully kept their backs to us. From the smell, they were dipping hot tortillas into the pot of *salsa* while they chatted, but nothing was as sweet as the feel of Valentina's bare breast against my lips.

Giddy with love, I left Valentina and looked down the tracks in both directions, and on the bank behind the sheet-iron shelter. Nothing—nobody! We were safe for now, anyway.

"*Mi vida*," I said, going back and taking her in my arms again. "I love you so much it hurts, do know that? But we must go our separate ways for a little bit till I figure out how to hide you, to keep you from that ugly Father Eusebio. I wouldn't doubt that he's snooping about in Torreón right now, trying to pick up your trail."

"I don't want you to leave, Benjamin!" Valentina clung to me. "I'm afraid now!"

I tried to comfort her. "Afraid? Afraid of what? I will ask these good ladies to hide you until I can find a better place!"

She took a deep breath, shook her head, ran a small hand over that wealth of blue-black hair that showed fiery glints in the dwindling fire. Maybe the old women were running out of wood. Still, they sat like black statues and I heard against the rain the humming of their talk. As near as I could make out, they were telling jokes; I caught enough of one to make me blush. Ah, those women of Mexico, the *viejas*, the old ones, like poor dead Victoria! The backbone of the country, they were!

"What's wrong?" I asked. "You look troubled."

She took another deep breath, sitting cross-legged on the blankets and looking gloomy.

"Now I cannot fight for the revolution anymore!"

"Well," I said, "that's no matter. You have done your duty, and can now honorably rest after your escape from that horrible place where they punished you so."

In the dying glow of the fire her eyes were somber, deep dark pools. "Am I not going to have a baby now? Am I not going to have your son, Benjamin?" She began to weep. "Is that . . . what we did . . . not the way to make babies?"

I was flabbergasted, not knowing what to say. Did doing this—every time—mean a baby? I wasn't too sure how it worked. *Just once, was all it had been. Only once! Yet . . . a baby?*

"Maybe," I said. "That is to say . . . well, I mean . . ." *A baby? My baby? Our baby, from this too-brief moment?*

"I think it will happen," Valentina said in a low voice.

Benjamin Wilkerson a father? Oh, no! It was too much. Back in McNary fathers were people like Mr. Ballard at the sulfur mine, Mr. Claude Teasdale with his blood, Mr. Mose Allison with his mules and the contract plowing he did. I didn't signify for beans as a father alongside of them! Still, maybe when you're man enough to make a baby you've got to be man enough to face up to facts and act like a father, even if you don't *feel* like one. Still, *me* a father?

"I know a little about such things," Valentina murmured. "A very little, really. But there is a way to tell if I am going to have a baby. It will take a few weeks, but . . ."

I felt like a pillar of ice; no feeling was in me. What had I done in my love for her? Made a baby? Now she was my wife, although we hadn't stood up before a padre and signed any papers. I felt dizzy. Wavering to my knees, I reached down and drew Valentina to me.

"I will talk to these good ladies and give them money to take care of you and hide you from Fierro until I come back, Valentina."

She looked bewildered. "Come back?"

"Yes, we've got to do a lot of arranging things. You see, General Villa is giving up the fight for a little while. He and some of us are going into the sierra to think things over and regroup for a new campaign. I've got to go with him, because I believe in him, and maybe . . ." Aware I was beginning to sound a little pompous and immodest, I started again. "I guess I do some sort of a service for him—"

"I want to come with you, Benjamin!"

"Good Lord, no! Fierro is going too, and you must not be seen by him! Anyway, if you are going to have a baby—our baby—you can't go up into the sierra!" There was a rift in the clouds—maybe good weather coming for our retreat into the sierra. I pointed toward the jagged peaks, ghostly pale in moonlight. "We'll be lucky if we all come back down in the spring!"

Before I left I gave one of the old women—Alicia Rivera, whom Valentina knew and liked—a handful of silver pesos to take care of Valentina.

"*Sí, sí, señor!*" She tucked the money into a fold in her skirt. "I have a cousin in this city, *señor*, a good woman whose husband was killed at Chihuahua City. She has a little house on Calle Fuente in Torreón and will appreciate the money." She spat into the dying embers. "I know that *cabrón* Rodolfo Fierro! May dogs eat his bones and crows peck out his eyes! No, *señor*, your little Valentina will be safe with my cousin! You will come back in the spring, you say?"

"That is a matter for God to decide, *señora*. But I hope to come down from the mountains in the spring with my general, and we will fight once more for freedom, for the people, for the land and the tools to work it as they have for so long deserved."

It was a flowery speech but I meant it. The old lady grinned a toothless grin and whacked me on the back.

"Go, with God, *señor!* And do not worry about your little bird!"

But I did worry. The time had been enough. Just before General Villa and his diminished party left for the sierra, Valentina found she was pregnant. I was now a father—or more exactly, in nine months or whatever it was, I *would* be a father!

In my new unexpected role as a father, or rather a father-to-be, I had to make further arrangements. Valentina laughed at me for some of my worries, saying she was small but strong as a mountain pony. In fact, it seemed to me that she was much less concerned about her state than I was. I suppose it is something in every female's makeup; that is to say, from thousands of years of childbearing they treat it more casually than do men. I had at times seen women working in the fields with huge bellies. Ojo Parado explained to me that it was not uncommon for them to have their babies in the cornfields and go right on working. Well, my Valentina would not suffer needlessly; I had made up my mind to that! So my good friend Ojo Parado loaned me some more money to pay for Valentina's keep. The general's small party might be in the sierra for a long time. For that matter we might be ambushed by the Carrancista forces before we got well up into the sierra, and I wanted Valentina to be taken good care of for as long as I might be away from her.

Ojo Parado, taking the silver pesos from the small leather poke he kept always around his neck, mentioned something else.

"You know, the general has sent Fierro on a scouting expedition to the base of the Sierra del Gamón."

I knew.

"And I have not seen that rascally Father Eusebio around and about—not yet."

"*Verdad*," I said, beginning to understand his point.

"Let us hope, then, that Fierro will return quickly so that we can get started up there." He pointed to the snow-basted peaks in the distance. "Get on our way before that damned prick Eusebio meets Fierro with the news that his little pigeon has again escaped the cote!"

I nodded. For too long I had been dancing on a string, with Fierro waiting to cut that string, and my throat into the bargain. Now, with Ojo Parado's words still sounding in my ears, I recognized that the string I spoke of was becoming dreadfully frayed.

Fortunately, we moved quickly into the sierra. As soon as Fierro returned, the general got everything moving in a hurry. I didn't even have a chance to say a proper goodbye to my wife. Instead, I was kept busy loading pack animals, writing messages to General Villa's other allies, telling them of his plans, and getting my own kit ready. At the last moment I thought I had an hour or so to spare, and could hurry to Calle Fuente to say good-bye. But it was not to be. General Villa called for me and said I should ride near him. He was already astride Siete Leguas; that splendid beast was capering about with excitement and he had to jerk hard on the reins to keep her steady.

"For," he said, "I will dictate things to you while we ride and you can take them down in that little notebook of yours, Benjamin. Someday I may write the story of my life, and your notes and your help will be invaluable to me."

I was very nervous while the general organized the train, and greatly relieved when at last we started toward the outskirts of Torreón and reached the open country beyond. Fierro, riding grimly to himself, apparently did not yet know that Valentina had once more escaped Father Eusebio and that terrible prison for girls called a convent. As we rode through the foothills above the town, I felt my spirits rise.

"Benjamin, *chamaco*," the general said when we paused at a spring to let the horses and pack animals drink, "you seem happy this morning. What has set you in such a good mood, eh?"

Rodolfo Fierro was on the other side of the pool, smoking a cigarette and looking dour. One of his Yaqui scouts approached him to say something but Fierro cursed him and stared down into the ice-rimmed pool, the cigarette hanging loosely from his lips.

"Well, sir," I said, "it is such a beautiful sunny day for late autumn, and I am glad to be with you wherever you lead."

He grinned at that, and swung up on the mare. "Ah, youth! It is a fine thing to be young and full of life!" Raising his arm, he pointed forward. "*Arriba, compañeros.* Up we go!"

It was during that terrible march to the Sierra de la Silla that I became sixteen years old. This time there was no singing of "Las Mañanitas," no cake, no gift from my wife Valentina. Technically, of course, we were not married, but in Mexico such ceremonies were for the most part honorary. Men and women lived together as man and wife for a long time before a priest on a donkey would visit their little village and sanctify the union.

During that march to the sierra I froze several toes, and they still pain me. If it wasn't raining again, it was cold as a well-digger's ass, like my brother Cleary used to say. Our party was small—no more than twenty-five or so. Colonel Aguirre went; the general could not do without Aguirre and his methodical ways and good counsel. Rodolfo Fierro rode with us, of course. Felipe Ángeles, that officer and gentleman, had been executed by the Carrancistas. A roving patrol, one of those that harassed us even into the sierra, had caught him riding toward a meeting with Tomás Urbina, Villa's most trusted general, and executed him summarily. As the news came back to us, it seemed that the good Ángeles nearly escaped but his game leg hampered him. It was reported also that he disdained the usual blindfold. Before a dozen hungry rifles, weight on his good leg, Ángeles made a final statement.

"I am happy to die for the good of the Mexican people. The flower of freedom must be watered with the blood of patriots!" His death plunged us into sadness.

A dozen or so of the general's most trusted Dorados came along also, including old Ojo Parado, who by now had advanced to the rank of sergeant commanding the detachment. We were all mounted, of course, and the Dorados each led a pack mule loaded with guns, ammunition, blankets, cornmeal, sugar, coffee, lard, and strings of hot red chiles. We rode higher and higher into the sierra, guided by Ramón, a wrinkled and leathery Indian who had known Francisco Villa since the general was born in 1878. I didn't know how old Ramón was, but from his stories he was an old man at the time and once carried the infant Doroteo Arango in his arms. It is hard to tell the age of an Indian, but spry Ramón must have been seventy-five at least, an advanced age to be going into the Sierra de la Silla in the winter season.

Higher and higher we traveled on a narrow trail outlined by huge frosted boulders. There was little snow as yet, except that which lay in hollows and pockets among the rocks. The wind was from the north, hard and bitter. As the atmosphere grew thinner, we had to stop frequently to let the animals rest, gulping air into their starved lungs. At night we rigged a canvas fly among the rocks and built a fire for tortillas, dried meat, and coffee. No one said much; the general was obviously moody. He still wore his favorite shiny and stained suit, with open vest and a collarless and gaudy silk shirt, a wool *sarape* around his shoulders, and a Texas hat with a scarf to pull the wide brim around his ears. He did not look like the great man he was, certainly, and would be again.

On the third day the sun shone, breaking out of a rack of scudding clouds. The air was so cold it hurt the lungs. We paused on a great outcropping and stared down at the state of Chihuahua, far below.

Gasping for breath, I asked Ramón, "How much farther, uncle?"

Sitting his tough little burro comfortably, he said, "Oh, not much farther, *señor*." He pointed. "Up there, around that great ledge that juts out like a man's chin, a tough man and a tough chin."

I swallowed hard. "Up . . . there?"

"Indeed, *señor*."

I went back to my place in the column with Ojo Parado. "Do you know where we are going?"

Mustache festooned with icicles where his breath had frozen, he grinned.

"*Por supuesto*, I know! Another few meters above that, we see God, Benjamin!"

Breaking camp the next morning, we all lingered for a last tin cup of coffee to warm us before we went toward God again. Colonel Aguirre, bundled in a bearskin coat, had just started to speak to me.

"Benjamin, I want you to—"

A shot rang out and the tin cup spun from his hand, spraying coffee and clinking down into the shale. "Take cover!" someone yelled. I think it was Ojo Parado, sharper of sight with one eye than the rest of us with two. "Everybody down!"

Grabbing our guns and dragging cartridge belts, we scrambled into the rocks. A thin snow started to fall as lead bullets spanged into the boulders and ricocheted off, whining like banshees. The general had whipped off his *sarape* and had a pistol in each hand, firing down the trail where the attackers must have come from.

"Stand firm, my boys! Get into a good position while I cover you!"

We had camped in a narrow canyon with steep walls and our unseen assailants were confined, their rifle fire only in a narrow field. But it would not be long before some of them climbed the rocks and flanked us, firing down like marksmen in a shooting gallery.

The general seemed to have recovered. A battle always put him into good spirits. "Luis!" he shouted. "You and Rodolfo climb the rocks there and make sure they are not coming up! Little Juan and Federico, go up the other side! The rest stand by me and pepper the bastards. You, Benjamin, and Aguirre and Rigoberto, saddle the horses!"

At first we didn't know who we were fighting. There were a lot of bandit gangs in the sierra; maybe all they wanted was our horses and supplies. But that idea didn't wash when we saw the green-and-white Carrancista flag whipping on its staff where one of our attackers had wedged it into a crevice.

"Fucking bastards!" the general gritted between clenched teeth. "Who would have thought they would follow us all the way up here!"

My little pistol wouldn't do any good. When Rigoberto fell with a hole in his chest you could put a fist through, I picked up his carbine.

"Don't bother with that!" Colonel Aguirre gasped. "Help me with this packsaddle!"

My ears stung with the sound of guns, not a single sound but a series of reports bouncing back and forth between the canyon walls. It was like being in a bass drum while a mad drummer was beating on it. A bullet smashed into a boulder behind Colonel Aguirre and sent out a shower of lead particles. Clapping a hand over his eyes, he sank to his knees.

"Colonel!" I dropped beside him. "Are you hurt?"

He shook his head, dug at his eyes with a fist. "No, I don't think so. But I can't see very well, Benjamin."

I tried to make him sit still while I looked at his eyes, but he got up, pushing me aside.

"No time for that now! Saddle Siete Leguas for the general!"

A man in a white uniform stood up on a distant rock and leveled his piece. I shouted out a warning to General Villa; as the man fired, the general snapped off a shot with his pistol. The Carrancista fell off the high rock, slid down a rocky escarpment, and disappeared.

"*Cabrón!*" the general shouted, shaking his fist. Then he dropped his revolver and slowly sat down with his back against a flat rock. While I watched, he rolled up his pants leg.

"The general's hurt!" I yelled.

Colonel Aguirre stared here and there, still fumbling at his eyes. "Hurt? The general? Oh, no! I can't see! Where, Benjamin . . . where?"

I ran to him. "Shit!" General Villa said. "Benjamin, look at that, will you?"

Some of the Dorados came near, mouths open, concern in their eyes.

"Get back!" The general waved his hand. "Go get them, boys! Don't mind me!"

The wound in the general's right leg had apparently been from a soft lead Remington bullet, entering a few centimeters below the knee and breaking one of the bones. I didn't know what it was then, but later found it was the tibia. I looked around for a piece of rope or a leather strap to act as a tourniquet, but the general shook his head.

"No, *chamaco!* It has already stopped bleeding. But look at that damned fucking bone sticking out there! *Válgame Dios!* I have seen such wounds before, and—" He broke off, tried to rise "I must be on my feet again!"

I do not remember whether I pulled him back or whether he just fell. "Jesus!" he muttered. "Oh, blessed Jesus! I cannot put any weight on it!"

As if angered by the general's wound, Ojo Parado and

his Dorados were driving the Carrancistas back down the trail, whooping like mad dogs as they ran down survivors. Rodolfo Fierro kept up a steady fire from a high crag. From where I crouched beside the general I could see several crumpled white figures in the rocks. Ojo Parado sashayed up, very proud, to report.

"We have driven the whelps off, General! Who are they, those *cabrónes,* to think of coming against Dorados?" Then he saw the general's wound and his face fell.

The general grimaced in pain but his voice was steady.

"*Amigo*, how many men did we lose?"

Ojo Parado blew out a great breath that stirred his mustache. Fumbling with the breech of his rifle, he muttered, "Too many, General! They came on us very quickly, as you know. The Dorados are all brave men, but—"

"How many, damn you!"

"Well, then . . . the Arrieta brothers, both of them, and Catarino Estrada. Also, Rigoberto Cruz is alive, but not for long. He was shot through the lungs. And some more have wounds."

"How many wounded?"

"Scratches, really," Ojo Parado said. "A few small wounds, here and there. Hardly worth mentioning, General." Seeing General Villa looking at his trousers, Ojo Parado put a hand over the gaping hole. "Missed me, it did—that is, my prick. But it did terrible damage to my pants, sir."

In spite of the fact that we drove them off, we had been pretty well mauled. Rigoberto Cruz soon died, and we buried him in a shallow grave with the others. The soil was too hard and rocky to do more, but we piled stones on top to keep away the wolves and the vultures. Another man, whom I did not know, died on the upward trail the next day. He had been shot through the belly but did not want the general to find out.

"For," he said, "that will only grieve him more."

The thin snow, driven by winds of violence, changed to heavy flakes. Soon we rode like cotton-swathed statues. Luckily the wind dropped and it grew a little warmer. Still, the going was hard in new snow on top of old, and under the fleecy blanket was ice. The sun disappeared, to be replaced by murky twilight.

Colonel Aguirre took off his sombrero, flapping it against his thigh to clear it of snow. His nose was red and he kept blinking his eyes. I had tried to pick out some of the lead on a brief rest stop but there were tiny grains that seemed embedded.

"Enough!" he said. "I thank you, Benjamin, but any more digging like that will ruin my eyes for good!" He glanced over to where Rodolfo Fierro was changing a bandage on the general's leg. It had been rudely splinted with a stick and more bandages. General Villa was obviously in pain, biting his lip, swarthy face pale. "I am no doctor, Rodolfo, but I do not like the looks of that wound," he muttered.

We had a small store of permanganate of potash. When Fierro cautiously swabbed the wound with the stuff, the general cried out a muffled oath. Then he grinned and said to Fierro, "I sing, Rodolfo! It did not hurt that much, really. It was only a small melody to God that he allow me to recover and go again after those Carranza pigs!"

Now, after five days, it seemed we could go no higher. There seemed nothing above us but the sky, a brutal and metal-hard canopy that never ran out of snow. It was hard going; another of the few Dorados simply walked away in the night and we never saw him again. Maybe he died in a snowbank, maybe he got back down the mountain and survived with the knowledge that he abandoned General Villa, to his shame. But Ojo Parado knew the man, and said, "He had an inflammation of the lungs and knew he was going to die. So he just walked away rather than burden us."

Patriots all, men who loved freedom and found it easy—well, perhaps not exactly easy . . . perhaps appropriate—to die, and in so doing strengthen the resolve of those who were left. I thought again of Felipe Ángeles' last words before a firing squad. *I am happy to die for the good of the Mexican people. The flower of freedom must be watered with the blood of patriots.*

With only a few of us left, and the general slipping into

delirium, Rodolfo Fierro moved into command. General Villa, carried on a litter, protested weakly, then slipped back into a merciful coma.

"Damn you!" Fierro snarled at old Ramón. "Do you know where you are leading us, old man?" He took out his revolver. "Tell me—where are these fucking caves you talk about? How far? Tell me the truth or I will blow your head off here and now!"

I think old Ramón had lived so long he did not care much whether he lived or died. With great dignity he answered, "*Señor*, it is only . . ." Calmly he squinted toward a snow-packed saddle above us. "It is only a matter of another hour or so. Put away your gun, *hombre*. I am not afraid of your gun and I do not fear death so I do not fear your damned gun! Follow me and I will lead you to a big cave where there are painted on the walls men like sticks and queer animals. People have used that cave for more years than can be counted with numbers. Let us go quickly now, before the snow gets heavier."

Once across the saddle, floundering through snow so deep it reached a horse's belly, we emerged at last on a rubble-strewn plateau protected by sheer canyon walls. It was a kind of deep cleft in the summit. Near the base of the cliffs was a black hole hardly big enough for a man to pass through. Ramón went ahead, carrying a torch improvised from a bunch of twigs dipped in resin.

Once inside, the rush of wind died away. In the light from the flaring torch I saw indeed crude paintings on the walls, a parade of odd sticklike figures and curious-looking animals, puzzling symbols, mystical circles that probably represented the sun, a flight of dark birds I recognized as crows. The drawings were all crude, at least from a professional artist's viewpoint, but they were touching and powerful, a distillation of long-ago nature, done by people who lived close to the earth, close to life, close to whatever gods there may have been at that time. The crows, especially, were somehow so real that I could almost hear them squawking over a cornfield, as they still do to this day.

"As I promised," Ramón said, kneeling to mutter a short prayer, perhaps thanking the blessed Virgin for our delivery, or perhaps only as an obeisance to the ancient gods. Mexicans are a queer mixture of Catholicism and paganism.

Booted legs spread wide apart, fists on hips, Fierro stared at the drawings. "By God, here we are!" He didn't look much like Rodolfo Fierro. I guess none of us resembled anything more than ragged scarecrows. Fierro's face was raw and chapped, his beard long and tangled, the patrician nose dripping inelegantly. "Here," he said to Ramón. "Take this for your trouble!" Drawing a silver peso from his pocket, he offered it to the old man.

The weathered ancient drew himself up proudly. "You insult me, *señor!* A man does not take money for trying to save his country from the damned Carrancistas!"

Fierro shrugged. "For your grandchildren, then, let us say."

Ramón bowed, accepted the coin, dropping it into the leather pouch he carried over his shoulder. "In that case, then . . ."

Quickly we busied ourselves unloading the pack animals, starting a small fire from twigs and grasses in a smoke-blackened niche in the stone wall where people had made fires thousands of years ago, perhaps. Ojo Parado boiled coffee and Federico Morales lit a tiny gasoline lantern from one of the packs. Weary, exhausted, we lay down on dirty blankets while Colonel Aguirre bathed his eyes in melted snow. Rodolfo Fierro, legs crossed, squatted beside the general, trying to feed him a broth of jerked beef soaked in hot water.

"Eat!" he urged. "It will give you strength, Francisco."

Outside, the wind attacked the cliff walls. Where it blew across the opening of our cave it made a low droning noise, almost like the sound of blowing across the lip of a jug to make music, the way Grandpa Johnson used to do when we had dancing and play-parties in the summer at the Teasdale barn. Now there was nothing merry about this sound. It was more like a dirge, a dirge for a lost cause.

Almost hypnotized by the endless drone, I slept, and had bad dreams. I saw Valentina walking toward me, a baby in her arms. But she slipped and fell into an unseen chasm. I screamed out and sat bolt upright. Colonel Aguirre, propped against a wall, opened inflamed eyes.

"What is it, Benjamin? What is wrong?"

Chilled, feeling feverish and my joints aching, I got to my feet, wondering if I was catching an inflammation of the lungs too. My head ached, though it was probably only from the high altitude, or possibly the weight of my thoughts. Anyway, I had to keep well to see my Valentina again.

"Nothing," I mumbled. "Nothing at all, Colonel."

It was soon my turn to go on guard duty. Wrapped in the fur coat Colonel Aguirre loaned me, I took my rifle and a bandolier of cartridges and went outside. Dazzling sun on the blanket of snow nearly blinded me for a moment. My head throbbed so I was afraid it was going to explode. Gun in one hand, scrambling for purchase with the other, I climbed to the rocky pinnacle where Jorge Cruz, brother of the dead Rigoberto, squatted behind a makeshift parapet of piled rocks.

"Look, *hombre*," he called, waving his hand. "*Por Dios*, look!"

It seemed the whole state of Chihuahua was spread out below us like a map. It was really the first clear day for a long time. Torreón, Matamoros, even Hidalgo del Parral far to the north, were visible. Of course, I did not know then what was to happen at Parral years later, or things might have turned out differently. Anyway, the smoky smudges on the horizon were certainly those cities, now in the hands of Venustiano Carranza.

Far below I could see the foothills where the dun-gray land, broken by cultivated fields and tiny buildings, gave way to patches of white from the storm. Higher came the deeper snows, at first pierced by the rough outlines of the rocky slope but finally blanketing everything in a mantle of white, softening the harsh outlines. It was dramatic, thrilling; I sucked in my breath at the beauty of it.

"And look!" Jorge pointed with the barrel of his rifle. "Do you see that tiny black speck down there? Well, that is old Ramón with his donkey making his way to the little *jacal* where he raises corn and beans and dogs. Ay, dogs!

The old man loves dogs and has dozens of them." Stamping his feet to warm them, he slung the rifle over his shoulder and prepared to go down into the cave. "A sight, eh, Benjamin? My Mexico, my *tierra!*"

"My *tierra* also," I said.

He clapped me on the shoulder. "Keep a good eye out, *hombre!* Those Carrancista shits may still be chasing us, hoping to catch up with us before they freeze their balls off." Then he was gone, stepping carefully through the rubble and whistling "Adelita."

When he was gone I remembered the field glasses Colonel Aguirre had loaned me. With them I saw what looked like ants raising a long tail of brown dust. That was probably a Carrancista patrol. But they were very far away, and from the direction they were going, it looked like they had given up the pursuit. Anyway, in our narrow canyon hideaway it would take an infantry regiment, along with good artillery, to dislodge us. We were safe, at least for a time.

Daily the general sank lower. Rodolfo Fierro insisted on tending the general himself. For long periods he sat by the rude bed of pine boughs and blankets with chin on hand, listening to the delirious babble. The stink of the leg wound seemed to hover in the cave like an evil miasma. We had run out of permanganate of potash and now the wound filled with greenish-yellow pus, which had to be scraped out each day.

Ojo Parado gathered pitch from a withered pine, all straggly and bent from holding fast against the mountain winds for years. He melted it in a cup and mixed it with fat from one of our horses that had died from starvation. Only a few of the toughest Durango ponies were left, and they pawed the snow for dead grasses and looked at us with sad eyes as we passed by. Anyway, Ojo Parado said the mixture he was brewing was an old Oaxaca remedy for wounds which his Tía Cecilia, his aunt, had taught him. Although General Villa, when in his right mind, would steel himself against any pain and only set his teeth hard, as the melted resin fat was dribbled into the gaping wound he screamed, a piercing birdlike scream that set our teeth on edge.

Just relieved from sentry duty, I stood beside Colonel Aguirre, watching the experiment. It was like a scene from some medieval painting I dimly remembered from a book of art prints; a sick man, Rodolfo Fierro hunched beside him with chin in hand, onlookers in the dim edges of the painting, snakes of black soot on the walls where we were burning our last candles stuck into cracks and crevices.

"Stop it!" Fierro cried at last.

Perplexed, Ojo Parado looked up. Fierro knocked the tin cup of Oaxaca remedy from Ojo Parado's hand.

"It's only hurting him, you fool! It was a stupid idea, anyway!" Fierro's eyes filled with tears, and he angrily rubbed them away with the back of his hand.

"But I only—"

"Get out!" Fierro jerked his head. Ojo Parado shrugged, moved away to pick up the fallen cup where the stuff had spread over the floor of the cave. Fierro weeping! I could not get over it.

I hated Rodolfo Fierro with an intensity I cannot describe, yet I must give him this. He loved Francisco Villa, and Villa loved him, a love that had nothing to do with sexuality. It was the kind of love that can exist between two brave men who have fought together, risked all together, saved each other on many occasions at the risk of one's own life. It is a kind of love a woman can never understand, just as a man can never understand the depth of a woman's love for a man.

"Aguirre!" Fierro called.

Colonel Aguirre's eyes were still inflamed and he had broken one lens of his spectacles. Hooking them over his ears, having a little trouble with that because of the long uncut hair hanging over his ragged collar, he said, "Yes, what is it?" He was always cool with Fierro.

"I ask you to look to our general while I am gone."

We were all surprised. Finally Colonel Aguirre asked, "And where are you going?"

Fierro got up, rubbed the back of his neck, still staring

down at the unconscious form. "I am going down to bring a doctor to him."

Colonel Aguirre shook his head. "That is not wise, as you must know! You will give away our location to the Carrancista patrols, and then we will all die, after a while!"

Fierro did not seem to hear. Turning to one of the Dorados, he said, "Luis, go out to the horses. Find the best one and saddle him for me. Pick out a good lead horse, also."

"Look here, now!" Colonel Aguirre was upset. "This is a foolish thing to do!"

"Fuck you," Fierro said casually. "But take good care of him while I am gone or I will reckon with you later."

We started murmuring among ourselves. In the dead of winter, with winds howling down the canyon and everything veiled in a mist of falling snow, Fierro might perish on the trail. Too, with the general out of action, we depended on Fierro as the next in command. With him gone also there was only Colonel Aguirre left, and the colonel was more a scholar and a secretary than a warrior. Also, as Colonel Aguirre had pointed out, Fierro might put the Carrancista dogs on our trail. While it would be hard to dislodge us, they could ring us below and starve us out. But when Fierro looked around with a hard stare we all fell silent. Very few people crossed Rodolfo Fierro and lived to brag about it.

"Adiós, hombres," Fierro said, pulling on a ragged woolen sweater and getting into Colonel Aguirre's fur coat without asking permission. "I will be back soon, trust me for that, and I will bring a doctor to treat our general." He wound a scarf around his head and ears, knotting it under the ragged golden beard, now a nondescript dirty gray, and pulled down a furry cap. Where he borrowed that from, I don't know, but no one objected.

Without another word he strode out into the wind. A moment later we heard the shrill neigh of a horse. Then the light in the cave dimmed as the rider passed the narrow entrance, brightening again as Fierro rode by on his perilous way down from the sierra.

"Well!" Colonel Aguirre muttered. Absentmindedly he

took off the spectacles to huff on them, forgetting the broken lens. The glass fell out, tinkling on the floor. "Well!" he said again. Someone shuffled his feet, and the sound was loud in the silence. "Well," the colonel said for third time, "it appears that I am left in command here." He shrugged. "My present orders are merely to carry on, *hombres*." Hooking the spectacles back over his ears, he sat down beside General Villa, who, thank God, was sleeping, or perhaps he was unconscious. Anyway, he was quiet.

After three days he returned. Yes, Fierro returned, bringing with him a frightened country doctor, a small man, saddle-galled, with a fringe of gray hair around a bald head and nearsighted eyes behind thick-lensed glasses. He carried a small black bag, and wore beneath a *sarape* a black frock coat and a heavy gold watch chain across his small pot of a stomach. The coat and chain made him look very professional, whether he was or not. Ojo Parado stared covetously at the gold chain, and I made up my mind to keep an eye on the old rascal. A physician come all the way up to the sierra in winter on an errand of mercy should not have his watch chain stolen.

"Can you help him?" Fierro demanded.

The doctor bent over General Villa, eyes blinking behind the thick glass. "Hmmmm," he said. In medical school all doctors are taught to say that, I understand.

"Dammit!" Fierro exploded. "Answer me, you—"

"Yes, yes!" The doctor quailed, drew back, very nervous. "Give me just a moment, please! This case is very serious." Opening his black satchel, he took out a pair of forceps. Gingerly he probed in the wound. The general, unconscious as he had been for the last several days, groaned.

"Aha!" The little man drew out a chunk of bone, held it up for all to see. "This, gentlemen, is what is causing the infection! This man would not have lived a day longer with this thing festering in his flesh and poisoning his system."

Folding his arms, Fierro looked fiercely at the doctor. "Do you know who this man is—your patient—Doctor?"

The doctor, still holding the chunk of bone in his forceps, wet his lips. "Well, I don't know . . . that is to say—"

"You damned well know! This is the savior of our country; the general Francisco Villa! And as I warned you, if and when we let you return, I, Rodolfo Fierro, will hunt you down and kill you if you mention to anyone, to one solitary person, even your wife, that you have attended General Villa!"

Personally, I thought Fierro's manner was unnecessary. In Chihuahua it appeared that most of the people were in favor of Carranza now. It would be considered treasonable to give aid and succor to "the bandit Villa," as Carranza called him.

Dropping the fragment of bone, the doctor wiped the forceps on his trousers with a shaking hand. "Yes, yes . . . of course! I understand, believe me! A physician is sworn to uphold the privacy of his patients and their complaints!"

Kneeling beside the bed, Fierro holding a dripping candle, the doctor located other splinters of bone. The wound cleansed, he took from his satchel a sack of the paddlelike blades of the nopal cactus. Peeling them with a penknife, he packed the sticky green cactus flesh into the wound.

"There are new medicines," he explained, "but I am too poor to buy them. After all, the people pay me only in corn and beans which they raise, and sometimes a peso or two. Therefore I am forced to use old remedies. These nopalitos will draw out the poisons. Each day they must be taken out and replaced with these extra ones which I leave you."

Taking out a roll of bandage, he wound it around the general's leg. "Not too tightly," he said, "because that would restrict the flow of healing blood to the wound, and not too loosely, because that would allow dirt and foreign matter to enter." Satisfied, he wiped his hands on his trousers again and stood up.

"Will he live?" Fierro asked.

The doctor shrugged. "He is in a very bad way, I would say. Still, he seems a powerful man! If he has survived this long, he has the will to live."

We all breathed a sigh of relief.

"Well, then . . ." Fierro took a deep breath, almost a sigh. "You can go, Doctor."

Picking up his satchel and draping the *sarape* over his shoulders, the doctor looked startled.

"I can go? You mean . . . ?" He dropped the satchel. "Surely you, or someone, will escort me down to the foot of the mountains, at least?"

Fierro shrugged. "We cannot spare anyone, Doctor. I must stay to command, and every man is essential to the defense of our high outpost."

The doctor's face was ashen. "But that is murder, *señor!* I am a city man! What do I know of these wild mountains? I will die in the snows!"

"May God preserve you" Fierro said.

"But—"

Fierro gave him a shove. "Get out, now! Emiliano here will saddle you up a horse, a good one." He winked at Emiliano Herrera. "One of our best, Doctor."

Head bowed, the doctor followed Emiliano to the entrance of our cave. For a moment he paused, a small dark figure against the backdrop of falling snow. Then he turned and walked out. Angry at Fierro's evilness, I slipped out after him. Emiliano, a hazy figure in the snow, was saddling up one of our most emaciated and sickly mares.

"Doctor!" I called.

Turning, he looked dull-eyed at me. "Yes, *hombre?*"

"I am sorry for what happened. Fierro is an ugly and heartless man. If he does not kill people one way, he manages to do it in another. But if you do go down safely, and come back to your office where the people pay you only in corn and beans . . ." I dropped into his hand the few silver pesos I had put away. "Will you do a favor for me? Something that is my life to me?"

He stared at the silver, then looked up. "A favor, *hombre?*"

"There is a girl called Valentina. She is living in Torreón, in a little house of a Señora Eulalia Gutiérrez. As quickly as you can, go to her and tell her you have seen me and that I am well. Tell her . . ." I broke off, my voice unsteady. "Tell her I love her, and will see her soon, no matter what happens. You see, Doctor . . . well, she is my wife, and she is going to have a baby."

The little man closed his eyes, seemed to sway a little on his feet. "Yes, a baby. Well . . . new life comes and old life goes, eh? There is a kind of balance to things."

Emiliano brought up the poor horse and helped the doctor mount, tying the satchel to the saddle for him. "Down, Doctor," Emiliano muttered. "Go down, that is all I can tell you! *Vaya con Dios!*"

The doctor rode away, a black smudge soon fading, and there was nothing left but the curtain of falling snow. Emiliano and I watched for a while, then trudged back to the cave.

"He is a brave man, but a bastard, that Fierro," Emiliano muttered.

Inside, Fierro sat once more by the general's bedside. We were silent, watching. Finally, exasperated, he turned.

"What are you all looking at? Isn't there anything for you to do? Isn't there firewood to be gathered, snow to be melted for coffee, someone to clean up this sticky stuff on the floor?"

Among us were some of the toughest rascals ever. Yet I think they were all horrified at what Rodolfo had done to that good little physician.

"After all," Fierro said, "it is certainly better that we make sure he doesn't talk!"

I got a rag to clean up Ojo Parado's mess, and someone went out to search for a few twigs from the barren cliffs. Rodolfo Fierro continued his silent and intense vigil.

— 17 —

Snow almost buried the entrance to our cave. Many of our little Durango horses died and we ate horse meat. Everyone had colds approaching pneumonia. Three more Dorados died, one from a broken neck when he fell from the lookout point, one who went out to search for anything burnable on the mountainside and became lost in a sudden squall, and a tough old man named Victorio who merely lay down and did not get up.

That winter was unusually bad for all of northern Mexico, and in a way it was lucky for me. The convent where Valentina had been imprisoned—might as well put the proper word on it—was at a place called Chimahuatlin, far south in Durango, in the mountains. It was pretty well isolated; no trains were near, and the rugged terrain, Valentina said, made it like the end of the world. Consequently, while Valentina's escape had been detected at once, getting the word out to Fierro would be difficult until better weather came along. Valentina was safe with the widow, old Eulalia, until I could come to her again. Of course, I knew that sooner or later the church bloodhound, Father Eusebio, would report to Rodolfo Fierro, who if he thought I knew where his daughter was, would have me tortured by the flat-faced and sullen Yaqui scouts of his brigade. I had heard from Ojo Parado that the Yaquis were very inventive. Torture, he said, was a religious act for them.

In those bitterly cold mountain nights I dreamed of her: Valentina huddled under the bandstand at Ciudad Juárez, Valentina dressed by old Victoria in looted finery after the battle, the *soldaderita* Valentina, the blooded Valentina who had killed her man, although she was sorry about it and cried afterward, Valentina coming to me in the corrugated-iron shanty by the railroad tracks, Valentina lying soft and warm in my arms while the old ladies gossiped and heated tortillas and *salsa*, graciously allowing the consummation of our relationship in their hovel. There were so many Valentinas, and the thought of her warmed my chill bones. Valentina . . . ah, Valentina!

In spite of what we thought of as our impregnable fortress, we were astonished to hear a lookout challenge someone coming up from below. Two or three peasants, anxious to see General Villa and help his cause, toiled up the sierra with burro-loads of cornmeal, cheese, chiles, and freshly butchered cuts of beef, lamb, and goat, the latter frozen hard from the arduous journey. This time it was an old man named Tomás and his two strapping sons. Tomás grinned at our surprise, leathery face crinkling in a monkeylike grimace. We were puzzled that they knew General Villa's whereabouts. And if *they* did . . .

"But," old Tomás said, hat in hand, "how would we *not* know, *señores*, where our leader is? And how should we not find our way to him, wherever he may be?"

General Villa, though gradually improving, often lay for hours in a kind of coma and Colonel Aguirre did not want to wake him.

"*Muchísimas gracias, compañeros,*" Aguirre muttered, taking off his lensless spectacles and huffing on them to hide his emotion at these people who risked not only snowy death on the upward trail but also certain retribution if the Carrancistas learned of their generosity to "the traitor, Francisco Villa."

Old Tomás brought with him a few newspapers, several weeks old. "I cannot read," he apologized, "and my two good-for-nothing sons never went to school, but I thought you gentlemen might enjoy the news."

I had been without reading material for a long time. Eagerly I reached for one of the newspapers, devouring it like a hungry man goes after a steak. One small item caught my eye and I read it aloud. General Obregón, it was reported, had sent a telegraphic message to President Carranza, saying, "I have the honor to inform your excellency that the bandit Francisco Villa seems to be nowhere and everywhere."

Guffawing, Tomás slapped his thigh. "They cannot find our general!" He winked "*We* know, the farmers and little people, but Carranza and his thugs do not know! Every time someone robs a bank in Torreón or throws a bomb into a police station, they think it is our General Villa! But he is here, in our great sierra!" He took off his hat, almost as one entering a church. "*Señores*, may we, my boys and I, look at our general?"

Fierro, squatting in the snow and sharpening a machete on a flat rock, called out, "The general is sleeping and must not be disturbed!"

Colonel Aguirre put on his spectacles again. "He is asleep, *amigos*, but if you are very quiet . . ." Ignoring Fierro, he led them to the cave entrance. Pulling aside the old *sarapes*, he pointed toward the bed, a guttering candle beside it. "One short look, *hombres!* That is all we can allow! General Villa has been very sick, though he is now recovering."

Awed, the three peered in. Old Tomás' face shone in religious exaltation. The two oafish sons towered over the old man, looking also. One asked Tomás, "That is our great leader, *papá?*"

Tomás' voice was hushed. "That is our Pancho, boys, our champion!" With a gnarled finger he sketched a cross on his wolfskin coat. "May the Mother of God heal him quickly, bring him down to us again to take up our cause!"

Colonel Aguirre urged them away from the entrance. "That is enough, *hombres!* When he wakes I will tell the general about your generous gift."

They bobbed their heads, drew their clothing about them, and went quietly to the burros tethered to a snow-laden juniper. The few of us who were left had a feast: barbecued goat with a sauce made from a string of red chiles, plenty of tortillas to dip in the hot spicy sauce, real coffee (ours had long ago run out), and a chunk of goat cheese. The cheese was hardly good old rat-trap cheese from Hawley's grocery store in McNary, but it was rich and filling. Though General Villa could as yet keep little on his stomach, I cooked up a kind of soup from the sauce, mixing it with meat drippings, and carried it to him along with a steaming cup of real coffee. For the first time in months, he ate a good amount.

"I am glad you are enjoying it, sir," I said. "Old Tomás and his sons ran a great risk to bring us the food."

He nodded; his eyes misted. To cover, he laid down his spoon, saying, "This soup is good, Benjamin, but awfully damned hot!" I started to turn away, but he called me back. Propped up in bed, bandaged leg resting on a folded blanket, he said, "*Hombre*, people like Tomás and his two sons trust me. They are the good hardworking people of Mexico—my people. They are waiting for me." Rolling over, he sat up, gingerly putting a little weight on the bad leg. "I will not hide here any longer! I must go down and—"

"Sir!" Horrified, Colonel Aguirre hurried across the sandy floor of the cave. "You must not try to walk—not yet! The doctor told me—"

The general scowled at him. "Fuck the fucking doctor! Is this my leg or his? Aguirre, you are an old woman!"

Rodolfo Fierro, squatting near the fire and sipping a tin cup of the good coffee, grinned. "That is what he is. Aguirre—an old woman! Gather your skirts, *señora*, and pat us up some fresh tortillas!"

Aguirre colored, stammered. But the general caught his hand, saying, "Pay no attention to that wild man Fierro. I know you spoke out of concern for me and I am grateful for such loyalty. You are dear to me, Aguirre. When we take over, you can be my minister of finance."

Fierro shrugged at the rebuke, went back to his coffee.

I think it was that day when the tide turned. Of course, we were a long way, horizontally and vertically, from any tides, but that is the expression that came to me. An old sailor man once came to McNary to live out his years. His front yard was always full of rusty chains, anchors, and the weathered hulk of a boat he was building. Anyway, Captain Blythe was always talking about the ocean—the turn of the tide, a red sun at night is the sailor's delight, and things like that.

Christmas came and departed. Along in late March, I think, came an unseasonable warm spell. The ground about the cave was soaked with water from melting snowpack; you squished up to your knees in mud when you walked. A bit of green actually showed and our starving horses broke tethers and ran to rip up the stuff with stained teeth. Below, it appeared to be raining. Up where we were the sun was strong and hot, and the rocks held accumulated warmth through the night. The cave smelled more like an outhouse than anything else and we were all grateful to lie in the sun, feeling its warmth soak winter chill from our bones. For some days the general had been hobbling about on a stick-crutch Ojo Parado had made for him. Now he paused beside me where I was sunning myself on a blanket. Quickly I scrambled up.

"No, *chamaco!*" He pushed me back. "I am not royalty, that one needs to stand in my presence. I am Pancho Villa, a simple man from Durango."

I shook my head. "You are a great man, sir. Everyone knows that."

He stared down at the flatlands below. Tilled fields alternated with desert bald as a billiard table where no irrigation water reached. "*La tierra,*" he muttered. "My land, down there, where I was born. Who can keep me in the sierra, playing invalid, when *they* need me?" He took a deep breath. "Benjamin, *hijo,* my son, they used to call me the Friend of the Poor, the Inspirer of Patriotism, the Hope of Mexico."

"Yes, sir," I said, not quite understanding what he was driving at.

"So . . ." Setting his teeth, he hurled the makeshift crutch far out into the mountain air. In a descending arc it tumbled over and over. When it hit in the rocks below it was so far down we did not hear the impact. Standing awkwardly, trying to keep his weight on the good leg, the general cupped his hands and yelled out.

"*Hombres,* it is time! It is time to go down there and cut off Carranza's balls—if he has any, that is!"

They came out of the cave mouth, down from the lookout station, scrambling up the hillside with bundles of twigs and brush. Ojo Parado, who had been trying for days to carve himself a new eye from a pine knot, dropped his knife and stood up, brushing wood shavings from his ragged pants.

"It is time, *amigos*," the general repeated, still waving his arms. "Let us ride down in style, and show the bastards where Pancho Villa is!"

We were certainly few, very few, now. I don't think that I, or anyone, had really acknowledged we were so few. The general, Fierro, Colonel Aguirre, Ojo Parado, myself, and several others constituted the División del Norte. But we cheered General Villa until I thought that on a road somewhere several thousand meters below us a Carrancista cavalryman must have looked up at the noise and discovered us.

Colonel Aguirre did not cheer. He looked troubled, but said nothing. Rodolfo Fierro ran into the cave and brought out the old and tattered red-green-and-white flag of the División, waving it exultantly.

The general, grinning, said to me, "Benjamin, *chamaco*, do you remember my favorite story with which I bore people? How I crossed the Rio Grande with only three men, four horses, two pounds of sugar, a pound of coffee, and a sack of salt?"

"Yes, sir," I said. "I remember." I had heard it many times, but each time there was some small change in the statistics.

Wincing a little as he shifted his bad leg, he said, "Well, things are getting better, that is plain. Now I have a dozen men, more horses, still a small amount of sugar and salt, although we are out of coffee. It is an improvement over those early days, it it not?"

"Yes, sir," I agreed. "A real improvement!" In spite of my misgivings, I could not help smiling at his indomitable spirit.

I would not like to bore anyone with the details of what followed, but there are a few things. Riding through the foothills of the sierra in a cold spring rain, we were greeted with celebrations and tears of happiness at every turn of the road. Hastily improvised bands played loud and off-key; the peasants plied us with food an *pulque*. They pressed cigarettes on us, insisted on sewing up pants and jackets to replace our own mountain-worn winter clothing. One old lady made a new red-white-and-green flag to replace the tattered banner that was now worn out from waving in most of northern Mexico. Somehow the Singer sewing machine seemed to have found its way into every brush hut in Durango and Chihuahua. There were *abrazos* all around as old friends met old friends. Ramón, our guide into the sierra, had died, but his oldest son greeted us, proud of the role his *papá* had played in the revolution. In his exuberance the general "married" a local girl in San Vicente, one Faustina Díaz.

As we rode, gathering up recruits, we sang "Adelita." The people followed us in a ragged band, carrying scythes, machetes, and old muskets. The general beamed.

"Carranza, eh? Who said the people had gotten to prefer that old shit? Look how they adore me!" Of course, he had admitted before, in public speeches and interviews, that his popularity seemed to be waning, and that the people preferred Carranza. But he had forgotten that, and I did not remind him.

Of course, most of these poor farmers were middle-aged or elderly men, had families depending on them, and would not make adequate soldiers anyway. Still, it was nice to have them marching along with us, at least until suppertime, and we did manage to enroll a dozen or so young bucks. The general promised them modern rifles, plenty of ammunition, warm *sarapes* and good leather boots when we ambushed our first Carrancista patrol.

Whenever we paused in a little villiage, Ojo Parado tired to drill the recruits into a semblance of soldiery but finally despaired.

"Dolts!" I heard him scream. "You are all scoundrels, fools, the lowest of the low, with no more brains than a fucking cow! Close up there or I'll . . . I'll . . ." Words failed him. He sat down in the melting snow, holding his head in his hands.

"Don't be discouraged," I told him. "Remember what the general's first army must have looked like!"

The general emerged from a Chinese restaurant, belching and loosening his belt. In every little town the Chinese, hardworking and industrious, had monopolized the hotels and restaurants. For a moment he looked at the milling recruits—charcoal burners, pack-train drivers, miners, goatherds. Then he mounted Siete Leguas and trotted over to the bleak cornfield where Ojo Parado was trying to make soldiers.

"*Oyen, hombres!* Listen to me. We cannot whip Carranza's Federales unless you begin to look and act like soldiers of the revolution! There is more to being a soldier than just shooting a gun, you know, just as there is more to properly loving a woman than merely sticking your prick between her legs! Is that not true?"

They got that, all right, and roared with laughter.

"Now, *hombres!* Will you follow me wherever I lead you?"

There was an eager chorus of *"Sí . . . sí . . . sí!"* Someone shouted, *"Libertad!"*

"Will you fight like devils for your families, fight to own a little plot of good land for your own and raise corn and beans for yourselves, not for the *hacendados* and the government?"

They broke into cheers, shouting, *"Arriba General Villa!"* Now he had to shout to make his words heard.

"Then listen to my friend Señor Ojo Parado. He is an old campaigner and knows all kinds of tricks to keep a man alive so he can dance at our ultimate victory in Mexico City itself!"

I would not believe that a handful of ragged peasants could make so much noise. In spite of his protests, they hoisted the general onto their shoulders, careful of his mending leg, and bore him around the plaza, cheering and singing while one of them tootled on a homemade reed flute:

> With Carranza's whiskers
> I'll make a new hat band

> For the sombrero of my general,
> General Pancho Villa!

Now, years after, when I look back at that scene in the plaza, one of only many scenes in many plazas, I do not think that any man before or since, with the possible exception of Alexander the Great, could sway a band of soldiers the way Pancho Villa could. It was a gift I think he hardly knew he had, or appreciated. It certainly was not a matter of modesty, because he could brag endlessly about his exploits with women; he just took leadership as a given. After all, as he often claimed, he was born to fight, and for a man to fight successfully, he must first of all be a leader.

As we traveled, our little band grew. Many of the general's old comrades-in-arms came out of hiding, returning from *jacales* and adobe shacks in the hills, abandoning wives and families and hard-scrabble cornfields to be again with "Our General," bringing long-hidden guns and sacks of carefully preserved cartridges. *"Arriba Villa!"* they shouted, brandishing Krag rifles, Enfields, Mannlichers, handguns, even ancient muskets, galloping agile little ponies around, firing into the air until the general himself had to admonish them.

"A shot fired into the air is wasted!" he shouted. "*Amigos*, save those bullets for the fucking Carrancista bastards!"

Across Chihuahua the ragtag army crawled in a welcome early spring, almost as if the weather was making amends for the bitter winter. Sprouts of green pushed through a thin blanket of snow. The hooves of horses wore wads of sticky mud which had to be cleaned off frequently. Wherever we went, the people met us with poor but generous offerings—cornmeal, coffee, a butchered sheep, jugs of *pulque*, precious hoarded cigars, even a silver peso or two taken from a chink in the wall or dug up from a garden patch. Everyone cheered, crowded forward to shake the general's hand. He was exultant, perhaps too exultant, as conservative Colonel Aguirre worried.

"For," as Aguirre told me, "a man can be made a fool of by the clamor of a crowd."

The colonel had great difficulty in seeing. That spattering bullet on our journey up the mountain had badly damaged his eyes. Much of his influence with the general had as a result passed to Rodolfo Fierro.

"What do you mean?" I asked. "Here, sir, sit on this bench and rest."

He sat down, squinting in a ray of sun that escaped from a cleft in rain clouds. "It is very heady, this adulation, and can addle a man's judgment. Do you know that the general and Fierro are seriously considering a plan to raid Mexico City itself and kidnap Carranza?" Carranza was by now President, for all practical purposes.

The idea was so outlandish I could not believe it.

"It is true!" The colonel dabbed streaming eyes with a soiled handkerchief. "Instead of a slow and steady campaign, he is taken with the idea of a daring cavalry attack on the capital itself, forcing Carranza to abdicate!"

I said nothing; there was nothing to say. I could not help thinking, however, that if Colonel Aguirre himself could somehow get to Mexico City there might be eye doctors who could restore his sight. But that was as farfetched as Fierro's raid. Aguirre would be turned in and executed at once as a traitor.

He got painfully to his feet. "Well, there is no remedy for it, or for my eyes, either. Benjamin, will you guide me to my horse? I have in my saddlebags a bottle of brandy. Lately I have taken to drink to ease the pain in my eyes."

Our descent from the sierra did not go unnoticed. Patrols of Carrancista cavalry quickly discovered us. It was their bad luck, however; Villa's ragtag army went after them like hounds after a hare. Knowing the land so well, they pursued the luckless Carrancistas into box canyons, trapped them at streams swollen from melting snow, outrode them across stubbled cornfields. The men returned in high spirits, wearing warm Federal-issue clothing—thick *sarapes*, high soft-leather boots, woolen shirts. They brought rifles, ammunition, even a U.S. Browning machine gun that had found its way to Mexico, along with a small mountain cannon that could be taken apart and carried by three men. Now we had mule-drawn wagons loaded

341

with supplies following us. Even our wild mountain men were now grave and purposeful; the long column was beginning to take on the semblance of a genuine army, although it was no longer the famed División del Norte.

Rodolfo Fierro, daring as always, sneaked into Chihuahua City in ragged clothing and a tattered straw hat and came back exultant.

"They do not know we are so near! I tell you, Francisco, the fucking soldiers play cards and pick their noses all day. No one expects any trouble. Now is the time to move against them!"

Colonel Aguirre protested weakly but was overruled. Fierro was sarcastic.

"A blind man is cautious, that is true! But blind men do not capture cities, Aguirre. Go get yourself a tin cup and we will find a street corner for you in the city."

The general was very rough with Fierro. "That is enough, *hombre!* This man has fought with me for a long time. He was a respected lawyer who gave up a big income to join the revolution. I will not have you speak so to him. Do you understand?"

Fierro shrugged. "I am sorry," he said. He could afford to be generous. "But about Chihuahua, now, Francisco . . ."

It was not exactly correct to say the resurgent Villistas took Chihuahua City. It is more correct to say they raided the city, stayed for three days, then left quickly as Obregón's troops moved to cut our escape route. The general freed prisoners from the state penitentiary, made a ringing speech from the balcony of the government palace, promising to return soon, and left with sixteen automobiles and trucks loaded with sacks of gold from the banks, rifles and cartridges, dynamite and medical supplies, cases of Scotch whiskey and American bourbon. Everyone thought it a great victory, a black eye for Carranza, but standing in the plaza, listening to the general's speech, I worried about a kind of apathy in the crowd. The citizens of Chihuahua City had once adored General Villa. Now they began to doubt his power, realizing it was Obregón and his advancing armies they would soon have to make their peace with.

Villa withdrew with a few casualties after having, as he said, "kicked Carranza's ass." But new recruits to his cause dwindled, and Obregón's Federal troops rode everywhere, eager to run down the once-powerful "Centaur of the North"; a price of fifty thousand pesos was on his head. Learning of this, the general preened his mustache and grinned. "So many pesos for such a little head, eh? My brain must be worth more than I thought!"

Again he wore the soiled greasy suit, a striped silk shirt without a collar, a battered Texas hat. Perhaps it wasn't the same suit I had originally seen him in at Cuitla on that long-ago day. Maybe it was just that he had a way of quickly ruining clothes. Anyway, egged on by Rodolfo Fierro, he moved quickly about Chihuahua, raiding here, slashing there, cutting rail lines as of old, taking no prisoners. He seemed unable to realize, as some of us were beginning to suspect, that this frenzied activity might be a last paroxysm of the revolution. Colonel Aguirre was despondent.

"*No sirve!*" he muttered. "It won't work!" It was a phrase the general himself often used in the old days when making tactical decisions. "No, Benjamin, the revolution is in the last phase, I am afraid. What the general does not realize is that he is getting to be a minor character in a drama that daily becomes more political than military. Fierro is using him, and there can be no good in it."

In spite of misgivings, Villa's army continued to snatch victory narrowly from defeat. With only a thousand or so men he continued to harass Carrancista strongholds. Rodolfo Fierro urged him on; Fierro was happy, burning, looting, slaughtering prisoners. The general had twice before taken Torreón, only to lose it again each time. Now, for the third time, he took Torreón in a brilliant maneuver, sweeping away the demoralized defenders. Two Carrancista generals were killed. A third committed suicide after the ignominious defeat. Staying only briefly in the city, General Villa forced a "loan" of thousands of pesos in gold and silver from the banks and merchants. But the wealth had a certain irony to it. Being constantly on the move, there was little opportunity to spend it and our supplies dwindled. It became more a responsibility than an asset, since the heavy canvas sacks required a wagon to transport them.

Lingering shots still echoed in the streets of Torreón when I asked Colonel Aguirre for permission to visit my wife Valentina in the house on Calle Fuente. A courageous Torreón physician had treated his eyes with salve and picked out most of the crumbs of lead. One eye was bandaged and the other almost swollen shut.

"I cannot give permission anymore, Benjamin," he told me. "I am only a weary old soldier, ill-used, who has been pushed aside by younger and more able people."

Time was short. I knew the Villistas would, in a day or two, perhaps only a matter of hours, retreat toward Ciudad Juárez before Obregón's eager troops, who smelled that huge reward. General Villa was sitting in the bar of the Hotel Metropole, drinking, while Ojo Parado squatted in a corner, rifle across his knees. The general had always refused alcohol. Now, discouraged by the desertions from his cause, he began to drink anis, the powerful licorice-flavored brandy.

"Your woman, eh? You have a woman, *chamaco*? Right under my eyes you have grown into a man, Benjamin! Women are good for a man, that is true. But I hope you married the woman, as I do."

Well, we were not married yet, although we would remedy that shortcoming when there was a chance. It wasn't exactly lying when I replied, "She is my wife, and I love her, sir."

"And where does she live, *chamaco*, this precious little dove of yours?"

I didn't want anyone to know about the little house on Calle Fuente.

"In Torreón, sir."

He laughed, poured himself more anis. "You do not tell me a great deal, Benjamin! Still, I understand. These affairs of the heart are very precious, and are best handled in private lest another suitor come along, eh, and cut you out?"

"Yes, sir," I said uncomfortably.

"Well, go then, *chamaco*, and have your little tryst!"

I hurried from the hotel. Fierro, as usual, took splendid quarters in the Hotel Paraíso, where I had a tiny cubicle also, without any of the amenities. But there were so many people in town for some kind of *fiesta* that I was grateful for even that. Coming down through the crowded lobby, I paused in alarm and stepped back. A tall man with a great blade of a nose and severe priestly habiliments was inquiring at the desk for General Fierro.

"Father," the room clerk said, "he has left orders not to be disturbed."

Father? Father Eusebio, of the convent, Valentina's pursuer? I had never seen him, of course, but he fitted Valentina's description. If it was Father Eusebio, come all the way from Chimahuatlin, he was about to advise Rodolfo Fierro that his daughter Valentina had again escaped. Behind a potted palm in a hugh brass urn I watched; the Hotel Paraíso was lush with greenery.

The gaunt black-dressed padre became insistent. In a funereal kind of croak he said to the clerk, "I am Father Eusebio Garza from the Convent of Santa Ynez de la Fe Sagrada in the small town of Chimahuatlin several hundred miles from here. I have traveled a long road to bring the general information which is very important. It will go hard with you if you do not advise General Fierro at once that I am here!"

He bamboozled the clerk, all right. When he turned and sat down on a wicker chair in the lobby to await Fierro's summons, I fled from the hotel, anxious—deadly anxious—for Valentina.

That night the streets were filled with roistering Villistas, drunk on *pulque* and *mescal* and imported German beer. In the plaza pranced unsteady soldiers, seizing any woman nearby and reeling about while the Torreón *policía* peered uncertainly from windows and darkened storefronts. Someone had broken into a shop filled with Chinese fireworks and the sky quickly filled with a cloud of yellow and red and green shooting stars. Looking over my shoulder, hunched down in the *sarape* to better escape notice, I hurried away from the merriment, taking a zigzag course through quiet dark streets, the only light a lattice of gold where a candle shone through shutters or a gasoline lantern burned. Again the city power was off. City power has always seemed to me to be the first casualty of a revolution.

By a crumbling adobe wall I stopped short and waited, listening. Was someone following me? I could see no one, but Fierro might have sent one of the Indians from his brigade, one of those stone-faced Yaquis who moved like shadowy cats and who could follow the trail of a ghost. Indians could see at night, Ojo Parado said, just like cats. Well, I hoped that one wasn't watching me on my way to my beloved.

Skulking along, I stayed close to the walls. Opening a door suddenly, a woman threw out a pail of slops, narrowly missing me. Cursing under my breath, I froze, motionless, until the door closed again. There was nothing but the faint popping of firecrackers and the distant hiss of rockets and pinwheels, an occasional streak of colored light as something soared above the rooftops. Going on, counting streets, I came at last to Calle Fuente. At the door of the house of Eulalia Gutiérrez, widow, I paused, looking around again to be careful. Nothing—nothing but a skinny gray cat sitting on a *carreta* licking its fur.

Softly I knocked. the light leaking through the cracks of the heavy plank door glimmered quickly out. No one answered my knock. Well, that figured. With the city occupied by drunken soldiery, it was well to be quiet!

Putting my lips to the rough stuff of the door, I whispered, "Eulalia? Valentina? It's me—Benjamin. Open the door, please."

There was still only silence. Then came a hesitant, wondering voice. I knew that voice. "Benjamin? *Madre de Dios*! Can it be you?"

The door creaked open. Eulalia stood there holding hight a candle. "Señor Wilkerson, is it you? Truly?" Behind her—oh, happy sight—peered Valentina, eyes glowing with unshed tears. Hurrying past old Eulalia, she threw her arms about me, pressing her lips against mine, crying and laughing at the same time. "Benjamin! Is it really you?"

I tried to hold her to me but there was an unfamiliar bulk between us. Eulalia laughed. "Don Benjamin, now that she is getting pretty big, you cannot hold her that way!"

Small Valentina was certainly no longer small. I was dismayed by her bulk, but Eulalia only giggled. "Do not look so shocked, Don Benjamin! After the baby comes she will look the same again!"

My arm around her shoulders, I walked her to the sagging divan and sat beside her, holding her hand. Somehow or other, this still seemed unreal. A baby? A flesh-and-blood baby, in her and by me? Well, it was true, all right! This was the way God made babies, though I certainly had something to do with it too. I began to feel nine feet tall, a nine-foot father.

"Feel!" Valentina urged me, guiding my hand. Suddenly timid and embarrassed, I let her hold my hand against her stomach. "Do you feel him? There—he kicked, Benjamin! He knows you are here!" She never looked lovelier—that is, if you didn't look at her swollen stomach—dark eyes shining in the candlelight, her smile lighting up the shabby little room and investing it with her own beauty. "You know, he is to be called Benjamin. I would not have any other name for our little son!"

Eulalia brewed scarce coffee and took a few little cookies from an enameled box. "I bought *galletas* for Christmas but saved some till you came, Don Benjamin." Then she withdrew behind a burlap curtain, first stoking up the few lumps of charcoal that glowed in an iron pot. "I leave you two alone to talk. Young lovers do not appreciate an old lady within earshot."

"*Señora*, you . . . are welcome to . . ." I faltered. She was already gone.

Valentina was insistent that I tell her everything that had happened to me. From time to time she touched her stomach and whispered "*Oye*, little Benjamin! Listen to this brave father of yours who has done so many brave things for our blessed Mexico!"

I was embarrassed. "That is not right, Valentina! I have done very little myself. But a lot of brave men fought and died so that someday our little new Benjamin will grow up in a good country."

Finally the coffee was gone, the little cakes eaten, good old Eulalia snoring behind the burlap curtain. The charcoal was only a dusty settling in the iron pot and the room was getting cold.

"I must go in a few minutes," I said. "But before I do, Valentina, there is something important I must tell you."

She must have seen the concern on my face because she was instantly quiet, almost fearful.

"Yes, Benjamin?"

I thought hard how to say it. Well, there was only one way.

"Father Eusebio has finally come up from the convent. While we were in the sierra there was of course no way to reach your . . . your father. But now he has come after a long journey. I saw him in the hotel asking to see General Fierro."

She looked down at her clasped fingers. "My . . . father."

"Yes."

She raised her chin. "I have no father, Benjamin. You know that. Now I have only you. I do not admit to a father." She began to weep, rocking back and forth, hands locked awkwardly around her knees. "Oh, Benjamin, if you could only know the grief, the disappointment . . ."

"I know," I said, kissing her eyelids gently. "There . . . do not cry. We will handle this, you and I, and someday soon we will raise our family in peace. But for now you must be very careful! Neither Fierro nor Father Eusebio knows where you are, and we must keep it that way until I can carry you away from Torreón and to safety across the border."

"What . . . what must I do then, Benjamin?"

"You must stay out of sight. Do not go into the streets. Let good old Eulalia do the marketing, the errands, whatever is necessary. But *stay inside* until you hear from me again, my sweet. Do you understand? This is a very risky business for both of us, and for that little Benjamin who will soon come."

It was nearing midnight; I heard a nearby church bell clearing its throat to sound the hour.

"But must you go, Benjamin?" she asked. "I . . . I cannot bear to have you leave me again!"

Reluctantly I wrapped the *sarape* about me. "It will not be for long, *mi vida*. To me it seems that things are coming to an end soon."

Her face darkened, a fleeting shadow. "An . . . end?"

I would say no more. "Trust me. I will come back soon. In two months, Eulalia said."

"Two months, a week, maybe a few days more." She held up her fingers, counting on them. "Eulalia is very wise. She knows about such things, exactly."

I kissed her, moved toward the door. "Take good care of our son, Valentina, *mi preciosa*."

Still she clung to me, quietly weeping. "Why do you have to go?" In sudden contradiction she added, "This is not even your country, Benjamin! You do not have to fight for Mexico! Take me with you to El Paso so we can be rid of this war! Please, Benjamin!"

Gently I took her arms from around my neck. "Listen, Valentina. Listen! You are right. I do not have to do this. But I want to, do you understand? No more do I belong to Texas. I am more Mexican now than many of the people. Though things do not look very good these days, I have made up my mind to stay with General Villa until the last, the very last." I took her trembling chin in my fingers, tipped up her tearstained face. "I think I am obliged to do it because General Villa is a great man who has been good to me and I admire him. But even more"—my own eyes began to sting a little—"even more, I am fighting for little Benjamin. Do you understand?"

I led her back to the divan, and she sagged into it awkwardly and heavily.

"Yes. I understand. Of course I understand. It is a thing that must be done. Men go to war and the women wait. It is hard, but that is all we women can do. The good Eulalia told me not to be surprised. 'That is the way,' she said. So I will wait. I will wait forever, if that is what is needed."

I slipped quickly out into the night. That image of her,

of Valentina sitting awkwardly on the sofa, almost childish body swollen with my son, our son, and the resignation in her voice as her eyes followed me, was vivid in my mind. I would never forget it.

Outside the wind had risen. There was only an occasional rocket from the plaza, a few drunken shouts, once a lonely pistol shot. The skinny cat meowed, rubbed against my boots. At the end of Calle Fuente, where it turned into Camino Ruíz, a dark bundle lay in the shadows. Wary, I skirted it. A body? I did not want to find out. But a sound behind me, a shuffle of leather on cobblestones, made me whirl, reach for the little Spanish pistol I always carried.

"Don't bother," Ojo Parado said. "Someday you will get yourself killed, *hombre*, thinking that silly popgun protects you. Well, did you have a nice visit with little Valentina?"

For a moment I was so startled and relieved I couldn't find my voice

Ojo Parado went on. "As for me, I prefer the knife." Taking a rag from his pocket, he wiped stains from the horn-handled blade he carried at his belt. "A knife makes no noise, kills fast, and never needs bullets."

I saw what that dark flat bundle was—one of Rodolfo Fierro's Yaqui scouts.

"Well, shall we go?" Ojo Parado slipped the knife back into the sheath and jerked the body upright by the long black hair.

Taking my arm, he pulled me at a trot toward División headquarters, dragging the body of the Yaqui after him and disposing of it in a trash barrel some distance from Calle Fuente.

"Very small people, those fucking Yaquis," he said, dusting his hands, "but they can be dangerous. Come, *hombre!* We must hurry. I understand that our victorious army leaves Torreón in the early morning."

— 18 —

The confrontation with Rodolfo Fierro that I dreaded wasn't long in coming. The next morning, as I was on my way to the general's headquarters, two of Fierro's wooden-faced Yaqui scouts grabbed me. With a knife to my back they hustled me off to Fierro's suite in the Hotel Paraíso. Our army was packing up, getting ready to leave Torreón for Chihuahua City. The streets were filled with wagons, trucks, staff cars, hubbub, and confusion. No one likes to make noise more than a Mexican! When given the opportunity to drive a motor vehicle, they love to race the engine to an ear-splitting scream punctuated by barrages of backfiring.

At any rate I soon found myself standing before a . . . What? If it were three hanging judges, it would be called a tribunal. Maybe this was a dosbunal, or some such thing. In any case, Rodolfo Fierro and Father Eusebio sat side by side at a long mahogany table covered by a silk runner. I faced them with the heavy door locked, the windows barred by the hotel management against the excesses of Villa's troops, and two impassive Yaqui scouts behind me.

"So we meet again, eh?" Fierro asked. He seemed very nervous, and lit another aromatic cigarette before the first had been hardly smoked. "You, Benjamin—my onetime friend, and now traitor!"

I always talked more than I should have. Later on, at least by my twenties, I began to try keeping my mouth shut. But right now there was, I figured, nothing to lose by calling a spade a spade.

"I was never your friend, nor your *maricón* either," I blurted, "and I am no traitor to the revolution!"

Fierro turned to Father Eusebio, tallow-faced in his black robe. I could understand why Valentina and the girls at the convent feared and hated him. Rodolfo Fierro was evil, there could be no doubt about that. But this Father Eusebio radiated a different kind of evil, and evil the more monstrous since it was clothed in the habiliments of the church.

"This, Father, is the Texas boy who violated my daughter—my Valentina! My daughter was the one good thing in my life, you see. When her mother died I protected her, shielded her from the wickedness of the world, devoted my every effort to keeping her pure and unsullied in memory of her sainted mother, who, like me, came from the province of Aragon, in Spain. But this dog of a Texan has compromised her!"

"I did not compromise Valentina!"

Father Eusebio took a metal crucifix from somewhere under his robe and held it up.

"Do you swear by this holy relic that you—"

Angrily Fierro knocked the cross from Father Eusebio's hand; it went sailing across the room to land at the feet of one of the silent Yaquis. The man stared at it, then seemed to shrink back. The Yaquis were not Christians, of course; they had their own mysterious tribal faith. They not only were not Christians, they were not Mexican subjects. A handful of them had joined General Villa as scouts only to show their contempt for the present government.

"Fuck the damned cross!" Fierro yelled. "There is no truth in the little bastard, nor in any Texan! Where is my daughter?"

Father Eusebio rose to rescue the crucifix. Stubborn, he held it aloft and started to moan and groan. "Lord, look down on the evil boy and send swords of fire and lightning to punish him! Show him thy divine wrath, for he has greatly sinned and—"

"I'm not a boy!" I cried. "I'm a man, a Texan, and I'm not afraid of you or Rodolfo Fierro either!"

Of course it was foolish to sound off that way. I was in deep trouble. I should have been diplomatic, played for time, bent my mind to some way out of this deadly trap.

Rodolfo Fierro would have me killed in that hotel room after some ingenious torture by the Yaquis.

Father Eusebio sat down again, laying the crucifix on the table before him as if it were a pistol. He had little rat eyes, did Father Eusebio, and a yellowish parchmentlike skin that hung in wattles under his chin.

"Where is my daughter?" Fierro repeated in a voice that trembled with passion.

"I don't know." That was a lie, of course, and Fierro recognized it as such.

"Last night you went to her, to my daughter Valentina, and had a visit with her—a carnal visit! I know that, Benjamin! And my best Yaqui scout was found dead of a stab wound! Violated my daughter, eh? Killed one of my best Yaquis? I will cut off your balls and make you eat them!"

Below the barred window were sounds of rumbling trucks, grinding of gears, colorful curses, horses neighing, the crack of a teamster's whip. General Villa was preparing to move out of Torreón. By now my presence—or lack of it—must be noticed at the general's headquarters. Would someone come to find me, maybe, and get me out of this awful trap?

"I don't know where Val . . . your daughter is! And as for one of your Yaquis being stabbed, I don't know anything about that either!"

Someone knocked on the heavy door. "General Fierro?" The voice was muffled by the thick planks.

"Go away!" Fierro shouted. "I am busy!"

The voice persisted. "But the general says—"

"Fuck the general!" Fierro yelled, motioning to one of the Yaquis to chase away the intruder. When that had been taken care of, Fierro rose. The next thing I knew he had struck me across the face, a blow that sent me reeling.

"There is little time! Will you talk, or will my Yaquis make you talk, you damned scum!"

I think I already said somewhere that Texans are proud people and do not allow others to shame them. Scrambling up, I doubled my fist and hit Fierro in the nose. Blood spurted; he took a step back, holding his split nose, astonished.

"Why, you little . . ."

Father Eusebio was standing on a chair, apparently trying to get a little closer to God. "Lord, we beseech thee to carry off this evil sinner of a Texan who has soiled the dove of thy servant Rodolfo Fierro and caused me, your servant, to be put to much trouble and pain."

Fierro's lean bearded face, that elegant face of the Spanish grandee, was spattered with blood. I had hit him a good lick, and drops of blood—his blood—stained the silky beard. He seemed not to believe what had happened. When he raised a hand in a signal to one of the Yaquis I decided I was done for anyway and might as well go out in style. Before the Yaquis could grab me I rushed forward and gave him another blow, knocking the lean ascetic nose even more askew.

Mexicans, or rather Spaniards, I guess, don't know much about fistfighting, but I guess every Texan is brought up on it. I had been in a lot of fistfights in Mr. Dinwiddie's schoolyard. Dazed, Fierro slid down and sat, booted legs stretched out before him, propped against the massive mahogany table.

Ready for a knife in my back from one of the sullen Yaquis, I tried hard to think of a profound statement to memorialize my last moments on this Chihuahua earth. It was a failure.

"Don't you ever lay a hand on me again!" I yelled. Maybe I could have done better, but there was a hammering on the door and I heard General Villa's high-pitched voice, rising even higher in a crescendo of curses.

"Rodolfo! Fierro! Are you in there, you damned bastard? Open this door, I command you!"

Fierro tried to speak but could only mumble.

"Open this fucking door!" When nothing happened immediately, there was the roar of a heavy pistol, and splinters flew into the air. One hit me in the cheek, and that was the only blood I lost in the bizarre encounter.

"Open!" A heavy boot struck so hard that the iron bar that barred the general's way bent. Another kick sent the bar flying; I dodged it as it cartwheeled across the thick rug.

"There!" General Villa cried, breathing hard. "That for your damned door, Rodolfo!"

He paused, looking at the strange tableau: Father Eusebio still on the chair chanting prayers, Rodolfo Fierro trying to stanch the flood of gore from his nose with the end of the silken runner, me pressed flat against the wall saying my prayers to whatever God there might be.

"What in hell is going on here? Rodolfo, we are ready to pull out! I sent a runner to you and he told me you would not listen to him. By God, who runs this army, Fierro? You?" Villa spat on the carpet. "No, not you, my friend! *Me!* I run this army, and when I say come, you come—do you understand me?"

I think in a way it helped that Fierro and the general had been on strained terms ever since that meeting in El Paso between Villa and the U.S. authorities. By now it was no secret; from what Mr. Wickwire had told me, and the scraps of gossip I heard around headquarters, the general was actually going to take the offered American aid and in return give Black Jack Pershing's soldiers a little field exercise in Chihuahua. Many of the general's officers disapproved of the idea, and Rodolfo Fierro was the chief complainant. In fact, it was known that he had, at one time anyway, sounded out some of the others on a scheme to withdraw support for Villa and carry on their own war against Carranza.

"Ah . . . ah . . ." Fierro staggered to his feet, holding his nose and spitting blood. "This pup has—"

General Villa cut him off. "I know! Do you think I am an idiot, Rodolfo? I have several sets of ears and eyes at my service, and what has gone on here is obvious." He called to Father Eusebio, still perched like a huge blackbird on the table and mumbling prayers.

"You, there! Whatever your name is, get the hell down off that chair and go away somewhere that the sight of you will not make me vomit! To hell with you and your rascally church that is propping up that old perfumed bastard Venustiano Carranza!"

Father Eusebio fled so fast that the black robe stood out behind him like a starched shirttail, clattering down the stairs as if Old Nick himself was after him.

"And you, Rodolfo! I am losing patience with you. Some of those eyes and ears I have spoken of have brought me tales that worry me a great deal."

Fierro made a croaking sound and spat blood again. "This Benjamin . . . this traitorous Texan . . . has—"

"Speak!" General Villa said to me. "Tell me, *chamaco*! Do you know where Rodolfo's daughter is?"

Texans—proper Texans—do not lie. Oh, of course they may exaggerate things a little, but that hardly counts; it is only cockiness. Still, I had never lied to the general.

"I am in a hurry," General Villa growled, examining his dusty boot where that last massive kick had crushed the toe. "Speak, Benjamin!"

I lied to him. "I don't know where Val—his daughter, I mean—is. And if she has been compromised, I didn't do it!" A lie on both counts, if compromise meant that I had . . . well, had relations with her.

"Well, then, you see, Rodolfo?" The general put his boot back on and shoved the puzzled Yaquis out the door; they did not know Spanish, or very few of them did. "Benjamin has told you the truth and I have confidence in Benjamin, so you have no reason for all this crazy behavior! I am going back to my headquarters again, where I intend to hold a brief staff conference before we depart for Chihuahua City—a meeting to explain the latest plan."

The plan was, of course, to make it undisputed fact that the División del Norte was going to take on a new role, that of the fox hunted by President Wilson's green recruits.

"Come with me now, this instant," the general ordered. "There is no time to waste, Rodolfo! Banda and Urbina and the rest are already there awaiting my coming."

Fierro protested, "My nose—"

"Fuck your nose! There is work to be done." He turned to me. "Come along also, Benjamin! I will need you to take notes. Some of my generals are opposed to this new plan of mine, and I must knock a few heads together!"

The three of us left Fierro's room, Villa striding across

the courtyard, Rodolfo Fierro, badly beaten, trudging after him, nose in bloody handkerchief, and me. Fierro did not say anything to me, did not turn, but I knew that I was a dead man as soon as he could arrange it. I was under the general's protection; the general himself had made that clear to everyone and I was grateful for that. But Fierro had a long arm. There were ways he could get at me which General Villa could not prevent. I thought of that old warning in the División del Norte: "Look out! Here comes Fierro!" Soon there might be a new saying: "There went Benjamin, the Texas *gringo* fool who dared to strike Rodolfo Fierro!"

It would have been nice if our victorious army had continued to be victorious, but it was not to be. There were victories, of course, but they were small ones and did not have the flavor, the pulse-racing spirit, of Ciudad Juárez and Torreón and Zacatecas. Somehow the air seemed to be slowly leaking out of the revolution. Venustiano Carranza was now in fact President of Mexico, and his General Obregón had secured over eighty percent of the country. The people, General Villa's beloved peasants, saw the end before we did. They seemed to realize that the great days of the División del Norte were passing under Obregón's steady onslaughts and that they had better cheer for the new government rather than support the Centaur of the North. At first the change of heart was not apparent. But bit by bit the cheers became less ardent, people were less willing to feed us and clothe us and pay General Villa's "taxes." Even a few public executions of "Traitors to the Revolution" did not stem the increasing tide of indifference, then resentment, and finally downright anger when we rode into a town. The people knew that Obregón's troops would soon arrive to punish any gesture of sympathy for Villa's waning popularity. You could not blame them, of course. The Mexican citizen has endured much, and out of this has come a shrewdness that permits survival—survival above everything else.

In rainy winter Obregón drove us back toward Ciudad Juárez, scene of the general's first victory. The mood at headquarters was black. In the south Zapata was still ineffectual, contenting himself with minor actions. Obregón disregarded Zapata, keeping up his relentless pursuit of General Villa's diminishing army. No more were railroad trains at our disposal; the famous red caboose was long gone. We were short of ammunition. Most of our fieldpieces had been captured by Obregón. There were a few desertions, then more and more, and finally almost wholesale departures as once-proud soldiers of the revolution sneaked out of camp to go home and prepare for spring plowing. General Villa himself became moody and withdrawn. He would cut out pictures of the victorious Obregón from the El Paso *Morning Times* and pin them to a wall, afterward riddling the photos with his pistol, cursing all the while.

"*Carajo! Bribón! Fantoche!*" He could not think of anything vile enough to fit the victorious Obregón. "May he catch the clap and not be able to piss, so that he swells up and bursts like a balloon! May his balls fall off and be eaten by crows! May the devil run his pitchfork up Obregón's ass and twist it till his guts fall out!"

Rodolfo Fierro so far did not harass me. I think it was a combination of things. I was under General Villa's protection, his rascally Father Eusebio had been sent packing, and probably he realized that as long as I stayed close to General Villa there was no way for him and his damned Yaquis to torture the truth out of me as to Valentina's whereabouts. Maybe he figured he could wait, bide his time, and catch me unawares. But I was onto that, and stuck to the general's coattails like a leech. Too, things were going from bad to worse on the revolutionary front. Fierro was not able, at staff conferences, to push for a last violent cavalry charge on Mexico City itself, Venustiano Carranza's capital. Wrapped in a cloak, he sat all day in his suite, staring moodily out the window where the once-invincible banner of the División del Norte hung limp and wet on its staff in front of the hotel.

At this dreary time, what pained me most was the departure of my old friend Colonel Aguirre. Now almost completely blind, he gave me a fumbling *abrazo* while his nephew waited outside the hotel to take him home near Guanajuato.

"I will miss you, *chamaco*," he said, touching my cheek with trembling fingers. "My wife and I—we have been childless, and now we are too old. But I wish I had a son like you, Benjamin."

I hugged him tight in a most unmanly way. My eyes filled with tears, and I was glad and yet unhappy that he could not see them.

"Sir, I will always remember you. I want to tell you that you have a son, wherever you go or whatever happens. I *am* your son, Colonel, and proud to be so!"

The Ford touring car skidded away in the mud of the rutted street, Colonel Aguirre sitting erect and military in the rain while his nephew drove.

In our discouragement I think the only cheerful one was old Ojo Parado. He never lost his faith in the revolution. The golden uniform of the Dorados was by now colorless and ragged, the lost eye and empty socket ungraced by a glass substitute. He squatted under a canvas fly making bombs from our scanty store of dynamite, singing quietly, almost to himself:

> I'm a soldier and my nation calls me
> To fight in the fields of strife.
> Adelita, Adelita of my soul,
> For the love of God do not forget me!
> If Adelita left me for another
> I would pursue her endlessly
> In a warship if she went by the ocean
> In a military train if by land!

The División del Norte, thousands strong, used to roar out "Adelita" in a mighty chorus, bringing fear and destruction to the enemies of the revolution. Now an old man sang softly in the rain, making pitiful small bombs and refusing to give up his dreams.

"*Amigo*," I said, squatting beside him. Taking out my mouth-organ, I played an accompaniment while rain hissed on the leaky canvas.

"There!" He held up a hide-encased stick of explosive. "Someday I will stick this up Obregón's ass and blow him straight into hell!"

I knocked the spit from my mouth-organ and put it back into my pocket. "*Hombre*, you are the man that can do it!"

He rolled and lit a limp cigarette. We were out of tobacco again and all that remained was the rank *macuche*. "You sound downhearted, *chamaco!*"

I sighed. "Things do not look good."

"Look here, Benjamin!" With surprising vigor the old man jumped to his feet, waving the bomb under my nose. "Do not talk like that! I did not think you were one of these whiners! Maybe I should stick this thing up *your* ass to teach you loyalty to the revolution! No, we will succeed! We have *got* to succeed! Do you think I am going to go back to Oaxaca and chop weeds again for the *patrón*? Do you think I am going to give up our hope of freedom, our hope of enough food and schools for our children and the right to go about as men, not slaves?"

I was taken aback, muttering something stupid; I don't remember what.

"I thought better of you, *amigo!*" The old man was almost weeping. He clutched my arm. "We cannot fail! We *will* not fail! We will all go to hell together, singing 'Adelita,' before Obregón whips us!"

There was more bad news, at least for me. The El Paso *Morning Times* was now available to us, and I managed to keep up with the current state of world affairs. The European war was in black headlines every day. The Central Powers had run roughshod over Belgium and France, and the British and French had lost thousands along strange-named rivers like the Somme and the Meuse. Many political leaders feared that the United States would soon be drawn into the conflict and worried that our military forces were scanty and ill-trained, no match for the spike-helmeted Huns. But President Woodrow Wilson was reelected, the Democrats praising ". . . the splendid diplomatic victories of our great President, who has kept us out of war!" Nevertheless, military men worried that the hour of decision was soon to come. On a back page I came across a small item that saddened me even more. A black-bordered announcement told of the passing away of Mr. Henry Wickwire, special correspondent for the El Paso *Morning Times*. "After a lengthy illness," it read, "Mr. Henry Wickwire of this city died yesterday at his residence on Houston Street. Mr. Wickwire had a long career as a reporter, and leaves only his wife." Such a life, to be encapsulated in a few words of newsprint! Staring into space, the *Morning Times* on my lap, I remembered the indomitable Wickwire, ruining rented automobiles, stubbornly refusing to let the hostile Mexican desert keep him from a story, sniffing out news with casual disregard for his own safety, casually bearing scars for the sake of the Kernel of Truth. There was to be some kind of a memorial service in a week or two, and I made up my mind to be there. It was the least I could do to pay homage to an unrecognized great man. I folded the paper and muttered under my breath, "*Ave atque vale*, Mr. Wickwire!"

In the depths of despond, something happened that injected new life into the revolution. I want to describe this very carefully, because much of the story has been claimed to be false. But I experienced part of it myself, and can vouch for that part, at least.

Daily the general was consuming a full bottle of anis. In a black mood he sent me out to buy a fresh bottle of the stuff. When I came back he was talking to a young man, a *gringo* in civilian clothes, a ramrod-erect young man with close-cropped hair in a military cut. I thought I remembered him from the time when the general traveled to Fort Bliss.

Waiting for a break in the conversation, I finally handed the general the bottle. "Here it is, sir. Your anis." But for some reason, excited, he waved me away. "Later, Benjamin! I am busy now!"

The next day both he and the young man disappeared. No one seemed to know where the general had gone. Rodolfo Fierro, sour and ugly, trapped me in the lobby of the Hotel Rey Moro.

"Now where is he—our general? Drunk, and lying in

some gutter? You always know where he is, Benjamin.''
Gripping my arm, he stared at me with bloodshot eyes. He had not shaved for a week and his breath was foul. "Tell me, dammit!"

I twisted away. "How the hell would I know?"

"You know a lot more than you are willing to tell, you little sneak! The general tells you things he does not even tell *me*, his good friend!"

I shook my head. "All I know is that he must have gone away in the night. Maybe he went with that shaved-headed young man that came to visit him yesterday."

"Shaved-headed?" He peered at me. "A soldier, perhaps?"

"I guess so."

"A *gringo* soldier, then?"

"Probably."

Spitting out an oath, he flung the cigarette away. I guess he had run out of the expensive Egyptian brand, and was smoking a rank Mexican cigarette called El Tigre. "I do not like what is going on!" he growled.

Maybe Fierro knew what was going on. I really didn't. Although I was beginning to have suspicions after that El Paso meeting with Black Jack Pershing. But with the general, my insurance policy against El Carnicero, gone on a mysterious errand, I was getting scared. My string was running out, as they say.

"You are lying, Texas whelp! I should have killed you that first day in Cuitla, before Ciudad Juárez, and had done with you! Tell me, what is this fucking thing that is going on?"

Some of the Dorados, always anxious to see a fight, hurried over, watching from behind marble columns and potted palms.

"I don't know," I repeated. "I tell you, I don't know. And that's all there is to it!"

With a glare Fierro sent the onlookers packing. The manager hurried over, anxious to prevent violence in his hotel, but Fierro waved him away and undid the flap on his holster.

"I have killed many men for less—for much less—than

what you did to me, Benjamin." There was a ghost of a smile on his lips. That, I knew, meant danger—great danger. But I didn't flinch. Foolishly, perhaps, I turned my back on him and walked away. At any moment I expected to hear the report of his pistol, to feel a thwack between my shoulder blades, then . . . nothing. But he didn't fire. Outside, in the pelting rain—God, would it never stop raining?—I looked back. Fierro stood on the porch of the hotel, pistol in his hand.

"Turn around, damn you!" he yelled. "I will not shoot you in the back!"

My stomach filled with ice water, I kept on walking down the street. Had I pressed my luck too far this time? But Fierro threw down his pistol with a curse; it went off, shattering a hanging basket filled with flowers. I had been very close to death. I knew. *Next time?*

Exciting everyone's curiosity, General Villa returned one day, very cheerful. I looked on in surprise as he stripped off his sodden garments. They were U.S. khaki, and the shoes good U.S. government leather.

"Go find me Rodolfo Fierro, Benjamin," he instructed me. "Quick, now—there are important developments to discuss!"

"Yes, sir!" I blurted, mystified.

Fierro was slumped in the hotel bar, two or three empty shot glasses in front of him while he sipped at another. When he saw me he staggered to his feet swaying, squinting through bloodshot eyes.

"This is business!" I said quickly. "I am to tell you that the general has returned and is asking for you. You had better drink some coffee and sober up before he sees you in this condition."

Staring at a puddle of liquor on the bar, Fierro ran a finger through it, making a small design that was reflected by the lights along the bar. "Yes, I know he is here. How should I not know, after all these years?"

"Then you had better hurry."

Unsteadily Fierro downed the cup of coffee the bartender brought. Brushing past me, he walked upstairs and opened the general's door without knocking, as he usually did. I started to follow, but he slammed the door in my face. They say curiosity killed a cat, but I had a stake in this revolution too! Especially I yearned to know why the general slipped away in the night and came back wearing U.S. khaki. Squinting my eyes shut, I put my ear against the door; there was no one else in the long hallway with its dusty palms and worn carpeting.

At first, what with the drumming of the rain against the window and the sound of vendors huddled below, crying their wares in the deluge, I could not make out anything more than vague sounds—the tenor pitch of General Villa and Rodolfo Fierro's deep-voiced responses. Pressing my ear flatter and flatter, I finally made out a few words. Fierro was angry, shouting at the general.

"No, no!" I heard him bang the table with his fist. "I will not be a running target for—"

A truck roared by below, throwing mud as high as the second-story windows, and I lost the rest of Fierro's words.

As the noise of the truck dwindled, I listened again. The general was trying to convince Fierro of something; his tone was wheedling. "There is no need, *hombre*, no intention, to carry out—"

Another damned truck! Then old Ojo Parado in his faded uniform came along, carbine over a shoulder, and demanded to know what I was doing.

"Nothing," I said.

He squinted, one-eyed, at me.

"What the hell is going on in there?"

"I don't know."

He scratched his head. "There have been rumors."

"Now, you know, *hombre*," I reminded him, "that there are always rumors in an army!"

Hands in pockets, I sauntered away, whistling; butter would not melt in my mouth. Still and all, I was puzzled. *I will not be a running target for* . . . And *There is no need, hombre, no intention, to carry out* . . .

Before he left for Russia, John Reed once said to me,

shaking his head in wonder and amusement, "A Mexican, Ben, would just as soon order a portrait, or a piano, or an automobile, so long as he doesn't intend to pay for it. I guess it must give him a sense of wealth!" Well, I guess I was getting to be a Mexican—*puro mexicano*. We of the revolution were penniless, not having been paid for months. Of course there were still funds in General Villa's safe in his room at the hotel—several thousand in silver. But that, he explained sorrowfully, must be conserved for the day when we would sally forth again to fight the Carrancistas. Because I intended to travel to Mr. Wickwire's funeral, I bought a new suit on tick from a Jewish tailor in Acosta Street. Years later I went back to pay him this old debt, but Meyer Jacobson was dead and buried. I gave ten U.S. dollars to his widow without explanation, and hurried away, still feeling guilty.

Anyway, it was still raining when I crossed the Stanton Street bridge and satisfied the immigration man I was a Texan. He believed me but *I* didn't, really.

The sparsely attended memorial service was held in a shabby Baptist church which I doubt the irreverent Wickwire had ever seen the inside of; I figured that Mrs. Wickwire was the churchgoer. A bored man from the *Morning Times* was there, along with a handful of friends and relatives.

Mrs. Wickwire took my hand between her own withered ones, weeping. "It was nice of you to come, Mr. Wilkerson! Henry was so fond of you, you know. He said you would go far."

Go far! I was a poverty-stricken volunteer in a ruined revolution! Still and all, I would not have been anything else.

"I am glad to be here, ma'am," I said. No, that wasn't quite the way to say it. "I mean," I bumbled, "that Mr. Wickwire was a great man, and a friend to me. I will never forget him, ma'am."

My new suit already sodden in the rain, and beginning to run a greenish dye down my hands—damn that tailor—a sudden thought came to me. What was that ridiculous story Mr. Wickwire told me when I last saw him, that time he lay in bed in the little house on Houston Street in El Paso?

365

They're going to try to work some scheme where U.S. troops go across the border and chase Villa all around Robin Hood's barn so as to give our green troops a workout. Blood them, you might say, so when they're shipped to Europe they'll be veterans that know which end of a gun the bullets come out of! Yes, now it added up. The general's trip with the shaved-headed U.S. lieutenant, sneaking into El Paso and out in a U.S. sergeant's uniform, the angry conference in the hotel room, with Rodolfo Fierro protesting, "I will not be a running target for . . ."; it all added up. Still, I could hardly believe it, it sounded so farfetched! Would General Villa lend himself to such a charade? Bewildered and disillusioned, I declined Mrs. Wickwire's invitation to cookies and tea and wandered off in the rain, going back across the Stanton Street bridge in utter confusion—and sadness.

When I got back the rain had stopped. My new green suit was running up my back like a window blind. Something had obviously happened while I was gone; the División del Norte was forming again. Decimated, we were less than a thousand. Still, there was spirit in the men as they looked toward battle.

"Did you hear?" Heavy with studded bandoliers, Ojo Parado clumped into my room. "We are on the move again!"

I threw the wet suit on the floor and got into my old shirt and jeans. "On the move, *amigo*? To where?"

He grinned a gap-toothed grin. "Who cares? A man is born to fight. It is not important where!"

Well, the "where" *was* important. We raided Columbus, New Mexico. It was, I learned later, part of the deal—the arrangement with General Pershing and Ambassador Henry Wilson, whom I had first seen so long ago crossing the Stanton Street bridge in a motorcar with General Hugh Scott. Villa was to create an incident that would justify the crossing of the border by U.S. troops. I doubt if Pershing and Wilson realized the magnitude of the "incident" General Villa had in mind. Anyway, on March 9 we trailed into the sleeping town at four in the morning, hoofbeats silent in drifted sand. The Thirteenth U.S. Cavalry was at Columbus and they were all asleep, not expecting any attack by the defeated General Villa. In the darkness before dawn, befuddled cavalrymen ran this way and that, cursing, shouting, dragging horses from the stables and trying desperately to mount a counterattack. Almost without opposition we ran them down, shouting *"Viva Villa!"* We got away with over a hundred of their horses, along with several Lewis machine guns, but the action was not without losses on our part. Almost a hundred of our people were killed or wounded. I read later in *Excelsior* that about twenty Americans—soldiers and civilians—had been killed, and another dozen or so wounded.

In terms of the great battles at Ciudad Juárez and Torreón and Zacatecas, the Columbus raid was a minor engagement. But it certainly put the general's name in headlines around the world. In the States there was immediate demand for retaliation. The incident had Mexican repercussions too. The resurgence of General Villa's popularity worried Venustiano Carranza, who would be glad to see the general captured or killed by anyone, U.S. forces or not. Even in defeat the general worried Carranza. "You can cut up a snake like Villa in a thousand pieces," he was reported to have told a reporter, "but each piece will grow another snake!"

As the agreement must have promised, our meager supplies were quickly replenished by the U.S. Following the Columbus raid, our raggle-taggle force withdrew into Chihuahua, holing up in the foothills of the Sierra de las Tunas. By this time there was no secret among the Villistas as to what was happening. There were loud and frequent arguments between General Villa and Rodolfo Fierro, overheard by everyone. I sat on a rock in the dusk, watching dusty brown U.S. trucks trundling in, loaded high with wool blankets, cases of cartridges, rectangular boxes with Enfield rifles packed in Cosmoline, field rations, medical supplies. Sergeant Thibeault, in command of the convoy, sat down beside me and lit his pipe.

"You *habla inglés*?" he asked in the abrupt way of Anglos. He did not mean any offense; he was only ignorant of the polite and indirect way a Mexican would frame the question.

"Damn right," I said.

He stared at me. "You U.S.?"

"No," I said. "Mexican. *Puro mexicano*."

He considered this, puffing on the pipe. "Well, you speak pretty good English, for a greaser."

I disregarded that. In spite of his words he seemed to be a nice man, although ignorant, and didn't know any better.

"That Villa over there?" He pointed with the stem of the pipe to where the general and Rodolfo Fierro were looking by lanternlight at a map spread on a rocky ledge.

"Yes."

"He don't look like such a much!"

I disregarded that also, but I was beginning to get a little nettled.

"What the hell they arguing about?"

They were indeed arguing, having been at it ever since the Columbus raid.

"How would I know? I'm just a buck-assed private in the rear rank!"

However, I did know. Everyone knew. The argument went on long after the lumbering truck convoy unloaded and trundled back toward the border. Miserable, I sat on a sun-warmed rock in the moonlight, listening to them wrangle.

"I will not be a damned duck in a shooting gallery for a fucking *gringo* general!" Fierro shouted. "What has happened to our revolution, eh? Are we whores, to be bought off by *gringo* gifts? Tell me that, Francisco!"

The general was going to hell in a hand basket. It was an old expression I once heard Mr. Claude Teasdale use, although I didn't know exactly what it meant, except that things were getting bad. Our revolution appeared to have been bought by the U.S., the general and Fierro were at cross-purposes—I felt sad, very sad. But something the general said made me sit up, listening.

"Rodolfo, you know me better than that! I tell you I take their guns, their bullets, their rations—whatever the fools will give me! Then we go back to fighting that prick

Carranza again! That is why I agreed to it! By god, Rodolfo, do you think I am some kind of pimp, to sell out my cause to that prissy President Wilson of theirs? You should know me better than that! If you do not . . . well, then, I spit on you!"

Fierro still grumbled, but appeared somewhat mollified. I, however, felt a surge of elation. The general never had had any thought of selling out! The revolution was back in business again! There was still a chance of unseating Venustiano Carranza and placing General Francisco Villa in his rightful place as President of the new Mexican republic. Like the dye-running green suit I had discarded, my doubts disappeared, fading away in the light of truth. *Arriba la revolución!* I did a little jig in the moonlight. One of Fierro's gang, on guard duty at the general's tent, approached me.

"*Compañero*, are you crazy? What are you doing? I have heard that moonlight sometimes makes men very strange!"

Throwing my arms around him, I gave him a big *abrazo*, kissing him on his whiskered cheek.

"Here! What are you doing?" Scowling, he rubbed his cheek.

I guess I was strange that night, although not from moonlight. I was crazy with renewed promise, and jigged away. Though it was well after midnight, I could not sleep. In the light of a waning moon I curried my mystified nag, gave her an extra ration of oats, which surprised her, and sat on a rock breathing softly into my mouth-organ till the rising sun bathed the slopes of the Sierra de las Tunas in a pink mist. Bemused, I sat there for a long time, playing, almost unaware of the growing activity around me as the Villistas pried open cartridge chests, exulted in unfired Enfield rifles, draped U.S. woolen blankets around their shoulders against the dawn chill.

The sun crept higher. The jagged mountains—the tawny peaks that hitherto had looked to me like merciless lions waiting to spring on hapless revolutionaries—now seemed almost soft, rounded, feminine in the growing golden haze. And suddenly I realized what was on my mind in this

Mexican dawn, and was ashamed to have forgotten in a flush of revolutionary fervor. I was a married man . . . well, not technically married, but nevertheless married. My Valentina was still in Torreón, ripe with my son, our son. Ashamed, I knelt—covertly—behind a bush and prayed to whatever God there was. Maybe he forgot Mexico at times, but perhaps he would hear me out, hear a soldier of Mexico.

Please, I muttered, *please keep and protect her, Lord! She is so small and so helpless! Let her know I am thinking of her, and will come to Torreón as soon as I can, for it must be nearing her time.*

Wiping grease from a brand-new Enfield, hands black with the stuff, Ojo Parado sauntered up, grinning. "You pray, eh? I did not know you were one of those, Benjamin. Still, I suppose it does no harm and it might be well to pray before a battle."

I nodded noncommittally and went to saddle my sullen old mare. We seemed always short of horseflesh, and I was lucky to have a horse, evil-tempered as she was. As always, she tried to bite me but I did not scold her. Thinking of Valentina, my Valentina, I was charitable toward anybody, even that tough-mouthed continually farting old Durango mare.

— 19 —

At first it was fun, exciting. I had hardly realized how Mexican I had become. Revived, with many guns and fresh horses, we dashed about the country stinging Carranza strongholds. We were back in the saddle again, where the general said a proper Mexican ought to be. Excited also, a few recruits joined us from Bosque Bonito and Gallego and Carrizal, some even riding down from Santa Clara, high in the sierra. But I had to admit they were few. In general, the people had lost their enthusiasm for General Villa and his wild sweeps across Chihuahua and Durango. Venustiano Carranza was also tightening the screws, executing anyone who had given aid and comfort to the rebels against his regime. His troops were everywhere—guarding railroad lines, searching the canyons, riding in force across the plains to interdict us. In that first flush of enthusiasm, however, the fact that we could now muster only a few hundred men was hardly noticed.

I still do not understand how the messages were forwarded but I do know that from time to time the general received information from an exasperated General John J. Pershing that he should leave off fighting Carranza and act as a proper target for the U.S. cavalry that was bumbling about in Chihuahua in search of him—the bandit Pancho Villa.

"Fools! Idiots!" Gleefully the general tore up a warning telegram, and with Rodolfo Fierro set about planning another wild sortie. First we hit Chihuahua City, setting fire to a warehouse full of cotton. On we rode, making a feint toward the Presidio itself, then swinging back to Hidalgo

371

del Parral, where we routed a small contingent of Carrancistas and took several thousand silver pesos of ransom to free the mayor and the city council, who had turned into ardent Carrancistas in our absence. Then we rode into the Sierra de la Tasajera to rest for a while and regroup.

In all these operations we had lost only a few men, but now we were again running low on ammunition. A Mexican never fires a single shot at anything. Even a fleeing deer would suffer volley after volley of .30-caliber bullets. Sometimes the meat was so full of lead it was dangerous to eat it for fear of broken teeth and no dentist.

General Pershing finally became furious. U.S. newspapers were criticizing the decision to send U.S. troops into Mexico. "After all," the Boston *Globe* complained, "the effort to date has been utterly futile. The bandit Villa continues to romp around Chihuahua, making fools of General Pershing and his bewildered cavalry. Perhaps the chase should now be abandoned before our troops become sunstroked, ill, and discouraged. Pancho Villa has shown that he is more than a match for the unhappy pursuers, who have yet to approach within miles of the wily bandit."

Well, it was true. So far, Pershing's cavalry had never come near us. They did, however, fight a pitched battle—not with us, but with Carranza forces at Carrizal, some eighty miles south of Ciudad Juárez, under the command of Carrancista General Felix Gómez.

The whole affair was incredible, and caused great if short-lived merriment in the sierra where we were holed up resting. We did not know all the details until much later, but on the twentieth of June Troops C and K of the Tenth Cavalry were scouting near Carrizal, vainly searching for us. General Gómez rode out to greet them, warning that they should not approach Carrizal too closely; he considered the Americans foreign troops apt to menace his town. A Captain Boyd, commanding the scout party, suspected that Carrizal was harboring Villistas. Dismounting, he led a party on foot to investigate.

General Gómez, very nervous, gave an order to fire on the invaders. The general and seventy-four Mexicans were killed in the ensuing battle. Captain Boyd and his second in command were also cut down by a burst of Mexican machine-gun fire. The U.S. troops lost eight dead, and twenty-three of the party were captured by the Mexicans. In addition to the fruitlessness of Pershing's pursuit of Villa, the U.S. press was merciless in its criticism of Ambassador Henry Lane Wilson and General Pershing. The whole so-called "Punitive Expedition" became a laughingstock, especially in the Sierra de la Tasajera.

However, our laughter was short-lived, as I have said. Waiting in the sierra for another promised shipment of supplies, General Villa had second thoughts when the stuff did not appear. Rubbing his chin, he looked thoughtful. To Fierro he said, "Well, Rodolfo, I think we have had our fun. Now we have made Jack Pershing mad, and he has cut off our supplies. I suppose we will have to do something to encourage him."

Fierro was sullen. "What do you have in mind, then?"

It was a fine hot day in July and the Villista flag fluttered in the breeze over our mountain hideaway while the plains below sweltered. Squatting on a ledge, cleaning my little Spanish pistol, I was thinking about Valentina. My love for her was largely spiritual, I believed, but there was also that tingling in my groin when I thought of her yielding body in lamplight, the ripeness of her breast, the indefinable fragrance of her hair, of Valentina. Aimlessly, lost in pleasant musings, I ran the cleaning rod back and forth in the barrel, thinking that the action was very like my thing in Valentina. Gross, certainly, was the thought; I was repelled by such grossness but went on with the action mechanically, eyes half-closed in pleasure.

"Dammit, no!" a voice shouted, waking me from the reverie.

Startled, I opened my eyes. Fierro crumpled a map in his hands, threw it down, stamped on it. "I will not be a party to such foolishness, Francisco!" Breaking into French, which he still used occasionally, he shouted, *"Je refuse . . . je refuse!"*

General Villa, booted feet propped on a rock, hands folded across his middle, glowered. "Don't talk your fucking French to me, *cabrón!*"

Fierro stood his ground. Agitated, he said, "We are

supposed to be fighting that idiot Carranza! It is our duty as patriotic Mexicans, sons of the great revolution! I refuse to waste what we have on a foolish charade that gets the revolution nowhere!"

The general's brown face suffused into a pinkish cast. His voice became quiet, almost inaudible. "I give orders here, Rodolfo. No one refuses my orders without dying as a traitor. Do I need to remind you of that—you who have killed so many with less reason?"

Fierro shrugged, sullen. "My life is worth no more and no less than theirs. But I have made up my mind. I will not do it!"

Ojo Parado and some of the others were cleaning guns, repairing saddles, grilling deer meat over a blaze of pine twigs. Stopping their usual banter, they avoided looking directly at Villa and Fierro, but kept quiet, aware that something important was going on.

"Listen!" the general said, trying to be reasonable. "Listen to me, Rodolfo. We have a lot of pesos in those bags over there, but no place to spend them. We are running out of bullets. We need spare parts for the Lewis machine guns we captured. Our horses are worn down from so much riding. We need medical supplies and blankets and cornmeal and bacon and coffee and sugar and a lot of things. General Pershing promised me these things as I required them. But we have not heard from him for weeks! He is mad at us because we are making fools of him and his toy soldiers. If we are to remain a force in Mexico we have got to make compromises! I propose to go down to Villa Ahumada and let the poor fools chase us for a while, that is all! That will save Jack Pershing's face, and then he will send us what we need. Now, what is wrong with that—tell me!"

Fierro scowled, tugged at his untrimmed beard, said nothing. "Come, now, Rodolfo! We are old friends!" Still in that greasy suit—it must have been made of boiler-plate iron, to last so long—the general rose and clapped him on the back, offering him a cup of scarce coffee from the blackened pot that simmered on the fire beside a rack of deer ribs. "Come, now, let us be friends again! Humor me this one time, even if you do not agree. Then, when we have diddled this Black Jack or whatever he is called, he will be pleased to resupply us. What do you say, eh?"

Fierro sighed, shrugged. "I suppose I must agree. It seems I have no other fucking choice, does it not?"

I still had my doubts about Fierro. Cruel and vicious as he was, he still burned with a desire to free Mexico of Venustiano Carranza and the tricky politicians who surrounded him, an unsavory lot at best. He had agreed, I suspected, too quickly. Maybe going to Villa Ahumada was a diversion, but it was only temporary. I could not conceive of treachery on Fierro's part against his old friend, yet I worried about it.

Well, my doubts were soon resolved. Rolled in a blanket against the chill of a mountain night, I was sound asleep when something cold and hard pressed against my throat. Tight with fear, trembling, I opened my eyes in starshine to see the carved idollike face of another of Fierro's Yaqui scouts.

"*Ven conmigo*," he murmured. "Come with me quietly or I will slit your throat, *hombre!*"

With his knife pricking my neck as a warning, he tossed away my little Spanish pistol and herded me across the grassy clearing and into a copse of scrub oak. There, out of earshot of the camp, Rodolfo Fierro waited with three horses.

"There you are, little bastard!" Fierro greeted me, slapping a leather quirt into his palm. "Benjamin, we are going on a small journey now, you and me and my good Yaqui friend here!"

Wildly I looked around for a chance to escape but there was none. As a caution, the grim-faced Yaqui drew a little blood from my neck with a prick of his knife.

"*Cuidado*, Benjamin!" Fierro said mockingly. "Alberto is a cousin of León, whom you stuck with your knife that night in Torreón when the men were having so much fun with fireworks. Alberto would use any occasion to kill you, that is clear! Blood is very thick among the Yaquis. If a Yaqui is killed, the crime must be washed out with more blood—in this case, *gringo* blood."

The Yaqui's face was as impassive as ever. I doubt if he would have changed expression even when he killed me, as I knew he was anxious to do. I hadn't killed his cousin, of course; old Ojo Parado had done it to protect me and Valentina. But Fierro and the Indian obviously thought I had done it. Well, there was no point in trying to explain. *Ay, chingado!* My balls had crawled so far into my belly that I figured they would never come out again.

"I have a villa not too far away," Fierro said conversationally, tying canvas sacks to his saddle. I recognized them; they were the silver pesos the general had taken at Carrizal. "For now, we must travel fast, before that lunatic Pancho Villa realizes that I am gone, you are gone, and his silver pesos are gone. But when we reach my Las Delicias I will have my way with you, Texas boy—and then Alberto will sweat out of you the whereabouts of my daughter Valentina, the flower of my life whom you have ruined!"

Aghast at his treachery, for some perverse reason more appalled at that than by his threats to me, I spoke out.

"You have betrayed our general and the cause he fought for! You are betraying the people of Mexico! You have betrayed the revolution itself!"

While Alberto pinioned my arms behind my back, Fierro beat me with his leather quirt until I sagged to the ground, head reeling and the warm salty taste of blood in my mouth. Huddled on the dew-wet sand, I guess I groaned; Fierro smacked the palm of his hand with the quirt, smiling.

"You will howl much louder, Texas boy, when we reach Las Delicias! After Alberto has finished with you I will do what people do to dead dogs—throw you on the garbage heap!" He laughed and went about finishing securing the heavy bags of silver to his saddle.

"Get on your horse!" he ordered.

When I did not move quickly enough, he kicked me hard in the ribs. The pointed toe of his boot was like a stiletto. I bled again; I could feel the manta shirt wet and clammy against my bruised side.

"Get up, damn you! I cannot afford to have old Pancho catch up with us—not at *this* stage!" He gestured. "Alberto, throw him up on the saddle!"

As Ojo Parado had said, the Yaquis were small, but Alberto was very strong. Tossing me onto the saddle, he mounted his own horse. Fierro pointed into the darkness.

"Let's go!"

In almost total darkness—no moon and few stars—we moved down the mountain, guided by the Yaqui. It was said they were part cat and could see at night. We rode through dense brush, down boulder-littered canyons, across cold bubbling streams, slipped and slid over water-polished ledges, emerging at first light on the plains below. There was a shabby village in the distance. I could see smoke curling from mud chimneys, and a dog barked, a faint and far-off stirring of the misty dawn.

"We stay away from villages," Fierro muttered. "No villages! I will leave no trace."

Moving quickly, we skirted a rocky ledge and rode along the foothills of the sierra, keeping close to the jumbled boulders for cover. At noon, the sun only a faint glimmer in the overcast, we stopped. Fierro took some scraps of *chorizo* and a few stale tortillas from his saddlebags. He and Alberto ate, washing the food down with swigs from a canteen of cold coffee. I got nothing. I couldn't eat anyway; I was too scared, not only for myself but also for Valentina. I wouldn't tell Rodolfo Fierro anything, even if Alberto stuck lighted splinters under my fingernails. Or would I? Almost I wept at my predicament. Maybe I murmured something, because Fierro, getting up and belching, grinned down at me.

"No food for you, Texas boy! I want you weak and pliant when we come to Las Delicias!" Stretching his arms, he yawned. "Did you know, little worm, that Las Delicias is where my Valentina was born, so many years ago? And Las Delicias is where her mother, my sainted María Luisa— Marucha was my name for her—died. It is only fitting, you whelp, that this business comes to an end at Las Delicias!"

Late in the afternoon we turned away from the foothills and followed a willow-bordered stream, milky with snowmelt from the peaks towering above us. Pausing to let the horses drink, Fierro scanned the mountains with his field glasses.

"Good! Nothing stirring except a wagon or two on the road. I have good friends in Ciudad Camargo. When we reach there this evening we can get food and fresh horses."

It started to rain, a foggy misty rain that soaked me to the bone. Having been rousted from sleep by Alberto, I had had no time to dress properly. Clad only in shirt and pants, I shivered in the cold. Hands bound, the Yaqui Alberto riding behind me with his carbine slung loose across his arm and Fierro just ahead, I was caught for fair. Even if I had figured out some way to escape, I probably couldn't have brought it off—I was too weak, and my legs felt like rubber. In agony, physical and mental agony, I twisted in my bonds. Alberto, wary, struck me over the head with the barrel of his carbine and I cried out in pain. Fierro looked back.

"You are softening," he said. "I see that, Texas boy! It will not take too much to loosen your tongue!"

In the distance patches of sunlight glowed on sprouting grain. Ducks, migrating ducks and geese, sailed on shallow pools among the green shoots. Distant farmers, looking like dolls, flung stones at them. When they saw us coming the farmers fled, taking us for bandits. Fierro swore.

"If Pancho follows us, they will tell him where we have gone. But there is no cure for it, so we must hurry. He whipped up his horse and the Yaqui jabbed the ribs of my weary mount with his toe. The mare rocked into an awkward gallop. Weary, saddle-sore, and scared, it was all I could do to keep my seat.

At dusk, a blood-red sun sinking in the mist, we stopped for a few minutes to rest the horses. "Not much left in them," Fierro said, eyeing them. "A thing like this is difficult. We must move fast to escape old Pancho's wrath, but we must also conserve our horses. A nice balance must be kept!"

Before us lay a shallow pool of water fifty meters or so wide, where the set of the field had not permitted the rains to drain off. Slowly, so as not to alarm Alberto, I slid off my mount and stood on trembling shanks, swaying a little at the feel of solid ground under my feet.

"My wrists hurt!" I complained.

Fierro grinned. "Suffering ennobles the soul, they say. At Las Delicias you will become so damned noble that you may ascend to heaven without any aid whatever! So suffer, Texas boy! Suffer as you have made me suffer over what you have done to my Valentina!"

A newborn gosling, waddling out of the reeds along the green-slimed border of the pool, ventured too near where Alberto was hunkered down smoking a brown-paper cigarette. With a catlike move he snatched up the little thing and wrung its neck, tossing it back into the muddy pool. The mother, half-seen among the reeds, squawked loudly and fluttered about, half-rising from the water and then falling back in distraction. Fierro chuckled.

"You see, *chamaco*, it is ony Alberto's way of showing you what he would like to do to you for knifing his cousin that night, although other things will probably precede the final event! How did León die, exactly, Benjamin? I would not have thought you so murderous, or León so careless!"

With Fierro's glasses Alberto was scanning our back trail. Fierro spoke to him in what must have been the Yaqui language; it was no Spanish *I* ever heard. Fierro was a brilliant man—I had to give him that. He was well-educated. Someone once told me that he had been to school in London and Paris to study economics or some such thing.

Alberto answered him in the same gibble-gabble and Fierro muttered, "No pursuers yet! Well, that is good. But I do not doubt the old man will come down on us soon if we do not hurry." He looked suddenly pleased with himself. Ah—*comes down on us* indeed! I remember poetry: "The Assyrian came down like a wolf on the fold, and his cohorts were gleaming with purple and gold." Of course, it loses something when translated into another language.

Rest over, we mounted again. My wrists still tied, now terribly sore and chafed, and my hands left without feeling, like two wooden blocks, Alberto hoisted me onto the weary mare. She was still puffing and blowing. I doubted she would last long.

"*Adelante!*" Fierro shouted. "Forward!" Digging his

cruel spurs into the ribs of his mount, he galloped straight into the shallow pool, the gelding's flailing hooves sending up a shower of greenish spray sparkling in the setting sun like a handful of emeralds flung into the sky. Wearily I kneed my own mount. She moved toward the water, the watchful Alberto following me, carbine at the ready.

Suddenly there was a great splash, then a turgid rolling aside of the green slime as Fierro's horse slipped, struggled, then fell sideways into the water. Mud roiled up, turning the green water to brown. Fierro's leg was pinned under the gelding. Cursing, he struggled to free himself.

"Ah! Fucking horse! Get off my leg, damn you! Mother of God, my leg is broken, I think! *Merde!* Ah, *merde!*"

The Indian scrambled down, still carrying the carbine. Splashing through the water, falling and picking himself up again, floundering as he staggered toward his master, he carried the carbine high so as not to foul the barrel with mud or water.

"*Arena!*" Fierro called, a note of panic in his voice. "*Arena movediza!* Ah, *merde!*" I knew what that meant—quicksand. Old Ojo Parado said that steers, seeking water, often were sucked down into such pools. I remembered the time when the División del Norte was stalled in such a pool while men worked to free trucks and wagons that had been thus trapped. I had seen one Dodge truck settle down, canvas top and all. Slowly it disappeared while cursing soldiers tried to save dozens of cases of scarce cartridges before the truck gurgled completely under.

With one hand the Yaqui was trying to pull Fierro free. But with his leg pinioned under the thrashing horse, Fierro was only sinking deeper. With his free arm he pushed Alberto away.

"Go untie Benjamin, you fool! Quick! He will help you!"

Uncertain, the Indian looked at me where I still sat my horse, wrists tied behind me.

"Yes, go, stupid fool! Go! *Apúrate, cabrón!*"

Uncertainly Alberto splashed his way back to me. Drawing his knife, he cut my bonds. On rubbery legs I slipped down, rubbing my cramped wrists. Electrical charges seemed

380

to dance through my arms as the pent-up blood began to flow.

"Hurry, dammit, Benjamin! Come quickly! Alberto, you will have to shoot the horse—he is dragging me deeper!"

The Yaqui, seized by an idea, ran to his mount and snatched up the braided-hair lariat that hung on the saddle. Confused, perhaps, by the sudden emergency, he laid down his carbine, propping it against a fat barrel cactus. Uncoiling the lariat, he turned, probably meaning to tie one end to his master and the other around his saddle horn to pull Fierro free.

Laying down the carbine was the last mistake he ever made. I picked it up and levered a shell into the chamber. Facing me, still as impassive as ever, the Yaqui stood like a statue, coil of rope in his hand, assessing the situation. Slowly he advanced toward me, uncoiling the lariat. I remembered seeing the Indians do tricks with lariats; they made good cowhands, I had heard.

I couldn't take any chances with this *hombre*. Drawing a quick bead, I shot him through the head just as the hair rope snapped whiplike toward me. My arm was shaking so that for a minute I thought I missed him. No—he took a few faltering steps, dropping the rope, and pitched headfirst into the water, crumpling on hands and knees into the ooze until only his manta-clad rump showed above the water.

"Benjamin!" Fierro's voice was frantic. "What the hell are you doing?" He who had killed so many now stared white-faced at the muzzle of the carbine. The mother goose was squawking in terror at the report of the gun and flapped madly into the sky, abandoning the rest of her brood.

"Don't worry," I said, "I'm not going to shoot you, Rodolfo!"

He struggled as the water inched up toward his chin. Painfully he was craning his neck, trying to keep his head above water. "But—"

"Shooting is too good for you. It is too quick. I understand a bullet through the skull is practically painless." I walked gingerly into the pool, assuring myself that he was pinned securely under the frightened horse, rolling its eyes widely in fear.

"What are you going to do, then, *chamaco?*" He struggled some more, and spat out water.

I think the gelding had already injured a hind leg. "But the horse," I said, "must not suffer." I put the carbine to his ear and pulled the trigger. I could not bear to look—the gelding was a fine animal. He thrashed for a moment, then lay still.

"Benjamin, help me!" Fierro cried. "Look how I am sinking!" The weight of the dead horse, along with the bags of silver tied to his saddle, bore him deeper into the sucking mud. "Surely you are not going to leave me here to drown, Benjamin! Listen, *chamaco*—I am Valentina's father!" Her name—Valentina's name—was sacrilege on his lips.

I splashed back to the bank and squatted, the carbine across my knees. Hungry, I ate a tortilla from Alberto's saddlebag.

"Look!" Fierro pleaded. "Take the sacks of pesos, Benjamin! Take them for yourself and go wherever you like! Only get me out of this fucking mud! I would not like to die this way!"

Now there was little of him above the green waters but one arm and his head. Slowly the dead gelding settled, bearing him down.

"I love you, Benjamin! Believe me, *chamaco!* How can you do this to me, *chamaco?* Ah, *merde!* Blessed Virgin, help me!"

Fierro calling on the Blessed Virgin! I doubted if she had ever heard of Rodolfo Fierro, although I knew that the devil was well-acquainted with him. I ate another tortilla and washed it down with the few drops of coffee left in a canteen.

"I don't want the money," I told him. "Take it to hell with you! Maybe it can buy some water there to dampen the fires that are certain to roast your ugly soul!" I laughed, and remember it as a kind of high-pitched cackle—crazy, hysterical. After all, I had been through a lot.

"Benjamin!" he screamed, a blood-curdling sound. I

continued eating while the light died on the tableau of the brackish pool, Rodolfo Fierro and the dead horse, the Yaqui Alberto apparently kneeling in prayer.

Fierro spat mud and gurgled something. His precious beard was sodden and muddy; the water was now nearly over his mouth so that he had to puff and blow to keep it out.

"Only a little time now," I told him. "Then you will meet the souls of all those you murdered. They are waiting for you, Rodolfo Fierro, in the pits of hell!"

In the loneliness of dusk his voice rose shrilly in a last gasp. "For God's sake, Benjamin, shoot me then! I cannot die like this, in mud, drowning in mud! Save me, for the sake of my poor daughter Valentina!"

I threw away the crumbs of tortilla and dusted my hands. Feeling unreal, as if it were all a dream, I shoved the carbine into the saddle boot of the Indian's horse and took the bridle of my own mount.

"Benjamin!" It was a shriek so piercing that a crow flying overhead wheeled in fright and pumped madly away, sounding a cry of alarm to brother crows. "Benjamin, do not leave me!"

Sitting the Indian's horse, a better mount than mine, I watched for another few minutes. Fierro's head was underwater now; only a few strands of the long golden beard floated on the water to mark his passing. As I watched, even those disappeared, pulled down by the sinking body. A few bubbles came up and some yellowish stains too; when a man dies, his bowels are released. As I rode away, leading the other horse, the crow flapped back, curious. For a moment he circled the pool, suspicious. Then, reassured, he soared down to a skidding halt, cocking his head at the Indian's tilted rump. *Rodolfo Fierro was dead, dead, dead—and I never got to use my little Spanish pistol on him.*

A day later I rode into a small village. I was sick, very sick, from some disease that the local *curanderas* did not know, but the people took good care of me. I gave them the extra horse, and later sent them money for their kindness. Mexicans are always good to the sick, hurrying to make them well lest evil spirits come into the village in search of the dying.

That horrible happening in the quicksand still does not allow me rest. Certainly Rodolfo Fierro deserved, richly deserved, to die that ugly and lingering death; it was only just payment for his sins against God and man. And yet I still wonder about El Carnicero, Francisco Villa's Butcher. *I love you, Benjamin! Believe me, chamaco! How can you do this to me?*

Certainly he could, at any time, have squashed a frightened Texas boy under his boot like a bug. Of course I was under General Villa's protection, but Fierro often disobeyed the general. The murder of a bothersome Texas stripling would have been only one, and perhaps the least one, of the hundreds of deaths he was responsible for. And yet, though often furious with me, Rodolfo Fierro always restrained himself against a simple and effective remedy: shooting Benjamin Thomas Wilkerson as he had so many others, like the young Berlanga.

I love you, Benjamin! Well, perhaps he *had* loved me in his own perverse way. I myself loved several men, but not in Rodolfo Fierro's fashion. There can be great love among men—among the brotherhood of brave men—patriots, fighters for freedom, men like good old Ojo Parado, who are dedicated to a cause. I loved Ojo Parado and I loved others also for their dedication and bravery, men who risked death to save others, even courting death with a smile and a joke. It is a kind of love I doubt if any female can understand and is perhaps a greater love than that of a woman for a man. Yes, "love" is the only word for it!

But Fierro's love for me was not that kind of love. His love was an ugly and bizarre thing. Still, in his crazed mind perhaps it was all that the Butcher had to offer me.

Who can understand these things? It was, I concluded, God's business and not mine.

— 20 —

Numb, not believing and not wanting to believe what I heard, I sat in the small parlor of Señora Eulalia Gutiérrez on Calle Fuente in Torreón. To this day I remember every detail of that humble place as if it were a photograph—withered flowers in a mason jar before the portrait of the Virgin, the big pink-and-white seashell that was her proudest possession because she had never seen the sea, the faded crayon portrait of Eulalia and her husband, Luis, dead at Ojinaga to the greater glory of the revolution. They were both in wedding finery, Señor Gutiérrez in an unaccustomed high starched collar that seemed to be choking him. There was in the air the Mexican smell of beans cooking on a charcoal brazier, the rich scent of chiles laced with fresh *masa*, the dough from which women pat the tortillas which are the daily bread of Mexico. There were sounds, too: children playing *pelota* in the narrow street outside, the chords of a lazy guitar, a flapping of pigeons overhead as they flew back to a rooftop cote.

"We could do nothing, *señor*," Eulalia Gutiérrez said, dabbing at her eyes with a handkerchief. "There was a little money from that which you left us, and I went for the doctor. The first one said that the money was not enough. Then the kind English lady I clean for helped me to find another, a good doctor, and she paid him what I could not. When he came . . ."

She broke off, handkerchief to her beak of a nose. "*Señor*, it is hard to tell! Anyway . . ." Taking a deep breath, the ragged lace at her throat rising and falling, she went on. "He said, the doctor, that she was very bad. It seems she was so small. You know that, *señor*. She was so small that the baby could not come out the way it should! He sent for an ambulance to take her to the hospital, but before it came she gave out a great cry. Valentina called your name, *señor*. A wild look was in her eyes. She grabbed my hand so hard it hurt, but I did not mind. 'Benjamin!' she said. "Oh, Benjamin! Come, Benjamin—please!' Then she was gone, gone to God, along with the poor baby. When the ambulance came, it was too late."

I sat motionless, fingernails digging into flesh. I could not weep. Before she died she called my name! *Benjamin! Come, Benjamin—please!* All alone, except for old Eulalia, while I was skyhooting around Chihuahua with General Villa. Valentina, all alone . . .

"Please, Don Benjamin!" Eulalia came to me and put her arms around me. "Do not just sit and stare like that! Weep, *señor*! Here—I lend you my skinny old shoulder! Weep, for the love of God!"

I could not. I got up, feeling numb and lifeless, like a badly made wooden doll.

"*Señora*, I thank you. I owe you a debt I can never repay. I have a little money." Digging into my pocket, I came out with a few pesos, but she pushed my hand away.

"Keep your money, *señor*! This is not a matter of money. Valentina was like a daughter to me. Anyway, I clean for the Englishwoman and she pays me enough."

Still uncertain on my feet, I went to the door, dazed. Somehow I could not yet feel the meaning of what had happened.

"Please!" Señora Gutiérrez said. "Wait a moment, *señor*, and pray with me—pray for her!"

We knelt at the rude door which was nailed together haphazardly so that light showed through. In winter it must have been cold in the little house, and Valentina must often have shivered. I saw her face before me as I stared at the mud wall. *Valentina!* Head bowed, I knelt.

"She was very small, Lord, and very brave. She loved this man so much it hurt, but she was always brave. Every night she prayed he would be well, that you would bring him back safely. Even at the last, Lord, she forgot her own pain to pray for him. Someday this man will join her in that glorious heaven where angels sing and all is happiness and two lovers will be reunited with their little baby. Until that time, Lord, keep her and comfort her—our Valentina!''

There was an eloquence in the old lady, a simple eloquence that broke the wall I had kept between me and Valentina's death. Suddenly I started to weep. Ashamed, I tried to hide my grief. Old Eulalia pulled me to her skinny bosom as if I were a child, a great lubberly child who had suddenly known grief.

"There, there, Benjamin!" Her voice was gentle; she smelled of hard soap and scrub brushes. "Get it all out of you, *muchacho*. It is better that way!"

Ashamed of my blubbering—after all, a man in Mexico is always *muy macho*—I tried to move away but she held me with astonishing strength.

"Weep, my son! It is nothing to be ashamed of!"

After a while I managed to gasp a deep breath and swallow the great lump in my throat.

"There, now." Smoothing her black dress, she nodded with satisfaction, as with a floor well-scrubbed. "Will you have a cup of tea with me before you go? The Englishwoman gave me some India tea that is good."

I drank tea with her and went away feeling a little better. But there were long days to come, days when Valentina was in my mind almost as in actuality. I talked to her as I wandered about, and got a reputation in Chihuahua as *un poco loco*, a man slightly "touched," as they say back in Hudspeth County.

I had had enough of the revolution, of wars and blood, machine guns and Carrancistas. But the war went on. The "Punitive Expedition" of General Pershing petered out when the United States entered the Great European War on the side of England and France. General Villa was left without funds, without support. Still, he and his loyal bodyguard continued to raid Chihuahua, miraculously staying one step ahead of the vengeful Carrancistas, whom he was making look foolish. Then something happened, a decisive

387

thing that came out of nowhere, the way things often happened in Mexico.

While I was wandering around Chihuahua like a lost dog, Obregon fell out with Carranza, and Mexico churned with new violence. Half mad, and without the opportunity or desire to read such newspapers as made their way into the hovels where I begged for food or slept, I did not know the facts until much later. At any rate, that big-bellied, blue-bespectacled prick of a Carranza looted the treasury and fled Mexico City, aware that Obregón's forces outnumbered his. At Tlaxcalantongo, a poor village of wattled huts with earthen floors, a place of sickly chickens and sickly children, a local peasant leader, Rodolfo Herrero, met Carranza and his party and offered them shelter for the night. On Friday, May 21, 1920 gunfire broke out in Tlaxcalantongo. The circumstances remained unclear, but Venustiano Carranza, the potbellied blue-spectacled *perfumado* so hated by General Villa, was killed. It was believed that Obregón himself had signed Carranza's death warrant, though it was never established for certain.

In any case, Carranza was succeeded by the governor of Sonora, Adolfo de la Huerta, an honest and forthright man, and no relation at all to the bullet-headed Indian, Victoriano Huerta, who was briefly President of Mexico. De la Huerta brought a measure of peace to bloody and embattled Mexico, calling together all the rebels with promises of remedying their grievances. Only General Villa remained on the loose, prowling Chihuahua like the fierce "Lion of the North" he had always been. Now, however, my general seemed more than ever filled with bloodlust. His great plans for Mexico had been blocked by the hard rock of the new President and greatly superior forces. The Dorados, gold greatly tarnished, swept into Chihuahua villages, demanded ransoms, then vanished into the sierra, leaving behind terrified peasants, those very people Villa had once professed to be fighting for. Villa sought out old enemies and killed them with his own gun. One of his lieutenants, Baudelio Uribe, whom I did not know, specialized in cutting off ears of civic officials. In Santa Rosalía de Camargo, where a de la Huerta garrison had been taken by surprise and wiped out, the Villistas executed the soldiers' women and children. In Jiménez General Villa burned the feet of a poor man with live coals until the *anciano* gave him permission to marry the old man's daughter. At Satevo, where a fifteen-year-old girl was bearing Villa's child, he forced the parish priest to confess paternity, abandon his vows, and marry the girl. He made long rambling speeches before terrified communities, and wept as he described his long career as a revolutionist, how he had been betrayed first by Carranza, then by the new President de la Huerta. It was a wild, sick campaign, led by a great man now wild and sick himself. I grieved for him and for the death of the revolution.

I was wild and sick myself, perhaps a little insane. I wandered about Chihuahua, taking odd jobs here and there, drinking too much, having bad dreams, seeing Valentina's face constantly before me, consumed with grief and self-blame because I had left her to die alone, bearing my son. Yes, it would be a son; we both knew. Benjamin, he would be called. My own life descended into the abyss along with that of General Villa. I slept with many women, was cruel to them, and unsatisfied. I repaid kindnesses with surliness, and once stole money from a rich *hacendado* who befriended me. I bathed infrequently, grew a mangy blond beard, and smoked marijuana cigarettes. On the great military trains of General Villa, in those glorious early days, I used to refuse a proffered cigarette, though everyone else smoked marijuana, roaring out the chorus of "La Cucaracha," including the part about *"marijuana que fumar,"* marijuana to smoke. I rode about Chihuahua for three years on a spavined old mare, half-dazed with marijuana. I do not remember all I should of those bad days, but at least the drug served to dull suffering. I was a very young man, but as old as the brown hills of Mexico.

At last, I think even the fierce Francisco Villa tired of carnage, bloodshed, the baseness to which the revolution had descended. Through bleared eyes I read an article in *Excelsior*. He had written a conciliatory letter to the new President de la Huerta:

*   *   *

In writing to you I am guided solely by love of country. In order to achieve a definite pacification of the country I am disposed to give a brotherly embrace to you. If you are ashamed to be my friend, reject me. I am ready to fight against injustices, without fear of the danger or the number of the enemy. I will listen and follow the voice of justice. If you would deal honorably with me, send me a letter signed by you and we can begin to discuss the well-being of the republic. In the meantime I am suspending hostilities."

It was signed, "A brother of your race who speaks with his heart—Francisco Villa."

The letter was a breakthrough. De la Huerta, an honest and responsible man, answered promptly. "What a proud thing it will be for my government," he told friends, "to bring to order the most feared *guerrillero,* the only one still in arms!"

One day I was hoeing cotton near Bermejillo, that place south of Torreón where the great battle for that city had begun in a long-ago March, the battle for Torreón where my friend Mr. McFall had been killed, and where I somehow won the medal the Villistas joked about, the Cross of Military merit, for a foolish assault on the water tower where the Federales were holed up. Long ago I had lost that medal; it was so long ago it all seemed part of the life of another man. But to come back to Bermejillo. Hot and sweating, I dropped my hoe and squatted to drink from an *olla.* Noting the other hands looking around, I laid down the *olla* to see a whiskered face staring at me from the back of a nice little Durango gelding.

"You are Benjamin Wilkerson, *hombre?*"

Slowly I got up. There was something familiar about the rider.

"*Dígame, hombre!* Are you the same?"

Uncertain, I nodded. Had the theft from the rich *hacendado* found me out? "Yes," I admitted. "I am that Benjamin Wilkerson."

The whiskered face split in a grin. "The *gringo* Benjamin Wilkerson, the boy spy for the bandit Villa, the one they once offered a thousand-peso reward for?"

It was true. Once, at the post office in a little town at the base of the Sierra de la Silla, I saw the poster, and was amused by it. Well, I had done some spying for the general, though I was small potatoes compared to the other heroes—Felipe Ángeles and Tomás Urbina and Colonel Aguirre, even the damned Rodolfo Fierro. But was this a de la Huerta policeman who had come to take me back for some kind of punishment? I looked around for my hoe, intending to defend myself, but suddenly laughed, almost hysterical, seeing the glass eye screwed into the face of old Ojo Parado. It was a magnificent thing, full of colored swirls like a Swiss paperweight, the pupil a diamond sparkling in the morning sun.

"*Hombre!*" I dragged him from the mare to embrace him. "Old friend! Can it really be you?"

He gave me an immense *abrazo*. For such a fierce old warrior his eyes became misty. "Benjamin, *amigo!* I have found you! It was the very devil's work looking for you! No one knew where you had gone. The general sent me out to find you, saying, 'Don't bother to come back, you old rascal, unless you find him!' But you know how he is!"

"The general?" I was puzzled. "Why does he he want me, *hombre?*"

Ojo Parado squatted in the cotton while his mare chewed at grasses between rows, and offered me a pull at his canteen of *mescal*. Suddenly ashamed of my wastrel ways, I refused, saying, "*Buen provecho, amigo*"—enjoy it yourself.

"Have you not heard the news, Benjamin?"

I looked down at my fingers—nails broken and grimy, rough with calluses. Once they had been capable of sending Morse at high speeds; I was proud of my "fist."

"Out here," I said, "there are no newspapers."

"Well, then!" Ojo Parado wiped his mouth, corked the canteen. "We are all in clover, *hombre!* Maybe we have lost the revolution but this new man de la Huerta has been generous. He is giving the general a big hacienda near Parral, a fine place for cattle and grain—twenty-five thousand acres, imagine it! All of us old soldiers get a year's pay. We are invited to join the Federal army at our previous rank if we want to, but my teeth are falling out and my hair also and I myself have had enough of saddle sores and short rations. That man de la Huerta is a good man, Benjamin! He whipped us, that is true, but he recognizes that we fought for the people, as the general always said, so he has been very kind."

I was dumbfounded. Wanting to ask questions, I could not stop old Ojo Parado's torrent of news.

"We were treated as heroes, *hombre!* The government sent a train to take us to Durango but we insisted on our horses that had served us so well. We rode as conquerors! In town after town, in Coahuila and Chihuahua we were cheered and made much of. In Parral, near the hacienda he has been given, the general made a great speech that brought tears even to my glass eye. 'I love you all as if you were my own brothers,' he said. 'I salute you for your courage and your loyalty. Now we leave off fighting and turn our hands toward peaceful tasks to rebuild our mother country, good Mexico!' "

"But me!" I interrupted. "Why does he want *me*?"

Ojo Parado clapped me on the back. "Why does he want you, *hombre*? Why, you are part of it, of course! He wants you to come to Parral and be his private secretary. He wants you to write down the story of his life." Taking off the new sombrero, he scratched his grizzled head. "But first we must give you a bath, *amigo!* Good Christ, you smell like something that has been dead three days under a very hot sun!"

So I went to Parral, where the general embraced me.

"Benjamin, *amigo! Válgame Dios*—how you have grown! You are a big fellow now, but as handsome as ever!"

"And you, sir," I said. "You have not aged."

He grinned, shrugged. "A little gray in the hair, *verdad*, but I can still handle any woman in bed!" Frowning, he pulled at his lip, stared thoughtfully at me.

"You know, *hombre*, I have never learned exactly what happened to my former friend Rodolfo Fierro. I imagine he took you with him the night he stole all my money and ran away. Oh, the great cocksucker, with his elegant ways—his damned Frenchy talk and Egyptian cigarettes and all! But where is he now, eh? What can you tell me? How did *you* get away, Benjamin?"

I shook my head. "I don't want to talk about it, General. All I can say is that Fierro is dead."

"Oho!" He raised his eyebrows. "Is that all, *amigo?*"

"It is enough," I replied, and would say no more.

Sitting together in the big hacienda, we drank coffee while he told me his plans. He was prosperous now. With the generous pension the new government gave him he was rehabilitating the place, ordering farm machinery and blooded stock. His loyal Dorados, now in blue workshirts and cotton jeans, had abandoned their lives in the saddle and were riding tractors to clear the land and put it back into production. The general had built a school for the children and insisted on taking me with him to listen to their lessons. "For," he said, "I am still an ignorant peasant, Benjamin. I need you and your education to advise me."

While prosperous, as always he gave little attention to himself. I advised him to buy a new suit, but in a few days it was as shiny and greasy and baggy at the knees and elbows as the old one he wore at Ciudad Juárez and Torreón and Zacatecas. There was no changing him; Villa was Villa.

I sat for long hours taking notes while he dictated the story of his life. But in the midst of this serene existence, he was troubled. Obregón, the general's old adversary, had succeeded to the presidency and the general did not trust him. Also, de la Huerta was again campaigning for the presidency, and was challenged by General Plutarco Elías Calles, who had once trounced the Villistas at Agua Prieta. While de la Huerta and Villa remained on good terms, Villa hated Calles. He was suspicious that Calles would try to have him assassinated so as to remove him as a supporter of de la Huerta.

"He is after me, that Calles!" the general grumbled, oiling the revolver he had tucked in the waistband of his trousers. "One must always be on guard, Benjamin. I do not fear a fair battle in the field, but death done by sneaks . . ." Shaking his head, he loaded the revolver with shiny brass cartridges. "I do not relish that. It is no way to die, *hombre*—not for a man who always faced his enemies proudly."

General Villa was kind to me, giving me a good salary. I lived in my own room at the hacienda and took dinner with the general and his current "wife," who liked me and did my sewing and laundry. Realizing I must plan for the future, I invested the money in land, supplementing my own funds with loans from a bank in Canutillo which the general had bought control of for the purpose of making capital available to farmers at low interest. I had some luck, and before my twenty-fourth birthday was a well-to-do young man, at least by Mexican standards. While the general and his small body of guards went to cockfights and christenings, I stayed at the ranch to read books I ordered from Mexico City— real-estate law, torts, financial arrangements, politics. Seeing me at my books, the general slapped me on the back.

"I envy you, my good Benjamin! You know books so well, you study everything, you have education." He laughed, pounded his big thigh, powerful from long hours in the saddle. "When the people come to give me the presidency of Mexico, I will make you minister of education!"

There had been sporadic attempts on his life but he shrugged them off as the work of amateurs. On this day, July 19, 1923, I had a premonition. I spoke of it to Señora Villa, who told me she had had a bad dream about her husband the night before.

"Blood!" she muttered, ironing one of my shirts with a huge black flatiron taken from the wood-burning stove. "There was much blood, but it was thick, like a river, and I could not see who was bleeding."

That morning the general was to attend a christening at the home of an old friend, Sabas Lozoya, who lived at Río Florida, a few miles east of Parral. Of course, I intended to go with him and announced my intention.

"Eh?" Cigarette dangling from his lips, he pulled on his old battered boots, the ones he had worn through the revolution. The new boots his wife had bought him pinched his feet, he complained. "No, *amigo*, you stay here and read your books. I will be back soon to dictate more of my biography."

"But I think I ought to go, to be with you."

He scowled, a moment of the old fierceness returning. Then he shrugged. "All right, then! Come along!"

He first intended to ride to Río Florida with his Dorados. But at the last moment his wife pointed out that Sabas Lozoya was a poor man, unable to provide forage for all the horses. We went instead in the general's dusty Dodge automobile. Sitting beside me as I drove, he talked animatedly about the old days.

"You remember Cuitla, don't you? The *vaquero*, the crazy moving-picture star—what was his name, *chamaco?*" He had gotten to call me by that old name, in effect "kid," though I was now a grown man, sober and with responsibilities.

"Mix," I said. "Tom Mix."

"I am going to buy all his movies and show them to the children at Río Florida," he announced.

The christening was a wild and riotous affair. Such Mexican ceremonies usually are. The three Dorados got drunk. Even Ojo Parado, who regarded himself as the general's principal bodyguard, got drunk. There was a lot of drinking. Poor as he was, Sabas Lozoya had barbecued one of his scrawny steers in a big pit lined with oak coals. Still apprehensive, I drank no liquor and ate only a small piece of beef drenched with a fiery sauce.

A little girl in a ragged dress and bare feet followed the general to the Dodge automobile, tiny hand holding fast to his thumb. Dangling her on his knee, then carefully setting her down, the general was happy.

"See, Benjamin! See how the people love me! They know I am one of them, and have always fought to improve their condition!"

We stayed that night at the Hotel Hidalgo in Parral, which the general owned. At a few minutes past seven in the morning, the general himself took the wheel to drive back to the hacienda.

"Watch me, *hombre*," he joked. "I am a very bad driver, as you know. But perhaps you will instruct me as we drive!"

We moved down the Calle Juárez, Ojo Parado and three Dorados sitting in the back seat, rifles at half-cock. As we approached the corner of Cabino Barreda and Calle Juárez, a vendor with a tray of candies, chewing gum, and trinkets for the schoolchildren called out, *"Viva Villa!"* The vendor's shouted *"Viva Villa!"* was the signal for a withering fusillade from the vine-covered house on the corner. Villa cursed, twisting the steering wheel in an effort to get away. His big foot hit the gas pedal, and we crashed into a tree.

"Damn them!" the general shouted. His head was bloody but in that last moment of life he managed somehow to draw his revolver. Later I found that he had killed one of the assassins, Ramón Guerra, with that quick snap shot, though he should have been dead by that time.

The Dorados, all three wounded in that deadly hail, crawled behind the big tree, firing at the second-story windows of the vine-covered house. Ojo Parado, bleeding from a wound in the neck, lay across the general's body in the dust, still firing. One Dorado, Ramón Contreras, with an arm shattered and a gaping hole in his belly, hobbled to the safety of the Parral River bottoms. The general was still lying under Ojo Parado and I pushed the old man aside to drag the general into the reeds bordering the river, hoping he was still alive.

Feet squishing in the mud, I was in the reeds when the firing stopped. Several men hurried from the house and mounted the horses tied in front. Shouting "Death to the bandit!" they galloped away. None was ever positively identified but there is little doubt they were Calles' men, assigned to murder General Villa.

In the eerie silence after the fusillade I looked down at a dead body. The general did not look as big in death as he did in life. At Cuitla, that first day, I had come on him pissing into a sandbank. Now he had pissed himself again; a damp dark stain was at his crotch, and piss mingled with his blood.

After the crackle of gunfire and the mad clatter of departing hooves it was quiet—very quiet. The villagers peeked out of windows, looked around corners. An old man in a tattered *serape* shuffled near, twisting his straw hat in gnarled fingers, a look of wonder on his face. The vendor and his tray had disappeared somewhere. By twos and threes people approached, not too near, to where I stood spraddle-legged over the body.

"*Señor*," the old man said uncertainly, "it is he? It is our Pancho?"

I nodded. "*Verdad.*"

"He is dead, then?"

"Yes."

A woman started to cry; her husband took her hand in his. Finger in mouth, a little girl stared until her mother, awed at death, pulled her away.

"*Con permiso, señor?*" an old man asked, pointing to the body. I nodded.

The villagers bore his body back to the Hotel Hidalgo, where it lay surrounded by flowers for two days. People came from all over Mexico—*la gente*—humble people, small farmers, teachers, *bravos* from Jalisco, women in best Sunday clothing to hold up their infants, showing them the calm face of the man who had meant so much to them: "The Invincible General." Photographers took endless pictures of the corpse until I drove them away.

"Have you no respect for the dead?" I shouted. "Take your damned cameras and get the hell out of here!" I shoved the worst of them. "Beat it! No more damned pictures!"

Nevertheless, there were photos of the dead general hawked all over Mexico. I have since seen them in humble *jacales*, pinned to the wall next to the portrait of Jesus Christ. Someone composed a *corrido* titled "The Forty-Seven Wounds of Pancho Villa." I counted only three: two in his head and another in his chest, close to the heart.

The government, of course, dissociated itself quickly from the crime, with promises that the assassins would soon be brought to justice. Plutarco Elías Calles himself wore a black armband for a month, though everyone believed he had planned the murder. The government found a mendacious thief names Salas Barraza who "confessed" to being the ringleader.

Ojo Parado, my good friend, was indestructible. After

three days in the hospital he demanded to be let out, holding a gun on the flustered doctor. In addition to the wound in his neck, he had a broken arm and a wound near his ancient genitals. "That does not bother me so much," he said. "My balls are all dried up. But this bad arm pains me so much I cannot hold a rifle and go searching for the *cabrones* who murdered a great man!"

At Parral the general's wife wailed long into the night till Ojo Parado told her to shut up.

"He is gone and there is no need to go caterwauling about like an alleycat in heat!" he protested. "Shut your mouth, woman! Anyway, you are only one of his women, and not the best of them, either!"

Ojo Parado always got directly to the heart of the matter. She later made considerable money showing American tourists through the house where her murdered husband had lived, setting up displays titled "His Hat," "His Slippers," "His Gunbelt"— even "His Toothbrush," though I never knew the general to use one.

One more thing—an important thing. I built a small house next to the general's, and stayed there for several years, acting as manager of the hacienda for Senõra Villa. But in 1934, now in my middle thirties, the United States in the grip of the Great Depression, and Roosevelt churning out new legislation to be passed by a frightened and incapable Congress, I felt I had some unfinished business. That winter I went back to McNary, in Hudspeth County, Texas, where I was born, and lived until that frightful day I killed by brother Cleary and burned down Grandpa Johnson's house with my telegraph wires.

McNary had never been a metropolis but now it looked shabbier than ever. The sulfur mine had closed and men walked the streets looking for odd jobs—anything to put bread in the mouths of hungry children. Storefronts were boarded up and signs were plastered on houses where the bank had foreclosed on mortgages. About the only person I recognized was Mr. Claude Teasdale. He had been an elderly man when he helped put out the big fire. Now he was so withered and aged that he looked almost translucent, as if you could see through him to discover the network of bones and veins and nerve trunks. He was clerking in Hawley's grocery store. After all those years, the familiar smells of vinegar, harness, coal oil, and plug tobacco had not changed. He looked askance at me.

"Well?"

The loafers in chairs around the warm stove shifted their feet uncomfortably; I heard one of them mutter something about "greaser." I guess I did look like a Mexican, and Mexicans were always suspect in Texas. My suit was of Mexico City cut and I wore an embroidered vest under the sheepskin coat I used at the hacienda.

"You want something?" Mr. Teasdale demanded.

"I'm Ben Wilkerson, Mr. Teasdale. Grandpa Johnson's boy—Cleary Wilkerson's brother."

Squinting through square-rimmed spectacles, he hobbled forward, peering. "What say? Don't hear too good!"

One of the loafers explained. "He's Ben Wilkerson, he says. Wilkerson!" Cupping his hands he shouted at the old man. "Do you know any Ben Wilkerson, Claude?"

Mr. Teasdale's mouth dropped open. "Ben? Little Ben? Ben Wilkerson?"

"The same," I said. "I was wondering if you could tell me—"

"Ben Wilkerson!" He scratched an unshaven chin. "You was reported to be dead, someplace in Mexico!"

"Ben Wilkerson," someone said softly. "Do you remember me, Ben?"

One of the men pushed his chair back and came to shake my hand.

"Ben Wilkerson! Remember me—Charlie McCracken? You still owe me an aggie from the time you lost at marbles in the schoolyard!" Another said, "By God, you look different, Ben! But so do we all, I guess. It's been a passel of years, ain't it? Wasn't you in some kind of scrape down in Mexico?"

"You could call it that," I said. *Some kind of scrape!* History moves fast, and doesn't wait for anyone. To Mr. Teasdale I said, "I've been looking at the old house. Grandpa Johnson never rebuilt it, did he?"

Mr. Teasdale cut a thin slice of rat cheese from a moldy

wheel and offered it to me. Most Mexican cheese is very bland; this tasted good along with the cup of coffee he brought from the pot on the stove. The rest congregated around where we sat at a board atop a cracker barrel.

"Never did!" Mr. Teasdale said. "He swore the house had bad spirits in it. Died, saying that."

"I guess I was the bad spirit," I told him. "I did a lot of damage. I killed my own brother too, though I didn't mean to. Cleary, you remember."

One of the men hooted. "Killed Cleary Wilkerson? Why, you couldn't kill that old buzzard with an ax!"

I was stunned. "Cleary . . . not dead?"

"Oh, I guess you set fire to him pretty good," old Mr. Teasdale chuckled, "but he got well again. Constable put him in jail regular every day for public drunkenness, and Cleary got tired of looking through bars. Anyway, he went up to San Antonio and started making hooch back in the hills there. Last I heard, the revenuers caught him and he's serving ten to twenty in Leavenworth."

I took a deep breath. For all these years I had lived under a burden of guilt. Now it was lifted so suddenly I felt giddy. To cover my confusion I asked, "Grandpa is dead, I suppose?"

"And your ma." Mr. Teasdale opened a can of sardines and passed it around. I remembered he had always been tight as paper on the wall, but the years seemed to have mellowed him. "Lots has died since you went away."

I wanted to ask about old Mr. Ballew, the one-legged watchman and telegrapher. Mr. Teasdale anticipated my question.

"Old Ballew—remember him, Ben? Right after you left, he thrown himself in front of the last express to come through town before they gave up the line. Cut off his other leg and most of his fingers. He lived for a while in the hospital in El Paso, but died. At the last he was right out of his mind, babbling crazy things."

Cold wind howled around the little store, its shelves almost bare except for a few cans of beans, a mildewed saddle hanging from a hook, a small stock of lanterns, shovels, chewing tobacco—Red Man, Beechnut.

"Mr. Ballard?" I asked. "You know, the superintendent at the sulfur mine?" I didn't care a fig about Mr. Ballard; I wanted to know about Prue Ballard, that lovely thing I had coveted with a young boy's hot passions. Still, I could not say her name. My throat seemed thick and unwilling, and I felt again a small tingle in my loins.

"Too bad!" Mr. Teasdale said, shaking his head. "A lot of things hit that family. When the mine closed down, Mr. Ballard shot himself. Found him in his office at the mine, a forty-five in his hand. Then Mrs. Ballard died too. Don't know what ailed her, except she was used to fine living. You know, they had books and a pianny and all sort of fancy stuff, and I guess she passed plumb away from embarrassment. For a while her and her girl Prue—"

"Prue Ballard?" I asked. "That . . . that was their girl?"

"Yep! They took in washing and tried to make do. Then Prue up and married a drummer from Dallas. Name was Billings. Slick feller—sold men's furnishings on the road. He left her with two kids and went to Rio de Janeiro, they say."

"But Prue—"

"Coming to that." With maddening slowness Mr. Teasdale cut a paper-thin slice of cheese and handed it to me. "Still lives down near the railroad in a little shack by Murphy's Creek with her two kids. Railroad's been abandoned, you know. Folks takes stuff down there once in a while—old clothes and wore-out shoes and maybe some bacon and coffee. Poor girl, life used her hard! Brought up in luxury, you might say. Then dropped down into the gutter."

One of the men guffawed. "Town ain't got no gutters! We hardly got roads anymore! We ain't got *nothing* in McNary anymore, have we?"

"Just a figure of speech," Mr. Teasdale said mildly. "No, that's right, Ed. We ain't got much here anymore. I mind when . . ." Taking off the square-rimmed spectacles, he polished them absently with a shirttail. "McNary used to be a nice little town."

Following his directions, I walked down to the railroad,

or what had been the railroad. The rails were beginning to rust. Mr. Ballew's shack tilted to one side, settling into the mud and cinders. I paused, thinking of the mournful whistle of the mixed special, how it seemed to sing in the rain, sing an old song. The telegraph wires were broken, hanging down like discolored threads from the cross-arms of the tipsy poles. *Gone, all gone!* Walking slowly up the tracks, I came to a clearing in the overgrowth. A small house was at the end of a muddy road that probably led back to McNary. A cur dog snarled at me, running away when I shied a rain-wet cinder at it.

In the yard a wash-boiler was propped on rocks. There was a sagging clothesline, a wicker baby carriage without any wheels, and a boy about fourteen splitting firewood on a stump. The ax stuck in a tough pine billet and he swore. I called out to him.

"This were Mrs. Billings lives?"

He paused, staring at me, his brown cowlick sticking straight up in the air. "Yes, sir."

"I'm an old friend, come to see her. Will you tell her that Ben Wilkerson is here, please?"

Dusting his hands on patched jeans, the boy hurried into the house. I waited, noting the mud-chinked chimney topped with a rusty stovepipe, chickens pecking in the yard, the cur dog which sat at the front door as if daring me to enter. A moment later the boy came out.

"Mom asks if you'll wait a minute, please, sir, while she reds up a little."

Reds up! It had been a long time since I heard that expression. My own mother used to say that, and her mother, and probably all the mothers back to Eve—at least in Texas.

"I'll be glad to," I said, sitting in a splay-backed rocker on the porch. "What's your name, son?"

"Donald, sir. Donald Billings."

Even in the gray light of winter afternoon, that hair, its unruly cowlick sticking up, was Prue Ballard's hair—glossy, shining with inner light, a rich mahogany.

"How old are you?"

"Fourteen." He stood foursquare, facing me, hands

behind his back, not at all shy or embarrassed. Donald was probably the man of the family now that his father had run away, and took his responsibilities seriously. He might have been one man talking to another. "Almost fifteen now," he added proudly. So grown up, but only a year or so older than I was when I burned down the house and killed—no, just singed—my brother Cleary.

"This here," he said, "is my sister." She came around the corner of the house, dressed in a ragged sweater and holding a doll. "She's only eleven," Donald explained. "That's why she still plays with dolls."

She was Prue Ballard too, not quite firmed up the way Prue was at thirteen, but on the way. Her eyes were big and brown. Putting a finger to her mouth in a thoughtful way, she quickly withdrew it. I imagined her mother had scolded her about sucking fingers.

"I'm Beth," she said with the simple directness of a child. "Who are you?"

"An old friend of your mother's. My name is Ben Wilkerson."

The door opened and I stood up. If I hadn't known Prue Ballard I would not have recognized her. Prue was now thin and angular, the remembered chestnut curls tinged with gray and drawn back tightly in a bun that emphasized the leanness of her face, the unnaturally bright eyes, the thin lips.

"Prue," I murmured. "Prue Ballard."

She had put on a red dress that perhaps once had fit but now was too large. A shawl was pulled tightly about her shoulders, and the patent pumps were down at the heels.

"Ben Wilkerson! Oh, how good to see you! It's been so long!"

Even now, with childhood gone, her face showing hard times, there was something about her that stirred me—a kind of welling-up of feeling. There was something else, too—a sensation of betrayal. What had happened? What had she done to herself? Where was the old Prue, that creature of rich delights I dreamed about on my cornhusk bed in the loft of Grandpa's house? It was unkind to think that way; perhaps I had betrayed her too. I guess when we grow up, we all betray our childhood.

"Come in, come in, Ben! Donald, take Mr. Wilkerson's coat. Beth, put the teapot on."

She sat opposite me in the tiny parlor that smelled of cabbage from a pot bubbling on the kitchen range. There was not much furniture except a sofa, two chairs, some pictures on the wall, a crayon portrait of her father, the sulfur-mine superintendent, and the grim-faced Mrs. Ballard. On the table with a marble top was the stuffed bird in the glass bell that had been Mrs. Ballard's pride and the talk of McNary as the symbol of wealth.

"What brings you back here, Ben, after all these years?"

I told her a smattering of what had happened: Mexico, the revolution, my house in Parral close to General Villa's.

Donald's eyes brightened. "You rode with Villa, Mr. Wilkerson?"

"Yes. You see, I was kind of his helper."

"Gosh!"

I turned back to Prue. "Do you remember Mr. Dinwiddie, Prue?"

A thin hand played with the lace at her throat. "He was a wonderful man. He liked you a lot, Ben—I remember that! Of course, we girls weren't too interested in electricity and such things, but Mr. Dinwiddie was awful handsome. *That* interested us!" She laughed.

For a long time we sipped tea and talked over old times. Finally I became aware she looked weary. She began to cough, a racking cough, and dabbed at her lips with a handkerchief. That worried me. Anyone could see Prue Ballard wasn't at all well. Donald looked at his mother with sudden solicitude.

I struck right out. "Prue, are you all right? I mean . . . you don't look well at all!"

"Oh, I'm fine!" she said gaily. "It's just that once in a while I get these little spells!"

I was doubtful. In Mexico I had seen people look like that. They call it *calentura de los pulmones*—inflammation of the lungs.

"No, she ain't all right!" Donald protested. "She's sick. I keep telling her—"

"Now, you just be quiet, Donald Billings! Mr. Wilkerson

doesn't want to be bothered with talk like that!" Prue turned back to me. "You used to have some kind of a telegraph at your house, didn't you, Ben?"

"Look here," I said. "You're not at all well, Prue. Have you seen a doctor?"

Donald started to say something but a sharp glance from his mother silenced him. Quickly she went on talking.

"My, my—those were good days, weren't they, Ben? It was such fun, being . . . well, young and full of spirits and seeing all life before you, stretching way out wide!"

"Yes," I said. "Life was wonderful then." I had already meddled in her private business, so I figured a little more didn't matter. "I . . . I loved you, Prue. You were kind of a goddess to me!"

Sharp tinges of color brightened the pale cheeks. She looked away, thin hands tight on the arms of the chair. "My goodness! Well, I guess I don't look like much now, do I?" She started to cough again, this time violently, and Donald looked beseechingly at me.

"She's sick, Mr. Wilkerson! I better put her to bed."

With Donald's help she got to her feet, waving away my protests. "I . . . I'm sorry you have to see me this way, Ben. I guess it kind of spoiled our reminiscences, didn't it? But I get so weak at times, and the coughing—"

"You go with Donald," I said. "I'll be back to see how you're doing, Prue. Don't worry about anything."

When Donald came out on the porch, I talked with him. "Your mother needs a doctor, Donald. Has she seen one?"

White-faced, he swallowed hard. "There ain't . . . I mean, there wasn't anyone in McNary but old Doc Birkett and he passed away."

"There are good doctors in El Paso. She has tuberculosis, doesn't she?"

He shook his head. "I don't know to put a name on it, Mr. Wilkerson, but sometimes she coughs up blood."

"I thought so," I said. "Look, Donald, I've got a car in McNary that I rented in El Paso to come down here and visit. Is your mother able to ride? I want to take her to El Paso and get her a good doctor."

"She's pretty weak right now, but sometimes she gets

better after one of these spells. Maybe tomorrow . . ." He looked at me with desperate hope in his brown eyes. "You mean . . . maybe we could get her fixed up?"

I saw in him myself at fourteen: a creature of wild passions, extravagant hopes, great love, many misunderstandings, dreams, shattering disappointments—the whole pack of crazy things that make up an adolescent boy.

"We sure will," I promised.

Donald looked relieved but undecided. "But I don't . . . What I mean, Mr. Wilkerson, is . . . Well, why are you doing all this for my mother? It's very nice of you, but . . ."

"Donald," I said gently, touching his arm, "I owe your mother a whole lot more than I'll ever be able to repay. I don't expect you to understand this until you're older. But maybe someday I can tell you and you'll understand."

"All right." He nodded, satisfied.

There's not a great deal more to this story. In the hospital at El Paso, Prue began to improve. I paid for several months in an Arizona health resort for tuberculars, and finally she was well enough to come back to the little house in McNary near the abandoned tracks. I would have found a nicer place for her but that was home, she said.

We sat together in the cramped little parlor. Donald was again splitting firewood in the front yard, and Beth was in the kitchen making us tea. Prue had had a hard time of it, but now it looked as if she had it licked. With a bright red ribbon in her hair and a frilly dress, there was something of the old Prue in her—a softness in the brown eyes, more of that lovely color in the hair swept back from her face, a glow on the lips that might have been cosmetic but still looked good.

"We can never thank you enough, Ben," she said. "I guess you know that. And Donald and Beth know it too. You . . . you're like an uncle to them. They love you, Ben."

For a moment I had a wild idea. Here was a ready-made family for an old Chihuahua hand: a fine wife, two beautiful children, many shared memories.

"I want to tell you something, Ben," she said shyly.

For a moment she was the old Prue, or maybe it was just my eyes misting up a little as I thought of those vanished days when we were young.

"It's silly, maybe—you probably don't even remember. But when we were in school one day, you reached your foot over and touched mine. Do you remember?"

God, did I remember! It had seared my soul, although it had not dampened my ardor for her.

"I . . . I think so," I stammered. "Yes, I do. I do remember, Prue."

"I told you to get your clodhoppers off of me, didn't I?"

I was back in Mr. Dinwiddie's classroom again, my face burning with embarrassment as the pupils tittered. I felt like I could have walked under a snake.

"You *do* remember!" She closed her eyes and rocked a little, thin hands grasping the arms of the chair, a carved walnut rocker that was one of the few things remaining from the big house in the hollow where the Ballards lived. "It was cruel of me to say that," she murmured, her eyes looking through the window, past the front yard, beyond the screen of chinaberry trees, far back into a time long lost.

I was silent, looking back there too.

"Ben, I cried that night. I cried over what I said to you. It was cruel. Papa and Mama didn't know what was wrong with me, and I wouldn't tell. Papa said it was just female vapors. But I cried because I knew I had hurt you, Ben. I . . . I wanted you to know that."

I still didn't know what to say. If I claimed it didn't hurt, then that would make me out a shallow young fool. And if I said that it *did* hurt, I might make things worse.

"Now," Prue said, smiling, "I feel ever so much better! That cruel thing I did has been on my mind a long time, Ben."

Beth, in a new starched pinafore, proudly brought the tea and some cookies on a tray, and I thanked her.

"Good cookies," I said.

Prue patted her daughter's arm. "Beth is a great help to me these days, Ben. Without her and Donald—and you—I don't know what I would have done."

I chewed a cookie, sipped tea, thought. No, that would not work! Valentina, my lost Valentina, was still in my mind, and always would be. There could never be another woman. Lying in bed with Prue, I knew my thoughts would all be of Valentina, my Valentina, my small precious Valentina. *Before she died she cried, "Benjamin! Oh, Benjamin! Come, Benjamin—please!"* No, it wouldn't work. I had been a fool to even think of it.

Before I left, I set up an arrangement for Prue and her children, a monthly check to be mailed to her and a trust fund for the children to go to college. I didn't tell her anything about it, not wanting to be thanked, but when I came home to Parral I found a letter from her.

Although Prue was too frail to travel, Donald and Beth came often to Parral to visit me, bearing their mother's love. They were great favorites of old Ojo Parado and Eulalia Gutiérrez, two more of my "pensioners," although that isn't the right word and I didn't mean it that way. Rather, I was only paying back some of the great debt they had contracted for me—and for Valentina.

Donald is now an electrical engineer working for a research laboratory at Stanford. Beth, a handsome lady with Prue Ballard's old beauty, has married a lawyer in El Paso. They both have children, and sometimes we are all together at Parral, one large and beautiful family. My relationship with them is something I cherish, something that is too good for an old reprobate like me—a man who has done many foolish things, drunk too much *pulque* and *sotol* and *aguardiente*, killed too many men, taken the Lord's name in vain. But it pleasures me anyway.

— EPILOGUE —

Dr. Veláquez is in the room. I cannot see him because something has happened to my eyes, but I can hear him talking to Magdalena and Concepción. They are worried about me and I guess with good cause. My old heart is giving out. Oddly, there is no pain. But I am very weak and when I try to talk there is only a kind of wheezing. Long ago I froze my toes in the Sierra de la Silla, and they have always pained me. Now I feel them no longer.

How long have I lain here? I do not know, but I believe it is September again. A fine month, September! The air, I know, is clear and crisp as it always is in that season. The corn is tall and loaded with fat ears to make *masa*. The *maguey* stretches as far as a man can see, the tall spikes marching like troops to the horizon. In Durango the rivers will soon be filled with snow water from the Sierra de la Silla and the Sierra del Gamón. I cannot see these things anymore but they happen every year and in my mind they are very clear, like a good painting. Too, the mind's eye is never obscured by fog or rain, snow or injury, not even by a bad heart.

I want to show Dr. Velásquez the tin box, the box with my heart in it. Somehow I manage to make enough commotion so that Dr. Velásquez bends over me, ear to my mustache.

"What is it, old friend? What do you want?"

This is very important. My signs and wheezes do not make sense to him, but Magdalena comes forward. "The box, he wants," she explains. "Doctor, there is a tin box."

Magdalena has been with me long enough so that she thinks as I do; at least, so much as is possible for a woman. At any rate, she comes back with the box. No one but me knows what is in that box. From time to time I take it from the big rolltop desk and open it when Magdalena and Concepción are out shopping for *masa* and chiles. Now I manage to send them out of the room while I motion Dr. Velásquez to come closer.

"The box, eh? Open it?" He nods, and gently lifts the scratched and dented cover. Once it held papers—receipts and forms and such—in the general's office.

I cannot see Dr. Velásquez, or the box, now. From the sounds I know he has lifted out my old mouth-organ, then the barlow knife I gave Valentina. He is a little puzzled at that; she wore it on a chain around her neck, like a charm.

"And . . . the lock of hair?"

I have often told the good doctor about my Valentina. Now he understands. Old Eulalia gave me that lock of hair after Valentina died.

"Yes," he says. "The lock of her hair. Valentina's hair, eh?" For a moment he is silent. Then he says, "Old friend, it is still fragrant. It is the perfume of love, I think."

Yes, that was it, always. The perfume of love—still there after all these years.

Now they are talking about taking me to the hospital in Chihuahua City. I don't want to go, and try to tell them, but all that comes out is that fucking wheezing. Anyway, they do not pay any attention to me. Dr. Velásquez goes away someplace while Magdalena and Concepción hover over my bed, trying to make me drink from a cup. I don't want to drink. I no longer need food or drink; the fleeting soul does not need these things. Annoyed, they give up and go to the kitchen, where I hear them banging pots and pans. Through the clatter I can hear Dr. Velásquez on the telephone, trying to get a number in the States. A specialist, maybe? I am too far gone to be bothered with a specialist. All I want to do is to lie here and rest.

"Mr. Tom Mix," I whisper.

Dr. Velásquez has left the telephone and is standing again beside my bed.

"Eh?" he asks. "What did you say, Don Benjamín?"

My voice sounds like wind through dry leaves. Nevertheless, I say, "He did become famous. But he drove his car too fast in Arizona and broke his neck, I heard."

Is it night or day? Well, that is not important anymore; night and day are manmade conventions. In space, they say, there is no night and no day; it is all one. How strange that must seem to a man! Imagine, men flying about in space where there is no night and no day! And suppose, just suppose, one of those astronaut men should come on an angel flying the same course. What would they say to each other? Of course, there are not any angels, in spite of what Padre Lerda says. Sometimes I even doubt if there are men flying about in space, though they report it in *Excelsior*.

I suppose days are passing. I have no way of knowing; they keep the shades drawn in my room. Sometimes I wish I could look out and see the flowers in the patio, hear the splashing of the fountain. Fountain! *Fuente*, in Spanish. My Valentina and our baby died on Calle Fuente in Torreón. Summoning up a little strength, I try to raise my body on an elbow to better hear the fountain. But the old arm, broken in that airplane accident in Chihuahua City, fails me. I drop back. Well, my eyes have seen enough, my ears have heard enough. Now it is time to rest them.

Maybe it is not with a physical eye but with the mind's eye that I sometimes see shadowy forms in the corner of the room where the big bureau sits, the carved bureau with the vase of carnations. They grow in the patio. Once I wanted to dig out that bush because carnations reminded me of Rodolfo Fierro; always he found one to wear in his buttonhole. But Magdalena objected and I have to humor her. Yes, shadowy figures move about there, in the darkness, and sometimes I hear sounds—sounds like rifle fire, and maybe music. It is delirium, Dr. Velásquez says, but I know better. Never has my mind been sharper or clearer.

Old Velásquez is still on the telephone. It seems he has been calling for days and days—or is it nights and nights?

Velásquez is inclined to be a fussbudget. After all, people die every day; it is not remarkable! Few of them have specialists or whatever. Specialists—bah! What I need, perhaps, is a specialist in death. General Villa, I think with some amusement, was a specialist in death. He knew all about death except that final knowledge that comes when one's own death arrives.

Days and nights, days and nights; the clock on the bureau measures on. Now the shadowy forms are clearer, and the music louder. A violin? If it is, it is badly played. Only one man played a violin like that—Mr. McFall. When I laugh, Magdalena comes quickly to my bedside. But I make a sound of deep breathing and she goes away.

Now there is the drumbeat of galloping horses. What a stirring sound! The general's great mare, Siete Leguas, made a sound like thunder. I have never heard a horse make so much noise. Actually, Siete Leguas had tiny dainty hooves, and I don't know how she managed that drumlike sound.

Now there are more people in my room, talking, arguing, gathered around my bed. I hear familiar voices but don't connect them with anyone. I suppose my brain is going dead before I die; maybe that is the way it works. But I am dying, I know that.

A small hand takes mine and warms it. Who? I try to ask, but my voice fails; there comes out only a wheezing sound, and stuff runs down my chin. Dammit all! I open my eyes wide but see nothing. All that is left is feeling, sensation, but not much of that.

"Valentina!" I call, or try to. Did any words come out of my mouth, or do I only think I called to her? I try again. Angry that no one can hear me, I try to prop myself up on my elbows, but fall back. Someone bathes my head with a cool cloth.

So this is what it is to die, eh? Humiliating, but there is one good thing about it. Apostate that I am, still I feel that soon I will see Valentina—and the baby, my son, our son.

I try to form words, but nothing works. Instead I think the words, think them hard, flogging them like the old Durango ponies we rode, us Villistas.

I am coming, Valentina!

Those hooves pounding again, or is it the trapped blood thumping in my head? A bugle sounds. My mouth is full of Durango dust, or is it just phlegm? I try to spit it out, and someone holds a cold porcelain thing against my chin. Good Lord! To be handled so, when one is a man—or was. Furious, I fight to rise again from the bed, and unseen hands push me back. *Chingado!* Always *chingado!*

BIBLIOGRAPHY

1. *Insurgent Mexico*, by John Reed. International Publishers Inc., New York, 1969.

2. *20 Episodes in the Life of Pancho Villa*, by Elias L. Torres. Encino Press, Austin, 1973.

3. *Pancho Villa—A Biography*, by Jean Ruverol. Doubleday, New York, 1972.

4. *Peace by Revolution; Mexico After 1910*, by Frank Tannenbaum. Columbia University Press, New York, 1933.

5. *Heroic Mexico*, by William Weber Johnson. Harcourt, Brace, Jovanovich, New York, 1968.

6. *Anecdotes of Pancho Villa*, edited by Jessie Peterson & Thelma Cox Knoles. Hastings House, New York, 1977

7. *The Eagle & the Serpent*, by Martín Luis Guzmán. Dolphin Books, New York, 1965.

8. *The Legend of Pancho Villa*, by Halldeen Braddy. University of New Mexico Press, Albuquerque, 1955

9. *Pancho Villa—Un Intento de Semblanza*, by Marte R.

Gómez. Fonda de Cultura Económica, Mexico City, 1972.

10. *Omnipatria; A Mexican-American Biographic Chronicle*, by J. Arturo Gutiérrez. Privately printed, Pasadena, California, 1983.

About the Author

Robert Steelman is the author of many Western historical novels and has traveled extensively in Mexico. He served as a civilian electronics engineer for both the United States Army and Navy. He presently lives in San Diego, California.